SUMMER'S FAE

Summer's Fae: Fated Mates Romance

Book 1: Gravenshade Vows

Copyright © Juno Heart 2025

All rights reserved.

Cover design by Artscandare

Fae Prince Edition paperback design by Covers by Juan

Character illustration by Bloodwrit

Interior image by Covers And Berries

Ebook ISBN: 978-0-6458956-8-1

Paperback ISBN: 978-0-6458956-9-8

Fae Prince Special Edition Paperback ISBN: 978-1-7642040-0-2
Hardcover ISBN: 978-1-7642020-1-9

V260116

If you've ever dreamed of finding a hot naked guy doing chores in your kitchen... Guess what? This one's for you!

CHAPTER 1

Wynter

Finally, I have the human girl in my sights, only yards away and visible through the trees.

When I found her, I expected I'd feel strong emotions... triumph, joy, even anger.

I imagined my heart would hammer, air would rush through my lungs, depriving my brain of oxygen, and there'd be an unfortunate tightness in these cursed mortal pants. All the usual symptoms of being in her presence.

But never once did I picture myself hiding behind the trunk of an old oak tree, frozen with indecision as I battled the wolf tearing at my insides.

I've waited many torturous years to see her again. The girl whose sunshine melts the icy winter in my chest. Ignites fire in my blood. Scrambles every thought in my head.

Hers is a name I will never forget. A face I've been dreaming about every night since the moment I lost her.

And as always... she is the bane of my existence. The one thing forbidden to me—a prince of Faery—indulged in all things except the one I crave the most.

As I slink deeper into the shadows, my gaze fixed on the sunlight spilling across her bare shoulders, I take slow breaths, fighting the urge to shift into my beast with everything I've got. My thoughts swirl and tumble, not one of them rational, my control slipping away.

Don't make a sound, I tell myself. *Don't fucking move.*

I've found her... so now what?

Just don't scare her away.

My bonded wolf, Ivor, presses his warm, sturdy body against my leg, keeping me in place. Probably the only thing holding me together.

I tug a wider gap in moss-covered branches and watch the girl direct a stream of water from a garden hose at a bed of tomatoes tangling with sunflowers in the afternoon heat.

This is someone else's garden. Not hers. I can tell by the way it smells.

My eyes close as I breathe deeply, mapping her scent. It's a single, concentrated note in the mix of human smells that drifts on the breeze toward me, allowing me to trace her every movement from the time she entered the yard.

Beyond the garden beds, perched on a rise of shimmering green grass, a large house looms. White columns and window frames drip with ivy, and its red bricks are drenched with the stink of human greed.

During my family's visits to this realm when I was young, I saw the kind of humans who inhabited such homes. Despite their wealth, they still reeked of hunger. Stank of relentless longing, not for food, but for power, more prestige at any cost.

It's similar where I come from. The Land of Five. The emerald-and-black city of Talamh Cúig, teeming with fae who scheme for power, while taking whatever they can steal and barter if it's within the rules of their court.

The girl doesn't belong in this garden. This house isn't her home. The sweat beading her brow is the cost of her labor. She performs work to earn human money to buy food. To survive. My own mother, who was also human, served food to strangers at an eating hall, waitressing in Max's Vinyl City diner before she met my father, the Prince of Air.

Therefore, I am well-informed about human employment and jobs. Grim work without magic. Barely any rest. Such strange customs, slaving to earn just enough money to live like paupers.

Despite her toil, the summer girl's limbs move with grace and ease. Her dark hair flows around bare sun-kissed shoulders, and a gentle smile curves her bow-shaped mouth. She looks happy. Untroubled. Unaware that a predator stalks through the darkening woods, his teeth and bones aching with the need to let go and become something wilder. To claim her as his. *My* bones. *My* need.

Can't she feel me shivering nearby? Why doesn't she turn and look?

But humans have always been blissfully ignorant creatures. Choosing to remain oblivious to the monsters inhabiting the shadows. Like all Earth-dwellers, this one is reckless and, despite her mortal weakness, always rushing headfirst into danger without cause or reason.

That's how she found herself captured by the Shade Court eight years ago, at the tender age of seventeen. She likely fell for the Wild Hunt's sinister glamour. Was entranced by a pair of dark, glittering eyes. A slyly feigned smile. Landolin Ravenseeker himself.

Come with us, sweetling, he probably said. Come sample delights and horrors that'll make you spin forever, wide-eyed and astonished. A white palm extended toward her. Then a single stomp of a horse's hoof jingled a web of gold trinkets into a haunting melody. Bells in the distance—soft at first, then louder, sounding a death knell.

A moment later, she'd have been in the saddle, seated before the Wild Hunt's leader, and riding into hell. The whole thing quick and simple and over in a matter of heartbeats. A life stolen. Nothing good gained. Only heartache. In her land and ours.

Fucking Landolin.

Then, a year and a day of her life flashes by in a haze, every minute spent dancing, playing the fool for the grinning, spitting fae of the Raven Realm. If it weren't for my sister, Merri, the summer girl would still be there, spinning mindlessly day and night.

Perhaps forever.

Beside me, Ivor growls, his black fur ruffling in the warm breeze, hackles raised as he presses his weight more firmly against my side.

"Calm down" I tell my wolf, even though I'm the one losing my shit. "The girl is fine. Told you she would be."

Ivor whines and turns his shivering snout toward the woods, ready to leave the leafy bounds of Lake Grenlynn's suburban sprawl.

Unlike me, Ivor despises the Earth Realm and can't wait to return to Talamh Cúig. But when I was a boy, my parents—a fae prince and his human mate—often brought my sister and me to visit our great aunt. I fell in love with human cities, the intoxicating mix of beauty and decay. The way the people lived their short, brutal lives without magic, careening often fearlessly toward their deaths.

I may be fae royalty, but I'm a halfling and have always longed to understand the human part of me that allows half-truths to slide from my mouth with only the barest wince of pain.

"Go home if you want," I tell Ivor. "The portal should still be open. I'll be fine alone."

Orange eyes stare balefully at me as he faces the yard again with a resigned huff.

No way I'm leaving. Not yet. I've waited so many years to see the girl again, spent weeks dropping into human cities, searching, not finding a trace of her until three days ago. Finally. In this town. In this woodland and this garden.

I can't leave, but I cannot stay forever.

So why am I here? To make sure she's safe. That much is certain. I came to the Earth Realm to protect her, so she'll never become the Shade Court's toy again.

At least that's the tale I tell myself.

In this realm, I can shift into my wolf form if needed, hide my fae appearance with subtle glamours, but my Elemental earth magic is weak here. Now that I've found her, I can watch her, follow her, sleep in nearby woods, but the longer I do so, my powers will wane.

Before long, I'll need to return to the Land of Five and bathe in the renewing waters of the Lake of Spirits or get stuck here forever. Maybe even in my wolf form. Time's ticking, and I'm wasting it, staring like a love-sick mutt with my tongue hanging out.

And if not to protect her, what else do I want?

What does the blood burning in my veins tell me? My shaking limbs? The answer is simple. Before I go, I need to feel her gaze trail over my skin. I want her to see me. To remember.

As she sets a sprinkler in front of another flowerbed, the summer girl glances up, her free hand scraping her brow, smiling and squinting at the sun and watching an eagle glide above. Her pleasure shivers through my body, reshaping my flesh.

Her wide-set green eyes flick down, then back toward the woods, scanning the trees around me. As I begin to hide from her, sliding behind the oak, for a bare moment, our eyes meet. Shock, bliss, then pain shudders through me, tearing tendons and reconfiguring bones.

"Fuck," I grind out, nausea making me retch.

Ivor whines, and I groan through gritted elongating teeth as the change completes itself and my skin splits and fur breaks through. Great fucking timing. One look and I go full wolf.

Pressing my muzzle against his face, I whine in protest. My tongue lolls out, my panted breath hot in my lungs, drying out the roof of my mouth.

I step from behind the tree, Ivor close behind, and stop at the edge of the yard, letting out a gut-wrenching howl. Something small and metal drops from Summer's hands—a garden tool—as her eyes meet mine again.

Girl sights wolf. Fae imprints on human.

We stare at each other, the spell broken when she blinks and grimaces as if she can sense my strangeness, knows I'm not a normal wolf. That I'm... other.

She takes an unsteady step in my direction. The air shimmers, and the gossamer outline of two bodies form behind her—a man and a child, dressed like human gardeners from decades ago. Fucking ghosts. Annoying but harmless.

I falter, and my body jerks toward the girl.

For a split second, I think she might actually come to me. But she doesn't.

Before I do something stupid, I nudge Ivor's side, and we run toward the woods.

CHAPTER 2

Summer

The wolves are back again, staring at me from the trees beyond the wire garden fence. I toss my weeding tool to the side and stand up, wiping my jeans with dirty gloves.

I meet the taller wolf's bright-green gaze and lift my chin. "You don't scare me."

Its snout twitches as if in reply.

"You hungry?" I ask. "Go hunt some rabbits. You're apex predators, not yard dogs."

For the last two days, the large wolves have lurked at the edge of my client's garden, magnificent creatures with black coats that glitter like opals in the sunlight.

They hide behind trees, peering around thick trunks to watch me weed, frightening the ever-loving shit out of me at first. Not an easy task, since I basically live with ghouls in a crumbling mansion held up by the unpaid efforts of me and my best friend, Zylah.

Mom's family is old money, a big name in these parts, but they don't want anything to do with us anymore after Dad gambled all her money away on shady stock-market schemes. After all I've heard about them, I'm not exactly mourning the loss.

Yesterday, after repeated shouts and hand-shooing gestures failed to move the wolves on, I decided I didn't mind their company and chatted away like we were old friends.

Today they're bolder, stretched out in the sun at the bottom of the Vandersons' yard, eyes locked on me, occasionally flicking toward the Victorian ghost-gardener and his transparent son, busy planting invisible vegetables nearby.

I should probably address the undead elephants in the garden. My spectral associates. The first time I saw one, I was nine and had just nearly drowned in Lake Grenlynn. A pale lady with no eyes and rocks in the pockets of her gown was waiting for me on the shore, guiding me back to safety.

After that, I started seeing ghosts on the regular—young folk, old folk, even limp-limbed pets and half-squashed wild critters.

Alarming at the time, but I adjusted reasonably fast. Considering I grew up traumatized by the lack of my parents' love and attention, it's no wonder lost, creepy things felt right at home with me.

Given my ability to communicate with the dear and decaying departed, I've tried speaking to the macabre gardeners, hoping to learn their story. But they pretend not to hear me, their hollow eyes sliding over my laboring form, then skyward, as if asking the gods for the ability to tolerate my mortal presence. Honestly? They're rude.

A rhythmic thudding sound comes from the woods, like someone running fast in heavy boots, cracking twigs and bracken as they go, getting closer. The wolves shake onto their feet, fur bristling as they sniff the air. The spiked hackles along their spines shout *"danger"* loud and clear.

The smaller, bored-looking wolf with a pure black coat and orange eyes, I call Satchel. To me, he seems like a tag-along, reluctantly following his buddy into dangerous situations. I've named the big one Trouble, thanks to his frequent rumbling growls, intense stare, and rakish patch of silver around his left eye.

"What's up?" I ask. "Is your pack calling?" I don't believe that's true. No howls are tearing through the air, echoing off the nearby lake. And besides, these two seem like loners. Same as me. Fellow outcasts who slink through streets and corridors in huddles of two, sometimes three, defiance smoldering in their glares.

I have long, dark hair that frames a pale face and wide-set eyes the color of swamp water that are often described as unsettling. It's a rare day on the mortal plane that I'm not swaddled in funerary shades or wearing a deep scowl on my brow.

Not very welcoming, the jocks at school used to say after I snarled at their buffoonish advances. There was a reason for the chilly exterior. I wanted them to fuck off. And stay fucked off forever.

Eerily silent, the wolves stare through trees, unmoving. I whistle to snap them out of it, but it has no effect.

With a shrug, I grab a pitchfork and urgently toss mulch over a garden bed as if a hungry vampire were breathing down my neck. Dusk will fall soon, and I want to be out of here before the Vandersons arrive home from work.

As far as clients go, they're nice enough, but they ask too many questions. And other than tight, neon-colored tube tops, that's the one thing I can't stand. Busybodies.

Insects buzz through the humid air as I take a break from forking mulch to wipe sweat from my face and swat a mosquito on my arm. Frogs croak and chirp from the pond under the willow tree, and I grab the handles of the old metal wheelbarrow, tipping it forward with a grunt to dump the last load of mulch.

Then a whoosh, whomp sound draws my attention. One of the wolves yelps, and I whirl around, searching the edge of the garden, finding Satchel standing over a bloodied sprawl of dark fur.

Dammit. Trouble's hurt.

Without thinking, I run down the grassy incline, through the back gate to the edge of the woods, and drop to my knees beside the fallen wolf with blood oozing from his shoulder. Trouble whines, then pants, his tongue lolling out, gold-flecked green eyes fixed on mine, as if imploring, begging me to do something.

"What happened?" I ask, not expecting either of the beasts to answer, of course.

Right now, I should be pissing my pants this close to wild animals, especially a wounded one. But a weird sense of calm has taken over me, and I have the strangest feeling it's coming from the wolves. That they're emitting this soothing energy to keep me there, helping them.

The wolves exchange a volley of low rumbles and snarls—an argument of sorts. Then Satchel nudges me toward the house with his forehead, casts one last worried look at his friend, and runs into the forest, deserting him. Or perhaps he's hunting down the perpetrator.

The other day, I thought I imagined someone watching me from behind the trees—tall and dark haired. Maybe he was actually real. A sicko wolf hunter.

"Is your friend coming back?" I ask, receiving another whine and a wolfish eye roll in reply. The blood on the animal's shoulder oozes around an arrow of all things, thick and barely flowing. Not a fatal wound, so he'll probably live as long as he gets some help soon.

"Oh, you poor thing. Who the hell runs around the lake looking for wild animals to shoot with a bow and arrow? A psychopathic lunatic is my best guess."

The wolf nods his head as if in agreement, and I pull out my cellphone, wondering how long it'll take wildlife rescue to get here late on a Friday afternoon.

He bares his fangs and shoves his nose into the side of my leg, pushing me away.

"Hey, I'm not gonna hurt you, you big old bit of chaos. Relax. Let me put some pressure on that wound," I say, placing my phone on the grass and whipping my bandanna from my jeans pocket.

Taking care, I wrap the cloth around the arrow, which is oddly made of a dark, glossy metal that almost looks like glass, and gently press down. With lumbering effort, the wolf lifts his head and licks the underside of my forearm.

My gaze slides to my phone. I should put in that call. Get someone over here to help before Mrs. Vanderson and her devilish pigtailed twins turn up. But as I lift one of my hands from the wolf's heaving side, he lets out a ferocious, rumbling growl.

For the first time in his presence, fear rushes through me.

"I said I wasn't gonna hurt you. Got a hearing problem?" I joke, attempting to settle my nerves. "I need to get you some help before a bigger critter comes along and eats you for dinner. Can't leave you here. You need medical attention."

Green eyes stare, begging, and I know I can't just abandon the poor creature to fend for itself in the woods. It's all alone. Wounded. And will likely die if I don't call for back up in the next few minutes.

Wolves are dangerous, no doubt about that, but in the past couple of days, I didn't once think they wanted to hurt me. Strange creatures, really. More stalker-ish than malevolent. Best if I make the call and wait here with him until a wildlife rescuer arrives.

Decision made, I reach my hand down again, and the wolf snaps at my cell. Three times I try to pick it up, and on the last attempt, his fangs crack the glass on the phone's screen.

"You're making it hard for me to save your life. I can't leave you here, and you can't come home with me. What am I meant to do?"

Instantly, the growling stops.

No way. Absolutely not. *Nope.* I can't be thinking what I think I'm thinking.

"I must be crazy," I mumble, and the wolf gives my arm a wet, encouraging swipe of his tongue. I pocket my cell and get to my feet, shaking my head at the green eyes intent on mine. "You sure are lucky I live not far from here and my housemate is an actual vet nurse. What were you thinking attacking my phone like a heathen and preventing me from calling for help?"

After warning my furry friend not to move, an unnecessary waste of time given his condition, I fetch the wheelbarrow and a large weeding mat, giving the Victorian gardeners a quick wave as they watch me with ghoulish interest.

"Okay," I say, panting over the wolf. "This might hurt a bit, but if you want to come home with me, you're gonna have to get in this thing for transportation purposes. Think light. Pretend you're a floating, non-biting feather."

It takes multiple tries—he's a dead weight and slippery with blood—and the barrow nearly tips sideways twice as I wrestle his bulk inside.

As I bend close, it occurs to me he doesn't smell wolfish, all musk mixed with blood, like I expect. Instead, his scent is earthy and clean, like a freshly watered garden bed. My favorite smell in the whole wide world.

Bleeding wolf secured, I tap out a quick message on my cracked phone to let Mrs. Vanderson know I've borrowed her wheelbarrow for the weekend. Then I hike my rucksack onto my back and press down on the barrow's handles, testing the weight. The front wheel wobbles like it knows we're both in way over our heads, and it's heavy as hell.

Fortunately, with all the digging and shoveling I do in my part-time job, I've developed a few muscles that should help me trundle a wild creature across the woodsy neighborhood and prevent us from ending up sprawled in the gutter.

"You're very cooperative for a slavering beast," I say, spreading the plastic mat over his body and tucking him in tightly.

I take a big breath and then head up the hill toward the side gate and the street, wondering if I'm making a terrible mistake. At least the wolf-shaped lump beneath the tarp is well-behaved, lying still.

As I follow the path along the side of the house, I tell him, "I think I'm going to call you Hank. Sounds a lot sweeter and cuddlier than Trouble."

CHAPTER 3

Summer

"Hey, Zy. You home?" I holler as I wheel the injured wolf into the near-dark room, bumping into the scarred oval table that takes up most of Gravenshade Hall's kitchen. "Got someone I want you to meet. Hurry. He's injured."

The wolf whines, and I shush him as a sugary voice travels up the stairwell from the basement. Footsteps clunk then my housemate Zylah appears in the open doorway, clutching her latest failed experiment—a half-stuffed squirrel she's been practicing her taxidermy skills on.

She pushes a long spiral of auburn hair that's escaped from one of her space buns out of her golden eyes and sets the critter on the dusty marble bench, leaving its little head hanging upside down, onyx eyes glaring at me like I've just insulted its mother.

"*He?*" Zylah says, pointing at the heaving lump under the tarp. "Is there a small child under there? Or have you brought home another three stray cats? Aren't the five we already have enough?"

"Always room for more," I say as one of my aforementioned rescues, Ollie the sphinx—all tufts and scowls, like a grumpy little gargoyle who lost a glue fight with a rabid toddler—winds around my legs, yowling in disgust at the wheelbarrow.

Zylah and I share the crumbling mansion I inherited from my parents with five cats, a basement full of partially taxidermied roadkill, and a few ghosts that provide enough jump scares they *almost* render our coffeemaker pointless. Who needs a caffeine infusion before work when a rotting corpse might randomly appear in your bathroom mirror to get your heart pounding?

"Take a look," I say. "I'm pretty sure Hank won't bite.'

With a huff, Zylah tucks a scalpel behind her left ear and stalks forward. I grab the wheelbarrow handles, ready to wheel Hank to safety—wherever that is, I'm not sure—if my housemate freaks out.

She flips the edge of the tarp, her eyes flaring wide as she stumbles backward. "Shit, Summer, that's a wolf. A huge one stuck with an arrow who does *not* look like a Hank!"

"Of course he doesn't look like a Hank. He looks like a furry death machine with teeth the size of my fingers. But I panicked, okay? And naming things makes them less likely to eat you. That's an unspoken rule."

"How the hell did you get him up the front stairs?" Zylah asks.

"Used a garden plank as a ramp. Highly recommended technique if you want a hernia."

"Oh, Summer." She shakes her head and bends to inspect the animal's wound. "Ever heard of asking for help?"

"I'm asking now," I say.

"Okay. Turn some more lights on."

I nod and hurry to do as she bids.

The wolf's tongue lolls out, his side rising up and down with short, panted breaths. He whines as she pulls back each eyelid. "What in the scrambled hellfire hash browns made you think it was a fine idea to bring a mangy, possibly rabid wolf home?"

"Well, I live with a vet nurse so... And as you can see, he has a thick, perfectly *healthy* coat of fur. And I decline to answer the first part of your question until after I've made us a jug of Vodka Lemonade and drank at least half of it."

"Wound doesn't look too deep," says Zylah, ignoring me and bending over the patient again. "He's one lucky wolf. That arrow missed all the important bits. Even so, I think I should call Theo and arrange to take your Hank into the surgery."

"Your *boss*? No. Wait. Think for a minute. If it's not too bad, you can stitch him up yourself, right?"

She lowers her chin and looks at me over red-framed cat-eye glasses. "I could..." she says slowly. "But for safety, he needs to be kept caged while he recovers, until he can be rehabilitated and released back into the woods by, you know... *wildlife experts.*"

"I'm not sure that's a good idea."

"Why not?" she asks.

I step closer and point at his glossy fur, his perfect, overlarge form. "I mean take a good look. Does he seem like a *normal* wolf to you? And the arrow shaft. Weird-looking metal. Who runs around the woods shooting arrows at wolves?"

Always dressed well, even when skinning roadkill in the basement, her calf-length orange-and-green dress swishes as she glides around the other side of the wheelbarrow, Doc Martens whispering over the tiles.

Zylah looks like a goth but wears bright colors, slashed with only hints of black, and she's never without her neon winged eyeliner. I prefer black jeans and T-shirts. Although on a stinking-hot night like this, I should be changing into a cute black dress at the earliest convenience.

"It's weird that Ollie isn't scared of him," says Zylah, watching my cat.

"He knows Hank can't move right now. Knows he might not be a normal wolf."

Zylah sighs. "Maybe you're onto something being the girl who sees ghosts and all that."

"Are you thinking what I'm thinking?" I ask, hope making me rise onto my tiptoes.

"If you're thinking that animal there is some kind of supernatural werewolf creature hailing from Bon Temps, Louisiana, then I'm thinking you've lost the final, unhinged, wonky marble in your brain."

"But you said—"

"I was being sarcastic. Help me get him up on the table and grab my kit from the basement before I change my mind."

Hank lies limp while we huff and puff and spread him out carefully on the kitchen table. I run down to Zylah's lair and return with supplies just as Hank lets out a dramatic whine. Zylah preps him fast and gets to work, snapping on gloves and assembling cloth, gauze, iodine, and the whole vet-in-a-bag setup.

Out of the corner of my eye, I spot the ghost of the old groundskeeper leaning in close, eyeing the wolf like he's about to offer a second opinion.

"Unless you've got an extra-special, spectral bandage in your pocket," I mutter, "go haunt someone else's ER."

He vanishes immediately, looking offended.

"Was that old Ned again?" asks Zylah.

"Yeah. I think he's bored because we haven't been in the garden much, keeping him company."

"Maybe we should muzzle him," she suggests.

"Ned? He's a ghost!"

"*No*, the wolf."

"Hank, won't bite, will you?" Bright green eyes meet mine. Steady. No fear. Just an intense kind of calm that reaches out and hums deep in my bones. I brush my hand over his fur, rub the frown between his eyes. "I think he knows we're trying to help, Zy."

"Wonderful," she says with another dose of sarcasm. "If you don't mind getting your face ripped off, please do your best to keep him calm."

While Zylah cleans the wound with antiseptic, I cup the wolf's forehead with one hand and stroke his neck with the other. With steady, careful pressure she pulls on the arrow.

I hold the wolf more firmly, but instead of snarling or growling, Hank releases a long sigh of relief as the arrow slides from his flesh and Zy presses a pad of gauze over the hole to staunch the bleeding.

Working quickly, she flushes the wound with saline, stitches his skin with practiced hands, applies antibacterial ointment, and then, together, we wrap a bandage around the animal's torso and shoulder.

While the wolf lies still, only his chest rising with panted breaths, Zylah inspects the arrow tip. "No missing pieces. Got it out clean, so he should recover well. But look at this damn thing, Summer. Fancy silver shaft, but the arrowhead is made of rusty metal. Strange combination, don't you think?"

I nod, but there's a buzzing under my skin. That weird sense again, like I should know exactly what this means. "I could've sworn the shaft looked like it was made of black glass in the Vandersons' yard," I say.

Taking the arrow from Zylah, I turn it over in my palm, feeling its lightness. Its oddness. A strong sense of recognition rushes through me, as though I've seen something similar. Perhaps in a dream.

"I feel like we're being watched," says Zylah, washing her hands in the sink.

"That's because we are," I mutter, glancing up at the ghoulish heads peeking through the ceiling beams like curious bats. "By three ghosts. They're just debating if Hank's going to eat us when he recovers."

"So am I." Zylah laughs. "Spirits, huh? If only they brought snacks instead of intrusive opinions. You know what's weird?"

"What?" I ask, patting my head. "Is it my hair today?"

"No, that's fine. But I think I'm losing my mind. One of my stuffed ravens has started talking to me. Not all the time. Just snippets every now and then. Strange shit, too."

"That'll be all the chemicals you use in the basement. Formaldehyde isn't great for your brain."

Cursing and straining, we lift Hank into the wheelbarrow and shut him in the basement with some drinking water and a bowl of leftover chicken from last night's dinner.

"I'll get some tranquilizers from work tomorrow in case he wakes up grumpy and tries to take us out," says Zylah. "But you should think about calling the wildlife rehabbers. He's not a cute little stray we can house train to pee in the kitty litter and shake hands for treats." She pushes her glasses up her perfect nose and yawns loudly. "And I'll take a rain check on the Vodka Lemonade. I've got an early start in the morning and lots of reading to do."

"Hopefully the fun kind," I say, knowing how much she loves dark romances featuring heroes that'd never be allowed out of prison in the real world.

"Nope. Prep for an exam on Monday."

"You've been working so darn hard at vet school, Zy, you don't even need me to wish you luck. You'll ace it, I'm sure. And I promise I'll think about getting the rehabbers involved." I grin before dropping a grateful kiss on her cheek. "I'm sorry about this... unless you're planning to stitch up werewolves for your thesis, in which case—you're welcome."

CHAPTER 4

Summer

As I head up the creaking stairs toward my room, I admit to myself that Zylah was right. Hank's wound will need care, and it won't be so easy to treat when he's feeling sprightlier. And by that I mean pissed off and bitey.

Despite the warm summer evening, my room is as chilly as the long-term storage section in a morgue. Probably due to the ever-present paranormal activity. A haunting usually drops the temperature by several degrees, which means some needy ghost is lurking nearby, wanting attention.

Dumping my work bag on the four-poster bed, I scan the faded velvet drapes, matching peeling burgundy wallpaper, and cobwebbed chandelier for any signs of ghostly mischief.

The dust and musky scent of the old wood vanity and flooring make me sneeze, and then the drip, drip, drip in my private bathroom draws me toward the sink to wash my hands then twist the faucet closed tight. Damn thing is always leaking. Every part of the house is in dire need of major maintenance.

Keeping my eyes lowered, I dry my hands with brisk movements, hoping to avoid the notice of my least-favorite paranormal roommate.

For several moments, all is quiet, and I risk a glance into the mirror, meeting a set of narrowed pale-green eyes. "Hi, Mom," I say cheerily. "It's been a hell of a day, and I'd prefer to avoid an argument, if you'd be so kind."

It's really too bad that ghosts don't get tired. Or too hoarse to nag their daughters.

When her icy stare stays fixed on me, I sigh and decide to be nice. "How's the afterlife going?"

Her gray curls bounce around her lined face as she shakes her head, ghostly expression scornful. "You were a strange child, Summer. Unpopular, disobedient, but bringing a wild creature into the house is a new one. Let me give you some advice. A distraction *that* big and dangerous won't help you finish counseling school any faster and begin earning the full-time income needed to maintain our beautiful home. This *wolf* brings bad tidings. I feel it in the *ether*. All the gray ladies are saying so."

The gray ladies. Not them again. That's what she calls her spirit friends who've been dead decades longer than her on account of their washed-out, monochrome color. Or lack thereof.

"Mom, you shouldn't be spying on me," I say gently. "You're dead. Waft off and enjoy the afterlife or go find Grand-paps. I'm sure he'd be thrilled to see you again."

He sure would be. Father and daughter were like two bitter peas in a pod—so alike in their sour, hypercritical natures. Perhaps that's what wealth and power do to people. Gives them superiority complexes. Makes it impossible for them to ever be pleased by their own children.

"Stay awhile, Summer. Read me a tale from the Fenian Cycle. The one about the Tuatha Dé Danann and the warrior Fionn mac Cumhaill. You know it's my favorite, and I'm bored. The undead only like to speak of themselves, you know. It gets rather tedious after eight years in the underworld."

My mother was an academic, specializing in Celtic History, so I understand why she enjoys the old stories. But I don't like them at all. At the mere mention of the Tuatha Dé Danann, my blood runs cold. I don't know why, but it happens every time my mom invokes the name of the old folk of Ireland.

It started on the night I reappeared in Lake Grenlynn, about a year after my parents were killed and I learned Mom's spirit was still hovering around the Hall, haunting me like a grouchy nightmare.

I brush my teeth and rinse my mouth, Mom watching my every move. I need to shut this conversation down before she starts blaming me for her death again.

"Anyway, I've got an early start tomorrow and a book I want to read." Best not tell her it's a romance about a knife-wielding stalker. That won't go down well considering the way she and Dad had died. Speaking of my father.

"Any sign of Dad among the deceased yet?" I ask.

She sniffs. "Of course not. He's most definitely been sent downstairs, the adulterous rat."

By *downstairs*, she means hell. But if that were true, surely Mom, Grand-Paps, and ninety percent of our ancestors would be down there, too, boiling away in a vat of past lies and misdemeanors.

The Astellia banking dynasty wasn't known for its benevolent actions. Quite the opposite. I may be estranged from the conniving, living relatives on that side of the family, but truthfully, I'm grateful for it.

"Night, Mom. Rest well."

A scoff hisses from her mouth. "Thanks to you, there's no rest for *me*. I'm stuck behind mirrors, vapor behind walls, bored as a potato rotting in a pantry."

"Depressing imagery. Anyway, I have an early start tomorrow so…"

"On a Saturday?" Mom asks. "Why?"

"I have things to do. People to see. And a wolf to visit." I say the last part under my breath before blowing her a kiss, returning to my room, and hopping into bed to read about a psycho hero and his librarian obsession.

The next morning, the first thing I do after dragging on clothes is hightail it down to the basement. I find Hank curled up asleep where we left him on a pile of blankets in a corner under Zy's workbench. A green eye surrounded by a patch of silver fur opens, but he doesn't move a muscle or snarl.

Zy had messaged me earlier, saying she checked our patient before leaving for work and that he was calm and happily ate some spaghetti with meatballs for breakfast. As I inch closer, speaking nonsense in a low, soothing voice, I notice his breathing is a lot better than last night—rhythmic and even.

The wolf shivers as I stroke his head and rub behind his ear. Bumps erupt over my skin as I pat him. A quiet pulse of something weird but comforting coils through me, tugging at the edges of my thoughts and lulling me into staying cross-legged on the floor for far too long.

At some point today, I should call Zy's boss and talk about getting Hank moved. As soon as he's well enough to stand, we won't be able to contain him safely in our basement. Even feeding him will be impossible without risking getting our throats torn out. No way he'll be this docile at full strength.

A memory of him watching me from the woods in the Vandersons' garden fills my mind, his steady gaze, intense rather than ferocious, brimming with intelligence.

I don't know why the idea of releasing him fills me with dread. I know it must happen. But I feel connected to him in the same way I would if I found an injured stray dog. Like we belong together. Like he's mine, and I'm his.

Placing his huge paw over my forearm as if to keep me in place, he groans, then wriggles in discomfort.

"Don't fret, Hank. I promise we'll get you back to the woods soon. Hey, I wonder if your friend is still out there, waiting for you. Bet you're looking forward to running free again, hunting rabbits."

He whines and licks my hand.

"Oh, Hank, you're a real sweetie, you know that? If only Zy could see you now, she might want to keep you, too."

A heavy, black tail drums the concrete floor as if he approves. I stroke the silver patch around his eye, and he moans, pressing closer.

"I've gotta go out, but I'll swing by the store on the way home. Bribe you with a juicy bone. Sound good? So behave and don't even think about attacking any of Zylah's stuffed pets." I hitch my thumb in the direction of the shelves of tattered, preserved specimens. "She loves them like children. Seriously."

As I close the basement door, the wolf lets out a high-pitched yelp that sounds exactly like: "Hey, get back here."

"Sorry, Hank," I say from the stairwell. "I've got a cold case to crack and a very critical ghost to dodge. Don't want to draw Mommy Dearest down here. She's not very nice company."

CHAPTER 5

Wynter

Did I just wag my tail at her like some desperate, love-starved pup?

Yes. Yes, I did.

And of all the curse-ridden, idiotic names in the realms, did she just call me *Hank*?

Hank!

Son of a gods-damned, blood-sucking draygonet.

Fuck.

CHAPTER 6

Summer

The night my parents died was the end of my life as a so-called normal seventeen-year-old. I lost a whole year of memories, including the details of the horrific night itself. To stay sane, and so I can stop blaming myself, I really need to get those memories back.

I have to know what happened. And, unfortunately, there's only one person who can help me.

I check the time on my cell. Almost ten a.m.

A creature of habit if I've ever met one, I know exactly where he'll be on any given Saturday morning—Angelina's. Downtown. And thankfully, an easy fifteen-minute walk from Gravenshade Hall.

As I set off down the street, I double-check my outfit, making sure I didn't forget anything important, like shoes—or pants.

I'm wearing a black mesh top over a fitted tank, the tattoos on my arms of creeping vines and purple irises on full display. And finally, black cargo shorts and ankle boots. Good. No accidental nudity today.

It's peak Saturday morning vibes in the neighborhood. Everyone's pretending they're not hungover and playing happy families while guzzling iced lattes. A guy juggling oranges on a unicycle rides by like that's totally normal, and I smile at the third golden retriever I've seen since I locked my front door.

Halfway to the cafe, I hear the squeak and rattle of Zylah's thrift-store bike before I see her. I look up just in time to watch her swerve around an elderly man with a shopping bag and give him a jaunty wave.

She pulls up alongside me, the outside of her closed basket decorated with flowers she dried herself—baby's breath, lavender, and marigold. Without looking, I know it contains her roadkill-collecting kit, a morbid contrast to her bright lipstick and the orange-and-green shift dress she wears over Lycra pants.

"Hoping to find some new victims for your dark arts on your way back from jujitsu class?" I tease as she grins and swings off her bike, then pushes it beside me with a jaunty bounce in her step.

She wipes sweat from her brow on the sleeve of her dress. "I almost nailed a shoulder throw today," she says proudly. "Except I forgot to let go, so I kind of flung myself straight onto the mat. Ten out of ten for drama, zero for technique."

The cicadas screech louder with the rising heat of the morning, either complaining about the weather or trying to get laid. Guess I'll never know for sure.

"That's unlike you," I say. "Your moves are usually lethal."

"I was a bit distracted."

"Why?"

Zylah grins. "Heard on the taxidermists' forum a family of armadillos caused a car crash this morning on Myrtle Street, just past the quail farm. If I'm lucky, I might find a reasonably intact critter to work on."

"Mm, tasty. I was wondering what was on tonight's dinner menu," I joke, earning myself a poke in the ribs that I immediately return, sending Zylah and her bike wobbling over the sidewalk.

She laughs as she steadies it. "Hey, I just read your post on the McGonnamy Murders. So creepy. Bet you'd like to run a ghost tour through their house someday soon."

"Thanks. And, yeah, I sure fucking would." I pop a last bubble of my tasteless gum, then fold it in its wrapper before pocketing it. "Five family members taken out on the same night by a cousin that they'd kept in the attic his entire adult life. The paranormal angst in that house will be off the charts. And who knows, one of the sadly departed might even know my dad."

Something cold tickles the back of my neck. I glance over my shoulder. Nothing there now. But I bet there's a shy ghost hiding behind a nearby tree, expecting me to sort out its afterlife.

Frowning, Zylah clicks her tongue. "Summer, *I* know you didn't kill your parents. Deep down you know it too. If there was even a chance you're the culprit, you'd probably be in prison right now. When will you let it go?"

"Probably... uh... never."

"You're hopeless, and no doubt heading off to ruin you-know-who's breakfast again," she says, glancing at her cellphone. "Shit, I'm running late for my shift. Better scoot. See you for dinner when we'll talk about that rather large wolf sleeping in our basement, right?"

My shoulders drop, and I sigh.

"*Right?*" she presses.

"Right," I reluctantly agree as she cycles off down the leafy street, ringing her bell at a pedestrian, even though she's the one who should be riding on the road.

Given Zylah's obsession with the dead, she should be consumed with jealously because I'm the one who can see ghosts. But she's not. She's a happy little sunshine-hearted creep. Unlike me... a depressed, potential murderess.

A soft voice brushes my ear. *Don't forget to ask him about the ash.*

I flinch, spin, but the ghost has already done a runner. Of course.

Ash? What the hell is that supposed to mean?

As soon as I push the cafe door open, the smell of coffee and bacon hits me. I scan the mix of families and college students enjoying their rowdy breakfasts and find my target in his usual booth, reading the paper old-school style, like he's in his sixties, not fast-tracking out of his mid-thirties.

The booth cushion lets out a sigh as I slide along the seat opposite him. "Detective Perez," I say as he looks up and scowls at me from under thick, dark brows.

"Summer. Not again. You know I can't talk to you."

"Come on, Rich. What's the harm in a little chat? Please. I'll get down on my knees and beg in front of everyone if I must. Just tell me everything you remember one more time. That's all I'm asking."

"You can stick to calling me *Ricardo*. No, wait, better make that Detective Perez."

"Sure, Detective Perez. Anything you say." I smile and point at his overloaded plate. "Eating Spanish donuts for breakfast again? That's not very healthy. I can take one off your hands, if you like. I'll be doing you a favor, and I'm starving. Didn't have time to eat breakfast. Couldn't chance missing you here."

"Don't worry about *my* health. I've earned the donuts. Spent the last hour running around the lake," he says, pushing the plate toward me like the good-hearted man I know he is. "There's no need for me to ask what *you're* doing here."

I pretend to study a hanging fern near the window, grinding my teeth and counting fast to twenty-seven. Honestly, I'd prefer not to beg further, but I will if I have to.

The whir of the coffee machine, bursts of laughter, and the clink of cutlery fade as I shrug and snatch a donut, focusing my gaze on Perez's neat, square nails against his cerulean mug, then his trim mustache and narrowed dark eyes.

"I was just passing by," I mumble through a mouthful of sticky goodness. "Happened to notice you in here."

He barks out a laugh. "That's not what you said three seconds ago."

Raising my hands in a guess-you-caught-me gesture, I say, "Come on. *Please*. What would it hurt to go over it once more?"

"Once more until the next time you ask, you mean?"

A guilty smile tugs the corner of my mouth. "Okay, so, yeah, you're right. I'll probably ask again. But if there's the slightest chance you've forgotten even a tiny detail... something that's been hiding in your subconscious for the last eight years, then it's worth pissing you off on the semi-regular to tease it out of you. Right? Maybe it will mean something to me, unlock my memories."

He rolls his eyes and folds the newspaper, setting it aside, and I relax against the booth with a relieved sigh, knowing I've already won this round. I could hear this tale told a million times and never tire of it. It's a horror show, yes, but at least it's *my* horror show.

I've replayed the trauma enough times in therapy to earn a frequent flyer badge—and anyway, sarcasm pairs nicely with the anxiety meds.

"As you know, a neighbor heard a female screaming and called the police. Cops found you on the floor of Gravenshade's kitchen, covered in blood as you leaned over your parents' bodies, dressed in a long T-shirt, feet bare, like you'd just gotten out of bed. A kitchen knife was on the floor about three feet away, the back door open. You weren't crying or screaming, just staring at them. You'd gone into shock."

My breath goes shallow and tight. Numbers run through the background of my brain—7, 8, 9, 10, 7, 8, 9, 10, 7, 8, 9, 10—cycling on repeat. The room shrinks until there's nothing but the booth, the table, the numbers, and his words. "Was the kitchen trashed?" I ask. "Did it look like there'd been a fight?"

He takes a big gulp of coffee. "One of the dining chairs had been knocked over. There were long smears of bloody handprints on the wall beside the back door, your mom lying face down below them. Your dad was on his back partly covering her. Their throats had been slit. No other stab wounds or injuries. Your father's expression... he looked... stunned rather than terrified."

As I wipe my clammy palms on my pants, my heart beats like a drum in my ears, nearly drowning out Detective Perez's words. Leaning forward, I cross my arms on the cool surface of the table.

I don't even need to close my eyes to see the kitchen—the way it looked when my parents were alive. I remember the mundane details of the night so well. It was warm and sticky. A full moon. The soothing hum of cicadas. Barred owls hooting from deep in the nearby woods.

Pain twists in my chest, but still I push the hardest question through my lips. "And the knife definitely didn't have my fingerprints on it?"

"It didn't have *any* prints on it, Summer. None whatsoever."

A waiter appears at our table, wanting to take my order. I smile, point at the remaining donuts, then wave him away. "And the handle was covered in blood. It hadn't been wiped?"

He nods grimly.

"How is that possible?"

"I don't know. I'm hoping that one day you'll tell me."

"Me too," I say, taking a sip of his water before continuing the conversation. "So, there were no strange cars on the street. Nothing to be seen on the yard cameras. Neighbors heard my screams ten minutes before the first responders arrived. Right?"

"Yes. Exactly."

"But did I look scared? Angry?"

"No. Just..." Perez drinks more coffee and grimaces. He prefers it strong and bitter. "By all reports, you looked dazed. Like you'd been hypnotized. As I said before, in shock. Understandable considering what you'd just witnessed."

Stroking my favorite pendant of a raven picking at a silver skull, I groan. "None of it makes sense! Last thing I remember about that night was that I couldn't sleep, so I'd gotten up to make frozen-crust pizza and had cut up lots of mozzarella and cherry tomatoes. Eight years later, and I still can't look at a cheesy slice of pizza without gagging."

"I bet. Sergeant Brantson was the first cop on the scene. He pulled you off the bodies, you went easily. Quietly. But while he and his partner were talking, they lost focus on you for a minute, no more than three, turned around, and you were gone. Straight out the back door, over a small pile of ash."

"Ash?" So that's what the ghost on the street was whispering in my ear about.

"Yep. No idea where it came from, but it seemed odd. Out of place. A neighbor told reporters he'd seen you running toward the woods behind the house in your pajamas, but we later learned he'd made it up, enjoying his moment in the spotlight. We spent days dragging the lake, searching the surroundings, but not a hair or scrap was found until—'

"A year and a day later, I turn up in a parking lot wearing a finely made but shredded emerald-green dress. If I was kidnapped, at least the bastard had decent taste."

"Don't joke about it, Summer. Kills me to think what you might have gone through. You still going to those counseling sessions?"

"Not anymore. But I am still studying to become one—a counselor, I mean."

"Great! Stick at it. Help others learn how to deal with trauma. But if I could give you any advice? Deal with your own trauma first. That's the way forward."

I twist a napkin until the paper tears, then shred it into tiny pieces. "Does Brantson still think I'm a murderer?"

Perez shrugs. "There was no DNA on the scene other than yours and your parents."

"Right. So according to Brantson, there's no other possibility?"

"And no way to prove you did it either, Summer. Plus, you disappeared without a trace and claim not to remember a thing. Pretty fucking mysterious. Believe me, I'd love to solve the case just as much as you need answers."

I grab his hand as he reaches for the newspaper. "There has to be something you're missing. A neighbor you haven't talked to. Security camera footage you've missed. A suspect who didn't get questioned properly."

He leans over the table, the scent of coffee strong on his breath. "The way I look at it, you're the one holding the missing pieces. You were there when they died. Go back to therapy. Unlock those memories. Where were you for twelve fucking months?" He points at the beautiful but creepy designs on my arms. "Who the hell gave you those tattoos? And why don't you remember any of it?"

All good questions that I'd give almost anything to know the answers to.

"Go on, go home, enjoy your weekend, and leave me in peace," he says, picking up the paper and flicking it open.

"Okay. Sure. I'll leave you be... for now." I start to rise, then a fleeting thought freezes me in my seat. "Detective Perez?"

He groans and looks at me over the sports section. "What now?"

"The ash on the doorstep. You've never mentioned that before. It was a hot summer that year. We hadn't used the fireplaces in months."

"It was nothing—just black soot scattered on the threshold, trailing down the steps. No footprints in it or nearby."

"Not even mine, right? Don't you think that's weird?"

Perez stares at me, done with the interruption to his leisurely breakfast.

"But forensics photographed the ash?" I ask.

He nods.

"I need to see it. Or can you look at the photos and describe them to me?"

"I'll consider it. In the meantime, I need to find myself a new place that makes donuts as good as Angelina does."

"One last favor..."

He laughs.

"Would you let me see the case file?"

"No."

"Not the original... just some screenshots? Pictures of the ash on the steps?"

"Maybe," he finally says.

"Will you look over the footage from the cameras again?"

He sighs. "Yes."

"Rich?" I say as I get up.

"What?"

"Thank you for putting up with me. It means a lot that you still speak to me."

"Can't say it's a pleasure every time we meet, but I badly want someone to pay for what happened to your parents. And to you. Not a week goes by that I don't review the file anyway."

"Even if it's me who pays?" I whisper, the fear clamping down on my ribs like it always does. Fear that I did it. Terror that I forgot on purpose. Buried the memories down deep because I'm a monster.

Dark eyes remain on mine, unflinching. "Yes, Summer. Even if it's you."

CHAPTER 7

Wynter

Four nights I've been trapped in this basement, listening for her footsteps on the stairs. Always the third step, creaking like a snapped twig. Her spicy scent hits next—clean with grassy undertones intensifying as she gets closer. Then her laughter floats down as she talks to the other girl in the house. Always on her way to visit me.

Her voice is so different to how it sounded in Faery. Instead of hollow and wooden, her laugh is lighter, imbued with air and sunshine, and she sounds *happy*.

My summer girl, who fascinated me even then, seven long years ago, by human time.

My shoulder wound is completely healed thanks to the magic still working through my blood and sinews, even in this mundane realm of concrete and cold logic. I should be hunting the one who shot me—focused on the threat still out there. I'm fairly certain I know who it was. But instead, I spend my time thinking about Summer, *wanting* her, when I know very well she is forbidden.

Many years have passed since the insane air mage cursed me—at my sister's wedding to the Unseelie King, no less—outing me as the coldest heart in the realm, and declaring it would only melt for someone I could never possess. Even then, I knew she meant Summer—the girl I've dreamed of since I first saw her dancing, bewitched, at the Emerald Keep, after my sister rescued her from the Unseelie mage's grasp.

Eight years ago, she was stolen. Seven since I first laid eyes on her.

The words that sealed my fate echo now through my mind: "Prince of the barren earth, buried within it you must be for at least seven days and seven nights, and until you—"

Then her sister cut in, kind Ether, tempering the curse and twisting a torment into a promise of release that one day everything would be all right... if only I could surrender.

"Prince of the barren earth," she had said, "buried within it you must be for at least seven days and seven nights, and until your heart's love unearths you. Then free and forever blessed you shall be."

So, all I must do is simply let myself die and trust that the girl, who can only be Summer, will rescue me, all the while possibly putting her life at risk. I'm willing to sacrifice myself... but Summer... as much as I want to take her back to Faery again, I can't bear the idea of putting her in danger.

Before she left Faery as a thrall, I told myself she meant nothing. That it wasn't love—just some pathetic fixation born of my halfling human blood. That I only wanted to possess her. Cage her like a pet. But now, hearing her true voice unclouded, watching her move freely again, I know the truth. She is mine. My mate. The only one I could ever want.

The Shade Court once stole her away from her life, and if my suspicions are correct, the fae who loosed an arrow on me in the woods was one of them. The bastard must have been lurking around, spying for days.

But who were they watching? Me or her? Icy fear raises the fur along my spine. I won't let them take her again.

I'll do anything to protect her.

Such as lay here like another one of the ragged, stuffed beasts in the basement, pretending I'm still healing, drawing out the time I'm able to spend in her company. Feeling the giddy warmth of her touch, her fingers stroking my fur, scratching behind my ears. It's embarrassing to admit that such brief, innocent contact is so deeply satisfying.

Oh, how my sister would laugh if she could see me now—heartsick and pathetic.

But I cannot lie here forever. I can't stay away from the source of Elemental power for too long. I must bathe in the waters of the Lake of Spirits soon, or risk becoming stuck in this realm in my wolf form, trapped in silence. And unable to protect her.

That's all I want—to keep her safe.

I wonder which of my powers, if any, will remain if I change into my fae form. My mind-reading gift is sporadic at best. And ever since I've been stuck in the basement, not a single stray thought from either girl has reached me. If I shift, I hope I have more useful abilities and immense strength.

As if in direct response to my thoughts and fears, my muscles snap tight, and a sharp pain grips my gut, bile crawling up my throat. Gods, no. I stifle a groan of agony as the shift rattles and rages through my bones.

A wet pop sounds deep in my shoulder. Then another. Bones shift under skin like branches bending in a storm. I shudder, whine, then moan.

Fuck, no. Not here.

Not *now*.

CHAPTER 8

Summer

Tuesday afternoon, it's raining so hard I stop work early at the Vandersons' and walk home beneath a blackened sky, bag slung over my shoulder.

Rain pelts the sidewalk, soaking my tank top and pants until they stick to my skin like oiled cling wrap.

I pass mansion after identical mansion wrapped in old vines of ivy and tumbling roses. Many contain a blank-eyed ghost hovering in a high window or in the garden, their mouths working in silence, eyes brimming with hollow hope.

Darn beseeching ghouls with their sad, accusing stares. I feel sorry for them, trapped on this mortal plane, possibly forever, but I wish they'd stop pestering me. They expect me to ease their torment because I can see them and hear them, but I have no clue how to assist. I really wish I did.

If I could help even one of them depart their tormented limbo, I'd do it in a heartbeat. Especially if it were my mother.

I'd do almost anything to avoid being stuck with *her* for the rest of my days. She disliked me enough when she was alive, but since she's been dead, her disapproval has ascended to new heights now she considers herself an all-knowing, supernatural being.

A ghost she may be, but wise and omniscient she most *definitely* isn't.

I'd rather be haunted by all the creepy kids from every horror movie combined than spend another year with my mom looking down her translucent nose at me. It's the worst kind of hell.

I'm glad that Zylah works late on Tuesdays because I'm not in the mood for another lecture about how I should have given Hank up to the animal experts four days ago. I mean he looks perfectly healthy and content to me. What's the harm in keeping him a little longer?

His wound healed fast with no signs of infection, and he's so placid, not mean or aggressive. He just lays there, black tail thumping, a deep moan rumbling against the concrete floor while I pat him.

I keep telling myself that although he may seem tame, he doesn't belong to me, even though it feels like he does. Which I know is insane. I can't keep him. He's not a house pet.

He's kind of fussy with his meals. Won't eat canned pet meat, only fresh stuff, more akin to human food. And the way he stares at me, green eyes burning through all my defenses, I'm starting to believe he actually understands what I say.

One thing's for sure; he's a very strange wolf.

I wave at an apparition in Gravenshade's upper turret window, then race up the front steps, throw my work bag on the hall sideboard, and suppress a bolt of disappointment when I hear Zylah clanking dishes in the kitchen.

Bracing myself for the difficult "Hank-talk", I barrel through the doorway to ask why she's home so early—and let out a scream loud enough to wake any ghouls that might be asleep in the walls.

Why the scream?

There's a stranger in my kitchen! And not just any kind of stranger—a strange, *naked man* to be precise. A single earsplitting shriek is justified.

Thinking fast, I pick up the closest available weapon—a bunch of bananas—and hurl it at the back of his head, cucking into the hallway as they bounce off the tiles with wet-sounding smacks.

The naked man doesn't curse, shout, or come running after me, the soft clunks continuing as if he's doing the opposite of what a nude stranger in your kitchen should be doing. Unpacking the dishwasher or polishing spoons.

Could he be an apparition? A neighborhood ghost who's gotten lost? Even so, I'm not taking any chances.

Patting my pockets for my cell so I can call 911, I peek around the door frame. Yep. He's still there, back turned, stance wide and relaxed, like he owns the goddamn house.

The tiles beneath my feet blur, and I blink fast, hoping he's just a mirage conjured by rain-drenched exhaustion. I *must* be seeing things. Perhaps I've finally lost my mind to the soul-destroying guilt of possibly being responsible for both of my parents' deaths.

I rub my eyes and blink again, praying he's disappeared. Nope. Still there.

A well-muscled arm—connected to one of the finest-shaped backs I've ever seen, not to mention the statuesque planes of his perfectly sculpted butt—calmly sets the coffee pot on the stove as he turns toward me, grabbing the back of the kitchen chair.

The chair hides the more *gossip-worthy* parts of his anatomy, but not the ridiculous perfection of his face.

Who the hell is this nude psycho staring at me across the kitchen table as I stand mute and feel around the bench for a lethal weapon? A knife. A fork... Maybe some cat kibble. Anything I can lob at the subtly mocking smirk curling its way across his mouth.

"Time to stop smiling," I announce. "I'm calling the cops."

Other than arching a single dark brow, he remains preternaturally still. "Now why would you do that? I thought we were friends."

Oh, sweet hellish demon lords, he's got a voice made for sin, deep and raspy with a hint of a vague accent. Despite my dire circumstances, a hot chill races down my spine.

Why, oh why, aren't I running out of the house while dialing emergency services, terrified and crying like a baby?

I already know part of the reason... I don't have the best history of dealing with local law enforcement officers. But, eeeek, I really can't think about that right now.

"*Friends?*" I yelp instead. "I've never seen you before. You're a naked danger in my coffee, making house! *Ugh*. I can't speak straight." Holding the bench for support, I shake my head, rebooting my brain-to-mouth connection. "I *meant* to say, you're a naked *stranger* in my *house,* making coffee. How do you suggest I respond appropriately to *that* situation?"

"Sorry. Glamour's malfunctioning."

"The what now?"

The man shrugs, rustling the messy hair almost touching his shoulders. It's thick, dark, and shaggy with a chunk of silvery white in the long bang above his left eye, which somehow reminds me of Hank.

Hank!

My gaze shifts toward the basement where the door hangs ominously open. Where's my wolf? If this dude has let him out the back door into the woods, I'll personally strangle him, clothed or not.

"Join me?" suggests the naked stranger, pointing to a steaming mug of coffee on the table. "You like milk? Sugar? It's no trouble to make another."

"Oh, that's kind of you," I say, my words dripping with sarcasm and rising in a shrill manner, not uncalled for given the situation. "Stop talking about sugar and milk and tell me where my wolf is? What have you done with Hank?"

Laughter rumbles in his chest as he pulls the chair out and sits, but not before I catch an unwelcome flash of something girthful swinging in the breeze that I've, so far, only envisaged while reading Zylah's romance books that I borrow from her room on rather too frequent occasions.

Story of my life. For once, I find a guy with a decent-sized package, who going by his athletic build and sensual moves, might even know how to use it. But just my luck, he's forgotten to take his anti-psychotic meds and decided that enjoying coffee and nudity in a random person's house was a great way to spend his day.

Lord help me.

"So I'm guessing you don't want coffee?" he finally says when it's clear I've lost the power of both speech and movement.

Ollie appears out of nowhere and springs onto the tabletop, ears flat as he makes a truly bloodcurdling noise.

Naked-guy rears back, and says, "Draygonets, what is *that*?" Then he leans forward until his nose is an inch from my tufty cat's and lets out an unmistakable, low *growl*. Without another sound, Ollie scampers from the room. The little coward.

My mouth opens to reject the coffee offer for the second time, but only a zombie-like groan issues forth.

"Are you okay?" he asks, brow furrowing in what looks bizarrely like concern. *I'm* the one that should be feeling concerned right now. "The wolf you're worried about," he continues, "that's me. *I'm* Hank."

And cue the dramatic organ music to herald in the moment I realize exactly how badly this guy is fucked in the head.

He looks about my age, so no more than mid-to-late twenties, and his expression is calm, intense, a little arrogant, but neither of his eyeballs are spinning with madness. He swipes a chunk of black hair out of tilted, almond-shaped eyes, the green shade not dissimilar to mine, just more electric. An unreal fluorescent jade.

Those eyes are familiar. The naked, ripped body not so much.

"No, you're definitely not Hank. What you *are* is insane."

I rush past the table, down the basement stairs, and search every nook and cranny large enough to hide a massive wolf, but find only dead-eyed, dusty roadkill creatures staring back at me.

"You don't believe me," says a deep voice from the top of the stairs, infused with a note of hurt.

I feel like I just kicked a puppy.

"Sit back down or I'll call the cops," I shout. "Last thing I need to see is that monster *thing* of yours again."

"What monster thing?" he asks, dropping into a defensive stance and looking behind him.

"Don't worry about it," I shout up the staircase. "You won't be able to fight it off. It's connected to you. Just go back to the table and keep your distance."

When I reenter the kitchen, his head is in his hands, his elbows on the tabletop and fingers twisted deep in dark, glossy strands of hair, tugging gently.

"Listen," he says. "Even if you don't, I remember everything. Your name is Summer."

Crossing my arms, I lean on the opposite wall. "Could've learned that from looking at a letter in my mailbox."

"Okay. Last night, you gave me leftover butter chicken for dinner and told me it was the best one you've ever made. The night before, I had meat pasta. You visited me every day—told me about your gardening job, how you're hoping to finish counseling school next year. Now explain to me how I know these things if I'm not the wolf living in your basement. I'm a shifter. I can take this human-like form, or I can—"

"Oh my god. You're seriously pitching yourself as a real-life wolf-man?" I say as I realize the only way he could know those things about me and Hank is if he'd broken into Gravenshade and planted hidden cameras in the basement. Hopefully not in my bedroom.

He has to be a stalker. An insane one, too.

The room sways around me as I pat my pockets for my phone, noticing it on the bench near the door. Too far away. "You're crazy. I should call the police."

The edges of the room darken, and a warm, sickly sensation washes over me. Then I'm swallowed by a wave of black.

When I open my eyes, the guy is holding me upright, his bare chest too close, his expression worried.

As he loosens his grip on my biceps, I laugh for no good reason, feeling like I've drunk a whole jug of Vodka Lemonade. "You have freckles," I say, my hand reaching toward the dusting of gold speckled across his nose.

His brow creases. "My mom," he says, jerking his head away from my touch as if he's the one who has something to be afraid of. Maybe my girl germs.

I step out of his arms. "What about your mom?"

"The freckles... I got them from my mother, *Lara*."

He says his mom's name like it should be significant to me, but I have no clue why I should have heard of his *mother* of all people. But I admit that just the mention of her eases my fear a little. Guys who are about to kill you don't normally talk about their moms. Or... do they?

He strolls calmly around the table and sits down again. "I promise I won't harm you. I need your help," he says, then waves his hand over his body, indicating his lack of clothes. "As you can see, I don't have anything appropriate to wear for this realm. Don't live around here. I don't know anyone but you and the other girl who comes down into the basement occasionally."

I cross my arms and stay silent, contemplating making a wild run for my phone on the other side of the kitchen.

"My name's Wynter Fionbharr, but most of the Folk just call me Wyn." Then he unleashes a nuclear smile, flashing a knockout set of dimples that sets my pulse racing.

The Folk? He couldn't mean those Tuatha Dé Danann creeps, could he?

His face is gorgeous, all hard planes and striking angles, strong jaw, and yet those freckles and dimples somehow soften the lethal package, a bit like putting a ribbon on a bear trap. And damn, do they suit him. A little sweetness sprinkled on a predator who might be about to rip my throat out. It's disconcerting to say the least.

Marie, the young kitchen servant—who looks like she was around sixteen when she died—appears in the kitchen, hovering above this Wyn person's right shoulder like a translucent soothsayer, smoothing the blood-covered apron over her black dress. "*Believe*," she hisses through thin lips.

I point at Wyn and mouth, "*Him?*"

She nods, adjusting her white cap. "*Yessss. Help him.*'

Well, in all the years I've lived in this house, which is basically my whole life, Marie has never led me astray. She warned me that my junior-year crush only visited me to photograph Gravenshade's original black-and-yellow kitchen tiles for his interior design project, not because he was "into me" as he had sworn profusely.

Our ghostly servant correctly informed me that Dad cheated on Mom—not once but *three* times, with *five* different women (don't ask)—in the space of a year. That his finance business would fail, and his dodgy dealings would end up ostracizing us from Mom's side of the family, the wealthy Astellias, for good—leaving us screwed financially.

And that's not counting all the lost socks, hair ties, and school papers she helped me find over the years.

When Marie speaks, I listen. She's never failed me yet.

As her black-and-white uniform slowly absorbs into the pantry door and she disappears, I study the stranger sitting at my kitchen table, his expression somber, body patiently still.

Hank has vanished. No exit trail, no shredded screen door. Nothing. And now this guy sits at my table with the exact same eerie-ass eyes as my missing wolf. Either this is a very elaborate prank, or something deeply paranormal just waltzed into my life and made himself a cup of coffee.

But people don't just shift into wolves and then into men. That's fairy tale logic, not real-world physics.

And yet...

Heat prickles the back of my neck, and I narrow my eyes. "So what are you, then? Some kind of druid with a furry side hustle? A cosplay guy who takes things way too seriously?"

He doesn't answer. Doesn't even flinch.

I've not only lived with ghosts but observed them outside my home—in the streets, gardens, bars, stores of the city—for as long as I can remember. If I can accept them as part of my reality, then surely I must accept that other types of supernatural creatures exist. Like werewolves and shifters, for example.

Still. There's a big difference between believing in something abstract and watching it swing its supernatural schlong around your kitchen. I pace once across the room. Stop. Glance at him just sitting there like the world's hottest wax figure.

"Prove it," I say before I can stop myself. "Shift back. Go all Twilight on me."

He only tilts his head. Not quite a no. Definitely not a yes.

I wait... One second. Two. Three.

Aaaand... nothing happens.

No bones cracking, no fur sprouting, no dramatic howling at the ceiling. Just him, calmly watching me like this is all very reasonable. The worst part? He looks like he wants to explain something, but thinks I won't believe him.

And, yeah, he's probably right.

So thanks to Marie and my questionable decision-making skills, it seems I won't be calling the cops on this *Wyn* guy just yet. But I'd better not make a habit of trusting every random hot guy who invades the sanctity of my home to brew coffee in his birthday suit.

Especially if they think they're a wolf shifter.

CHAPTER 9

Summer

"Let me find you some clothes. Then we can talk about getting you some help."

His shoulders drop in relief, and he activates the deadly dimples again, smiling broadly as his eyes sweep over me, warm and unhurried. "Not sure your clothing will fit me."

"Don't worry. My housemate's brother stays here when he has blow-up arguments with his girlfriend and needs a peaceful night's sleep. You look close enough in size. Although, his shirts might be a bit tight around your chest. Wait there for a few minutes."

I race up the stairs, and footsteps thud behind me. "Hey, having a naked guy on my tail is a little... uncomfortable to say the least. Go wait in the kitchen."

The footsteps stop, a wooden stair creaking in complaint as it bears the full load of his weight. I continue along the hall to the left, then duck into Kurt's bedroom. Light illuminates dust motes as I fling open the dark blue curtains.

"There you are," a deep voice says, causing me to fling around expecting to see another pesky ghost. Nope, just Wyn the self-proclaimed wolf shifter, leaning on the door frame and looking hotter than a naked bat boy on steroids.

"I thought I told you to stay put *twice*," I scold.

"Stay *put*? What does that mean?"

I blink. Is he serious? Who hasn't heard that line before? Wolf shifters, I suppose. Not that I fully believe his muddled ravings. Or at least I hope I don't.

"Stay put means don't move. You're not from around here, are you? Where's home?"

His gaze slides over the birds and blooming florals on the peeling damask wallpaper like he's stalling for time. "I'm from a land of green and gold."

I frown. "*Green and gold*? Australia? Your accent's almost American, but there's something... off. You from Ireland maybe?"

"Um... Not Australia or Ireland. Somewhere in between the two."

Hm, feels like he's lying. Or something. "So, like... the Indian Ocean?" I say, hoping my limited geography knowledge lands the joke.

Dark brows knit together, his expression suggesting he thinks I'm insane. Fair enough. I think I might be more than a little crazy, too. But I'm *still* not the one loitering in a stranger's doorway, naked, with all my muscles on display.

"Do you and your friend live alone in this castle... *house*?" he asks, stumbling over his words and walking into the room with no sign of shame in his slow *nude* swagger.

To avoid another eyeful of his show-stopping *assets*, I dig out a pair of black jeans from the closet, then throw them on the bed. "That's right. Just me and Zylah live here. And as I mentioned earlier, sometimes Kurt."

God, this sounds like the start of every awful horror movie. Why am I telling him these things?

"Bit big for you, isn't it? And also old and eerie."

"Nothing wrong with old and eerie," I say, thinking of my high school science teacher, wrinkly as a raisin, dressed like an undertaker, but one of the nicest men I've ever met.

I rustle through Kurt's chest of drawers and pull out a pair of boxer briefs and a dark gray T-shirt emblazoned with an orange surfboard leaning against a green palm tree. "Put these on," I say, passing him the bundle of clothes and keeping my gaze locked on his eyebrows and begging my eyes not to flick downward.

Wyn raises one of the aforementioned eyebrows and tosses the underwear on the bed, then his head disappears beneath the T-shirt. Before it has a chance to reappear, I hurry through the door, calling out, "I'll be up the hallway if you need me. Meet me in the kitchen when you're dressed."

My bedroom with its own private bathroom is a few doors along the corridor, and Zylah's is at the very end, next to the gigantic arched window that overlooks the old swimming pool my grandparents added back in the forties. When empty, it was the stage for many drunken late-night skating sessions—and a few too many broken bones, including my own wrist. Twice.

Gravenshade has a second wing of bedrooms with their own bathrooms at the front of the house. If we wanted, we could easily spread out for more privacy, but given the house's ghostly inhabitants and general creepy vibe, we prefer to sleep close together. That way, if one of us screams, there's a greater chance of someone coming to our rescue.

As I enter my bedroom, the lace curtains flutter in the warm breeze, sunlight breaking through the rain clouds. The bougainvillea outside the window casts barbed, tangled shadows over the floor.

I hurry past my four-poster bed into the bathroom, hoping to scrub away the image of the six-foot-five naked guy loitering in my hallway—possibly from Australia, Ireland, or somewhere in the middle of the Indian Ocean—from the back of my eyeballs.

"What a time to be me," I say out loud, my shoulders dropping as I wonder how much crazier my life could possibly get.

When I look up, a pair of judgmental green eyes are staring back at me. Great. Just what I need right now, my ghost-mom's bleak opinion on the situation. She has the same pointy chin as me. Same steely glare. Same tendency to shut people out. But at least I never left a child to rot alone emotionally.

"You've always been drawn to chaos, Summer. If you ask me, you bring it on yourself. Always did love getting into embarrassing fixes."

"Well, I didn't ask," I reply, masking the usual flare of guilt I always feel when I see her—that flicker of doubt that maybe I'm the reason she ended up like this... you know... technically dead. "Anyway, you can't talk. Remember at Nana's seventieth birthday party when your false teeth shot across the table and landed in Dad's chicken parmigiana? Some would classify *that* as embarrassing."

"Accidents are different. And how many times have I asked you not to bring your father into our conversations? The gray ladies say he doesn't like to hear you speak his name."

Of course he doesn't. Like most people, he probably thinks, or *knows*, I killed them both. Yeah, that's me, just your average possible-parent-killer. Some life I'm living.

If ghost-dad doesn't like to hear himself mentioned, he should just stop eavesdropping on Mom all the time and agree to actually meet with her.

Always happy to get under her non-existent skin, I continue with the subject that most irks her. "But at the time, Dad didn't even *know* you had false teeth... so... if you ask me, that was pretty dishonest and very chaotic of *you*."

With a superior sniff, Mom's face wavers, dissolving into the mirror's surface at the same time the floorboard near the doorway creaks.

"Who are you talking to?" Wyn asks, fumbling with the zipper on his jeans.

Seriously, I wish he'd stop sneaking up on me like that.

"Just myself. What are you doing in here?"

"I need help. How do you fasten these... *pants*?" he asks as if he's never seen a zipper before. Or a pair of jeans either, for that matter.

"First, do up the button. Then hold the material below it. See the metal tag? Pull it carefully upward, toward the top, keeping tension in the denim," I say, waiting for him to laugh and fire back a shut-the-fuck-up-I-know-what-I'm-doing response.

Instead, he follows my instructions to the letter, brow furrowed, then gives me a sweet grin when he accomplishes the task.

Wow, this guy is seriously challenged in the life-skills department. "Well done," I say out loud, and for a moment he looks even prouder. I toss him a pair of Kurt's boots—the ones he wanted me to sell online. "Here, try these on for size."

Sitting on the bed, he slides his feet into the shoes, handling the laces like a pro. With an inquisitive *mraow*, Ollie springs out of nowhere, lands on the bed, and blinks a series of cat kisses at Wyn, having decided it's safe to befriend the intruder.

"Is that a cat?" Wyn asks with a frown. "Where I come from, they're sleeker... beautiful to look at."

"Hey, leave the love of my life alone. He's perfect as he is."

While Ollie purrs and rubs his head against Wyn's knuckles, Gravenshade's other feline residents enter the room. Wyn laughs as three wind around his legs, and the grumpiest, Mr. Smiles, a cantankerous orange boy, stands guard just inside the door, glaring at the newcomer with disdain. He's a hard guy to win over but very loyal once he's decided he can bear your company.

"Is Summer your true name?" Wyn asks, his tone intense as he lifts his gaze from the cats to focus on me.

True name? He certainly has some unusual turn of phrases. "Everyone calls me Summer," I say, my eyes shifting to the floor between us.

No way I'm telling him my real name. He might look me up online and find the news articles about my parents' murder. Or stalk my socials and flag my posts about haunted mansions, where I jump on tours and share what the *real* ghosts actually say about the attendees. It's not my fault ghouls have shockingly foul mouths.

Wyn says, "Given your answer, I'm guessing Summer isn't your birth name. Why do you call yourself that?"

Damn it.

Internally, I roll my eyes. "My dad started the nickname when I was young because I loved the sunflowers in our garden and called them summer suns."

"You remind me of a sunflower," he says, giving me an underwear-vaporizing grin.

Who says stuff like that? Also, it's kind of sweet. Dammit.

Then he continues, "One trapped in a vase and wilting. As all lovely things must eventually."

My breath catches. What the hell does he mean by *that*?

Forcing a smile, I say, "Nice. An insult wrapped in a compliment. Quite a skill."

"I meant only that this life and this realm are stifling you."

I laugh. "Come to spirit me away to a better place, have you?"

"If only I could tell you who I really am," he mutters, leaning his elbows on his knees and looking up at me beneath dark bangs, his eyes gleaming with something like hope, or madness. Hard to tell which.

"So... you're not a wolf shifter?" I say with a smirk.

"I am, but..."

"Go ahead, then. Shift and prove it. I asked you to earlier, and you ignored me."

Closing his eyes and balling his fists over his knees, he mouths a jumble of words that sound suspiciously like a spell or an incantation. "I tried to shift back to my wolf immediately after I changed into my current form in your basement. But I think the arrow injury has drained my power. I'm sorry. I still can't do it."

"Didn't think so. And if you *were* Hank, you'd have quite an obvious wound healing on your shoulder."

"Nope. My magic is weak, but it managed to heal the injury all the same."

Despite feeling sorry for his state of delusion, a laugh rushes out of me. "All right. Enough of that nonsense. We need to find you a shrink as soon as possible."

He grins as though I've just paid him a compliment. "I have no knowledge of these shrink creatures you mention. Are they mages? Healers perhaps?"

"Hm. Maybe the second option. Let's go downstairs and workshop whether to call Animal Control or Mythical Beings Anonymous." I head toward the door and turn back, finding him still sitting on the bed, staring at me. "Are you coming?" I ask.

"Are you going to send the dog catchers after me? Yesterday, I heard your orange-haired friend say you should."

"If you *do* change back into a wolf," I joke, not believing that he actually *can* shift into a magical creature, "then, yeah, maybe I will."

His footsteps trail me down the stairs, followed by his gravelly voice. "You have a forge in the house?"

I blink. "Forge? Like... for making swords?"

"Yeah, metal forge. The workshop you just mentioned."

"I used the *verby* version of workshop. It means to throw ideas around when faced with a problem. See if any of them stick and can help solve it."

"Oh. Right," he says, a confused but handsome frown still decorating his face.

I've no doubt this Wyn guy is crazy, but honestly, I kind of like him.

CHAPTER 10

Summer

I t's late afternoon in a client's garden, the heat is suffocating, and all I can think about is the oversized, half-feral man who showed up naked in my kitchen yesterday, claiming to be a wolf.

Yeah. *No*. Surely not possible. Except the crazy thing? Part of me actually believes him.

Anyway, he's currently lying low in the basement, keeping out of Zylah's way while she decides if he's safe enough to let him sleep upstairs. She thinks he's an old family friend with some mental health issues, just passing through town, and I'm supposed to hook him up with a doctor, get him new meds, and send him on his way.

I drive the spade into the dirt, leaning on it to catch my breath, sweat running in gross rivulets between my shoulder blades.

Mrs. Jenner wants her front garden "drought tolerant but lush," which is pretty much code for I'll be busting my ass for hours and she's guaranteed to complain anyway. Yeah, she's one of *those* clients. Impossible to please without a blood sacrifice.

I curse under my breath at a tangle of stubborn wisteria roots.

"Language, dear," a voice clucks behind me.

I don't even look up. "Hi, Mrs. Broussard," I mutter, yanking hard on the rootball.

She's been dead five years now, but still makes the rounds of the neighborhood, offering free and unasked-for critiques that, thankfully, most people can't hear.

"You're never going to get a man with that mouth," she scolds. "In my day, young ladies were classy and demure."

Mrs Broussard was probably around ninety when she carked it. So when she was twenty-five, she was probably chain-smoking in a Buick and pretending she didn't want to stab her husband with a carving knife.

"Who said I wanted a man, anyway?" I say, gritting my teeth and pulling until a root snaps and I nearly fall on my butt.

"Speaking of men..." She sniffs. "I see you have company today."

What? I look up as Mrs. Broussard drifts toward the edge of the yard, transparent skirt rustling in a non-existent breeze, then walks right up to Wyn.

My stomach sinks—and also kind of buzzes. What the actual hell?

Standing just inside the fence, arms folded, watching me with that unsettling stillness like some apex predator trying not to spook its prey is the gorgeous crazy man living in my basement.

"Oh, great," I groan.

Green eyes blazing, he stalks forward slowly.

"Hi, Summer," he says casually, hands stuffed deep in Kurt's jeans pockets.

I glare. "Don't you 'Hi, Summer' me. How long have you been standing there?"

He tilts his head, considering. "A while."

I jam the spade into the dirt and straighten up, my sweaty shirt sticking to my spine. "Define a while."

He looks confused. "Since you arrived, of course."

I squint at him. "You mean... all day? You've been standing there all day?"

"I lay down for a while too." He shrugs. "Under the willow tree."

I drag a filthy glove down my face. "Congratulations. You're officially a stalker."

Staring calmly, he says, "I'm not stalking you like prey, if that's what you mean. I'm watching over you."

"Same thing, Wyn."

Mrs. Broussard chuckles. "He's very... *masculine* and handsome, isn't he, dear? But there's something strange about the boy. Something not quite right."

"Tell me about it," I mutter.

Wyn's gaze flickers to where she's floating. But when I look at him, he's pointedly not reacting, and I wonder if he can sense her.

"You can't just hang around and watch me work like some creep," I snap. "It's not normal."

He frowns. "I wasn't... being a creep."

"You were lurking. That's literally what creeping is."

As he looks at the ground between us, his bangs slide into his eyes, the silver patch on the left side catching my attention—exactly where Hank the wolf's patch was.

"I was ensuring your safety," he insists.

I let out a sharp laugh. "My safety? From what? Killer gnomes? Rabid gardening tools?"

He looks at the ground. "I have... concerns."

"Concerns," I echo flatly.

He lifts his gaze, his expression earnest. "A few days ago, someone shot me with an arrow. They could've hurt you instead. I won't allow that to happen."

Wow. Protective much? And, also, he kind of has a point. Different garden, but there's possibly a lunatic running around Lake Grenlynn with a bow and arrow, and I'd prefer it if I didn't bump into them.

An image of the sunflower that I found mysteriously lying on my pillow this morning flashes into my mind. "Were you in my room last night, Wyn?"

Jaw set like stone, he replies, "Only to leave you a gift. You said you love sunflowers."

"A gift? Next thing you'll be telling me you slept on the floor outside my bedroom door."

Green eyes stare steadily, not blinking once.

"You didn't, did you?"

"I'm not gonna let anything happen to you, Summer. Not while I'm breathing."

I open my mouth. Close it. *Goddammit.* What is wrong with this guy? And why do I like it so much?

Mrs. Broussard gives an exaggerated, theatrical tsk. "I've changed my mind. He's a keeper," she croons, before fading out in a swirl of smoke.

"Who have you been talking to all day?" Wyn asks, voice carefully blank.

I cross my arms. "Nobody," I lie. "But I have been singing quite badly."

Flashing his dimples in a sweet but deadly grin, he stares for long seconds, the air between us crackling. I'm so screwed. I should be running away from this guy, but all I want to do is drag him closer.

I scrub a hand over my mouth. "Look, if you're gonna stand there all day, at least make yourself useful."

His dark brows lift. "Useful?"

I wave at the garden bed. "Help me dig."

We mostly work in silence, punctuated by my muttered curses and his weirdly formal questions, such as:

"This ground feels... tired. Did you drain its strength?"

"No, Mrs. Jenner likes me to use lots of chemicals on the weeds. I've told her it's bad for the soil. Bad for *her* health and *my* health. But she doesn't seem to care."

"Where are all the worms?"

"See my previous answer."

"Why do you arrange the plants in rows? They seem... controlled. Almost like prisoners."

"Many people in Lake Grenlynn really like order. They're usually control freaks."

"Why do you put shredded tree corpses around living plants?"

"Because we think mulch looks good and protects them."

"Do you curse at your tools because it helps you work faster?"

"No. Why do you ask questions like you're an alien from outer space?"

"Because I'm a Fff... don't worry. What's an alien?"

On top of his strangeness, his general presence is unnerving. Not just because he's tall and broad and absurdly good-looking in Kurt's borrowed T-shirt, which is a size or more too tight across the chest.

It's the way he moves. Controlled, smooth, and so not normal, I can almost believe he's not human. That he's a shifter as he claims.

And the worst part? I like watching him work. *Really* like it.

Strong arms flex as he wrenches roots free. The careful way he checks for rocks before digging deeper—as if he doesn't want to smash them unnecessarily. I mean, they're rocks. Don't they kind of exist to be broken into tiny pieces over time?

At one point, he looks up at me with such intensity, I have to snap my gaze away so fast I nearly give myself whiplash.

It's almost dark by the time we finish, and when I stab the spade into the ground one last time, I'm shaking with hunger.

He notices. Of course.

"You need to eat," he says.

"I know," I mutter.

"I'll... come with you."

I roll my eyes. "What a surprise."

We walk toward the corner cafe two blocks away, and I keep my arms folded over my chest, guarded.

The air's cooler now, cicadas buzzing their horny little hearts out in the trees, the sound summery and festive.

"You know," I say after a while, my voice low to cover my unease, "most people don't admit to being monsters on day one like you did."

He doesn't look at me. "You asked what I was. I told you the truth."

I snort. "You really don't get sarcasm, do you?"

"Give me time. I think I'm learning."

I shoot him a sideways glance. He's walking a half step behind, like a bodyguard. Like he's ready to fight to the death for me.

My chest goes tight as I think about how protective he is, and I wonder for the millionth time where Hank is—if Wyn really *is* Hank like he claims.

"Well," I say, "I probably won't believe you're a wolf until you actually shift in front of me and howl at the moon or whatever.'

A long beat of silence.

I glance over and find him staring at the pavement.

"I wish I could, but I can't," he says finally. "Not at the moment, anyway."

At the cafe, he squints at the menu like it's in ancient Sumerian, so I order us both cheeseburgers, large fries, and some juice from the dusty fridge.

The college-aged server with a man-bun who's usually here on week days ignores Wyn and leans over the counter. "Hey, Summer, did you come in for lunch yesterday? I didn't see you."

I blink. "No, I was working at a different client's on the other side of town."

He winks at me. "Well, don't forget about that party I mentioned. The one at Carly's place."

Wyn's head turns so slowly it's honestly terrifying, green eyes glowing like a wolf caught in headlights. He doesn't say a word. He just stares at the server as a low, rumbling sound vibrates in the air—a sound that's most definitely coming from his chest.

Oh, shit.

The server pales as I pay for our order. "Right," he says. "Uh... Enjoy your food."

I elbow Wyn. "Seriously? What was that?"

"He was threatening you," Wyn mutters.

"Nope, he was flirting."

Wyn frowns. "Same thing."

"Wow, maybe you *are* a wolf shifter after all."

"Listen, I don't have any money. Should I offer to work in exchange for the food?" he asks, leaning down to whisper near my ear. His breath gusts over my skin, and I shiver despite myself.

"Please don't offer to do that. Anyway, it's my treat, wolf-boy. You can pay me back by not murdering the cashier. We *do* need to find you a job soon, though."

He smiles like he's won the lottery, and my stomach drops at how stupidly gorgeous he is. How dare he!

Night has swallowed the last glow of twilight, casting heavy shadows over the sidewalk. We sit on a graffiti-covered bench out front of the cafe, streetlights flickering overhead. Wyn watches the other customers and passersby, head tilted like he's studying a new species. It's... weirdly endearing.

I unwrap my burger and take a massive bite. Grease drips from my chin onto the wax paper, and Wyn stares intently.

"You're very... efficient," he says, focusing on my mouth like I'm the meal he's hungry for.

I glare. "Eat. Before I make you wear it."

He sniffs the burger as if he expects it to explode. Then he bites, chews carefully, and swallows.

His eyes flick up to mine. "It's much better than it smells."

I bark a laugh. "Glowing review."

A pale, hunched form drifts out of the alley that runs behind the cafe. A teenager who died in a car crash two years back, wearing a hoodie, a baseball cap, and a sullen expression. I know him well, unfortunately.

"Hot date?" he snarls out.

"If you haven't got anything nice to say, Ethan," I reply, my mouth full of fries. "Go haunt someone else." He's always crashing the pop-up ghost tours I host around the old neighborhood, being an absolute, disruptive little shit.

Damn. I forgot Wyn can hear me supposedly talking to myself again. His jaw tightens, but he doesn't look at the ghost or say anything.

I narrow my eyes at him.

He's too still. Hyper aware.

I don't even know why I haven't told him I can talk to the dead. Maybe I'm just tired of being the weird one. Then again, this guy thinks he's a wolf. So perhaps I should come clean. When the stars align. Or I'm drunk.

When Ethan realizes I'm not going to engage, he flips Wyn off and drifts away laughing.

Wyn's shoulders relax, and he bites into his burger again.

We eat in silence for a while, then, finally, he speaks. "Zylah doesn't trust me."

I smile. "You're supposedly my long-lost, mentally unstable family friend who needed to be dragged off the kitchen floor naked. Can't imagine why she'd be wary."

He winces. "You told her I showed up naked in your kitchen?"

"No. I'm joking. I'm not that silly. She'd kick you out so fast your head would still be spinning when you hit the lawn. She has heard about your wolf-boy delusion, though. Wasn't too worried about that."

Electricity zaps from my arm to my heart when he puts his hand over mine. "Thanks. It means a lot that you're helping me, Summer. Anything I can do for you, just tell me. I want to make your life easier, better. Safer. I wish you didn't have to do this."

I frown. "Do what?"

He gestures around. "Work too hard like these people. And... be alone."

I laugh. "I'm fine. My mom and dad weren't the best at parenting, to be honest. So, other than Zylah and Kurt, I feel like I've been alone most of my life. That's the way I like it. It's efficient. No one to let me down."

He squeezes my fingers, his thumb brushing over my knuckles in a way that makes my brain stutter and reminds me we've basically been holding hands for the last few seconds.

"I want you to be happy," he says.

Oh, come on. That's a rather intense statement from someone I only laid eyes on a couple of days ago.

"Why do I feel like we've met before?" I ask. "Whenever I look at you, it's such a weird sensation."

An almost pained expression crosses his face, and he literally bites his lip, stifling words that look ready to bust out of his infuriatingly sensual mouth.

"Go on. Out with it. Say whatever crazy thing you're bottling up," I coax.

"I want to. But I can't. You won't believe me anyway."

Yawning, I stand up and drop my burger wrapper in the bin. "I'm beat. Come on. Let's go home."

We walk in silence, the backs of our fingers brushing every now and then, sending unwelcome sparks zapping through my body. The streetlights throw long shadows over the pavement that Wyn keeps an unnervingly focused eye on, like he expects them to rise up and attack us.

I huff a laugh. "If any of the lampposts offend me, I promise I'll let you know."

He nods solemnly. "Make sure you do."

Finally, when Gravenshade comes into view, I stop and cross my arms. "No following me to work tomorrow, okay? That's definitely weird. If Zylah found out, she wouldn't hesitate to cut your throat with one of her scalpels before you even got a chance to explain. Promise me."

"Uh... do I have to?"

"Yep, you do. Vow it, Wyn."

"Okay, sure. I vow I won't follow you to work tomorrow. Satisfied?"

"Hardly. Now swear you won't find your own way there separately and stand on bodyguard duty all day?" I insist. "Nor will you sleep outside my bedroom tonight or tomorrow night."

He sighs, big shoulders sagging in defeat. "Fine. I vow I won't guard you at work tomorrow or sleep outside your room tonight or tomorrow night."

I jerk my chin toward the house. "Basement's that way, wolf-boy."

He starts walking but glances back once, green eyes gleaming under the streetlights, like a cat or a... wolf. "Goodnight, Summer."

Smiling, I roll my eyes, trying to seem unaffected. "Don't make it weird," I say, my chest squeezing anyway as I watch him go.

CHAPTER 11

Wynter

As I roll over on the mattress, a thin ray of moonlight slants through the basement window, glinting off a stack of dusty newspapers in an open trunk set beneath a workbench.

Two days ago, Summer discovered me naked—glamour failing spectacularly—in her kitchen, and yesterday, I crawled out that window and followed her to work, watching from the trees to keep her safe.

Can't shake the feeling that whoever, or *whatever*, shot me with that fucking arrow might still be out there, watching her. Waiting for the right time to strike and steal her away again.

I'm so pissed off she made me vow not to follow her today or sleep outside her bedroom last night or tonight. But I didn't promise a damn thing about the next few days.

Unfortunately, it isn't just fear that lingers.

I can't stop thinking about the sweat shining on her collarbone yesterday while she worked, the way her fingers dug into the dirt like she loved the earth as deeply as I do. The stubborn set of her jaw when she ordered me to help. And the way she watched me at the burger place when she thought I wasn't looking.

Heat coils low in my gut, flooding my blood with need. My cock hardens, heavy and aching, but I refuse to give in to it like a creepy sex-offender lurking in a basement.

Eager for a distraction from the weird mix of impending doom and inconvenient lust, I shift Ollie, the bald, judgmental feline, off my chest. He makes the sound of a dying demon being wrung by its neck as I crawl to the suitcase and drag out a pile of papers, coughing as dust fills my lungs.

Earth is my magical element, so there's always something sacred about getting dirty, but the mortal particles have an irritating quality. Dry and acrid, they cling to the inside of my nose and make me sneeze till my eyes water.

Ollie jumps onto the stack of papers and butts his head against my shoulder. "Come here, bewhiskered, bald imp," I say, hugging him to my chest before setting him on the floor. I've grown fond of the strange creature and his near-constant, grumbling presence.

A death rattle echoes from the doorway. I whip my head around and find the oddly named Mr. Smiles glowering at me. He's the least joyful creature I've ever come across, and that includes the howling tomb-maggots of the Unseelie Mourning Mound back home.

"Feel free to leave if you're so displeased with me," I advise, but he only glares harder. I summon the wolf within, rumbling a low growl, and the foolish orange cat turns its back on me. An unwise move. If I were hungry, he'd make a very tasty appetizer.

I flip through a few newspapers near the top, then extract one from the bottom of the stack. The cover photo on a story dated eight years ago stops me dead. It's a dark image of Summer's house, looking in slightly better condition than now. The porch isn't sagging, and the roof has a lot more tiles.

The headline says: A HOUSE CURSED. A NAME TAINTED. The Bloodstained Legacy of Gravenshade Hall.

Celebrated Irish scholar Sorcha Brady, one-time heiress to the powerful Astellia banking dynasty, and her disgraced husband, former stock market speculator, Daniel Brady, were found dead in their Lake Grenlynn home Tuesday night, victims of what police are calling a brutal knife attack.

Their seventeen-year-old daughter, Grían Brady, known as Summer to her family and school community, disappeared before she could be taken into police custody. A neighbor witnessed the girl running toward the woods behind the property, advising police and reporters she was dressed in sleepwear and covered in blood.

I fold the paper shut, the edges trembling between my fingers.

Grían. Summer's true name is Grían.

And she may or may not have killed her parents.

If she did kill them, such an act would have released enormous clouds of dark energy that resonated through the realms, an irresistible summons to the riders of the Wild Hunt. To them, violence is a call to action they cannot ignore.

No wonder she ended up a captive of the Shade Court. I'd wager anything she was taken by them on the night her parents died.

Am I protecting a murderer? Have I been obsessed with a girl capable of brutally ending the lives of her own parents?

I put the newspapers back in the trunk, plumes of dust choking me, and drag it fully open. A cracked leather-bound book lies tucked into the side, and my fingers hover over it, hesitating. Whatever this is, it's been buried. Forgotten. Maybe even hidden by Summer herself.

What's in it? Somehow I know it involves her. I can *feel* it emanating from the book. Maybe she wouldn't want me to look. Maybe it's *too personal*, as humans are fond of saying. I pick it up anyway.

It's lighter than I expect, the cover warped and flaking at the edges. I settle back against the cold stone wall, drawing my knees up to brace it, and flick it open too forcefully.

The spine cracks, and there she is—Summer as a child, grinning, all teeth and wild, dark hair. Mud up her arms. Bare feet in the grass. Green eyes brighter than any glamour I could ever conjure. It's a photo album, like the ones my mom showed me when we visited my human great aunt in Blackbrook.

Heart pounding, I flick through page after page of images of her.

This is fucking gold.

I drag my thumb over one picture, smearing decades of dust off her face. She's laughing so hard her eyes squint shut. Someone—her mother or father?—has written in the margins in careful cursive letters. This one says: *Summer, age six. Wouldn't hold still. Ruined her flower-girl dress.*

She was so small. So fragile.

My chest tightens, and something hot and wet builds behind my eyes, burning. Not tears. Gods, no. I haven't cried since... well, since Merri sent Summer back to the human realm. Sent my mate away without telling me first.

I turn another page, and another, and another, and the years slide by. Age seven, eight. A gap where a photo's been torn out. Nine. Ten. She's changing, growing thinner and warier. That same spark is in her eyes, but by fourteen her smile is guarded. Closed.

And then...

My fingers freeze.

What's this one?

The background is the porch of Gravenshade, and Summer's leaning over the rail. She's wearing a black T-shirt with a man's scowling face on it, dark pants, and boots. Her hair is tangled, eyes smudged with black kohl—eyeliner, I think Summer called it. But the way she's standing... chin lifted with one hand on her hip, it's like she's daring the person taking the picture to fuck with her. To say no to something important.

She looks younger than she is now, about the age the Hunt took her.

I close my eyes and exhale slowly, a chill seeping through the stone wall and into my chest. The photo album trembles a little in my grip.

Fucking Landolin.

My throat tightens.

I flip back through the pages, my thumb brushing over her chubby child's face, paint-smeared and shining with pride. *If only—*

"Hey, Wyn." Summer appears at the bottom of the stairs, jolting me from my chaotic thoughts.

I snap the album closed and shove it behind me.

"What were you reading?" she asks.

I swallow hard. "Nothing." Technically, I wasn't reading...just spying on her entire childhood.

"Want to come out for a drink with me and Zylah?" she asks.

A *drink?* What does she mean by that? I shake my head and point at the faucet in the sink. "Thanks, but I have water down here."

"No, silly. I meant come out to a bar... for wine and conversation. A local place. Zylah's already there with her brother. We can walk over and meet them."

A *bar* must be a human gathering place, similar to a tavern in Faery. Or a diner, like Max's Vinyl City where Mom worked when she lived in the Earth Realm.

I get up from the basement floor, wiping my palms on the worn denim pants. Turns out jeans are a hell of a lot more comfortable than the leathers I wear at court, even if they don't turn as many heads.

"Oh, yeah, sure," I say. "A drink sounds good."

Her smile is sunshine, chasing away the bittersweet ache of the tragic story in the newspaper and the vulnerable child in the photographs. This girl is incapable of hurting a gnat, let alone ending anyone's life.

As we walk through the lamp-lit streets, memories of Summer's time as a thrall in the Emerald Court creep in. How she spun and danced, joy radiating in blinding waves of energy. How I could never take my eyes off her and only ever wanted to be close.

That hasn't changed.

Not when she's walking beside me now in a tight black singlet and a skirt short enough to make my teeth grind. She's radiant. And gods help me, I want to wrap my arms around her waist and keep every other soul in this realm from touching her. From looking at her.

I want to worship every inch of her and never let her go. She's not mine yet, but the wolf inside me howls to get closer and drink in her spicy scent. Is that so wrong?

I know I shouldn't scare her, but curiosity opens my mouth before I can stop myself. "You really don't remember Faery? Or me?"

Her narrowed eyes cut to mine. "For a second, I thought you said *Faery*. Like in the children's books. Celtic mythology. My mother wrote about the folklore of the British Isles and lectured on the subject. But maybe you already know that."

I stare at her for too long and trip over a crack in the sidewalk. "What? No. I might have said Fairly... a tiny island off the North Atlantic Coast. I thought I heard you tell Zylah about a night you "partied too hard" there and couldn't remember what happened." I wince, the pain of the almost-lies lashing through my muscles.

As a halfling, unlike most fae, lies usually roll off my tongue without too much effort. But that seems to be reversed in this realm, and I've gained an understanding of how difficult it is for full-blooded fae of my court to twist the truth to hide their intentions and ill deeds.

"Nope. As far as I'm aware, I've never been to this *Fairly* place you mention." She gives me a smirking glance that says she's not buying it. "Don't ever let Zylah hear you talking about shifters and faeries. She's got enough weirdness on her plate, managing her roadkill menagerie."

On her plate? What does that even mean? Humans and their strange food metaphors.

"I think I've convinced her to let you stay at Gravenshade for a while longer. If tonight goes well, she'll let you sleep in an actual bedroom instead of on the basement floor."

"Really?" I grin at her.

Summer told her housemate that Hank the wolf escaped and I'm a family friend from interstate, who's homeless due to mental illness, which I think means to be in possession of a fractured mind.

I grin, flashing my much-admired-in-the-Emerald-Court dimples. "Then I'll be on my best behavior tonight. Cross my cursed, black heart."

No idea why Zylah is concerned about *me*. I'm not the one who keeps a growing collection of preserved dead creatures and personally stuffs them with wood shavings. Still, she obviously cares deeply for Summer, and that makes her an ally, whether I like it or not.

Summer gives me a wobbly smile, and I can't tell if she is growing more comfortable around me or less.

In this realm, my erratic mind-reading skill seems to have vanished. Such a tragedy. I'd love nothing more than to know what Summer really thinks of me.

"Wyn, if you slip up and accidentally mention the naked-kitchen incident, just say it happened because you'd gone off your meds," she instructs. "And you're back on them now. Okay?"

"Sure. Are meds a type of potion?" I ask.

She cuts me another frowning glare. "Um, yeah. Kind of. What country are you from again?"

CHAPTER 12

Wynter

We arrive at a flashing sign that says Neon Velvet, and Summer reaches out to open the large, pressed-metal door beneath it.

I gently push in front of her and hold the door open. Her cheeks glow dark red, catching the flicker of pink light like warpaint as she enters the building, and I follow close behind.

The stench of cheap ale, sweat, and some overly floral incense hits me hard, a poor attempt to disguise the sour damp of spilled drinks and mildew baked into the walls and floor of the establishment.

Darkness cut by bursts of red and blue light, sweltering heat, and noise that rivals a fae revel assault my senses as I push through way-too-many humans shouting over each other. Their cheeks are flushed, and sweat slicks their temples as they press shoulder to shoulder in the long, narrow tavern.

I elbow Summer. "The minstrels are very loud in here."

She frowns. "Minstrels?"

"The musical performers."

"That's not a live band. The music is coming from those speakers. See?"

She points at thin rectangular boxes anchored on the walls, and a memory of Max's diner strikes me—myself as a child, dancing with my mother, while she laughed because I refused to believe the music wasn't played by invisible musicians. She'd explained how the sound was recorded, but even that process seemed like magic.

Summer waves toward one of the round tables that run the length of the room, where humans lean in close over tall glasses of ale, whispering secrets or laughing too loudly.

"Let's do this," says Summer, threading her arm through mine and tugging me along behind her.

She looks ridiculously hot tonight, and more than a few heads follow her progress. If anyone in here so much as looks at her the wrong way, I'll bury them under the floorboards. Quietly, of course. I'm supposed to be blending in. Laying low. Not mentally mauling possible suitors or mapping out which wall I'd press her up against first.

"Hello, basement-boy," greets Summer's housemate, Zylah, who I've obediently done my best to avoid over the past couple of days. "It's nice to see you out of your lair."

"Likewise," I say, making her mouth twist from a smile into a grimace.

As I take a seat next to a thin male with long wheat-colored hair, she says, "Wyn, this is my brother, Kurt. He thought he was a werewolf once, too. But that was after a bad mushroom trip. What's your excuse?"

Summer, who's sitting on my other side, gives me a meaningful look.

I shrug. "Guess I'm a... m-m-magical being and can't help it."

Fuck. I tried to say I'd "gone off my meds" as Summer taught me, but the words just wouldn't leave my lips.

Kurt throws his head back and laughs like I'm a court jester. "I'll get a round of drinks," he says. "What's everyone having? Wyn?"

I open my mouth to suggest ale, but before I speak, Zylah says, "How about a cocktail? They make a fantastic sangria here."

Cocks' tails? Did I hear that correctly? How are we supposed to drink them? Human traditions are worse than the Unseelie fae's. I glance at the drink menu, searching for rooster feathers. Nothing. Either I'm being lied to, or humans are even more perverse than I thought.

"Plum sangrias for everyone," announces Summer, clapping her hands together, like she's trying to redirect attention from me.

Kurt rises from the table and disappears into the crowd, returning ten minutes later with four long-stemmed glasses filled with fruit and a deep red liquid. I fish out a slice of plum with the end of a narrow tube, wincing at the tartness that's thankfully chased by a warm hit of cinnamon and rosemary. Not too bad.

Once I've eaten the fruit, I push my glass aside and focus on my companions' baffling conversation about jobs—their term for the contracts where they labor in exchange for enough reward to live almost as well as bridge trolls.

"Not finishing your cocktail, Wyn?" Summer asks. "Don't you like it?"

They stare at me as they slurp liquid through the narrow metal tubes called straws. I remove mine from my glass and gulp down the rest of the drink, wiping my mouth with a sigh when I finish.

Within moments, my head spins. My tongue thickens in my mouth, and, too late, I remember my father's warning. Human alcohol hits fae hard and fast, and he told me never to drink it.

I've fucked up badly, especially if I don't want Zylah to throw me out of Gravenshade Hall, away from Summer. All I want is to keep her safe and figure out how to get her back to the Land of Five, my home, without breaking her traumatized mind.

I consider rushing outside and purging the drink from my stomach, but the time for that is long past. My limbs are weak, my thoughts swirling, as if I'm on the seventh night of a sleepless revel.

"I'll go to the bar," says Summer. "Want another round, Wyn?"

"A round what?"

She squints at me. "Huh?"

"What round thing will you retrieve from the bar?" I clarify.

"*Get up.*" Tugging my arm, she rolls her eyes. "I think you'd better come with me."

"Why?" I shout over the music as I follow her through the crowd of humans, stumbling more than once.

"To keep you out of trouble. Remember you promised to act like a sane person around my housemate?"

I nod as we join a three-human-deep line at the bar.

"Well you're about to break your word if you're not careful. Alcohol doesn't seem to agree with you. Do you normally drink?"

"Not human alcohol," I reply. "It has an unusual effect on me."

Her gaze tracks from my face to my chest and back up to dance over my lips, fire tingling over my skin in its wake. "There you go again," she says, "talking like a crazy man."

People turn away from the bar and push past us, carrying large glass goblets full of ale. We step forward, and Summer greets a serving girl with hair as green as a sea witch's hanging down her back in thick ropes.

"Hey, Summer. Been to any cool new hauntings?" she asks before nodding at me. "Got a new friend?"

"Just the ones in my own house. But, yeah, this is—"

"Wynter Ashton Fionbharr," I say, inclining my head. "Pleasure to meet you."

Summer jabs me in the ribs as if I've just declared myself to be the Crown Prince of Stars, which, honestly, isn't that far from the truth.

"That's a rather large mouthful," she says, "so we just call him Wyn. Wyn, meet Rose, the best slam poet in the state, and she even has a trophy to prove it."

My interest piques. "I have a knack for poetry myself," I admit.

"Is that so?" Rose purses her pierced lips. "Let's hear something of yours then."

Ignoring Summer's glare, I spout the first rhyming lines I can think of—a little verse about the Shade Prince, my least favorite fae in the whole of Faery. In a loud voice, I begin my recital...

"By lemon twine and cursed-tusked swine, the Diamond Prince doth fucking whine. And whine and whine and whine. Like a baby troll. A shadow-wrapped doll. His blood shall weep, when I catch him asleep, and smash his brains out through his thick skull."

A stunned silence falls among the humans close by. Perhaps they prefer poetry with less death threats and more heartbreak. Cowards.

Rose sets down her cleaning cloth. "Oh. Not what I was expecting. Very... visually graphic. Do you live around here?"

"No, I—"

Warm fingers slip under my T-shirt, cutting off my words, and Summer pinches my waist so hard that I yelp out, *"Draygonets,"* before I can stop myself.

Rose must never have heard of the dreaded winged beasts of my hometown and narrows her eyes in confusion. I summon my wits, preparing to lie and tell her I reside in Blackbrook, where Mother lived before she married fae royalty.

Concentrating, I take a deep breath and blurt out, "I come from the Faery city of Talamh Cúig."

"Wyn!" Summer claps a hand over her mouth. "I give up," she says, laughing. "You're hopeless."

Rose shakes her head. "Talamh Cúig, huh? Where you have no doubt brought peace and harmony to the land you've reigned over for centuries. Am I correct?"

"Almost. I'm a prince, not a king."

For Dana's sake, why can't I lie anymore? Or at least keep my damn mouth shut?

When my father, a full-blooded fae, first followed my mother into the human realm, he found he could lie with ease, which wasn't possible when he lived in Faery. For me, it's the opposite. This realm has stolen my halfling ability to deceive with words and the alcohol removed my skill in twisting them.

Mental note: never drink human ale again.

The effects of crossing realms upon magical powers is not only unpredictable, but extremely inconvenient.

"You're a strange one," says Rose. "And outrageously easy on the eyes." Her dark gaze roves my face, then lingers on my mouth. "Would you like to have a drink later? I'm free all night after I close the bar."

"Better not," I reply. "I've had enough tails of the cock to last three lifetimes. They're lethal and—"

"*Anyway*," says Summer, interrupting me. "Can I get three plum sangrias and a soda water for this one?"

When the drinks are made, Summer hands me two, and we push back into the heaving crowd.

CHAPTER 13

Wynter

"You know Rose was hitting on you, right?" Summer asks.

"Hitting on me? I feel like I should know what that means."

"Oh, sweet mercy, Wyn. It just *means* she was trying to get into your pants."

I glance down at Kurt's jeans. "These? Why?"

"It means she wants to fuck you, silly boy."

I definitely know what *that* word means, no interpreter required, and hearing it come from my summer girl's petal-soft lips causes chaos to shudder through me. A riot of want and heat that I work hard to suppress so I can stay in control of my body. Even though I want the exact opposite.

An image of her head thrown back in ecstasy as I bite down on her neck tortures the wolf inside me.

A man shrieks in my face as I pass by, and I catch a glimpse of myself in a wall mirror, my glamour flickering. Sharp ears part my hair, which is undulating like it's lightning shot, and my eyes flash gold with the magic kindling through my blood.

Holding the male's gaze, I snarl, and he pales and turns away, likely pissing himself. Yeah, well. That's what happens when you stare at fae royalty mid-glamour malfunction. I ought to start charging for the excitement.

We thud the drinks on the table in front of our friends. Summer drinks some of hers, then whispers in my ear. "Come with me before you get us kicked out."

We exit a rear door into an alleyway, and she pushes me against the brick wall. "Snarling at a stranger? This wolf-shifter fantasy of yours is getting out of hand."

"You still don't believe me? Let me display my power, and you'll change your mind. Earth is my magical element. I can shake walls to the ground with a single thought, manipulate soil, produce gemstones at will. Spray glittering dirt. Move rocks, boulders. Shower you in diamonds simply by thinking about it."

Summer rakes a hand through her long locks, leaving an unruly dark halo around her head. "Don't be ridiculous."

She leans slightly closer, and all I can think about is the slope of her neck and how badly I want to taste the hollow between her collarbones.

Struggling through muddled thoughts, I tuck a wisp of hair behind her ear, then raise my hand above her shoulder and summon magic. Tiny stones fall behind her back. Not my finest work... but all things considered, better than nothing.

"Look!" I urge. "Turn around."

"No. Enough games. What's wrong with you? Have you really never drunk alcohol before?"

"The human kind? No. But more than my fair share at fae revels," I say, stepping close as I brush dark waves from her eyes. The sight of her exposed throat nearly makes me forget my own name. I know I should stop touching her. But I can't. "Seven hells, you're the loveliest creature I've ever seen."

She grips my wrist, heat searing my skin. "Thinking you're a wolf-shifter is bad enough, but a faery as well? That's going too far. Shit. We'd better get you home. You're not fit to be in public right now."

She's not wrong. I'm one minute away from shaking a glowing boulder out of my sleeve like a party trick. So much for being on my best behavior, like I promised.

When we return inside, I wait at the table while Summer visits the restroom after instructing me to keep my mouth zipped firmly shut.

Zylah tells a story about the time Ollie stole a dead baby opossum from the basement, and then toured the house on top of a remote cleaning device the humans call an iRobot with the stuffed animal clamped between his jaws and the other four house cats following behind yowling.

I laugh so hard at the picture her story paints that my glamour drops momentarily.

Zylah does a double take and let's out a small squeak. "There's something wrong with these cocktails," she decides after staring at her near-empty glass. "For a second there, Wyn, you looked... ah, different. Kind of like a cool vampire, but super strange."

Summer returns, saving me from sticking my foot in my mouth with another unacceptable explanation. We quickly say our goodbyes to her friends and begin the walk back to Gravenshade Hall through tree-lined streets.

This late, it's quiet, and there are hardly any cars around, but I make her switch sides so I'm walking closest to the curb. Protecting her.

Music drifts down from a high, open window of a house, drowning out the clicks and croaks of insects and frogs, as I take smaller, unsteady steps so Summer can keep up with me.

More than once she grabs my arm to stop me veering into the wrought iron fences guarding the mansions' rambling gardens. Every touch, each damn breath she takes, tests the vow I made not to tell her who she is to me and claim her as my own. But so help me, if her fingers graze mine again, I might just lose control.

"What happened to your parents?" I ask, dragging my mind out of the gutter and straight into a different kind of mess. A loaded question. Poorly chosen. But the only subject that might cool the heat burning through my insides.

After all, if she shares her personal secrets, she'll likely expect me to do the same. And I can't tell her why I'm really here in the Earth Realm—ultimately, to abduct her, just like the vile Shade Court once did.

A car horn blares in the distance as Summer takes a deep breath. "They were murdered when I was seventeen... apparently right in front of me with a knife from Gravenshade's kitchen. And I don't remember anything except making a late-night snack before it happened."

Questions tumble through the alcohol haze in my mind. "And after that? Were you imprisoned? Did you run away?"

She shoots me a glare. "The detectives suspected me at first, but there wasn't any evidence to make an arrest."

"Did anything strange happen to you afterward?"

She shrugs. "Well, I kind of lost a whole year of memories, but other than that, no. Nothing that I remember."

I know Summer went missing for a year and a day, and I'd wager the blade my father gave me that she was taken by the Wild Hunt that very same night. So either she killed her parents and the action drew the notice of Landolin Ravenseeker and the Hunt, or he was the one who murdered them.

"Do you think I killed them?" she asks as we turn onto her street.

An owl shrieks from the woods behind her home, giving me a moment to compose my answer.

"I'm not sure," I reply, unable to lie. "But I want to help find who *did* kill them. Even if it turns out it was you."

"You will? Why?" She stops walking, and her eyes search mine, like she's figuring out if I'm mocking her, or if I'm serious.

"Because I have a very... protective nature."

For a long moment, she stares open-mouthed at me, and I can't look away, even when I plow into another scrolled garden fence. "I'm very tired," I mumble, and Summer laughs and tugs me back on the path.

"You should probably eat something before bed," she says. "It'll help sober you up."

"Are you also tired?" I ask. "If so, I can carry you."

"You're not in any state to carry *anything* anywhere."

"Let me try," I murmur, wrapping an arm around her shoulders in preparation. "I could definitely carry you all night. Through a war. The apocalypse. I'm very strong."

She laughs, shaking me off as she keeps moving.

"Are you hungry, too?" I ask.

Summer rubs her stomach. "Yeah, I could easily demolish two or three fried eggs on toast."

My eyes linger on the smooth skin at the edges of her black singlet. "How about scrambled eggs? That's my specialty, unrivaled in any realm."

Summer's eyes widen comically. "Your specialty? Now I know you're definitely lying. Or crazy. You expect me to believe a supposed prince of a mythical magical land knows how to scramble eggs? The servants would do that, no matter the time of day."

I laugh. "If I demanded anything in the middle of the night, our head cook, Elowen, would spank the freckles from my face. Believe me, she's tried many times when I stole treats from her larder as a child."

"And this Elowen taught you how to scramble eggs?"

"No, my Mom did—Lara of Blackbrook. The secret is adding something I've heard you call soy sauce when they're almost cooked."

"Everyone calls it soy sauce," she says, opening the front garden gate. "Not just me."

I open my mouth to say that I meant all humans, not only her, but quickly slam it shut. No need to tell her how my mother, an addict of the salty sauce, had the necessary crops planted in the gardens and taught the cooks the year-long fermentation process so a bottle of her beloved sauce would always feature on our high table.

"Any decent Italian restaurants nearby?" I ask.

"Plenty. We can go tomorrow if you like."

My stomach growls at the idea.

There are disadvantages to living in this realm. I miss my family. My land. The full strength of my magic. But the advantages? I get to walk beside Summer now. Watch her move. Hear her speak without enchantment warping her thoughts. I get her totally unfiltered. Sharp-tongued and quick-witted. Laughing at her own jokes. Cursing like a hungover ogre on a bender.

And every time she looks at me like I'm not a monster, I come dangerously close to forgetting that I am.

And the next best thing? I get to eat my favorite dish—the one my mother taught the castle cooks to make—creamy Pasta Alfredo. Already, I'm looking forward to tomorrow. To the food. And for another chance to prove I deserve to walk beside this fragile, broken girl.

As we climb the stairs up to Summer's house, a chill skates down my spine. Someone is watching us, hiding in the shadows.

I glance back and see nothing. Feel nothing. No movement. No trace of magic in the air. But then I see her. A gray-haired figure frowning down at us from one of Gravenshade's high windows.

Summer's mother.

Dead and disapproving.

CHAPTER 14

Summer

While shoveling in scrambled eggs at the kitchen table, Wyn interrogates me about my parents' murder, and as he scrapes his plate clean, his bright-green gaze turns intense. "One last question. When you were making pizza that night, did you notice any strange smells in the kitchen?"

"What kind of smells?"

"A dark, smoky scent, tinged with something like burnt sugar?"

"No. Why do you ask?"

Shaking his head, he swiftly changes the subject and blasts me with another dimpled smile. "Some members of my family remember a time when this city was swampland, crawling with angry beasts with long snouts and even longer tails."

"Do you mean alligators? They're still out there. Take care if you walk behind the house near the lake. Do your ancestors originate from Lake Grenlynn, Wyn?"

Marie hovers by the stovetop, wiping it with a transparent cloth. I haven't the heart to tell her she's wasting her incorporeal energy.

As Wyn collects our plates, his lips twist and he avoids my eyes, fixing his gaze on the tabletop. "No. They're not from around here."

I touch his arm, flinching at the zap of electricity that shudders along my spine. "Leave the mess. We'll pack the dishwasher tomorrow after breakfast. We should go to bed."

Wearing a grin, he slowly turns to face me, his expression equal parts boyish mischief and barely leashed, extremely manly hunger. "Are you certain that's a good idea?"

Shit, no. But neither is microwave popcorn for dinner, and I've had that twice this week already.

"We have to sleep sometime, don't we?" I say, squeezing his bicep just because I can.

As we climb the stairs, he's so close behind me his body heat warms me like a radiator, and I'm pretty sure he takes a *big*, long breath through his nose, like he's... "Hey! Did you just sniff me?"

Please say no. Wait! Please say yes. *Dammit.* I clearly haven't decided if I'm flattered or freaked out.

"Is enjoying the way someone smells a crime in this city?" Wyn asks.

"No it's just creepy," I say, pushing him through the door of the spare room next to mine.

I'm lying. I don't feel creeped out at all. My skin tingles all over, and I'm having trouble thinking straight. I barely know him. But he's this perfect mix of hot and strong and vulnerable. And I'm so attracted to him. I don't want to be, but I simply can't help it.

"You can sleep in here, and Zylah will learn to deal with it."

His eyes light up as he checks out the room. "Really?"

"Yes, really."

Crossing his arms, he leans a shoulder on the door frame. "Sorry about drinking your scent in like a wild wolf before. I couldn't help myself. You smell amazing."

"I didn't have a chance to shower after work today. I must stink like—"

"You smell perfect," he interrupts. "*Really*. Couldn't be better."

I laugh. "You're still drunk. Time to go into your room, Wyn," I say, nudging his wall of muscle through the doorway again. A great excuse to touch him. "In this state, you're dangerous."

He makes a please-explain face, arching his brows, then his eyes smolder and darken.

"Why are you staring at me like that?" I ask.

"Like what?"

"Like I'm scrambled eggs."

"I think you know why."

Oh, shit. Here we go. He's not the least bit shy. The question is: what am I going to do about it? Give in, or resist my growing attraction to a possibly mad, clothes-optional stranger?

"Grían is the word for sun in old Irish," he says, leaning closer. "Did you know that? Makes sense that people call you Summer."

I swallow hard, unease humming in my veins. He knows my birth name? He must've read the old newspapers in the basement. Damn. I should have moved them. He says my real name like it means something. Like *I* mean something to him. That's what scares me.

"No. I didn't know it," I lie smoothly. Mom was an Irish scholar, so of course I'm aware of what my name means. I just don't understand why I'm lying to him.

Warm fingers stroke my cheek. "When you lie, Summer, the skin around your left eye twitches a little. Most wouldn't notice. But I notice everything about you."

"Sounding like a stalker again."

He grins, unashamed.

I smile back. "Those dimples of yours are lethal."

"Finest in the land that I hail from... or so I've been told."

"Humble, aren't you?"

"Not particularly," he admits. Stepping even closer, he rakes a hand through his hair and blows out a slow breath. "Gods, Summer. I want..."

Then before my brain catches up, his head dips lower. His lips touch mine, whisper-soft, the shock and feel of him curling my toes.

"Wyn," I moan like I've been waiting for this moment since I first saw him naked in my kitchen. Which is true, but honestly, I think I've been waiting my whole life for him.

Deepening the kiss, I lean into him, my fingers threading through his hair, the palm of my other hand cupping his cheekbone, not letting him come up for air.

Waves of heat pulse through me. I've never felt anything this good. When he groans and wraps his arms tightly around my waist, I push forward, into the bedroom, ready to take this all the way.

Life is hard, and I'm tired of not having nice things. Of sitting back waiting for the good stuff to happen. I don't want him to slip through my fingers and disappear forever. Not before I feel the full weight of him against me, skin to skin.

A tremor ripples through him, and then his hands are on my shoulders, cool air between our bodies. "I can't, Summer. Fuck, I want to. More than anything. But I can't because my sister—"

"Your *sister*?" Anger and confusion shudder through me as I sink onto the edge of his bed, rubbing my arms. "I don't understand. What's *she* got to do with who you sleep with?"

"You'll think I'm crazy if I tell you the truth."

"No shit. But news flash: I already do, so you've got nothing to lose."

"Where do I start?" The bed frame creaks as he sits beside me and expels a long breath. "I'm the only son of the Air Prince of Talamh Cúig, Everend Fionbharr. My mother is Lara Delaney from the human city of Blackbrook. I'm brother to the Unseelie Queen of Merits, and also, I have this pain-in-the-ass curse— "

I hold my palm up between us, shutting him down. "No, you don't. No curses. I don't want to hear any more of your delusions. It's best if you get into bed and have a good night's sleep. You'll feel better in the morning."

"The curse has nothing to do with why I can't touch you. It's just that I told Merri that I wouldn't. To keep us *both* safe."

"La-la-la-laaa," I sing, clapping my hands over my ears. "Not listening!"

"Come to bed with me?" he asks, his expression vulnerable. "To... sleep, I mean."

"*What*? Why? Because you're a glutton for punishment?" With a loud sigh, I stand up. "I don't think so. You can lie there all alone and think about what we could have been doing if only you weren't so worried about your imaginary sister's opinion, which is weird by the way. Hope you have the sleep you deserve."

If I sound seriously butthurt, that's because I am. I haven't wanted anyone like I want Wyn in years. But the feeling can't be mutual if he's making up bad excuses to avoid doing the deed with me.

"Okay. Goodnight, Summer," he says whipping his T-shirt over his head.

I bite my lip to stop myself from saying something stupid, like, *oh, wow, muscles*.

"Give my regards to the lady in the mirror," he continues. "I presume she's your mother."

Halfway to the door, I freeze. "You see the ghosts, too?"

"Of course," he says with a grin. "I'm not blind."

"Whenever I see my mom's ghost," I reply, "I *beg* my eyes to malfunction."

"Why? It's a talent, Summer. Only gifted folk see them."

Arms crossed, I pace in front of him. "I'm not convinced. Being forced to bear witness to their never-ending pain. Seeing them trapped in limbo. It's horrible."

Ollie appears in the doorway, announcing his presence with an urgent *meh-raow?* before springing onto Wyn's lap.

My cat vibrates in ecstasy as Wyn strokes him firmly from head to tail. "But you can easily release the spirits from the plane they're trapped in. The ritual is simple. If you know the dead person, you must forgive them for the harm they did you. If they did no ill, but believe they have, then you must say you forgive them anyway."

I tuck my unruly hair behind my ears. "It can't be that straightforward."

"It is. Just say the word, and I'll help you let your dear mother go."

"She was never that dear to me."

"Where's she buried?" he asks.

"Her ashes are in the garage."

He braces his palms on the bed, muscles straining as if he's about to stand up, bare-chested and everything. "Show me."

"*Now?*" I squeak. "Why?"

"I'll make sure we send your mom away for good."

"Dabbling in the dark arts while you're still drunk? No thanks. Too dangerous. Maybe tomorrow."

His earnest desire to help melts away any lingering resentment from his rejection. I bid him goodnight with a smile and a lazy wave over my shoulder.

While I'm brushing my teeth and trying to scrub the image of the sexy, crazy boy in the other room from my mind, my mother materializes in the mirror. "He's dangerous," she warns without preamble.

Although I agree with her, I pretend ignorance, shrug, and say, "Who?" through a mouthful of toothpaste. My plan to exorcise her from the house pops into my head, and hot shame rolls through my gut.

"The wolf-boy you were making out with."

Wait... how could she...? "I thought you could only see through Gravenshade's mirrors," I mumble.

"Perhaps that's what I wanted you to believe."

I spit into the sink, then rinse my mouth and toothbrush.

"Wyn's not as half as dangerous as the idea of you watching my entire sexual awakening in 4K, Mom."

Because that's just peachy. Who wouldn't want their dead mother witnessing every embarrassing moment of their lives?

I think of how wild and reckless I acted when I returned from my year-long-kidnapping event—or whatever it was. The hangover days I spent barfing over the toilet, my rage-filled self-destruction, the ridiculous songs I screamed out, drunk and hating on my parents for never loving me enough.

Oh, and let's not forget the times I spent in bed *engrossed* in Zylah's smutty romance books.

I really hope my ghost mother enjoyed all of that. Good *grief.*

"Right. So you can move anywhere you want around Gravenshade. Can you go outside, too? Why did you call Wyn a wolf-boy?"

She just smiles and melts into a ghostly cloud of gloom, destined to return tomorrow, like the world's most persistent nightmare.

I really must take Wyn up on his offer to perform an exorcism. I'll follow it up tomorrow and make sure whatever we do won't hurt her. I don't want her to suffer eternal damnation or anything too torturous, but I wouldn't be upset if I never saw her frowning, judgmental face again.

Realizing I've forgotten to take my anxiety meds, I slip into sleep shorts and an old band T-shirt and pad down the stairs and into the kitchen, the usual chill I get whenever I make this trip alone at night sliding down my skin.

I click on a lamp and find the benches reasonably tidy, which means Zy and Kurt are still out drinking. And just like that horrible night eight years ago, the moon is full and silver light is shimmering over the tiled floor.

Lunging on one leg, I peer under the dining table. No bogeyman. Good. It's just me and the creepy shadows.

After swallowing my pills, I crack open the back door and peek through it, certain I can hear music playing near the woods—wafting pipes and a low droning sound I don't recognize. Probably Kurt out there with a portable speaker, playing a cruel joke on me.

If it is, when I catch him, I'm going to bury him under the magnolia tree.

CHAPTER 15

Summer

Shivering, even though the breeze is warm, I step onto the back porch. The music from the woods quickens, the drums pounding faster, an eerie vocal keening higher and higher. The sound is... strange. And wrong. Yet I step down into the yard, unable to resist its pull.

"Kurt?" I call out, even though it doesn't sound like a recording, and there's no way his falsetto is *that* good.

A shadow moves at the edge of the trees, then a tall figure steps forward, pale hands loose at his sides, his outline glowing softly. Fuck. That's *definitely* not Kurt.

"Come here," he commands in a dark velvet voice.

Barefoot and heart pounding, I pad to the back gate and stare through the twisted iron bars. The night is silent now. No music. No owls hooting or frogs calling. Why am I standing here passive, like a virgin sacrifice minus the intact hymen?

The man moves closer, and I get a good look at him. Dark hair with blue tips framing coal-black eyes that glitter with gold flecks. A wide, petulant mouth. Sharp cheekbones.

Skin that reflects the moonlight. He's frighteningly, sickeningly handsome.

"What are you?" I ask, my voice barely above a whisper.

"Your destiny."

Oh good. A terrifying stranger with cheekbones that could slice steel and an epic god complex. Just what I need in my life.

Dark eyes scan my face, and he laughs.

A shot of adrenaline spikes, and my upper body jolts forward, but my feet don't budge. I can't seem to move my legs at all. I open my mouth to scream, but nothing comes out.

Shadows creep from the woods and wind around the guy's black-clad body, caressing his cold smile. Something about him reminds me of Wyn. Except Wyn makes me feel safe, and this one instills a nauseating kind of terror.

"Open the gate," he says.

Even though the urge to obey tugs at the muscles in my arms and legs, I shake my head.

In response, his fingers circle through the shadowy smoke, flicking a line of whatever it is toward me, ash trailing in its path. The gate opens, unseen fingers releasing the lock and lever.

I don't notice him move a muscle, but suddenly he's right in front of me, his vicious smirk widening. "It's good to see you after all these years."

"I've never laid eyes on you before. Whatever you're doing to keep me standing here, stop it. Please. Let me go."

"Sorry. I can't."

What does he mean? He can't, or he *won't*?

"Is this a dream?" I ask, my teeth starting to chatter.

"Oh, no. Not a dream. You're so close to finally waking up."

Whatever he means by that, I don't want to know. "Please," I say, hot tears burning my cheeks.

"As the oldest gods bear witness, what we make ours in the shadows remains ours. Always. You belong to us, and an ocean of your tears won't change that."

Blinking, I rub my eyes. This can't be real. I must have finally lost my mind, succumbed to the years of trauma.

"In case you're wondering, I'm as real as the night sky. *I* made you leave the house. *I'm* the one rooting your feet to the earth."

"Who are you?" I demand. "Tell me your name."

A cold laugh sends chills racing over me.

"You're not as foolish as most humans. Instead of screeching and howling, you have the presence of mind to ask the right questions. It would be a shame to take your sanity again. If you behave, perhaps this time we won't need to."

"*Again?* Listen, if I can't stop whatever's about to happen, you might as well tell me who you are. It won't make any difference, will it?"

Amusement flickers across his face, and his eyes glitter with calculation. "Some fae call me Landolin. Others, evil prick. But those in the second category don't tend to breathe much longer if they say it within my hearing—which, I must admit, is considerable."

Fae? Isn't that what Wyn said he was? A fae, a faery prince, like in the old books my mother studied.

"What do you want from me?"

He shrugs a velvet-covered shoulder, the white gemstones dotting the material flashing in the moonlight. "Only what we are owed," he says softly. "You were ours, and then you were taken from us."

What the actual fuck? Is *he* the reason I lost an entire year of my life?

"But first, some entertainment for the Wild Hunt," he continues. "To keep things intimate, we're a small party this evening. But we do *so* love to chase. Prepare to run, sweet thing. Run as fast as you can."

Did he say the Wild Hunt? Shit. I'm so, *so* screwed.

"I... I'm a terrible runner. Please don't—"

"Hush now. I'll give you a generous head start. Twenty-five slow breaths, one for each year of your life. But know this: the Hunt *will* catch you. The farther you get, the easier we will make your capture, and your subsequent return to my land. I vow this upon the shadows that feed my soul. Cross my heart. So... try to make it interesting, won't you?"

"Who's the '*we*' you mentioned?" I ask, scanning the dark trees for any more weirdos hiding behind them.

His fingers trace a fast pattern over his chest, like a priest. Or a total lunatic.

A loud jingling noise comes from the trees, and twelve horses appear, their silver manes threaded with glowing flowers. Eleven riders, beautiful and yet horrible to behold, sit astride the gleaming black steeds. One saddle is empty. Must be Landolin's horse.

I glance behind me, preparing to run into the house and lock myself in the basement, but three riders appear between me and the porch stairs. One lifts a curling horn to his lips, and Landolin mounts his horse, his sneer turning gleeful. "Ready?" he asks.

Nope. I'm absolutely *not* ready. And I think I'm about to die in my pajamas. Definitely not the best look for my ever-lasting ghost. But at least I'll be matching Mommy Dearest in the eternal-nightwear department. Fashion icons, the both of us.

Taking a massive breath first, I scream Wyn's name as loud as I can, and with a snort of surprise, Landolin looks up at the house, the glow around his body intensifying. He says something, but the horn blows, drowning out his words.

The muscles in my legs release, and an idea slips into my mind. If I can make it through the gap cut in the wire fence that's too small for a horse to fit through, then maybe I'll stand a chance. Fuck, I wish I had my phone.

I take off running toward the left side of the yard like hell just burst open behind me—because, hey, it kinda has.

The terrible horn sounds again as I scramble through jasmine vines hugging the hole in the fence. On the other side, I collide with the ground.

Landolin's voice rings out as he counts each breath. So far, he's only reached five, so at least he's kept his word and is taking his time.

I lurch to my feet and leap forward, crashing into a wall of fur. When I look up, the black wolf with the silver patch around one eye is standing in front of me. Hank. Or... Wyn.

It has to be Wyn.

After what I've seen tonight, I believe every unhinged word that's come out of his mouth. Fully. Completely. Fates help me.

The wolf huffs warm breath on my hand, and then moves forward, staring at me over his shoulder, begging me to follow, before taking off downhill in the direction of the lake.

The Wild Hunt's horn splits the air behind me, a low, bone-chilling sound that promises no mercy. Wyn streaks ahead, a dark shadow flashing through the moonlit forest. My lungs hurt as I pump my arms and do my best to keep up with him, my legs trembling and bare feet sliding over the ground.

My feet are probably bleeding, but I can't feel a thing. Other than fear.

Hoofbeats crash closer, the staccato rhythm relentless, drowning out the hammering of my heart.

Wyn's glowing green eyes slice through the darkness as he glances back every few moments to make sure I'm close by, rumbling low in his throat and urging me onward.

"I'm going as fast as I can," I choke out.

My heel slips on loose dirt, and I go down hard, a jolt of pain shooting through my knee. "Shit," I hiss, scrambling to my feet, the echo of Landolin's voice in the distance spurring me into action.

He's not counting anymore. Instead, he's laughing and joking with his monstrous friends, taking great joy in scaring the crap out of me.

"Run harder little human. Run for your life," he taunts over the piercing shouts of the other riders. "You have it in you, I know it. The longer the game, the better our aim."

Whatever that means.

Wyn skids to a sudden stop, looking right, then left, a guttural snarl ripping from his throat before he bolts off again, and I stagger after him, no clear thoughts in my mind other than, don't fall, don't fall. Just don't fucking fall.

The woods behind Gravenshade are a tangled mass of live oaks and cypress, Spanish moss twisting around their limbs, dripping like tattered cloaks. When playing here as a child, the forest felt alive to me, like a sentient, ancient being. Tonight, I imagine it whispering encouragement, cheering me on.

I yelp as I trip again and smash my nose into a tree trunk, the jangle of bridles, hoots, and calls of Landolin's Hunt growing closer, the riders gaining on us. I look behind me as an antlered silhouette lifts a glinting spear before leaning over his mount, urging it forward.

Fuck, fuck, fuck. We'll never outrun them.

"Wyn! Should we hide and wait for them to pass? I can't keep running forever."

The wolf doubles back and nips the air an inch above my arm, his meaning crystal clear.

No fucking way. Keep moving.

We leap over a fallen tree, push through low shrubs that open onto a flat, cleared space, the dark waters of Lake Grenlynn stretched out before us.

Now what?

Landolin is right behind us, his raspy laugh raising tiny hairs over my skin, his horse snorting and stamping the ground.

I taste blood in my mouth and wipe my nose with a clenched fist. "Wyn? There's nowhere to go."

"Let her come quietly," says Landolin, "and you can return home without punishment for interfering in Shade Court business, Prince of Mud."

Prince? Another thing Wyn wasn't lying about.

The wolf's hackles rise, his whole body shaking as a fuck-you growl rumbles in his chest.

Without warning, Wyn suddenly veers around me, then a blunt force hits the back of my legs, and I fall, tumbling sideways, rolling headfirst into the water.

The lake swallows my scream, dragging me down into its depths.

CHAPTER 16

Summer

"You're hurt," is the first thing Wyn says to me, finally noticing I exist after I've just spent five minutes watching his body writhe and reshape in agony on a bed of purple wildflowers. Quite the eye-opening experience.

Glad to see him back in his ~~human~~ um...*fae* form, I look around, amazed to find myself alive and not dead at the bottom of Lake Grenlynn with my lungs full of weeds and about to be fish food.

We're on a mountain in a small, sloped clearing that smells like crushed herbs and wet moss, surrounded by trees so tall they block out most of the sky. Also, it's daylight, which is weird since the spooky Landolin chased us through the woods well after midnight, and now it's like... *daytime?*

Whatever this place is, it has no respect for circadian rhythms.

"I'm fine, thanks," I finally reply, still in shock and already shelving it for later like a champ.

Sitting beside Wyn, I scrub the dried blood under my nose with a shaking hand and inspect the grazes on my bare feet. "Happy to be alive, actually. Now that I know every word you told me was true... I'm guessing we're in your world? Or realm—is that what you call it?"

"Yeah. You're in Faery. Told you I wasn't lying." He clasps his hands behind his head and lies back in the grass. "This realm is known as the Land of Five. Home of the Elemental Fae and the Seelie Court." Squinting against the light, he rakes his gaze over me, slow and hot. "You're breathing and not screaming. That's promising."

I sigh down at my sleep shorts and ripped T-shirt. If only I'd had the foresight to venture down to the kitchen last night wearing a pair of sturdy boots.

"So you knew that jumping into the lake would lead us here?" I ask him.

"I hoped the portal would still be connected. Took me a while to find one that spat me out close to your house. Now, it's my favorite one in all of the realms."

"Oh? Why's that?" I ask.

"Because it brought me back to you and allowed me to follow you to work and observe you for days without you noticing."

"Oh, I noticed you all right. Not too many giant black wolves hanging around Lake Grenlynn."

He shakes his head, a faint smile tugging at his mouth as he gets to his feet. "How do you feel?"

"You asked me that already."

"This time, I mean... in your mind. Now you're in Faery, are any memories racing back?"

"No, why should they?"

Wearing a miserable expression, he gives a half-hearted shrug.

"So I'm not dead or dreaming? Everything you said about being a fae prince, a wolf shifter... it's all true?"

He nods. "Yeah. Full-blooded fae can't lie, but my mother is human, so I'm a halfling, and it's much easier for me to lie in Faery, but strangely not in the Earth Realm. So everything I said while we were in Lake Grenlynn was the honest truth."

Brushing leaves off my legs, I stand up. "In other words, I can't trust anything you say here."

My comment wipes the dimpled smile off his face.

"Have you been trying to tell me I've been here before? Is Faery where I disappeared to on the night my parents died?"

"I'm afraid so. Do you... maybe remember me from your time here?"

Wait... what? He thinks we've met before he showed up in the Vandersons' garden, stalking me in his wolf form?

I study his face, transformed into something otherworldly, his human glamour gone. He looks like Wyn but turned up to eleven. His cheekbones and ears are sharper, eyes glowing and slightly tilted at the outer edges. The freckles dusting his nose sparkle like flecks of mica on wet stone. The patch on the left side of his bangs glows bright silver.

"No. Should I remember you? Hey, what happened to Kurt's jeans?"

Zylah's brother's clothes have disappeared, and Wyn's now wearing leather pants, a fine black shirt under a leather-and-velvet jacket with outrageous, silver-tipped shoulder pads that resemble armor.

He grins. "It's a glamour. I'm totally naked underneath, so don't stare too much. You might get a surprise."

Okay. And shame on me because I do stare. *Hard.*

Then a thought hits me. "But isn't that the way clothes work, too?" I say. "I mean, you don't wear clothes under your clothes just to avoid being naked beneath them. Or... wait. That's literally the point of underwear, isn't it? Never mind. Don't listen to me—my brain's scrambled from inter-realm travel and being chased by monsters on horseback."

He laughs but says nothing.

"Do your clothes disappear every time you shift?" I ask.

"Basically."

"Even the swords strapped to your hips are glamours?"

"Yeah. To scare off the feral pixies, but I can conjure a real weapon pretty easily."

"How does that work exactly?"

Leaning close, he whispers, "Magic." Then his head shifts back an inch, and he's so close I can count the gold flecks in his startling eyes. "We draw on our elements, mine's earth, and the magic around us and just... form stuff."

"Very scientific explanation," I tease.

"Listen, we need to get farther up the mountain—to the lake where I can recharge my power. Jumping through that portal zapped what little magic I had left after spending weeks in your realm. Pretending to be mortal is very draining."

"Sounds like a plan. And then what?" I ask.

"Then we'll travel to my home, the Elemental city of Talamh Cúig, and find a way to keep you safe from Landolin and the Shade Court."

"But when do I get to go back to *my* home? Zylah's going to be so worried. She'll contact Detective Perez. There'll be a search party. They'll drag the lake again. It'll be like history repeating itself. I can't do this again. I can't—"

He places both hands on my shoulders. "Breathe, Summer. Breathe. I don't have all the answers yet, but we'll send someone from the court to Gravenshade. We'll work it out. All will be well. Don't worry."

"Okay." I blow out a long breath. "Okay."

He steps back, gaze sliding down my bare legs. "You cold?"

"A little," I admit.

"Wait here." He scans the ground and stomps off toward a leaf-filled ditch, returning moments later with a patchwork cloak in different shades of brown and dark gold. As he wraps it around my shoulders and ties it with a cord from his pocket, I shiver at his touch.

"Better?" he asks gruffly, as if embarrassed by his gift.

"You made this out of sticks and dirt?" I ask, fingering a patch that looks suspiciously like it used to be part of a nest.

"Mostly leaves." He points at his chest. "Earth magic, remember?"

As we walk up the mountain, I yawn and blink at the silvery sun. "How close is your home?"

"Several days walk."

I groan, and he flashes me a cocky grin.

"Once I renew my strength in the Lake of Spirits, I'll carry you," he says, voice solemn like he's making some sacred vow. "That way, you can rest." Then his gaze slides over me, slow and appraising. "You look light as a feather. I'm sure I could carry you now."

"No, thanks. Hard pass. My legs are working just fine."

My heart thumps against my ribs at the idea of pressing against Wyn's chest... or clinging to his back, legs wrapped tight around his waist, my body flush with his warmth.

I said no thanks, but mentally I'm already curled up against him like Ollie in my lap in front of the fire in Gravenshade's library on an icy winter's night.

Back home, I wasn't afraid of Wyn—and even now, in Faery, I'm still not. What worries me is *me*. And this growing, inconvenient attraction to a supernatural being.

I guess I should be relieved that he's fae. Could be worse. He might have been a junkie or completely unhinged, like I first assumed when I found him naked in my kitchen, making coffee.

I yawn again, basically one belly rub away from curling up on the ground and snoring.

Wyn laughs, takes my hand to help me over a moss-covered boulder, and says, "Staring at the sun in this realm will make you sleepy. Feel free to look at me instead. Less likely to lull you to sleep. Or so I've been told."

"Tempting idea, but these trees are actually pretty spectacular. What are they called?"

There's a flash of movement in the shadows, and Wyn drops into a fighting stance, the stones, rocks, and ground around us shuddering.

Satchel, the other black wolf from the Vandersons' garden leaps through the air, jaws open and aimed at Wyn's throat. Instead of screaming and running for his life like I'm about to, Wyn laughs and rolls over the ground in a tangle of leather-clad limbs and fur, wrestling with the gigantic beast.

Just when I think they're about to tumble down the mountainside and leave me to get eaten by the next fae creature that wanders by, they stop and Wyn presses his forehead against the wolf's, then looks up at me. "This is Ivor."

I give a foolish, half-hearted wave.

"Good to see you, old friend," Wyn says. "Have you been waiting at the Lake of Spirits for me to return?"

A happy noise rumbles from Ivor's chest followed by a high-pitched yelp, then he trots over to sniff my knees with an enthusiasm I find uncomfortable. I reverse slowly until my spine hits a tree trunk.

"Stroke him," says Wyn, smiling. "He knows you well and is happy to see you safe."

He knows me well? *How* exactly? Losing a year of memories sure puts me at a disadvantage.

When I'm feeling settled and safer, I need Wyn to tell me everything he thinks I've forgotten. So far, nothing about this strange place looks or feels familiar. But after what I've seen in the past few hours, I'm willing to believe almost anything. Even that I've been here before.

I mean it makes sense. I went missing for a year and no one, not even the authorities, could find me. Being whisked away to another realm kind of sounds plausible. When it comes to my life, the most batshit theory is usually the one that sticks.

But who, I wonder, did the whisking? Was it that creep Landolin, like he claimed?

"Ivor will travel to Talamh Cúig and return with my horse, so we can ride home. In the meantime, I'll wait here with you," says Wyn.

My hand freezes on Ivor's thick coat. "You could shift and go with him, get home faster," I say.

"Sure, I *could* do that, but I won't leave your side until you're tucked away safe, where the Wild Hunt can't find you."

After we bid Ivor goodbye and watch him disappear into the trees, we continue following a glowing red river uphill until we reach the top of the mountain, where a lake sits in a crater surrounded by towering fir trees.

CHAPTER 17

Wynter

"This is the Lake of Spirits," I say, letting the pride in my voice ring clear.

"What's so special about it?" Summer asks, her toes sinking into the cool mud on the pebbled shore.

I gesture to the shimmering surface. "At the beginning of time, four sisters—our mages—sprang from the water, creating the rivers that are named for the elements they represent: Aer, Serpent, Fire, and Terra. The fifth sister, Ether, is connected to the lake. Some say she's the goddess of life itself."

Summer squints at me. "Cool. Is she gonna mind if I skinny dip in her beautiful lake?"

Seven hells, she sets one toe in that lake and I'm a goner. No chance in the realm I'll keep my hands to myself. "You can stay here while I bathe. Right at the edge where I can see you. Don't move."

She mock-salutes. "Yes, sir."

I can't help but laugh. Damn her.

I wade in. The water clings like silk, magic tingling under my skin as the glamour peels away. The cold bite grounds me. The heat in my chest does the opposite. I glance back and find Summer's eyes on me, watching. Of course she is.

Water sluices down my chest, and her gaze trails the droplets like she wants to follow them with her tongue.

"Stop thinking that," I say, unable to hide my grin.

She freezes, a blush rising up her neck. "Thinking what?"

"You *know* what."

"I was admiring the scenery," she mutters. "Maybe your ego needs a good rinse while you're at it."

I laugh and sink deeper, letting the water hide the evidence of what she's doing to me.

"Wait." Her eyes narrow. "Can you actually read my mind, or are you just creepily good at guessing when I'm thinking inappropriate things?"

I tilt my head. "Bit of both. It's an intermittent and unreliable skill of mine. Only works in Faery, where strong thoughts and emotions are amplified."

She groans. "Of course mine would be particularly loud."

"Right *now*, yours are shouting."

She does a little jog in place, clearly trying to kill her wicked thoughts, which, unfortunately for her, are now *mine*. Then she changes the subject. "Is that all you have to do? Just get wet, and then your powers recharge?"

"Essentially. The Lake is the source of our land's magic, as well as the power the Elemental mages draw on to control the five elements."

"Five?"

"Earth, air, fire, water, and ether—which is spirit."

She shades her eyes from the sun with one hand. "So if I went for a dip in there, would I come out glowing and speaking in tongues?"

"Come in and find out," I say before I can stop myself—because that's a brilliant move. Just invite temptation in and watch my self-control sink like a stone.

After folding her cloak of woodland scraps, she strips off her shorts and T-shirt. I spin around fast—too fast, the opposite of playing it cool. I hear water lap as she steps in. I focus on the horizon and not the fact that my mate—the only girl I'll ever want—is now in the water with me and possibly *naked*.

"What happens after this?" she asks.

"We'll camp near the river and wait for Ivor and Tier."

"Who's Tier?"

"Don't worry. Only my horse, and he doesn't bite... often."

I steal a glance, drinking her in. That pale, perfect skin begging for my touch. My breath catches. Fuck, I want her so bad.

She's close. Too close. Her scent hits me like wet earth after a storm. She stops, barely inches away, and I want... No. I clench my fists, arms crossed tight. Unconsciously, my thumb strokes the inside of my bicep as if it were *her* arm, *her* smooth, delicious skin.

I'm not touching her. I won't. But my gaze is stuck on her collarbone. Then her lips. Her lovely eyes. And the wolf inside me fights for control. Demands that I claim her.

I hold my breath and move an inch closer. Her gaze moves to my mouth. Then closing my eyes, I force myself to lean back a fraction, creating space before I do something I'll regret. The chasm of cool air between us feels realms deep.

She's likely still in shock, her teeth chattering and body trembling. After being hunted through the woods and yanked into another realm, she has every reason to be terrified.

"Wyn," she whispers. "I could really do with a hug right now."

My resolve crumples like wet parchment. How can I deny her anything? But if I touch her...

"It's just a hug," she adds, noticing my hesitation. "I'm not asking you to ravish me underwater or declare undying devotion."

"Just a hug?" My voice cracks. "There is no *just* with you, Summer. If I touch you now, I won't be able to stop."

"Fine. Don't stop."

"You must know I'd give everything, *anything*, to hold you... But the one thing I can't risk is you getting hurt. I promised..." My words drift away like leaves on a breeze.

I tear a hand through my hair, and before I can change my mind, I yank her into my arms. Gods. She fits perfectly, like she was made for me. Her cheek against my chest, her scent in my lungs. She sighs, melting against me. My arms lock tight, anchoring us both.

The words come unbidden—ones my mother used to say when I woke from nightmares as a child: *Don't worry, my love. You are safe. You are loved.* I whisper them over and over in the old language, stroking her spine, ignoring the less noble part of me currently pressing against her soft stomach. She doesn't flinch. She leans in. She wants this too.

She pulls back to study me, her gaze grazing over my face like she's memorizing every line. I hold still, even as her fingers tremble and brush my cheek, setting off a lightning storm beneath my skin.

Close the gap. Please. I want more. I feel the words bouncing off her skull into mine, torturing me.

I tilt my face closer and whisper her name. "Summer... I..." And then my lips brush hers once, twice before pressing more firmly, tenderly teasing her open. She hangs suspended in my arms. As lost in this as I am.

My arms tighten around her as I deepen the kiss, my cock hardening to the point of pain, my next breath filled with the earthy, human scent of her wet hair and damp skin. My breathing is a mess, caught in an erratic, ragged rhythm. She clutches my shoulders like she's drowning and I'm her only hope for survival.

The wolf rages beneath my skin, snarling with need. It doesn't care about vows or consequences. It wants her. And not gently. Not carefully. It wants to take and keep and mark her forever.

My control thins to a bare thread. The wolf claws at it, fangs bared, wanting, needing, *demanding*.

A deep sound, wild and desperate, rumbles in my throat, then a heavy splashing noise erupts nearby, and I let Summer go, turning toward the middle of the lake.

"Sounds like the ulaid is waking for her nightly hunt," I say. "If we don't want to be on the menu, we'd better move fast."

"What's an ulaid?" she asks, still breathless and shivering.

"Water dragon. They usually leave fae alone, unless the creature is injured or starving. Not sure about humans. You okay?"

I check her over, taking note of every inch. My body hasn't calmed down in the slightest, and her being mostly naked isn't helping.

Back on the bank, she dresses quickly, her gaze fixed on me as I rise from the water, my glamour curling into armor. Her green eyes devour every inch.

"Wyn," she says, bending and wringing water from her hair. "Can ghosts follow people across realms?"

"Don't think so," I reply, flopping beside her and unhooking my water pouch. "We've got plenty of wraiths. They're born of magic. But I've never seen a human ghost in Faery. At least not so far."

"Good. My mom doesn't need to see me clinging to you in the lake like a barnacle on a whale."

I take a sip of water and choke on a laugh. "What's a whale?"

"Giant sea creature. Similar to a kraken. Some are the size of boats. Bigger even. Don't worry, you're much more attractive than a whale, Wyn."

"Right. Thanks... I think. Do you always let your thoughts flow so freely?"

She shrugs. "Yeah. I have no filter."

We follow River Terra downhill until we find a small clearing. I summon bedding with earth magic, gather branches and moss, spark a fire. Then I conjure a spear and head to the river to catch our dinner. Or breakfast. Whatever the hells our next meal will be.

"How does shifting work?" Summer asks as my glamour dissolves and I wade into the water in something similar to Kurt's silky boxer shorts. "Can all fae do it?"

"Every royal male of Talamh Cúig can. My sister, Merri, thinks it's highly unfair, and she's not wrong. But as consolation, she rules the Unseelie fae with her husband, Riven. And still, she can barely forgive me my accidental birthright."

From the outside, it might sound as if there's a great rift between us, but that couldn't be further from the truth. I would do anything for my sister. Even lay down my life to keep her safe.

"Wyn," Summer says softly. "How did I get here eight years ago? What did I do while I was here? Tell me anything you remember."

I freeze and turn my back on her. "As you might have guessed, the Hunt stole you when you were seventeen. They kept you in Landolin's court for nearly six months before, Draírdon, the High Mage of the Unseelie Court bought you as a pet for the Merit Kingdom, where my sister is now the queen. Although, she was a mere visitor at the time."

"A pet? That doesn't sound good."

"At the time, the Merit Court was cruel under Riven's father's rule. During the four months you spent there, you were treated poorly. My sister rescued you, brought you back to Talamh Cúig, to my home, the place I first saw you. You stayed two months before she convinced Ether to remove the last of the Shade Court spell and return you to the mortal realm."

"What exactly happened to me at the Merit Court?"

Frowning, I look at her over my shoulder. "I don't think you need to hear all of the details. Not yet. But you were enthralled, ridiculed, and spent most of your days and nights dancing until you dropped."

"Right. How... horrid. That explains why, at times, I feel like my mind is a thousand-piece jigsaw puzzle. At least the recurring nightmares with weird music and existential terror make more sense now."

My heart breaks for her, for everything that she went through. One day, someone will pay dearly.

She starts whispering. "Seven, eight, nine, ten, eleven, twelve, thirteen—"

"Summer? What are you doing?"

"Counting. Makes me feel better."

I blink. She's counting. Maybe like a charm, or a ward. I don't understand or know the rules of her human coping rituals—but whatever this is, I'll let it stand if it keeps her from falling apart.

"And you and I... we were friends?" she asks.

"Not exactly. I was an admirer. A stalker, as you've charmingly called me. But I had your best interests at heart. My sister ordered me not to speak to you."

"Why?"

"Because our family harbors curses and secrets, and she was afraid I'd run away to your realm, where she couldn't keep me safe, and I'd never return."

"Will you tell me those secrets one day, Wyn?"

"Eventually. When I'm sure you can handle them."

She stands on the river's edge, searching for signs of fish glinting gold and green in the burnished light. "Can you shift easily anytime you like?"

I throw the spear and miss. Dammit.

"Not always. I can usually shift fast when needed. But in your realm, I struggled to stay in my wolf form. Certain... triggers."

She raises a brow. "What triggers?"

I flush and look away. "None you need to be aware of." My arm thrusts downward twice, and I skewer two fat, spotted fish on the end of my spear.

"Dinner," she yells, clapping like she invented fire.

As I step onto the muddy bank and summon another glamour, I grin. "Let's hope these fine specimens will satisfy your appetite. Your stomach's making more noise than Ivor during mating season."

"What's the plan after we eat?" she asks, mischief dancing in her leaf-green eyes.

Stepping closer, I lean in and murmur next to her ear, "I plan to rest. If you can keep your hands to yourself."

CHAPTER 18

Summer

Smoke curls through thick rays of afternoon light, wafting the delicious smell of cooking fish toward me, and my stomach growls like a bear waking from hibernation.

"Food's almost ready," says Wyn, grinning as he glances up through long, dark bangs.

"Brilliant. I was about to start munching on the firewood. I'll go wash up in the river before we eat."

"Summer, be careful. No talking to any stray creatures."

"Creatures? Where?" I scan the surrounding trees, searching for anything with claws or sharp teeth hiding in the woods. "What sort exactly?"

He shrugs a shoulder. "Sluaghs or redcaps. Their bites can be fatal."

"Oh, okay. But I wouldn't recognize either of those if I face planted on top of one," I say.

As I stroll away, I hear him call out. "Don't talk to anything, then. Not even yourself. Go quietly. You never know who's listening."

"Don't worry. I'm not going far," I shout over my shoulder, already breaking one of his rules.

I'm still reeling from discovering he can read my thoughts sometimes. Which is bad. Very, *very* bad. Also, Wyn might be the most overprotective male I've ever met, and I once owned a boy cat that bit anyone who so much as breathed on me.

Growing up with parents who just weren't that into me, I'm not used to being fussed over and worried about. It's a strange experience, and I'm still not sure if I like it.

When I reach the bank, I'm startled by a man bathing in the middle of the river, the water caressing his slim waist as he sways gently from side to side, as if in a trance. An alarm bell goes off inside me, and I glance back toward the camp, reassuring myself the fire smoke and Wyn are close by.

I should leave. Or call out for Wyn. But I don't do either. A molten warmth spirals through my veins, anchoring me in place. The woods around me are silent. No birds chirping or insects buzzing.

As I study the fae, the scent of damp earth fills my lungs. His elegant fingers trail through ripples of water, and his bare skin sparkles in the sunlight, as if his body is carved from gold-flecked river stone.

Midnight hair hangs in wet ropes over his shoulders. He smiles when he catches me staring, but his eyes remain cold, bottomless black pits.

Mesmerized, I smile back.

A thought slams into my mind: *Don't speak to him.* Then it's instantly washed away by the delicious warmth infusing my chest, making my head light, my mind euphoric, and my limbs heavy.

What a beautiful creature, I think, dizzy with pleasure.

"You're not afraid of me, are you?" the man says, his voice light and airy.

I shake my head and whisper, "No. Of course not."

"Good. The water temperature is just right for humans. Why don't you join me?"

"Is it safe?" I ask, even though I have no intention of taking my clothes off and swimming with a stranger.

His gaze skims the treetops, considering my question. "For some, yes."

That strikes me as a perfectly acceptable reply, and my pulse slows as I step toward the water's edge.

"What's your name, child?" he asks, wading closer to the bank. Closer to *me.*

Again, I shake my head and try to remember why I should leave. Why it isn't safe to speak. There's definitely a reason. I just can't seem to hold onto it, and it slips away every time I try.

My lips part before I can stop myself. "Summer," I tell him, and his eyes narrow to slits.

"Not your true name, which is a shame." His slick head tilts in a slow, unnatural arc, reminding me of a lizard or a snake. "Still, you should hurry and get in the water."

"I shouldn't," I reply.

A dry chuckle rattles from his pouting lips, as though my resistance amuses him. "You shouldn't, but you *will.* The water is lovely, and you're a tasty little surprise to find mere hours before dinnertime."

"Tasty?" My voice sounds weak, but I'm not afraid, even when my gaze blurs for a moment and an image of a gaping grin and jagged teeth superimposes itself over his handsome features.

In the back of my mind, I know I should run like the Wild Hunt's breathing down my neck, go anywhere but here, but that thought dissolves in a wave of incoming euphoria, and I clutch the cloak around my throat, and whisper a single word.

"*Wyn.*"

A faint metallic scent wafts from the river, coppery, like blood. The water darkens around the man's legs, ribbons of weeds twisting beneath the surface.

"Come a little closer," the fae says, his hissed words dripping with kindness. "So I can admire you properly."

A far-away part of me wills myself not to move, but I ignore it and step off the grass, my feet making a loud sucking sound as they sink into the mud near the water's edge.

"My friend will be angry if I swim with you," I say.

The fae lets out a growl, sniffing the air like a hound on the trail. "What friend?"

A bright light flashes to my left, then there's someone standing beside me. Wyn. His expression is calm, but a dark energy, like restrained violence, vibrates off his body. Just his presence clears my foggy mind a little.

"Enough," he says, the word ringing through the air. "Step away from her, or I'll tear your fucking throat out."

A vicious snarl splits the fae's lips as the water churns violently around him. "You dare interrupt my meal?" he hisses. "She's mine. She was coming to me *willingly*. Those are the rules you must abide by."

With a deep growl rumbling in Wyn's throat, he takes a single step forward, slow and deliberate. "She will *never* be yours.

You're not worthy enough to even *look* at her. She's belongs to me. *I* claimed her years ago. Don't you realize you're speaking to a prince of Faery? This girl walks under my protection. That makes her untouchable. To everyone. Including you. Understand this, whether broken or bloodied, as long as I can crawl, I'll be the one keeping her safe. And I will not fail. Do not test me on this."

Wyn claimed me? What does *that* mean? Saying it now must be his way of protecting me. He said he could lie in Faery, unlike other fae.

Wyn positions himself between me and the river, a soft golden light glowing in his palm. He turns his head just enough to speak to me over his shoulder, his voice low and gritty.

"Go. Back to the fire. Run."

I hesitate, confusion rooting me to the spot until Wyn barks, "Now!"

I stumble a few steps backward, my legs shaking as the roar of churning water and a bitter, metallic scent fills the air. "Why, Wyn? He wasn't doing anything wrong."

"Fuck's *sake*. Just trust me. *Go*," Wyn grinds out, and then the world explodes around us.

The river surges up, water winding in thick, writhing tendrils around the river fae's body before whipping toward us. The water knocks me off my feet, but Wyn doesn't flinch, his boots planted solidly on the ground.

I scramble up, grab his arm, and try to tug him away from whatever this is—some kind of fae pissing contest, but he slams a hand onto the bank, fingers splayed wide, and the earth beneath us shudders, then cracks. Tree roots burst forth like snakes striking, tangling and snapping on the riverbank.

I should do as Wyn says. Leave. Run. But I'm frozen, my breath caught in my chest as earth and water collide.

A shrill wail from the fae pierces my eardrums. He lunges, his hands slicing through the air, and Wyn spins out of his reach, raising an arm slow and steady. Dust coils up his forearm, veins glowing gold and green. Then the ground in front of him erupts, a wall of stone shooting up between them.

The fae's water magic glances off the rock, but the impact sends cracks spidering through it.

"Stay back!" Wyn snaps at me.

"Let's just leave," I plead. "He didn't hurt me." I stumble again, feet slipping in the mud.

My pulse pounds in my ears, the erratic beat urging me to run. But I can't move. I can't leave Wyn.

The fae surges forward again, the entire river seeming to rise behind him, but Wyn's hand twists, and the earth shifts underfoot. A jagged spike of stone erupts from the ground, driving straight for the river fae's chest, but he bends his body around the stone like he's made of liquid. He grins, his black eyes glinting with malice.

I scream as arrows of water magic skim Wyn's arm, tearing through fabric and flesh. Blood sprays, dark against the pale green of the water, splattering my arms and chest. Wyn hisses in pain but doesn't falter. He drops low, slamming both hands on the ground. The earth shakes with a deep, resonating tremor that almost knocks me off my feet.

Then the ground beneath the river explodes with a grinding roar, like the land is tearing itself in two, a gut-wrenching sound that makes my stomach lurch. Without warning, a blast of mud and stones shoots down the fae's throat, and Wyn charges into the water, his hands closing around the man's neck, shoving him under, choking him in a violent swirl of dirt and magic.

The fae thrashes, still resisting, but his strength is fading. He slumps forward, muscular torso draped over the bank, the river covering him from the waist down.

Moaning, I shield my eyes. "Stop. Please. You're killing him," I mutter through my spread fingers. "He didn't hurt me."

"He would've," says Wyn not looking back at me as his words turn to snarls, and he continues strangling the stranger. Murdering him right in front of me. "Anyone who even *thinks* about harming you will have to deal with me. And like this scum, they won't survive for long. I protect what's mine, Summer. *Always.*"

Long, pale fingers scratch Wyn's arms and chest, then the fae's body goes limp and still. Dead.

The crashing waves have retreated, the river's surface now smooth. A heavy silence wraps around us, and neither of us moves a muscle.

What the fuck just happened?

Wyn staggers from the water, blood dripping down his arm. He's breathing hard, shoulders heaving with each gasp. But he doesn't look at me, not yet. His eyes are fixed on the ground, waiting for me to speak first.

When I don't, he says, "That went well. Ready for dinner?"

I take a trembling step forward, my voice barely above a whisper when I say, "What have you done?"

"Saved your life." A beat of silence, then, "Do you think I killed him for fun?"

The water churns and bubbles again, and Wyn's jaw tightens as he scans the body lying in the river, making sure the fae is dead. He presses his uninjured hand to the ground one last time. A deep crack echoes through the air as the water settles, and the river fae still lies motionless.

Wyn finally turns to me, his green eyes burning despite the exhaustion etched on his face. The act of wielding magic must sap his energy. Take a toll. Everything in life has a cost, I suppose. Even in Faery.

"How can you be so cruel?" I ask. "Aren't you meant to be a prince of this land? Shouldn't royalty act with honor?"

"Honor is a luxury humans pretend to possess. In Faery, survival comes first."

"When you were an injured wolf trapped in my basement, I wasn't afraid of you. Even when you were a psycho naked guy making coffee in my kitchen like we were roommates, I felt safe with you. But now, I don't know what scares me more... what you thought that creature was about to do to me, or what *you* did to him."

My vision blurs with unshed tears as I spin and walk away, each step faster than the last.

"Summer, wait," Wyn yells.

I don't wait. I start running.

CHAPTER 19

Summer

Heavy boots crunch the ground behind me, growing louder—then Wyn's arms wrap around my stomach, pulling me back against his chest. He holds me tightly, like he's afraid I might vanish.

"What I did was necessary, Summer," he says, warm breath against my ear. "I promise. Let me show you why."

"You want me to look at that guy again?"

Wyn nods, his sharp cheekbone rubbing mine.

My skin tingles from the contact, and I shrug out of his arms. "I can't. I already see him lying limp like a dead fish every time I close my eyes. It's heartbreaking."

Guilt flashes over his face, then it's gone, his lips pressing into a flat line. "Too bad. This is something you need to see."

Before I can react, he sweeps me up and throws me over his shoulder. "*Finally*," he mutters, then marches toward the river.

"Wyn, if you don't put me down, I swear—"

"You'll what? Bite, kick, scream? I might enjoy all three. You have no idea how long I've been wanting to do this. Shame it had to be against your will."

I pummel his back with a fist, my other hand hunting for his weapon. "You are so lucky I can't reach your sword right now."

"Try my other side," he says. "You're welcome."

At the edge of the water, he sets me down next to the fae's lifeless body. I refuse to look, keeping my gaze directly in front of my feet.

"Summer, look at him. Please," he begs, his body a warm wall of strength behind me, fingers gripping my hips, holding me in place.

I open my eyes and focus on the limp form half-floating in the water.

The dead fae's handsome guise is gone. The corpse on the riverbank has slimy, mottled skin that stretches tight over long limbs and swollen joints, the bones jutting out at strange angles. Hair tangled like black weeds. Opaque obsidian eyes stare at the sky, his mouth a gaping maw oozing dark blood.

The water laps gently around him, a vortex of black, oily fluid rising to the surface. He smells like rotting fish. Serrated teeth protrude from a slack mouth, dark-green saliva still glistening between them.

"That's not who I was talking to."

"It is. He's a nix. A shape shifter that preys along the waters of Faery. When they die, all glamours dissolve. Even to human eyes."

"Okay," I say. "Now he doesn't look so friendly. Is there a chance he'll rise up and bite our heads off?"

"No, he'll stay dead. But next time I tell you not to talk to anyone, please fucking listen to me. I won't always be able to get to you in time. And if you die on my watch, I swear I'll strangle you myself."

"You know that doesn't make sense, right? I'd already be dead so..."

Wyn's steely gaze bores through me, snapping my jaw shut. From the trees, a bird sings a cheerful tune, as if the horrible violence never happened.

"How could I have been so stupid?" I ask.

"It's not your fault. Nixes cast spells on their victims to hide their true appearance. Creatures like him are exactly why I told you to stay away from all fae."

"To be precise, you said not to talk to anyone."

Wyn lets out an impatient huff. "Okay. And did you obey me?"

I stare at the trees on the opposite bank, unable to meet his gaze, feeling petulant and embarrassed.

"No, but why does it matter to you so much what happens to me? You're a so-called fae prince." My fingers place quotation marks in the air around the words fae prince. "And I'm a mentally messed-up human that you won't even fool around with to take our minds off all this shit. And that tells me how little I matter to you."

His spine straightens, and then he turns slowly to fully face me. "You matter, Summer. I care about what happens to you. Deeply. Nixes are dangerous creatures. Fae regularly disappear after straying too close to rivers when alone, never to be heard of again in any city or realm."

"Might just be rumors."

A muscle ticks in his jaw. "No. My sister was nearly taken by one in the Merit Kingdom. They're not usually seen so far north, but it was a nix, nonetheless. And you should thank Dana it wasn't one of Draírdon's half-mechanical monstrosities."

A cold shudder runs through me. *Draírdon.* For some reason, that name sparks a memory I can't quite grasp—glittery darkness spinning around me, wide, malevolent grins melting into sneers that mock and taunt. Did I dream this vision? Or did it really happen?

"By Dana, do you mean the ancient mother of the Tuatha Dé Danann?" I ask. "She's not going to pop out from behind the trees any minute, is she?"

"No, she's a goddess of the fae, no longer living."

"What a relief. Meeting her would tip me over the edge. So it was the risk to my personal safety that sent you into orbit? Nothing else?"

He shakes his head, staring intently, but saying nothing.

"Wyn, what if we were back at your court, and I'd been dancing with an Elemental fae you approved of, a nice guy for instance, and the dance turned into a stroll through the gardens, followed by a kiss that you happened to witness. Would you be all right with that?"

"No! By the gods, I would not be all right. And that *guy's* head would be removed from his neck before he could blink."

Fury boils my blood. He can't have it both ways. If *he* doesn't want me, he has no right to stand in anyone else's way.

"But that makes no sense," I say, pushing him against a tree trunk, my fingers twisting into the soft fabric of his shirt. "What do you want from me, Wyn? I don't understand you at all."

"I *want*," he bites out, "for you to be sensible and take your personal safety seriously." He looms over me, warm breath caressing my cheek.

"That's all?" I demand. "Nothing else?"

"Yes." His chest pumps beneath his shirt as he schools his features, concentrating on his next words. "That's all. Nothing else."

"I don't believe you," I say, catching the flicker of muscle in his jaw that signals discomfort, possibly even pain. "You're using your halfling ability to lie. Tell me the truth."

He drags a hand through his hair, sighing. "Look, I don't know... I want... I need to keep you safe. Definitely that. And to keep the Shade Court away from you." Then his voice drops, and he mutters something that sounds like: *everything. I want everything.*

For a moment, shock silences me, but I mentally shake it off and push him further. "And you're not happy about that?"

"No. I'm fucking pissed."

Then he does the last thing I expect.

He kisses me.

Furiously.

His hand curls around the back of my neck as his mouth finds mine, coaxing and consuming in equal measure. I gasp when his teeth graze my lower lip, a shiver rolling through me, one that has nothing to do with my near-death experience or the nix.

All logical thought dissolves as my fingers clutch at his shirt, pulling him closer, not allowing him to escape. The taste of him—smoky, sweet, and wild—feeds the heat kindling in my belly, turning it into a blazing wildfire.

Wyn pulls back just enough to murmur my name against my lips, his breath ragged, the space between us so small I can count each glittering, gold fleck in his irises. My pulse thrums in my ears, loud enough that I wonder if he can hear it too. His fingers trace my jawline, gentle, feathering up to the sensitive skin behind my ear.

"You drive me crazy," he says, voice rough as gravel. "I should save my sanity, drop you at the nearest warded stronghold. Walk away."

"Then do it. Go." My words are soft, a whispered dare.

Wyn's jaw tightens, frustration warring with something darker in his features. "I *can't*. No power in any realm could ever make me."

His other hand grips my waist, tugging me closer. And then I'm kissing him again, deeper this time, as if I can pour all my fear and confusion into him. As if he'll absorb every bit of it.

I might be the crazy girl who murdered her parents, who lost her mind to a year in Faery doing who-knows-what, and still can't remember any of it. But who cares? None of that matters when I have Wyn on my side, holding me tight. I can deal with anything if he's with me.

Anything at all.

I come up for air, soaking in the ruined sight of him, but he barely allows me a breath before his mouth crashes into mine again, and the ground beneath my feet shudders. His grip tightens at my waist, his fingers digging into my flesh like he needs this as much as I do.

My fingers tangle in his hair, tugging hard as his tongue strokes mine. Then an image flashes in my mind—the dead fae, broken and crumpled at the river's edge. Revulsion surges through me. And suddenly I don't know who I'm kissing.

I push Wyn's chest, putting space between us again as my head spins and my knees threaten to buckle. "I still can't believe you were so brutal. You didn't give the nix a chance."

"What do you expect? I'm a prince of Faery who turns into a feral wolf, not a wag-tailed mutt. Do I look like a lapdog to you?"

My gaze drags along his frame. Muscles tight with frustration, he looks infuriatingly gorgeous, standing tall with a predator's savage grace. "No, Wyn. Right now you look vicious."

"Good. Don't forget it. And you, of all people, should know that fae don't belong in children's books."

"Maybe not all nix are out to kill people."

"Keep thinking like that and I'll be digging your grave before sunrise. And then another one beside it for what's left of your murderer. The second one won't be very big." A thoughtful expression crosses his face. "Can you wield a sword?"

"Is that a joke? Of course I can't wield a sword. Can you parallel park a pickup truck during peak hour? Download an app on a cellphone? Have you ever even used one before?"

Almost smiling, he says, "Nope. Can't do any of that. But we could trade. I'll teach you to defend yourself, and you can show me how to summon the app. Stupidest name for a weapon, by the way."

A laugh bubbles up my throat, cut off by the appearance of a long, thin sword that materializes in Wyn's right hand.

He gives me a wicked grin, then turns the silver hilt toward me as he leans forward and whispers in my ear. "Lesson one, Summer. Be careful... I bite."

CHAPTER 20

Summer

"If only Zylah were here," I say, shifting my weight from foot to foot. "She's got jujitsu training and zero hesitation about turning anything into a weapon."

"I don't know what jujitsu means, but this sword isn't very long," says Wyn, flipping the hilt against his palm, sending the blade into three lazy spins before catching it with a smirk. He wraps my fingers around the hilt. "What's the worst thing that could happen? A few basic strikes is all that's needed to relieve someone of their entrails, Summer."

With swift movements, he swings his own weapon through the air in a series of crisscrossed flourishes, slicing up the space between us.

My throat clicks as I swallow. "I won't be any good at this."

"You might be surprised. Give it a go."

"Our dinner's getting cold."

"I wrapped it in leaves and kept it near the coals. It'll still be there when we're done."

"You're wounded," I say, pointing at his arm. "You were bleeding at the river."

"Nope. Magic healed it. Stop stalling."

The sword feels wrong in my hand, like someone swapped my pruning shears for a chainsaw and I'm about to destroy my favorite client's prized rose bushes.

Wyn stands a few paces away, his own blade balanced effortlessly in his hand, stance wide, breathing controlled. I'd find the composure impressive if that smile didn't look quite so smug around the edges.

"Hold it tighter or you'll be disarmed before you can strike a blow," he instructs, his lips quirking into a full-blown grin. "Now swing at me."

"Are you sure that's wise?" I ask, gripping it harder, anyway.

"Try the tree trunk, then," he says, nodding at a gnarled pine with bark like cracked, dried clay.

The leather-wrapped hilt digs into my palm, and a mix of embarrassment and anger rises up my throat. I'm not fond of doing anything I'm bad at in front of an audience. Especially an audience that looks like Wyn.

When I got dumped back into my real life after my lost year, I didn't just feel mentally broken and out of place. I felt alien—different from every other student in my senior year. Plus, most of my classmates suspected I'd killed my parents during a psychotic episode. So, yeah, feeling inferior and judged by others remains a major sore point for me.

But Wyn, who used to be a wolf and is now apparently a fae prince, told me to swing—so I do, bringing the blade up, then down in what I *hope* will be a clean arc. But even before it connects with the target, I know I've messed up.

My stance is too stiff, my wrists locked, and instead of slicing through the air, the sword wobbles, jarring in my grip. The impact sends a shock wave up to my shoulders, and I nearly lose my hold on it. I stagger back, heart hammering, fingers scrambling to keep control.

From the side, Wyn sighs loudly. *Too* loudly.

"Okay," he says, crossing his arms. "That was a... choice."

Ever the rebellious one, I pretend to inspect the blade. "Sure it wasn't great, but maybe you magicked me up a defective weapon," I tease, even though I wouldn't know a well-crafted blade from one made by a drunken blacksmith with a grudge.

Wyn steps closer to me, his boots crunching the dry grass. The river shimmers behind him, all blue-green tranquility, a stark contrast to the frustration building inside me.

"It's a perfectly balanced blade, Summer, and light enough for you to wield. The issue isn't the sword."

"So you're saying I'm the problem?"

"No, *you* said you wouldn't be any good at this. Remember?" His grin widens, and my heart stutters. "If you've already convinced yourself you can't do something, then what chance will you have? Why not declare you'll be brilliant instead? That's called magic."

"Why am I even bothering?" I mutter, glaring at a willow tree like it personally offended me. "As long as you're with me, I'll never need to use a weapon, which honestly, is a relief."

His expression softens, and he steps even closer, fingers brushing a wayward strand of hair behind my ear. "We could get separated. And if that happens... you need to be ready. Faery isn't safe. Not for you. Please, Summer, try again. I need you alive."

The fear in his voice steals my breath, and before I can think of a comeback, he moves behind me. The metal on his jacket brushes my shoulder blades as he adjusts my grip, his body heat weakening my knees.

"Relax your wrists," he murmurs. "Let the weight of the sword guide you."

I try to focus on his instructions, but his closeness makes it impossible. The warmth of his breath grazes my ear, and my pulse races like I've run up and down the stairs of Gravenshade Hall five times without stopping—with my mother's ghost on my tail.

"Summer," he says, amusement creeping into his tone. "You're holding it like a broomstick. It's a sword. Try again."

"If you weren't breathing down my neck, maybe I could concentrate."

"Breathing down your neck, huh?" His voice dips, teasing. I hate the heat that simmers in my belly... then sinks lower. And *lower*.

He claims it's too risky to touch me, but my hormones need a second opinion. I'm so turned on, it's embarrassing. What the hell is wrong with me?

I whirl around and face him, my sword dragging behind me. "Are you going to teach me how to use this thing or just make jokes and criticize?"

His grin falters, replaced by something sharper and hungrier, which doesn't make sense given how unhinged I'm behaving. For a moment, neither of us moves. The world around us—the river, the trees, the gentle breeze—it all fades to nothing.

Then he steps back, breaking the tension with a wry smile. "Lesson two: don't let your opponent distract you. Let's try again."

I grip the sword and raise it, ignoring the way my hands tremble. "Easy for you to say. You don't have to spar with a walking thirst trap."

His chuckle is warm, as he replies, "According to the ladies of Talamh Cúig, I was born distracting."

"No need to show off," I mutter. "Wait... do you actually know what a thirst trap is?"

He frowns. "Of course. A mortal device for catching parched prey."

"Oh my god. No. How could I possibly be sparring with one of those?"

He shrugs. "Mortal ways are indeed baffling."

Wyn retreats, the grin still dancing on his lips as he lifts his sword. "All right. Lesson three: the basic thrust. Step forward, keep your blade straight, and aim for your opponent's centerline. Controlled. Precise. No wild swings."

"Who knew wild swings were bad," I mutter, adjusting my stance. "They've served me well so far in life."

"They're not exactly bad, just sloppy," he corrects, circling me slowly, his eyes sharp and assessing. "And they can get you killed. Try a thrust."

Thrust. I hate it when he says that word. I mean, it should be illegal to utter it when you look like him.

I take a step forward and jab the blade out, but it feels awkward, like my arms have turned into disobedient strands of spaghetti. The sword wobbles in my grip.

Wyn rubs a hand over his jaw. "Good effort," he says, though the clear amusement in his voice suggests otherwise. He moves to my side and adjusts my shoulders. "Keep your weight balanced. Stop aiming for the sky. I'm not as tall as a gray man."

"A what?"

"You know the gray men? The fear liath mòr? Towering shadows from the mountains that feed on their victim's dread and confusion."

"Err, no. None of them inhabit any mountains near Lake Grenlynn, thankfully." I wonder briefly if they're related to the gray ladies my mom's always banging on about.

"Good. Aim lower and push out from your core."

My *core*? Why did he have to say that? Makes me think of... never mind.

"Can you hear my thoughts right now?"

He freezes. "No. Feel free to share them."

"Definitely not. I'm good."

I try again, this time with more focus. The tip of the blade slices forward, steady and straight, and a bolt of pride flickers through me.

"Better," Wyn says, circling back to face me. He swings his own sword, his movements sure and fluid. "Now parry. When I thrust, angle your blade to deflect. Small movements. Don't over commit."

I swallow hard. "Right. I'm better at this if I think about something else. Tell me how magic works in this realm."

"We're in Faery. You may as well ask how gravity operates in your world."

"If you can explain that, too, I'd be grateful," I say. "In science class, I mostly stared at the back of Brice Albright's golden waves instead of bothering to learn anything."

"Brice Albright." Wyn repeats the name of my high school crush like he's committing it to memory. "Does he live in Lake Grenlynn?"

"Hasn't for a long time."

"Good. Did this *Brice* person ever hurt you?"

"Only my pride by ignoring me."

A grin flickers at the edge of Wyn's mouth, then he lunges, his sword tip aimed at my chest. I smack the blade away with zero skill or finesse, my attention on his lips curving as he takes a breath to speak.

"Elemental magic follows the natural rules and principles that sustain life and, like in the Earth Realm, keep us from tumbling into the blackness of the multiverse. Magic is the energy that weaves through air, water, fire, earth, and ether. A creator. An unmaker. Life and death and everything in between."

The gleam in his eyes tells me that he's enjoying this, lecturing me while prancing about with his sword.

He strikes again, quick but measured, and I move to block. The force of his blade sends a jolt up my arm, but I manage to hold steady. In other words, I don't drop my weapon.

"Good," he says, stepping to the side. "Now, again. Watch your footwork this time."

We fall into a rhythm, moving in a slow dance around each other. He thrusts; I parry. I lunge forward; he sidesteps. Each motion flows into the next, and for a moment, I forget my frustration and focus entirely on the movements. The weight of the sword, the shifting of my feet, the subtle pressure of his blade against mine.

"Thrust, parry, sidestep," he says, his voice calm as he moves smoothly over the grass. "Keep your blade up. Don't leave yourself open."

"How are the realms connected?" I ask. "Are we literally on different physical planes, hundreds of thousands of miles apart?"

"No, the realms lie stacked on top of each other—side by side, twisting and sliding. Melded together, and separated only by the thoughts and ideas of their inhabitants. We'd feel our breath whispering over each other if we were brave enough to dissolve the veils in our minds—all the rules and reasons we construct in order to feel safe living in the chaos of infinite realities."

Wow, that's quite the revelation.

Stalking around me, sword raised, ready to strike, his eyes fix on mine too deeply. The double and triple meaning of his words collide and obscure his purpose and intentions. How many mentions of twisting and sliding and melding can a girl take before combusting?

Is he hoping to leave my skin raw and tingling? Burning for him to touch me?

If so, it's definitely working.

Before long, we've moved away from the water and closer to the edge of the woods, and I'm starting to feel a little more confident—until Wyn stops playing around.

His strikes come faster, harder, and I barely manage to keep up, my arms burning with the effort.

"*Wyn*," I gasp, blocking a particularly forceful thrust. "Are you trying to kill me here?"

"Just making sure you're paying attention," he says, smirking like he's going for gold in the Smuggest of Smug Bastard Olympics.

"Helpful."

Despite my grumbling, I can't deny the thrill coursing through me. The way we move together, the way his eyes never leave mine. It feels dangerous, and I don't mean in the I-might-get-physically-injured way.

After a while he lowers his sword and steps back. "That'll have to do. You're not improving anymore. But you weren't too bad for your first time. Just don't take on any dangerous fae creatures until you get some more practice."

I roll my eyes, panting as I let my own blade drop. "Thanks for the vote of confidence. Is that your usual method of teaching? Sexual innuendos and half-veiled insults?"

"Sex... *what*?"

I stifle a laugh. From his clenched fists and the dark blush on his cheeks, it's clear he knows exactly what *that* word means.

He tilts his head, his gaze softening in a way that makes my chest tighten. "Don't worry. You'll be able to keep yourself safe with a blade soon, Summer. I'll make sure of it."

"How about some constructive feedback? Something to mull over and improve on," I say, not really wanting any further sword instruction. But also not ready for his focused attention to leave me. I need to be near him for a little longer. Actually, a *lot* longer.

Wyn obliges and moves close, his hand now resting on mine over the sword hilt. His voice is a low rumble when he says, "Your grip is fine, but your footwork's still off. Step wider."

I try to focus on his words, but it's impossible with the heat of his body searing into mine.

The sharp, metallic smell of the blade in my hands blends with the scent of leather and pine that clings to his skin. His thumb brushes my knuckles as he adjusts my hold, and my pulse stutters.

Is he *trying* to drive me insane?

CHAPTER 21

Summer

"Like this?" I ask, my voice soft and strained.

Wyn leans closer, his breath a warm whisper against my ear. "Almost."

The sword is forgotten as my focus shifts to his solid presence behind me, the heat radiating from his chest, the way his fingers linger longer than they should. When he steps back, the sudden coolness on my skin makes me sway and burn for more of his touch.

"Try the lunge again," he says, his tone gruffer, as if he's trying to mask how he's feeling.

I obey, more to distract myself than any desire to hone my non-existent fighting skills.

My feet scuff against the ground as I extend forward, and he circles me, his gaze sharp. It's not just appraisal. The energy behind his focus is heavier, like a thunderstorm building in the distance. As if he's holding the reins of his control extremely tightly.

He's not as unaffected as he pretends to be.

"That looks good," he says, and the corner of his mouth lifts in a smile, dimples flashing.

A sharp ache blooms in my chest that's nearly unbearable.

I lower the sword, chaos churning inside me. "I think that's about all I can take of sword lessons today," I say softly. "You're definitely too distracting."

Wyn's eyes lock on mine, dark green and unreadable. For a moment, neither of us moves.

The forest that enfolds the creek is too quiet, as if all its creatures are holding their breath along with me, waiting for Wyn's next move.

Then he steps closer, close enough that I can see every glittering freckle dusting his nose and cheeks, the way his lips part as if he's about to speak—but he doesn't. Instead, he brushes a stray strand of hair from my face with an unsteady hand. His fingers trail down to my jaw, tipping my chin up.

"You're the distracting one, Summer," he murmurs, his voice rough. "And in the interests of full disclosure? I can hear what you're thinking right now. Loud and clear."

I could laugh or make a joke, but the air between us feels too fragile, too charged, and I don't want to break the spell. "Guess we're both a mess," I manage, though the words trip over my tongue.

He runs his hand over my arm, fingers tracing the dark vines and purple irises. "Nice glyphs."

"They're tattoos," I reply.

"*Tattoos*. That's what I meant."

"Did you put these on me?" I ask.

"*Me?* I'm not an artist. How can you not remember getting them? *Oh*—of course... it'd be those twisted Shade Court fuckers."

A chill rolls through me. I glance down at the ink staining my arms. What kind of asshole marks someone permanently without their permission?

"Please... let's not talk about *them* right now," I beg.

His gaze drops to my lips, and the world tilts. He leans in, slow enough that I could pull away if I wanted to—but I don't. When his mouth meets mine, it's like a match dropped in gasoline.

I'm instantly ablaze with wanting him. Needing to feel his weight pinning me down on the soft grass. Against a tree. Anywhere.

The kiss is firm, searing, and every nerve in my body lights up at once, buzzing so hard it hurts. His hands slide to my waist, pulling me closer, and I cling to his shoulders, the metal edges of his jacket digging into my fingers, grounding me as my knees threaten to buckle.

The faint taste of salt and something else—Wyn's own sweet flavor—floods my senses. His scent surrounds me, woodsmoke and pine, and I lose track of how to breathe and stop myself from whimpering like a fool. Then he backs me against the trunk of a giant elm tree, and I stop trying.

One hand wraps around the back of my neck, his thumb strumming a moan from my throat.

"Gods, yes," he says. "I've waited a long time to hear you make that sound."

His lips take mine again, and I smile against his kiss, panting into his mouth as I fumble for the fastenings on his pants.

"Wait," he huffs, seizing my fingers in a harsh grip and pressing them to his chest.

He distracts me by sliding his kiss down the long muscle of my neck, sucking and biting softly. His mouth trails fire along my jaw to the hollow below my ear. I shiver, heat pooling low in my belly as his breath skates over my skin.

The bark of the tree digs into my back, but I barely notice it. All I can feel is Wyn—his body pressed against mine, his hands cradling my face, his lips stealing my every breath. The afternoon sun filters through the leaves, dappling us in golden light. Somewhere nearby, water ripples and flows, but it feels like it's another realm away.

"Summer," he murmurs, his voice rough and uncertain. His forehead presses to mine, his hands trembling as they slip lower, framing my hips. "Tell me to stop."

Stop? That word doesn't exist in my vocabulary right now. I can't move, can't think past the way his thumbs brush over the waistband of my shorts, his fingers flexing like he wants to rip them off me. My breath hitches. Everything inside me pulls taut, straining toward him, aching for more.

"What if I don't want you to stop?" I whisper, my voice unrecognizable to my own ears.

"You don't understand," he says. His lips find mine again, hungry, desperate.

He kisses me like I'm something he can't have but can't live without, and I'm drowning in it, lost in the way he tastes like sweet, tortured longing.

"I do understand," I whisper against his lips to soothe him, even though I don't. Not fully. Not when his hands drift lower, his touch igniting a fire that scorches every part of me.

"Summer, I can't..." He pulls back just enough for our eyes to meet. "I won't let this go further. I can't give you what you deserve. What you need. Not tonight. Not here."

A hot knot of pain tightens in my chest at his words. I hate how much it hurts even though I know he's trying to protect me, trying to protect *us*.

His lips find mine again, harder this time, hungrier. His kiss devours me, like he's silently communicating everything he can't say out loud—fear, longing, the ache of almost losing me to the nix. His hand skims over the curve of my waist, then lower, sliding around to the small of my back, tilting my hips, pressing me firm against him.

I gasp at the hard heat of him, a raw surge of need shooting straight up my spine. He rocks into me, groaning, his movements jerky, like he's losing control.

He wants this as much as I do. And knowing that undoes me.

His hand glides over my stomach, then lower, brushing over the place where I need him to be ruthless, his touch maddeningly light.

My fingers curl around his forearm, desperate for something to hold onto as he circles and teases over the damp fabric. His thumb finds the right spot, and the perfect blend of friction and pressure pulls a sound from my throat that should embarrass me as my eyelids drift closed.

"Eyes on me, Summer. I need you to look at me when you come apart."

I obey, hypnotized by the molten gold swirling in his green irises.

"That's it. Let go for me," he says, his voice deeper, darker as he rests his forehead against my temple and dips beneath the band of my shorts, skin on delicious skin. "Fuck, you're so wet."

I can't answer, not when he shifts a little, his fingers pressing firmly enough to make me gasp. My head tilts back against the tree, eyes fluttering shut, lips parting as he works me to a crescendo of sensation that leaves me teetering on the edge.

"I said look at me, Summer."

My eyes fly open, and he gives a growl of satisfaction. His lips trail back to mine, claiming them in a kiss that's zero control and maximum chaos, even as his hand continues its tormenting rhythm.

The late afternoon sun feels too warm on my skin, amplified by the heat in my veins. Every nerve in my body is strung tight, every sense focused on Wyn. On the way he moves, slow, but unrelenting. On the way his whispers coax moan after broken moan from me.

When I finally come apart, it's like drowning and breaking the surface all at once. My body shakes, a low sound escaping my lips that he swallows in a desperate kiss before his teeth settle around the long muscle in my neck, clamping down as his hips buck.

Instead of panic, a wave of euphoria rolls over me as I wait for him to bite me. To mark me like a wolf would... like a mate.

But he doesn't. He just curses against my skin as I cry out.

For a moment, everything fades—time, place, doubt. Fear of what might happen to me in this strange land full of creatures like the nix. Fear of what's happening back at Gravenshade Hall. And the ever-present worry gnawing at my mind about where the crazy leader of the Wild Hunt has gone, and what he might do next.

It all disappears, and there is only Wyn, holding me as I shudder, his hands steadying me even as his lips press soft, lingering kisses to the corners of my mouth, my cheeks, my temples.

The world slowly comes back into focus—the rustling leaves, the brackish scent of the river on the breeze, the dying light of the sun filtering through the trees.

Wyn pulls back, his face tight, his jaw set as though he's forcing himself to let me go.

He doesn't say anything for long minutes. Neither do I.

Breathing hard, he brushes his nose against mine. "That was a hell of a lesson," he says, his voice ragged but laced with humor. "I learned quite a lot."

I laugh, soft and breathless, and reach for his sword belt. "About me? Weren't you meant to be the teacher?"

"A devoted pupil in this case."

Hooking my fingers in his belt, I tug him close again. "Your turn."

"Wait," he says, stepping back. "I can't."

A chill prickles over my skin, and my stomach aches from his rejection. "Wyn," I whisper.

He takes another step back, and then another. As much as it hurts not to be touching him, I refuse to reach out. I don't beg him to return.

Hands raking through his hair, he paces back and forth, then stops in front of me and finally speaks. "It might be forbidden to touch you, but that hasn't stopped me from thinking about it.

Every moment. Every damn night for the last seven years. I care about you, Summer. I always have."

"If that's true, then why didn't you come find me sooner?"

"I promised my sister—"

A hollow laugh erupts from me. "Your sister the Unseelie Queen?"

"Yes. I promised her I'd wait seven years before I tracked you down."

"She dislikes me that much?"

"No. While I was busy following you around like a wolf on the hunt, she was your faithful, constant friend. Brought you from the Court of Merits to the safety of Talamh Cúig, my home. Made sure you were sent back to the human realm. Kept you safe from *all* fae, including me."

"So what changed? Why did you suddenly turn up in the human realm, spying on me in the Vandersons' garden?"

"A fae's vow is unbreakable. As promised, I waited seven years. Merri hoped I'd forget you during that time. But I could never. The day after the time limit expired, I went through a portal in a cave in my land."

"Why?"

"To find you."

"But *why?*"

"Because I needed to guard you. Keep you safe. I feared the Raven Realm, Landolin's Shade Court, wasn't finished with you, and I was right."

"But why am I your responsibility? I don't even remember my time here. Or *you* at all back then."

His gaze drops to the ground between us, fingers twitching in anger or annoyance. Hard to say which.

"I can't tell you," he finally says.

"What?"

"I *can't* say why. It's not safe. When I can tell you, I will. I promise."

"Then at least explain why it's forbidden for us to go further?"

"I..." He swallows hard, a blush creeping up his neck. "My sister is overprotective. Years ago, not long before you left my court, a mage cursed me with a terrible fate, but then another gifted me with a sliver of hope, if only I could resist what I want the most. *You.* Merri thinks you're part of the curse unfolding, part of my downfall, and that I'll be fine if I stay away from you."

"That's ridiculous, Wyn."

"She forbade me from... getting close to you. To appease her, I said I wouldn't. She'll be furious when she learns I've brought you here—closer to danger."

"Well I'd be much worse off if Landolin had gotten his creepy hands on me."

"Undoubtedly. But then he'd suffer deeply for every harm he did to you. The hunter would become the hunted. I'd make sure of it." His lips press into a thin line as he steps forward and brushes hair off my face. "Come on. Let's return to camp and get some rest. It was the middle of the night when we left Gravenshade Hall, daytime here when we slipped through the veil. We've been awake far too long."

As he stalks off toward the trees, a thought occurs to me. "Wait... What did you say to me while we were in the lake earlier? In a different language?"

"Our dinner will be cold. Let's go eat."

"That's definitely not what you said."

He freezes, still facing away from me. "I don't remember."

"That's a lie."

"Fine." Twigs crack under his boots as he swings abruptly around, wild eyes flashing. "I said... don't worry, dear one. You are safe."

"Is that all of it?"

Several beats pass as his throat bobs, his gaze scanning the gnarled tree trunks and bramble behind me.

"It isn't?" I ask. "Then you'd better tell me the rest, or I'll think you're a coward."

"You are loved," he mutters.

"Pardon?"

"I *said* that you are loved."

"Do you mean by my dead family?" I ask. "The distant, living relatives that won't speak to me?"

He shakes his head.

"No? Then you must mean I'm loved by Zylah and Kurt."

"No, by Merri... and me." He spins on his heel and stomps through a narrow pathway between the trees, his dark hair lit by the last rays of a burnt orange sunset.

Okay. He loves me. So does his sister, apparently.

I take several long breaths to calm my racing heart.

"Summer," he shouts, his voice close, as if he's waiting nearby. "Hurry up or you'll get eaten by a two-headed othrius. Don't make me come and get you. I'd love nothing more than another excuse to throw you over my shoulder again."

I spend a moment hoping he'll do exactly that. Then I remember a fae beast might be hunting me, let out an embarrassing squeak, and scurry after Wyn.

CHAPTER 22

Wynter

"Get into bed," I tell Summer, jerking my chin toward the root-woven frame draped in moss and lined with ferns, built by my magic and set near the crackling fire.

Throughout dinner, I could barely speak as I fought the impulse to drag her to the ground and finish what we started by the river. Even now, my words are slurred, my blood a hot ache in my veins, and the wolf within longs to shift and run through the woods, find something to kill, and crush this lust with an act of unrestrained violence.

Summer stares at the bed like I've just suggested she spend the night in a pit of writhing vipers.

"It's safe," I say, crossing my arms, mildly offended she doesn't seem to appreciate my efforts. Or look even a little impressed. "My magic will keep crawling insects and small creatures at bay. You'll be fine."

"What about the larger ones?" she asks, arching a brow. The stars in the sky glitter behind her head like a crown of diamonds.

"Well they'll have to get through me first, and I won't let anyone or any*thing* harmful touch you. Ever."

"Okay. Thank you. But why make only one?" she asks, grinning like a manic pixie.

"One what?" I rake my fingers through my hair, then my sluggish mind catches on. "Oh, *bed*. Well because—"

"Let me guess," she interrupts. "Is it because we'll be warmer if we sleep close?"

I sigh, bone weary and aching for the relief of sleep, if only to stop thinking about her. Remembering how she looked, her lips parting with a moan as she came apart in my arms. "Of course we'll be warmer. But if you'd rather sleep on the ground and freeze, then by all means, do so."

If she chooses the ground, I'll be right there beside her, suffering in discomfort.

"I'm wondering how you'll resist me, Wyn, if we're lying close, breathing the same air," she teases. "Because right now you're staring at me like you're imagining something delightfully wicked."

The fire crackles and sparks swirl into the sky as I shake out a magic-woven blanket and drape it over the bed. "I'm actually picturing strangling you," I say. "But thanks for assuming my intentions are only dishonorable rather than murderous."

I swallow as she removes her cloak, revealing pale skin and a smile that makes me forget where I am. Or indeed, *who* I am.

"Your turn," she says, lying back on the bed as if it's no big deal, her T-shirt riding up just enough to fry my last sensible brain cell.

Moonlight catches the curve of her stomach like it has a personal vendetta against my self-control. I place my sword beside the bed and slide in next to her.

She doesn't make room for me, and I find myself half lying on the hard ground.

"Can you move over a little?" I ask, her crisp, apple scent invading my senses.

"Sure. I can do that."

When I settle my weight onto the bed, without warning, she lurches up and straddles my hips while I lie there blinking like an idiot, contemplating pushing her off. Which I should do. And I will. Yeah... soon.

"I don't think this is good idea," I manage, even as my hands betray me, my fingers curling around her hips.

"Remind me why we shouldn't," Summer says, leaning down to trail soft kisses along my neck, a curtain of dark hair blocking out everything but her delicious scent and warmth.

The wolf inside me roars to life, hungry for its mate. Desperate to flip her over. Pin her down. Make her mine.

She tilts her head up slightly, and her lips graze my jaw. My restraint hangs on by a fraying thread.

I take slow, deliberate breaths. Right. She wants *reasons*. And I did vow to make her happy. To give her anything she wants. Even if that promise was only to myself.

"Well..." I begin. "I have the self-control of a starved wolf. I might not stop until it's too late. Until I break you."

She hums, not the least bit deterred. "You wouldn't hurt me, Wyn."

I risk meeting her gaze, instantly regretting it. She says it like it's a truth carved in stone, but she doesn't know what happens when I lose control. What I'm capable of. She's smiling, soft and sweet. Like she already knows how this ends. Like she *knows* I'm so close to cracking.

"Also, this bed is not the finest I've made, and I'd rather not ruin my back for eternity." Most pathetic excuse I've ever come up with.

She makes a small, amused noise. "You're a supernatural being. I don't think your back is at risk."

I exhale, pinching the bridge of my nose. "Fine. How about this? My sister, the *Queen* of Merits, will have my head if I make you mine and bind our fates together."

"Sleeping with someone doesn't bind their fate to yours. At least not in the human realm."

"Oh, lucky we're still there, then."

She smacks my head lightly. "Stop it."

"Merri will probably take *your* head, too. Maybe she'll be doing us a favor."

Summer scoffs. "Ridiculous."

"Since you don't remember meeting my sister, you're not in a position to judge. But fine. We're in the middle of a *forest*. I refuse to bring you what will be the greatest pleasure you've ever experienced while a pinecone stabs the back of your ribs."

Summer chuckles, still watching me closely, waiting for me to cave.

"And I'm kind of... possessive about those I'm fond of," I say, strengthening my argument. "If I let myself have you tonight, I'll never let you go."

"And that's a bad thing, Wyn?"

A laugh catches in my throat, but it sounds more like a moan. "Yes! I might start writing you poetry. And you'll have to pretend to like it, which won't be good for either of us."

She sighs, the sound causing heat to explode inside my chest. "You told Rose at Neon Velvet you were an excellent poet."

"I was *drunk*." I shudder as her nails trace lazy patterns over my bicep. "And another reason I can't have you," I continue, "I'll be required to fight off every fool in the Land of Five who so much as looks at you. After a while, that will become exhausting."

"You'd enjoy it," she teases.

I close my eyes and curl my fingers into fists, fighting the urge to kiss her senseless. "Gods help me, I probably would."

Silence enfolds us as she traces a path along my collarbone, featherlight, making every inch of me strain toward her warmth. "Plus, there's the significant age difference," I add.

"Okay, then. How old are you?"

"Twenty-five."

"Wyn, we're the same age!"

"Yeah, but in fae years it's kind of closer to a couple hundred years."

Her eyes narrow to dubious slits. "How does that work exactly?"

"You don't want to know. It's complicated."

"None of those are real reasons," she whispers.

Groaning, I tilt my head back against the bed, fixing my gaze on the stars glittering through the trees above us. My fingers flex at her waist. "True. They're not," I admit, adding silently, *except for the one about my sister.*

Merri really *will* kill me if I get closer to Summer and set my curse in motion. And if Merri's right, then before long, I'll be dead. Buried beneath the soil forever.

It's on the tip of my tongue to reveal what Summer told Merri while she was still a thrall at the Merit Court—how she said she didn't want to leave because she was waiting for the winter prince to find her. Believed she was fated to him. And how my sister thought straight away of *me*. And recognized my mate.

I recall the bitterness I felt when our High Mage returned Summer to the human realm without informing me. How I fell into a drunken depression, telling myself it wasn't love that I felt. Assuring myself that like the Shade and Merit Courts, I too only wished to own her. Control her.

But that was never true.

All I want is to bask in the warmth of her smile. To see her happy. Keep her safe.

The tips of our noses touch. She's so close I can see the moonlight reflected in her eyes. Smell her sweet, musky desire. Close enough that I could cast my doubts into the soil beneath me and stop fighting this insane longing. The desperate need to make her mine. To mark her as my mate.

I let my thumb stroke over her lips and revel in the way she shivers. "I have many more reasons to list."

"Let me guess. Is reason number nine that I talk too much?"

From what I know of humans, she speaks exactly the right amount. I huff a breath and move on. "If we do this, you'll be stuck with me, and I'm more than a little cursed. My uncle was cursed, and my father before him. Mine's somewhat... tempered, but still. Fate's made it clear I'm not allowed happiness, so that can't possibly end well for you. And also, what if I shift during the event? You might end up fucking a fur-covered—"

"Wyn, will you ever stop?" she asks.

"Why would I? You clearly can't get enough of my witticisms."

"Is that what they call being annoying here?"

I wrap a length of silky hair around my fingers, tugging gently. "Also, you did ask for *reasons*, so I'm happy to provide a long list and—"

Her palm presses over my mouth, cutting off my ramble. "Wyn... shut up."

"Okay."

Summer's bare thighs and steady gaze hold me in place as her teasing smile challenges me to make a move. Any move other than lying here like a lump of clay, hypnotized by her scent and the feel of her bare skin.

Summer.

Right now, my summer girl is exactly where I've always dreamed of having her. Correction—*almost* where I've dreamed of having her. The wolf in me wants to drag her under me, rip away every barrier between us, and claim her roughly, hungrily. Like the animal I am.

I close my eyes and reach out my senses to check for danger in the woods. Other than the sound of our rough breathing and the rustling of a nearby night creature, all is quiet. I detect no encroaching magic. No strangers lurking.

As I stroke her cheek, then rub her bottom lip, dipping my thumb into the wet, soft flesh, she wriggles her hips, and my cock pulses, straining against the last of my control.

"Wyn," she says. "Can you hear what I'm thinking?"

"*Ohhh*, yes. And it's *exactly* what I'm thinking."

"Go for it," she whispers.

Three little words, and all rational thought dissolves.

All that's left is *her,* and the need to make her mine.

"Fuck it," I say, tugging her down. "Let's do this."

CHAPTER 23

Summer

Wyn surges up and rolls me beneath him as if I'm made of feathers and sunlight instead of flesh and bones. Every muscle in his body radiates strength, the kind that could crush me in an instant—but his grip is careful, almost gentle.

And I can't wait to feel him inside me.

A growl rumbling in his chest, he crawls over me and licks my neck, his teeth sinking into the long muscle there, causing just the right amount of pain but not breaking the skin.

I hiss in a breath, and his head rises. "Okay?" he asks.

"I'm fantastic. Hurry. Please don't waste any more time talking."

"Patience, love. I've waited an age for this. I plan to enjoy every moment."

"Me too. It's been days of torture, wanting you, needing you. I can't stand a moment more."

His gaze snaps to mine. "*Days?* Summer, I've been dreaming of kissing this neck... these delicious berries... for *years*." He bows his head and sucks gently through the material of my top. Chills ripple over my skin. "So don't speak to me about torture."

He pushes my T-shirt up and palms my breasts, thumbs stroking my hard nipples. His hands are warm, fingers callused and reverent as they mold to the weight of me.

Kneeling, he lifts my hips and slides my shorts down my legs. When they catch on my foot, I fumble to kick them off.

"Allow me," he says, hooking a finger in the waistband and flicking them into the air.

"I'll allow a lot more than that if you'll only just hurry."

A feral grin shines white in the darkness. "Of course. I'll get to work."

Then, without further delay, he whips my legs apart and sinks between my thighs. "You're so beautiful. Every inch. I can't believe how perfect you are."

As he presses wet kisses on my inner thighs, I tug his thick hair. "No, Wyn.... Wait. I want us to... We should... Oh, *my god*."

His lips graze my folds, his hot, ragged breath a delicious tease, and then his tongue traces my seam, thumbs parting me to the cool night air as he licks and nibbles.

"What are you doing? That feels amazing."

"Still want me to stop?" he murmurs against me.

I smack the top of his head. "Absolutely not. Stay there, wolf-boy. I like the way you feast."

"You taste so fucking good. Sweet, earthy, wild, and like..." He groans, low and rough. "Like mine. Fuck, I may never stop."

Writhing against his tongue, I sigh and moan, the most delicious feeling building in my belly, in my core. As my legs shake, he grips my hips and lifts me against his mouth, his tongue plunging inside me, his teeth scraping and nipping. My whole body trembles as I wind my fingers deeper into his silky hair, so close to breaking apart.

I make a ridiculous sound as his teeth clamp around my clit, and he sucks hard and plunges his fingers inside me, masterfully guiding me through an incredible climax as I spasm around him, drawing him deeper.

"Good girl. More. Give me more," he commands, watching me intently, his big body shuddering as if my release were his own. "I want everything you have to give me. All of it."

When the waves of bliss subside, and I catch my breath, I tug his face to mine. "Wynter Fionbharr, where have you been all my life?"

"Watching you from every shadow, waiting for you to see me, to remember me as the one who would give my life to keep you safe. Someone who would destroy anyone or anything for a chance to call you mine."

I tug at Wyn's shirt and then his belt. "Off, I want all of you. This thing's just a glamour, right?" I ask.

"Easy now." He chuckles and sits back on his heels. "So impatient. I'm not going anywhere tonight. Not without you." He waves a hand, and the glamour melts away—shirt, pants, everything but hard muscle and smooth, firelit skin—gone in an instant.

Desire trembles through me as his magic moves over my stomach, chest, throat in a rolling wave of heat—its essence deeply comforting, like the calm I feel after a day spent with my hands working in rich, beautiful soil. Grounded. Alive. Thrilling.

A sigh parts my lips as his palms cradle my face. "No matter what happens, Summer, we'll always have tonight. Promise me you'll remember every moment. Swear it now."

Wyn's desperation cracks me open, and I need his strength—the solid weight of him—to hold me together. I'm not sure what he's afraid of, but whatever it is, I won't give it the power to ruin this. To destroy what we might become.

"I'll remember every moment with you, Wyn. Always. Whatever happened to me before, I trust you. Whatever chaos is waiting for us tomorrow or the next day, I choose you. I choose this."

He smiles then crashes into me like a landslide, one hand in my hair, the other on the bare skin of my waist and inching higher as his lips meet mine, coaxing them open. Tongue exploring, he moans into my mouth, our ragged breaths loud and in sync.

"Are you mine, sweet thing?" he asks between kisses, his cock hard against my inner thigh.

"Yes," I breathe. "Always and forever."

Gripping my jaw, he stares deep into my eyes, my very soul. "And no one else's? Promise."

"Yes, Wyn, only yours... Please," I say, gripping his hips and dragging him closer, dying to feel him inside me.

His hands slide slowly down my body, worshiping every inch of me, his lips following in their wake, then back up to latch onto my nipple, sucking and biting until I cry out. "Stop teasing me and do it."

"Anything you want, little sun," he says as his fingers slide under my hips, lifting me, lining me up with his weeping tip. "I'm here to make you scream, to give you everything you ever dreamed of."

Little sun? Great. First the mind-melting sex talk, now a devastatingly sweet nickname. This man needs a warning label.

He swears under his breath, his fingers skating over my most sensitive skin, each glide and press drawing full body shudders from me like he's a god commanding an earthquake. I grip his length, so hard yet silky smooth, my thumb stroking as I squeeze another satisfying curse from his lips and a groan from his chest.

"So fucking wet," he murmurs. "You smell so good. I want to roll in your scent and coat every part of me."

A smile tugs at my lips as I picture him rubbing his thick, black fur in my desire like a randy wolf. "Start thrusting and you'll be getting closer to that goal."

He growls, one hand steadying himself at my entrance, the other cuffing my neck as he enters me inch by delicious inch, stretching me in the best possible way. Raising my hips, I bite my bottom lip, moaning.

"Please, Wyn, more. Hurry."

His snarl of approval rumbles over my lips, and he draws back slowly, then thrusts forward, burying himself deep and thick to the hilt.

Gasping, I rake the rippling muscles of his back with my nails, urging him on. Needing more. And more. And more.

"Seven hells," he says, driving into me over and over before claiming my mouth again, his grip on my body tight enough to leave bruises. Tomorrow, I'll treasure each dark bloom on my skin.

Settling into a perfect rhythm, relentless and punishing, he whispers words against my lips, slurred and broken by groans of pleasure.

Wyn's pace slows, his incantation shifting into a low rasp. "By the Powers of Five, you are mine, Summer Brady. True name,

Grian. Bound in flesh, heart, and soul. I will never forsake you. I will never love another."

As my eyes close and my breaths turn into short, labored pants interspersed with whimpers and moans, his pace picks up again. "Look at me while I fuck you."

I obey without question.

Magical energy builds around us, leaves and raw gemstones glittering in the moonlight as they swirl faster and faster, in sync with the wildness coiling through my body.

Pleasure spikes as he raises his chest, the change in angle driving deeper, grinding against nerves that make my toes curl into the moss beneath my feet. "It's always been you, Summer. From the first moment I saw you... I knew you were mine... That I would forever be yours... Even if I could never fully claim you."

"Wyn," I moan, the fire inside me burning hotter as I claw at his arms, urging him closer.

He falls over me, mouth everywhere—my breasts, my lips, my throat—devouring each with feverish urgency. His weight presses me into the bed, his grip unyielding, perfect, as his tongue moves in rhythm with his hips.

"You're the only thing that matters... you in my arms... I'd give up everything to keep you here where you belong, little sun. Everything."

All my muscles tense, heat and madness coil inside me like a spring... then it breaks, and I come apart with a helpless cry. As I pulse around him, Wyn's pace quickens, growing faster, harder, more erratic.

Then his movements slow, grow tighter and more deliberate, like he's holding back. A strange heat churns low in my belly, mirrored by the wild energy flowing between us. I feel it where our bodies meet, a subtle, pulsing swell of magic... and then...

Something shifts. His length thickens inside me, pulses, then swells. I feel stretched. Overwhelmingly full. But also... incredible, if I'm being honest.

My breath hitches as the sensation deepens, anchoring me to him.

He growls, teeth clenched, body trembling with restraint. Whatever's happening it's more than a climax for him. It's instinctual. Changing him. Preparing to...

Oh. Wow.

"Wyn?"

"*Summer.*" He growls my name like a warning, a devotion. "Fuuuck," he breathes as he follows me over the fevered edge into oblivion.

All his muscles lock tight, and he freezes. "Don't move."

I wriggle my hips. "I can't anyway. What's happening?"

"My knot. It's temporary. Just breathe through it... please, Summer."

"Your *what*?"

"It's a wolf's knot. It happens when the bond... when the need goes too deep."

"Is that a bad thing?"

"For me, it's fucking great, but I can't pull out yet. Can't risk hurting you. Never want to hurt you."

"It doesn't hurt at all. Just feels like I'm yours. In fact, I could probably fall asleep like this."

He gives a tortured laugh. "That's not advisable."

Panting, he tilts his face toward the moon and howls like the wild creature I'm far too aware he is. Then he kisses me slowly, cool strands of inky, dark hair spilling down and tickling my skin.

After a while, he begins to move. "It's easing," he says, voice strained. "I have to... slowly. I'll stop if it hurts."

"Don't you dare. God, Wyn, that feels..."

He swallows my words with another slow, bone-melting kiss.

"You feel so damn good, like you were made to hold me. The perfect fit."

"Stop talking like that, or I'll be demanding more knot swelling."

With a laugh, he carefully moves off me and rustles through a nearby bag. "Are you okay?" he asks, producing a cloth and pouch of water.

"I've never been better."

Gently, reverently, he cleans my thighs, my stomach. The cloth is warm and damp, his hands steady as he wipes, the crackle of the fire the only sound. He presses kisses on my dry skin then gives me sips of water from the pouch.

"There," he says, looking me over as he crawls into bed. "Now you can sleep comfortably... as well as anyone can in the middle of the woods in the Land of Five. Rest easy, Summer. I won't let anything happen to you."

Wrapping my arms around his neck, I pull his heavy weight onto my chest and kiss him back until we're both breathless.

"I wish we'd done this the first day I saw you naked in my kitchen," I say. "Think of how much time we've wasted."

The scent of crushed wildflowers fills the air as Wyn lays beside me, smiling as he swipes hair from my cheek and tucks it behind my ear. "I was contemplating eating you when I met you in the kitchen. Might have been dangerous."

I smack his arm. "You were not."

"Well, not consuming you *whole*." He lets his gaze trail down my body. "Just feasting on certain parts of you."

"We're different species. I can't get pregnant, can I?"

Sighing, he rolls onto his back, head resting on his fingers linked behind his head. "I'm starting to think your mother wasn't really an esteemed scholar of the Wild Folk." He lets out another deep sigh while I contemplate the glorious sight of his skin shining in the moonlight. "It has been known to happen," he admits. "Especially when the couple are deeply connected. Fates entwined by circumstance, mutual obsession or..."

"*Love*," I whisper. "Just like your parents. What was I thinking? Of course humans can birth fae children. I've just slept with the evidence."

"That's me—a halfling torn between two worlds and not fully at home in either."

"Poor baby," I say, dropping a kiss on his cheek.

"Holding you is the closest I've ever felt to belonging, like I'm right where I'm meant to be."

My heart expands, my ribcage too small for the emotions swelling inside me. "I'll be your home, Wyn. Together, we'll be fine."

"More than fine, little sun. We'll be the talk of all of Faery, written into ballads and stories. Whether they despise or celebrate us doesn't matter to me."

When I eventually meet his sister, if she hates me, I hope Wyn won't mind too much. That he'll still be mine.

"Wyn, before you said Merri told you not to speak to me when I was a thrall living in your city. Did you ever disobey her?"

Dimples pop as he grins. "Of course. Every chance I got. Following orders is not my strong suit. Danced with you, too. And when you wouldn't stop spinning, I held you in my arms, rocking you for hours. If I couldn't remove your enchantment, the least I could do was try to ease your discomfort."

Warmth blooms in my chest, soft and aching. "Maybe that's why I wasn't afraid of you when you turned up at Gravenshade. Deep inside, I know you. Remember you as a friend."

"Much *more* than a friend now."

"Most definitely. But if we're not friends, what are we exactly?"

"You and me? We're everything I was told I could never have. I belong to you, Summer. I'll crumble your realm and mine to dust before I let anyone come between us. Wherever you go, I'll find you. Always. I think what that makes us is *forever.*"

Forever. I like the sound of that.

The fire crackles, the dusting of freckles over Wyn's nose glittering like flecks of gold. The weight of his arm around my waist anchors me in place, the slight rasp of his knuckles brushing my ribs as he pulls me against his chest. I breathe in the scent of his hair—smoke, moss, and wood.

"Careful. Keep looking at me like that," he murmurs, voice thick with exhaustion, "and I might start thinking you're madly in love with me."

I hum, tilting my head up to meet his gaze. His emerald eyes catch the firelight, something soft and hopeful glinting in them. "Might?" I tease. "You *know* I am."

He huffs a laugh, then kisses my forehead with such soft sweetness it steals my breath away.

"Go to sleep," he murmurs. "Even sunshine needs rest. And don't dare put a toe off this mattress without waking me. I'm serious, Summer, don't move without telling me. Faery isn't a safe place."

I tuck myself closer, my fingers curling against his chest. The worry of wanting, wondering, and waiting is gone. In its place is warmth. Safety. This man's love. Perhaps forever as he promised.

"Wyn?" I whisper.

"Mm?"

"Don't be gone in the morning."

The quiet stretches between us, thick with tension. Firelight flickers across his jaw as I trace it lightly with my thumb.

Another beat of silence, then his arm tightens around me. "I marked you. You're my mate. For better or worse, you can never get away from me, Summer."

"Huh? You did what?"

"I said I marked you. You're mine. Forever. This life and the next. And the next... and the next..."

"Good," I say, watching his frown disappear. "Wouldn't want it any other way."

He squeezes me tight, and I let my eyes close as Wyn's steady heartbeat and the soft crackle of the fire lull me to sleep.

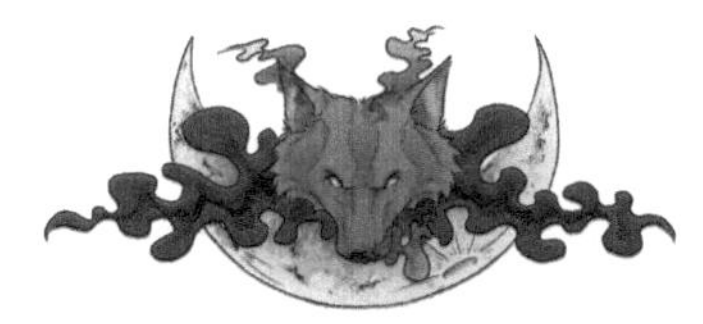

CHAPTER 24

Wynter

A two-headed othrius howls nearby. I bolt awake, the night air cold on my bare chest, with no body curled beside me for warmth.

Where the fuck is Summer?

Heart pounding like a war drum, I fling my hand out and pat the ground in case she's tumbled off our bed mid-dream.

Nothing.

No, no, no... Fuck.

After her encounter with the nix, she wouldn't be so reckless as to wander off alone in the dark without waking me first. Would she?

Knowing her independent nature, *yes*. Yes, she fucking would.

Fear surges as I shoot out of bed, landing in a crouch. My clothing glamour snaps into place as my palms press against the cool soil. I send my magic into the earth like roots, reaching for the familiar voices that speak to me through my element.

The ground whispers back in a staccato pulse, relaying a disturbance. A panicked struggle. Shadows curl behind my eyes, and my blood runs cold in my veins.

Fucking Landolin.

I stumble to my feet and run to the river, eyes scanning the scuffed earth near the shoreline. Drag marks veer into the woods. Summer's feet, small and bare, have left a wild pattern next to a larger set made by heavy boots that are firm and sure.

A primal moan rips from my throat, echoing through the trees like a war cry. If that shade prick has hurt her, I'll strangle him with his own shadows and rip his flesh to ribbons.

My pulse hammers in my ears as I kneel again, shoving my fingers deeper into the soil. "Show me," I command.

The earth's answer comes quickly—a dense fog of foul shadows, twisting and concealing all but Summer's kicking legs as they no doubt drag her away to the depths of Dorthadas, the capital of the Raven Realm.

Fuck!

Landolin, that shadow-born shit stain, has taken Summer again—eight fucking years after the first time he stole her. He's the one who killed her parents at Gravenshade. I know it. Dragged her to the Shade Court like a trophy. A mindless toy for them to abuse.

But if she mattered so much to them back then, why sell her to Draírdon, the High Mage of the Merit Court? Why let her drift into my sister's orbit—only to rip her away again eight years later? What the fuck are they playing at?

Fury burns in my chest, scorching away fear, leaving a boulder of rage in my gut and my spine rigid with the compulsion to get her back, no matter the cost ... Even if it kills me.

The forest groans as I unleash my power with a single whispered word, vines and roots surging to life at my command. They ripple through the thorn-choked undergrowth, carving a path around thick trees as I follow its direction deeper into the woods, each step I take reverberating over the ground.

"Summer," I shout, my voice's echo swallowed by a hovering stain of dark magic.

Ahead, shadows writhe, creating an unnatural, smoky void in a small space between a copse of silver wraith pines. Remnants of Landolin's magic. His scent clings to the air, smoke and cold ash.

I press a hand to the ground, and the forest answers. Tree roots surge higher, weaving through the darkness, searching for traces of Summer.

"Let her go," I roar, my voice cracking as the ground trembles in response. "If you hurt her, Landolin, I promise I will dedicate my life to the destruction of everything that's important to you. I'll tear down your home, strip the life from your lands so that not a blade of grass will grow where I've walked. And when you have nothing left, I'll make you beg for an end that will never come."

A low chuckle rumbles from the center of the void, and then I hear it, Summer's voice, weak but fierce.

"Wyn."

Relief wars with terror. She's alive. Still in this realm. But for how much longer? I tear through the trees, the earth rising underfoot and propelling me forward. Landolin's shadows lash out, but I raise my hands at my sides and vines strike back, surging to shield me as I near the void.

Landolin slips from the shadows, blue-tipped hair gleaming, grin sharp as a blade. "You're late, Wynter Fionbharr. A moment longer and she would have been gone."

The ground rumbles as I brace my stance, breath steady, my power coiling, ready to rip him apart. Of course he waited for me. Couldn't give up a chance to gloat. To watch me suffer.

"Correct me if I'm wrong," he continues, "but finders keepers is a law in your land. You should remember exactly who found this girl all those years ago. *Me.*"

Summer's thoughts come through loud and clear. She's stress-counting again—373, 374, 375—when she suddenly breaks off to send me a message.

Run, Wyn. Go. I'm not worth dying for.

Bull. Fucking. Shit.

I'll never desert her.

Fury overtakes me as I drop to the ground and slam my hands down. The earth erupts, vines bursting upward to shred Landolin's shadow magic. Thick smoke solidifies into a shield that erupts with a boom, forcing my vines away.

"The Hunt has no right to her," I say through gritted teeth. "You sold her to the Merits, relinquished your claim."

The void behind Landolin pulses, its coldness seeping into the air around us as it splits open, revealing Summer suspended in the center, her body bound by vibrating tendrils of shadow.

Her eyes are wide with fear, and when they find me, they fill with a desperate hope that ignites something feral in my chest.

"*Landolin,*" I grind out. "Give her back. Now. She belongs to me."

"Ah, Wynter, if only you'd woken from your sweet dream sooner, perhaps you could have stopped me. But dirt is slow and thick, and I walk with the Hunt's immunity to your realm's Elemental laws. Your magic breaks apart before it even touches me."

"And still you have no right to her."

Centuries ago, the Raven Realm won sovereignty over the Wild Hunt from its original masters, Yurendyl, the oldest of the fae realms. Rumors persist that, bound by blood to its ancient will, the hunt is slowly destroying Landolin in body and mind. I don't know how, but I pray to Dana this is true.

If there exists a way to bring his fate forward, I only wish I knew it.

Landolin takes a step closer, a long jacket of dark leather swinging around his calves. "I lead the Hunt. I go where I will. You know what happened the first time I took her. Your land upholds the law of finders keepers. Your sister's husband's court stole her away from me. What I do now only rectifies past wrongs."

"The Merits *bought* her from your father. You have no claim over the girl. So let her go."

My fists clench, my ragged breath sawing in and out of my lungs. The ground beneath me trembles, cracks spidering outward as my magic surges forward.

Landolin laughs, low and cruel. "You don't understand, do you? This girl has always belonged to my court. Belonged to the Hunt."

"She chooses where she belongs, and it's not with you." I thrust my hands downward, and the earth groans. Jagged spikes of rock erupt from beneath the forest floor, spearing toward Landolin, but shadows coil, swallowing him whole, and he disappears before the stone can reach him.

He reappears at my back and whispers against my ear. "You're so predictable."

I spin and a wave of roots bursts from the ground to trap him, but again he disintegrates into shadows and slips through the cracks like water through fingers. He darts in front of Summer, a demon in the dark smirking up at her barely conscious, limp form.

But I have no interest in his games. Not while Summer's life is at risk. I slam both hands toward the earth, and the area beneath Landolin's boots buckles.

If I can bury him alive, it may take centuries for the Hunt to find him.

The ground begins to collapse and swallows him up to his knees, then his waist, his body sinking inch by inch.

Landolin's smirk falters. "Enough." He raises his hand, and the shadows enveloping him twist, forming a row of arrow-like shards. I brace for the strike, but he flings them at Summer, not me.

"No!" My focus breaks as I turn to face her fully, my roots lashing out to intercept Landolin's magic. They deflect it, but while my attention is on Summer, Landolin springs his trap.

A shadow flies through the air, sharp as a dagger, and plunges into the side of my head. The pain is blinding, forcing me to my knees. I try to shift into my wolf and tear the shade prick's throat out before he has time to dematerialize, a skill that only certain Unseelie fae possess, but my body refuses to obey.

My magic falters, the ground rising around Landolin, lifting him from the grave I built.

"You should know better, Wyn," Landolin purrs, his coal-black eyes gleaming as he steps close. "Letting your heart guide your decisions makes you predictable. Vulnerable."

"Better that than be a life-long asshole," I spit out.

I try to get to my feet, to summon the earth again, but a smoky veil invades my mind, slowing my thoughts. Suffocating my rage. My breaths come shallow as the Shade Prince poisons the air with dark magic, choking my connection to the land.

I can't move. Only feel consciousness seep from my mind. *Summer.*

"Poor Seelie prince. I know you can't help but fight for her," he says. "Being told you were a hero by the simpering Elemental Court has woven the idea into the very fabric of your being. But know this, you will lose every single time you challenge me." His shadows darken around the void, obscuring my view of Summer. "Do you know why?" he asks.

"Let me guess. Because you'll keep cheating?"

"No, because I'm willing to do what you won't."

He flicks his hand, and another arrow shoots toward me. I watch its progress, unable to even flinch from its trajectory. I fight the pull of the shadow, trying to lock Summer's face in my mind—the shape of her reaching for me, her mouth open in a scream I can't hear. Then Landolin's magic engulfs me without mercy, her name on my lips as I collapse.

Some time later, I jolt awake with a sharp pain thudding behind my eyes and a sense of suffocating dread. I rub the side of my head, and my fingers come away sticky with blood. I groan, pushing up onto shaking arms, and freeze.

The moonlit clearing is empty, and I'm not at the campsite, in bed with Summer beside me. What the fuck happened? The last thing I remember is falling asleep in her arms, blissfully happy, followed by a nightmare full of shadows.

I reach for Summer through the soil, and then it hits me. Those shadows were real. I remember her voice screaming my name. The feel of my head cracking under that dagger of shadow magic. The fight. That fucker Landolin. It wasn't a dream. It happened.

I stagger to my feet, my legs weak beneath me as I stumble back to the campsite. Our bed is strewn across the ground. The cloak I made for her is missing. My heart slams against my ribs as I bolt through the woods to the clearing again. My gaze sweeps the area, searching for anything. Anything at all.

And then I see it. A disturbance in the earth, a violent smear of scuffed dirt and grass. My knees hit the ground, my fingers pressing into the soil. I reach for Summer, letting magic seep through the land like quickening tendrils.

The story unfolds in a rush—boot prints too large to be hers, the drag of a body, Summer's body, pulled unwillingly into the trees. A void of shadows. Me, trying to bury the Shade Prince alive.

"No." My voice cracks, terror shuddering through me.

Landolin came for her, just as I'd feared, and I hadn't been able to stop him.

I hadn't protected her like I promised I would.

A tremor runs through the earth, mirroring the rage rolling in my chest. I slam my palms down, forcing my power deeper into the ground.

"Where is she?" I growl to the soil, the roots, the bones of the Land of Five. "Answer me, dammit."

A flicker. A pulse of something warm and human. My magic catches it, clings to it. The remnants of Summer's bright energy.

I surge to my feet, the ground rising and rippling as if urging me forward. The trail leads deeper into the woods, a path still wrapped in the shade-rat's foul shadows. My vines lash out in the dark, clearing the way as I sprint forward.

With each step, Summer's voice echoes in my mind. Her laugh, her fire, the way she spoke my name when I was inside her, closer than I'd ever hoped to be. The memory of her scent, her smile, pulls me forward through a waking nightmare.

I won't let Landolin have her.

Not again.

The trees thin out, and as I stumble into a small clearing, I drop to the ground and plunge my hands into the dirt again, desperate for clues.

"Please. Please. Please," I beg, but the earth offers only silence in reply.

For one agonizing moment, I can't draw breath. Can't move. But then the ground softens, opening to me, and I feel the pulse of her heartbeat, faint and fragile. Still alive.

Fists clenched, I rise, the ground trembling as I turn in the direction of Talamh Cúig. *Home.* But I won't be there for long.

"I'm coming for you, Summer. And when I find Landolin, if he's hurt you, I'll tear him apart."

But to reach his land, I'll need an Unseelie monarch to open a path to the Raven Realm.

Which means...

Fuck me sideways.

I'll have to ask Merri.

CHAPTER 25

Wynter

A flash of silver ripples in the clearing, and my horse, Tier, steps out of the shadows, hoofs silent on the mossy ground. Ivor pads after him, his black coat gray in the mist, flanks twitching as he sniffs the air.

Ivor bounds forward and knocks me to the ground. We roll around, and then I push onto my haunches, rubbing his ears, as I call my horse to join us.

"Hey, Tier," I say, standing and pressing my forehead to his nose, breathing in his familiar scent. "It's good to see you. The foolish mortal has gone and gotten herself kidnapped again, so you're off the hook. I don't need a ride back to the Emerald Keep anymore."

He gives an indignant snort, ruffling my hair.

"Don't be offended. I know you're faster than Father's órga falcons. But if I shift and run with Ivor, we'll blend into the land, be less noticeable. My family can't know I'm back, or they'll never let me leave. Return home. All going well, I'll see you soon. You understand, don't you?"

Tier blows a hard breath, ears pinned and stamps his hoofs like I've insulted him in five languages before plodding toward the Lake of Spirits, whinnying over his shoulder every few steps.

"Take a swim in the lake," I call out. "Replenish your magic. Then the trip won't have been for nothing."

Ivor barks, growing impatient, and I shrug off the guilt of abandoning my horse and prepare for the change.

The shift comes with a searing bolt of heat that shudders through my bones. My limbs snap and change, my senses stretching beyond my bond with the earth element, now fused with the power of fang and claw. Fur bursts across my skin, and the sharp tang of pine and rot fills my nose, soil humming beneath my paws the moment they strike the ground.

Ivor gives a huff beside me and thrashes his tail expectantly. His favorite times are when we run together, hunting. I shake from my nose to the tip of my tail, releasing the tension from my spine, and then we turn toward the woods.

The wind rustles my fur as I run, paws drumming the damp forest floor. Ivor lopes beside me, silent and sure, a black streak in the darkness. Together we wind through towering trees and bramble-wrapped groves, the rhythm of our movements tuned to instinct and magical bond. Above us, clouds scatter across a waning moon.

We cross the lowlands under the cover of mist, the Emerald Castle's spires glinting in the moonlight, growing closer with every breath. As we race over the bridge, the city's waterfalls roar beneath us, and part of me aches to slip through a side door, and crawl into bed for some much-needed rest. But I can't stop. I'll never stop. Not while Summer needs me.

Instead, we bypass my home, taking an overgrown path that snakes around an outer wall, ducking beneath knotted tree limbs and weaving past the ruins of Castle Black—the old seat of my kingdom, where the air still thrums with ancient magic and curses.

The grass grows sparse near the sea cliffs, giving way to gravel paths and jagged stone. We pass the old tournament grounds, thankfully, not running into any nosy sea witches, ready to flap their gills to the court about my presence.

And then, there it is—the Moonstone Cave, mouth yawning wide like the maw of some sleeping beast. It shimmers subtly, as if it remembers us and is ready to do our biding. Which is a ruse. Only mages or queens can open this portal. I had to enlist Ether's help many times to journey to the Earth Realm to search for Summer until I finally got spat out near Gravenshade Hall.

I shift to my fae form with a shudder, summoning a courtly glamour of leather and armor. Ivor whines and paces behind me as I step inside, the stone glowing with bright veins of light underfoot. My hand slides over the familiar arch etched into the wall, the elemental sigils rough against my palm.

Thank Dana my sister can't read my thoughts—though I've read hers often enough to know I'm doomed. She's going to kill me when she finds out Landolin has Summer. I take a deep breath, but it snags in my throat, thick with guilt.

"Merri," I call out across the bond. "It's me, Wyn. I need urgent passage. I must see you."

Our connection takes a few minutes to snap into place, as if she's busy, occupied with court duties. I sense her confusion sharpen to recognition, then comes resignation.

"Of course it's you, brother dear," she replies. "You never knock politely, just barge in like a bog troll."

The air shimmers as the portal forms—an arc of rainbow-colored water licking the stone, widening until it encompasses the full width of the cave.

Ivor and I step into the pond, through the cascading wall of water, then everything goes black.

Regaining consciousness on the floor outside the golden doors of the Merit palace's Great Hall, I shake my head to clear it, then give the guards a brisk nod as I get to my feet.

"Evening," I say. "My sister is expecting me."

Ivor, ever the disagreeable guest, growls at the guards, his fur bristling. I hide a smile as a ram's horn sounds, and the double doors open wide. At least my wolf didn't raise his leg and piss on them.

"Wish me luck," I whisper, and step over a thin moat of flaming oil, momentarily blinded by the flashing gold and silver surfaces as I enter the hall.

Alternating red, black, and gold columns rise upward to bear the weight of the domed-glass ceiling that spills moonlight across the polished black marble floor. Beyond them, my sister sits on the Sun Throne, a regal vision in a glittering crown of silver meteoric spikes.

The throne itself, all sharp angles and gleaming metal, looking more like a weapon than a seat, fans out in bronze beams behind Merri that span the entire rear wall of glass. Beyond the glass, a sea of stars glitters like splintered crystals.

Even from this great distance, my sister's smile shines as bright as her vivid red hair.

On her right, wearing a matching crown of towering black, sits her husband—the silver-haired Riven Éadra na Duinn, the Unseelie King who saved my uncle and aunt's lives when they were imprisoned at this court many years ago. They now rule over the Land of Five, largely thanks to his benevolent nature.

A flock of mechanical birds swoops through incense-scented air, circling me in a blur of metal and motion. I swipe a hand above my head, and they squawk and flee, retreating behind the broad purple leaves of palm trees and tall copper braziers alight with green flames.

Though packed with Merit courtiers, the hall is hushed, everyone waiting to see what has brought a Seelie prince to their court in the middle of the night. All hoping for drama, no doubt.

A wild screech cuts through the air, then Riven's owl, a half-natural, half-mechanical creature, calls out, "The Wynter Prince comes. Where's Summer? Where's Summer?"

The damn owl knows everything. I swear she's a better mind reader than I am.

As I move closer, I notice Lidwinia, the king's sister and Merri's closest friend sprawled across the top steps of the dais, cleaning her teeth with a knife like the badass she is.

At her feet, my niece and nephew play—solemn, silver-haired twins. Their blue eyes widen, smiles stretching across their faces as I approach. They sit forward as if to rise, but Lidwinia presses them back.

"Queen of Merits," I drawl, offering an exaggerated bow, grin barely contained. "How fares the most regal of older sisters to ever exist in the realms?"

Before Merri can answer, Lidwinia, straightens, licks the knife with her thin, forked tongue, and says, "Ah, the Prince of Earth comes seeking favors."

I bow again. "You know me so well, Princess of Merits."

Laughing, Merri turns to Lidwinia. "What use is an older sister if she can't grant impossible favors to a charming but hopeless younger brother?"

A gold spider scrambles up the Merit princess's arm and hides behind her spikes of green hair. Rothlo may appear shy, but she is no ordinary spider. I once saw Lidwinia ride her into battle, the creature transformed into the size of a fomorian, the giants that roamed Faery thousands of years ago.

"My first favor is a humble request for a private audience with my sister and her husband."

The Merit Queen bows her head, and the entire hall disperses, most transferring by dissolving in the air like the ghosts that plague Summer in the human realm. Others raise leathery wings and flee through open windows, brave ones allowing their talons to scrape my head as they fly above me.

I crack my knuckles, and the walls shudder, dust gathering and swirling in a vortex in front of me before it erupts, covering the troublemaking fae on their way out.

"Shall we find Elas?" Lidwinia asks the children.

They nod, then hurry down the steps and wrap themselves around my legs before burying their faces in Ivor's fur.

"We forbid you to leave until you play with us," demands Brisa, a blast of her air magic tangling my hair.

"Air powers triumph over earth. We need you to help us prove our experiment," Eirian chimes in.

I dare not tell my fierce niece and nephew that I've let them win all of our battles so far, though sometimes I am quite tempted.

"I won't be at court long enough. But next time, count me in. Until then, stay out of trouble, chlann ghràdhach," I say, calling them dear children in the old language.

"We'll be up to say goodnight soon," Merri says, blowing Brisa and Eirian kisses that turn into a swarm of playful dragonflies that swoops around them.

As Lidwinia leads them off to bed, I conjure a handful of small gemstones—tiny earthborn baubles—and toss them gently after the twins. They squeal with delight, chasing the glittering arc of stones, their laughter echoing down the hall long after they've vanished around the corner.

Merri vaults from her throne, descends the red-and-black stairs in a blur, and flings herself into my open arms, knocking the air from my lungs.

"Oh, Wyn, it's so wonderful to see you. Let me look at you." She holds my upper arms and pushes me backward for her inspection, eyes narrowing with mock suspicion. Then she peers over my shoulder. "What, no bevy of pretty Emerald courtiers trailing in your wake?"

A dress of green gossamer strips, interspersed with stiff silver panels the same bright shade as her eyes, rustles and clinks as she moves. She looks queenly, intimidating, and I have to remind myself it's still Merri beneath the finery—the girl who once dared me to steal a draygonet's egg, then helped me wrestle it back in the nest when the screeching chick hatched in my arms.

I laugh, my cheeks flushing. If only Merri knew how little interest I've had in the Land of Five's courtiers these past seven years. The image she still holds from when we lived together in Talamh Cúig—me a carefree wastrel—seems to comfort her. And so I maintain it. But it's nothing but an act.

I haven't bedded anyone, fae or otherwise, since I fell for a girl made of sunshine and sorrow.

Cara, Merri's manic mire squirrel, squeals at Ivor, launches from Riven's lap, and chases my wolf around the edges of the hall, vaulting over channels of oil carved into the floor forming a vast triangle. Under Riven's father, those same channels ran crimson once a month, during the brutal Blood Sun Ritual.

Cruelty doesn't rule here anymore. This court, once obsessed with technology and machinery, has grown softer under Riven's reign. Though evidence of their tainted past lingers in their half-mechanical creatures, like the owl, Meerade—who rattles her metal feathers from the king's shoulder and coughs as if to remind me.

When Riven took the crown, the Merits returned to the old ways of the ancient Druids. And instead of dark magic and oiled gears, the air now smells of frankincense and cedarwood burning from the bronze braziers that flank the hall, and no fae have been sacrificed within these walls ever since.

"Has Dad finally driven Mom to madness?" Merri asks. "Is that why you're here? I haven't sensed you poking at my thoughts for at least a couple of weeks. I did wonder if you'd gone roaming."

"Yeah. I have been traveling..." I take a deep breath and meet her steady gaze. "...in the Earth Realm. And now the Wild Hunt has taken Summer."

CHAPTER 26

Wynter

"*What?* You promised you wouldn't go to her, Wyn." Merri paces a few steps, raking a hand through her hair. "The human girl was never a safe option for you, but I guess you've always had a death wish."

"Ether tempered Aer's curse at your wedding," I murmur, sinking to my knees in front of my sister. I clasp her hands tightly, pleading for understanding. "Remember her words, Merri? Prince of the barren earth, buried within it you must be for at least seven days and seven nights, and until your heart's love unearths you. Then free and forever blessed you shall be."

My sister's frown fades, and her silver eyes flick toward Riven, who watches from a smaller, crescent moon throne, silent but tense.

I smile to myself, recalling the final lines of the original curse of the Black Blood princes that foretold Merri's conquering of Riven and the end of doom and gloom for our family's bloodline. Well, for most of us.

A halfling defies the Silver King, from dark to light, her good heart brings. Enemies unite. Two courts now one. Should Merri win, the curse is done. Not Faery born, but human sworn. One celestial day, she'll wear his ring.

All along, my sister was the key. The silver hand that controls the Unseelie king's power. And Riven respects and honors her role and counsel and is often found sitting in the consort's throne, instead of the king's imposing Sun Throne.

I squeeze Merri's fingers. "If the worst comes to pass and I'm buried alive, Summer will free me. That's what Ether suggested would happen. And the High Mage's word is steadfast. As true as the four rivers that flow from the Lake of Spirits. All will be well in the end. Don't you see?"

Merri ascends the steps and takes a seat on her throne. "I can't let you risk your life, Wyn." She turns to her husband. "We'll send an envoy to fetch Summer from the Shade Court. Riven, can you recommend anyone for the task?"

The owl perched on Riven's left shoulder swivels her great head with an eerie grace. One eye gleams green, and the mechanical one clicks softly in its socket. "The mushroom mage deserves the journey," she croaks.

Riven's laughter echoes through the hall, his snow-white hair moving around his metal-capped shoulders. "Meerade, Draírdon is long dead," he scolds his bonded owl. "Recall how he betrayed Merri and the terrible punishment he earned for daring to plot against her. Have you forgotten how much you enjoyed telling me about his crimes?"

The owl coughs and fluffs her feathers, the metallic half of her body covered in scales tinkling like Beltane bells. It took a full year after my sister's wedding for Draírdon's betrayal to come to light. It took less than a few heartbeats for Riven to dispense his punishment.

Riven leans and caresses Merri's cheek. "I shall go myself, my love," he says. "The Shade King cannot refuse me an audience, and Summer will remember me. Does she recall her time in Faery, Wyn?"

"No. Not yet," I reply, my jaw tightening.

"Seven hells," Merri snaps. "If you think I'm letting you march into that shadow-cursed place without me, Riven, you're wrong. I'll chain you to this hall myself if I must."

Riven shakes his head, smiling, and I drop my gaze to the floor and reach out to capture my sister's thoughts.

Flashes come through fast: fear for her husband. Concern for Summer. The idea of going to the Raven Realm herself, quickly quashed by worries about leaving her children. Then an image that gives me hope flashes through her mind—me standing before the Raven King, Moiron Ravenseeker, in the ghastly Hall of Shades.

"Merri, you're considering giving me your blessing. Of course it's the right thing to do."

Her eyes narrow. "Did you just read my mind, little pest?"

I widen my eyes in mock horror. "Me? Intrude upon the Queen of Merit's private thoughts? Wouldn't dream of it," I say, wincing from habit even though in Faery, my barefaced lie causes barely any pain.

Riven chuckles. And Merri sends a blast of air magic to tear my hair upward and tangle the strands together. "Privacy is the last thing you care about, Wynter."

"You've ruined my hair. Quick send for a comb. If you start braiding my eyebrows, I'll declare war." I get off my knees and stride toward the dais stairs. "Fine. Fine. I may have taken a small peek at your thoughts."

"Why can't you let Summer go?" she asks. "You know the risk of being with her."

"It's not that easy. I—"

Merri claps her hands together, her gaze sharpening. "You've bedded her!"

My boots are suddenly the most fascinating items in the hall. "What? No. Well... yes, no...look—" My head snaps up, and I begin to climb the stairs. "How can you tell?"

"How can I *tell?* It's written all over you. Your freckles are glowing like powdered sunlight. Your magic is humming so loud I can hear it. And you're practically levitating, you poor enchanted fool. But you *said* you wouldn't risk Air's curse coming true, Wyn. You promised."

"Yes. Seven years. I vowed I'd stay away that long. And I did."

"You promised you'd forget her by then. That you'd never make her yours."

I lean in and kiss her cheek. "I love you, Merri, but I lied. And I made damn sure not to promise that I'd *never* make her mine. I love Summer, too. Right from the first moment I saw her. When you fell for Riven, I helped you sneak away to this very court, risking your life. All I asked in return was that when my time came, you'd help me make my way to the Earth Realm. But when the term of the vow expired, I didn't call in the favor, instead I found my own path."

"Because you had to," she says. "You knew how upset I'd be."

"Yeah, exactly. But now I'm asking you this... let me go to Summer. Let me die for love, if that's the price I must pay. The mortal, Grian Brady, owns my heart, and nothing in the Seven Realms will ever change that."

Merri's eyes shine with unshed tears. "Oh, Wyn. How can I refuse such a foolish and romantic request?"

She passes me a tray with a goblet of water on it and warm meat pastries dotted with honeyed figs. "Will you rest a little while, take time to formulate a plan? We should speak to Father or King Raff. You mustn't go alone."

"No. Not our father. No one from the Emerald Court. Please, Merri."

She frowns. Riven rests a hand on her knee, then blasts me with his intense blue gaze, cold as frost and steady as stone. "Let me at least send envoys with you, Wyn. A small band of warriors to ensure—"

"Fine, I'll eat," I interrupt, tearing into a still-warm pastry, barely chewing before swallowing. "Then I'll just... improvise." I set the food on the stairs, keep hold of the cup, and take a drink. "I need to go alone. In fact, I insist. If you refuse to help me open a portal, Merri, we're through."

Fists clenched, she rises from the throne. "Wyn! How can you say such a thing?"

"I've never been more serious. Not even you can keep me from Summer."

Tears spill down Merri's cheeks. "It's too dangerous. I insist you travel accompanied."

"No." The word cracks the air like lightning-struck stone. "No envoys. No warriors. And definitely no older sister or even her loyal husband." I force a breath through clenched teeth. "The Shade Court will take one look at you and Riven and call your presence a provocation."

She steps forward, silver eyes fierce. "And you think they'll welcome you with open arms?"

"No," I say quietly. "But they will tolerate my presence." I scrub a hand through my messy hair. "Landolin especially will want to gloat and sneer, toy with me. He'll know precisely why I'm there—to retrieve Summer—but my visit won't spark a political nightmare that after your death, your children might spend their lifetimes unraveling."

Merri's brows knit, and I feel her thoughts race along the bond—fear for me mixed with fury, love, and then finally surrender.

"You don't trust me to handle this properly," she says.

"I trust you with everything but this." I glance toward the shadows where her children's laughter recently echoed. "I won't have the Shade Court sniffing at your family's door because I dragged you into my mess."

Riven shifts on the throne, eyes narrowing. "And if you die?"

I let out a bitter breath. "Then I die. Better me than the whole damned realm if the Shade Court turns the Hunt against us."

My sister's lips press into a thin line, but the wet shimmer in her eyes tells me she understands. Even if she hates it.

Merri clutches the sculpted armrests of her throne, knuckles white as her head drops back, a vision overtaking her. Her body shakes, and Riven gently holds her shoulders, keeping her safe.

She mutters under her breath words I can't understand, except for the final few. "The dead waker... The shadows seek the dead waker." After a few minutes, her silver eyes open.

"What did you see, Merri?" I ask.

"Summer isn't who Landolin needs. He's taken the wrong girl, hoping to shape her into the Hunt's weapon."

"Sister, what are you talking about? Explain," I urge.

"That's all I've got. Tell Landolin. Convince him Summer can't help his court, and there's a good chance that he'll let her leave with you."

"I'll tell him. This is something positive at least. Now you can let me go with a lighter heart."

"Promise you'll be careful. I mean it, Wyn."

"Of course. I'll have no trouble getting Moiron Ravenseeker to see me. Convincing Landolin that he doesn't need Summer, that will be the difficult part."

"Remember that no matter how much you want to, you cannot kill Moiron or his son," Merri warns. "The truce between our realms still binds us to—"

Silverware clatters as I slam my cup onto the small table between the king and queen. "I know what the truce states," I say through gritted teeth, not admitting that I'd happily tear the treaty to pieces, destroy the peace in every realm if it meant I could save Summer from the Hunt.

"Calm down," commands Riven, power crackling through his hair.

I school my features into a serene mask, hiding the truth. If Merri knows how far I'm willing to go, she'll have me put under lock and key in the Merit castle. Possibly forever.

I cross my arms. "Then tell me... how do I travel to the Raven Realm."

Merri stiffens. "You're not seriously thinking of leaving right now without any—"

"I am." I meet her gaze without flinching. "I need you to take me to the portal."

Riven leans forward, composed as ever. "Our court's powers can send you anywhere, even to the lower Unseelie Courts. We will be honored to help you retrieve Summer."

I nod, my shoulders sagging with relief. "Thank you."

Merri's hand clenches over her chest. "Wyn—"

I cut her off with a warning glare. "I'm going. And now."

Resignation slackens her features. "Fine. But listen, Wyn, if you ever breathe a word of this to Father, if you tell him I helped you, I'll bury you in a bottomless pit of shadows myself. And not even your earth magic will save you."

"Understood. I'm ready to go. What should I do?"

"Come here. Let me give you a proper hug before I take you to the portal."

Merri opens her arms, and as I relax into her embrace, too late, I notice her give Riven a swift nod.

A flash of blinding silver light—then nothing.

CHAPTER 27

Summer

When I wake, I'm not snuggled against Wyn's solid, warm body. There's no sweet-smelling, mossy mattress beneath me, cushioning my butt.

Nope.

Instead, I'm lying across a crimson velvet couch, covered by a heavy blanket. I'm not sure if it's wool or silk, but it's softer than anything I've ever felt in my life.

Despite the crackle and heat emanating from a nearby fire, a full-body chill runs over me as I open my eyes and gingerly look around.

I'm in a bedroom. Quite a luxurious one, too.

The high ceiling is ribbed with what looks like rows of blackened bones arching into the gloom above. A bed framed by towering posts and hung with black velvet drapes sits against a deep burgundy wall, and silver threads in the dark-blue bedcovers sparkle in the firelight.

Is this Wyn's bedroom? Am I in the City of Talamh Cúig?

"Wyn?" I call out, rubbing my pounding temples.

No answer. I'm alone.

I slowly sit up, my bare feet landing on dark, polished marble that feels so good against my hot skin.

A minute ago, I was shivering. Maybe I'm sick and running a fever.

I consider lying down cheek-first on the floor and absorbing its glorious coolness into my body, but then think better of it. This place doesn't feel anything like the Bright Court Wyn told me about. If I was at the Emerald Keep, I'd remember arriving. And I probably wouldn't feel like shit.

Dread curls tight in my gut. Something's wrong. I know it. Automatically, I start counting in my head—a self-soothing habit I've had since I nearly drowned in the lake behind our house when I was nine.

25, 26, 27, 28, 29, 30, 31, 32.

A shadow flickers across the ceiling. I've seen magic like that before... the other night, when the Hunt showed up at Gravenshade Hall.

That's when reality hits me like a sledgehammer. Landolin must've taken me to *his* home, the Shade Court, Wyn had called it. So, instead of resting, I'd do better to figure out exactly where I am and how the hell to get out of here.

Poor Wyn. He must be so worried, boiling with rage that I got taken again. I only wish I could remember how. I hope he's safe and not doing anything stupid, like charging through Faery in wolf form, teeth bared, and tearing everything in sight apart.

Now that I'm upright and not seeing double, I take a stroll around the room. Maybe there's a mild-mannered ghost or two hanging around, ready to be recruited into espionage.

The fireplace mantle is the only bright thing in the room, ornate and carved from gleaming silver stone that resembles hematite. Even the light visible outside the open, arched window is a wan gray—the kind that feels peaceful, but also a little gloomy.

Opposite the bed is a wall made of smoky-gray glass. It reflects a hazy view of the room, and I get the creepy feeling that someone on the other side is staring back at me. Just in case, I give them my middle finger and a defiant, raised eyebrow.

If I'm some kind of prisoner, I refuse to show fear. Standing up to bullies is rule one. My counseling course hasn't covered fae psychopaths yet.

There's a wardrobe that's three times taller than me, a desk beneath the window, a bathing room behind a scrolled door, even a bookshelf that I hope contains stories like the ones Zylah (and me) love to read. But sadly, no friendly ghouls to speak of.

Are dark romance books a thing in Faery? I certainly hope so.

Thick, smoky shadows gather over the mirrored wall, concentrate in the shape of raven wings that beat the air, then Landolin steps out from the middle of them, dressed in black and indigo blue.

Forgetting my plan to stand my ground, I stumble backward until my spine hits the row of shelves beside the bed. "Shame. I was hoping you'd be a friendly ghost, not a kidnapping asshole."

A leather-bound book tumbles to the floor, and Landolin swoops in and sweeps it up, turning the cover over on his palm. "Careful, I like this one. A fine tale of the Wild Hunt's exploits as written by mother dearest. Not *my* mother, of course, *yours*.

It's not entirely accurate. But she knew things that a mortal shouldn't. Or couldn't. Why is that, I wonder?"

As he leans forward and tucks the book away, my gaze follows the upward arc of his hand and lands on what looks like a skull fixed above the bed. Its antlers stretch halfway across the wall and remind me of who Landolin is—the leader of the *actual* fucking Wild Hunt.

From what I remember in Mom's books, the Hunt isn't to be messed with. An ancient force of spectral riders, bound by blood and shadow, they're neither alive nor dead, existing in an in-between, liminal form, their sole purpose to ride and hunt at their master's command.

That same master who is currently grinning down at me with glee.

The stag's skull serves as a warning. To take care, watch my mouth, and keep my eyes peeled for clues on how to get out of here. Then I have to somehow find Wyn so we can both return to Zylah and Gravenshade Hall.

Faery isn't a safe place, and I'll need to convince Wyn to come home with me. Maybe Zy can get him job at the vet clinic. He should be good with animals. Especially dogs. Since he kind of *is* one.

Fuck. Fuck. Fuckity hell-fuck. How am I going to get myself out of this mess?

"Well?" says Landolin, snapping me out of my anxious spiral. "Nothing to say to me? You must have questions."

He's not wrong. I have about a thousand of them. "Is this still the same night you took me from Wyn's camp?"

"Not nighttime—it's late morning. In this court, we live in the gloaming no matter the time of day. And you've only spent one night asleep on that sofa, looking dead to the realms, neither waking for food nor water. I was beginning to think you might never open your eyes."

Landolin drags a length of hair off my sweaty cheek and slides it behind my ear, taking his sweet time and boring gold-flecked, black eyes into mine, as if he's hoping he might make me swoon and divulge some intimate secret.

Well, buddy, that's not happening. He's not my type at all. I like sexy sweethearts with grass-green eyes and tough exteriors. Wolfish guys—wink, wink.

Zylah, on the other hand, would have no trouble throwing herself off a cliff for this evil Gothic-fever-dream prince, wrapped in muscle-hugging black leather.

Is Landolin hotter than a food truck's secret sauce at five a.m. on the longest night of your life? Handsomer than the arrogant college jock your friends warned you about? Yes. And, *hell* yes.

But I like my men pettable, and sporting freckles and dimples, not sharp teeth and bitter smiles.

Landolin runs a palm over the vines and irises on my left arm, pouting unhappily. "These used to glow with magic when you were last in my realm."

"What? Did you give me these tattoos?"

"Not me. The shadow mages. Poor pet," he says, pinching my chin so hard my eyes water. "You look lost, confused. But you've always been a lonely, sad-eyed doe, haven't you?"

Zylah's face flashes in my mind. Bright smile, cat-eye glasses, and auburn hair twisted into space buns that she hides her scalpels in. Landolin is wrong. I'm not alone. Zy has always had my back.

"Did you shoot Wyn with an arrow in the woods while he was in wolf form?" I ask.

"Of course. I was just fucking with him. He'd do the same to me given the opportunity. And he would have healed fine without your intervention. No real harm was meant. Wynter knows this."

My skin chills as he pats my cheek. "Cheer up. I know just the thing to lift your spirits. I'm sure you'd love to learn the details of a certain full-moon night in the Earth Realm eight years ago," he continues, linking his arm through mine and ushering me in front of the mirrored wall.

My heart seizes in my chest, then pounds against my ribs in staccato bursts. I know exactly what he's referring to—the night my parents died. The night I possibly lost my mind and killed them.

"What night?" I whisper, feigning ignorance. "What are you talking about?"

Moving behind me, one arm winds around my waist, his other hand holds my chin in place, forcing me to stare at our mirrored reflection.

"All these years, you've imagined yourself to be a murderess. A pretty moon flower believing she's a weed to be torn from the ground before it destroys everything around her."

Despite my best efforts not to cry, a single tear tracks down my face. I wipe it away and glare at Landolin's smug image in the mirror.

"Hush now. The time for fretting is over. The truth must be revealed. Look into the glass. No matter what, do not close your eyes. Don't even blink. You'll want to remember every moment."

The mirror's surface ripples like a windswept silver lake, and a chill crawls down my spine. Landolin's feral gaze fixes on my face as images emerge from the blur of smoke-tinged light, clear and sharp, like I'm watching the scene on a flat-screen TV.

A girl stands in Gravenshade's kitchen. Me—at the bench beside the cooker, slicing and dicing tomatoes, busy making pizza.

Dread pools in my stomach, and I try to twist away from the sight. For years, I've longed to find out what happened to my parents, but now I'm terrified Landolin's vision might confirm my worst nightmares—that I'm a violent lunatic. A murderous freak.

The prince's grip tightens, gold shimmering in his cruel gaze like mica in polished obsidian stones. "Pay attention, Summer."

In the mirror, a tall shadow steps into my kitchen. Landolin Ravenseeker.

"What the hell? You were there!"

A deep chuckle sounds in my ear. "When fresh flowers are plucked from the human realm, the leader of the Hunt is always present."

"So this was all about stealing a human. Why? Why choose me? I don't have any special talents or hidden powers. I'm attractive enough—if you like dark hair and too much eyeliner—but nothing compared to the kind of supernatural beauty I'm sure fae are used to."

I choose to omit the fact I sometimes see and communicate with the dead. Where Landolin is concerned, it's probably best to proceed on a need-to-know basis.

"My father's instructions cannot be ignored," he says. "They follow the whims of his Shade Mages. Sometimes, their decrees seem odd, but there is always reason to be found in their madness. And as King Moiron's heir and the Master of the Hunt, it's my duty to see his wishes fulfilled, not to question them." He strokes from my earlobe to my collarbone. "In your case, the work of your mother, Sorcha Astellia, on the Celtic myths drew attention at court. That's probably how the mages initially found you and took an interest."

Great. Thanks Mom for getting me kidnapped. *Twice*.

"That still doesn't explain why you want me here at your court."

He gives a lazy shrug. "All will be revealed in time."

Whatever this is, I wish he'd just say it—rip the bandage off, plunge the knife in. The not-knowing is eating me alive. My heart's pounding so loud I swear he can hear it, but I keep my face blank. I have to. I can't fall apart. Not yet.

"Did I kill my parents?" I ask. "Did you somehow make me do it?"

CHAPTER 28

Summer

Landolin grips my chin and tugs my face back to the scene in the kitchen. "Take a look, human. And find out."

In the mirror, something clatters to the kitchen floor, and vision-me swears, stares down at the knife, then looks out through the open back door.

Over the hum of cicadas, an owl hoots in the distance. Then a horn blows—long and low—the tone bone-wrenching. Haunting.

I remember the first part of this night like it was yesterday, hot and sweaty, my hair had stuck to my neck, and the breeze blowing in from the woods was a cool relief on my skin. But that's about the last thing I recall, dropping the knife and staring at a slash of silver moonlight on the kitchen floor.

Then... nothing.

Absolutely zilch until about a year later when I turned up in the parking lot behind Zylah's work, scratched up and dehydrated.

My fingers twist into the bark-soft cloak Wyn made me, while in the vision, shadows peel off the yellow-and-black wall tiles, and my parents pad down the stairs and into the kitchen.

"Summer?" barks Dad. "Do you realize it's a fucking school night? What are you doing bashing and clanging and making pizza at this hour?"

"You know I have an early conference tomorrow morning," says Mom, filling a glass with water at the sink.

It's strange to see her alive. Pink cheeks and soft curls tumbled and glossy under the glow of the hanging light shade. The slight slump in her posture, the tiredness behind her eyes. She looks so ordinary. So human. So unlike the sour-faced ghost who haunts my bathroom day and night.

The girl in the mirror doesn't answer. Doesn't even glance at them.

Dad is wrapped in a brown silk robe, carrying a half-empty tumbler of the greatest love of his life—whatever brand of bourbon he could afford that week. His silver hair is coiffured to perfection, even though he has probably spent the last couple of hours lounging in bed, distracting Mom from her work.

Mom tugs at the cashmere wrap thrown over her indigo pajama set. "I finished translating an eleventh-century poem before bed, and what have you done, Summer? Spent the evening on your phone, contemplating stuffing your face? I hope you realize you take after your father's side of the family. So if you insist on eating cheese-loaded carbs at this time of night, before long, you won't fit through the front door. Summer? Stop pretending I'm not here and answer me."

Always ready to defend the woman who pays his bills, Dad puffs his chest out and shoves a hand on his hip at the exact moment three tall shadows swoop upon the knife I'd dropped. The blade swings in an upward arc, then slashes down and across his throat. Dad's eyes flare wide. A dining chair smashes to the ground as he stumbles backward, blood spurting between his fingers clutching his neck.

Someone screams and screams and screams.

Dad collapses near the back door, and Mom runs toward him. Shadow fingers spin the knife through the air again, this time slashing across her throat from behind. She turns and looks back at me, tries to speak, but only a bubbling gasp escapes, a sheet of crimson spilling down her chest.

The Shade Prince leans casually against the door frame of the stairwell, his face impassive as Mom's bloodied hands slide along the wall and a death rattle leaves my father's mouth. Dad goes limp, half-laying over his wife. Another choking gasp from Mom, and then they're both silent and unmoving.

Dead.

As though in a trance, the version of me in the mirror pads barefoot and silent to my parents' bodies and curls into a ball beside them, tucking my long T-shirt over my knees.

I stare at the bloody knife discarded on the floor about three feet away.

I don't scream. I don't cry. Don't move. Don't even glance at the shadow-wrapped fae standing in the corner of the kitchen and studying me with a fierce intensity.

A loud bang sounds, perhaps the front door being kicked open, then Sergeant Brantson barrels into the scene followed by his partner, a youngish female with braided brown hair who looks like she might throw up at the sight of all the blood.

Sirens scream in the distance, getting closer. Brantson helps me off the floor and says the ambulance will transport me to the hospital under police guard, and that I'll be questioned when I'm well enough. They freeze, and neither of them notice the shadows spiraling out the back door or Landolin stalking toward me, his closed-mouth grin poisonous.

But I see them all too clearly.

My eyes are on Landolin as he lifts his hand and scatters something over the doorstep, black soot or ash. Then he throws me over his shoulder and leaps across the threshold, disappearing in a cloud of smoky shadows.

The police snap out of their daze—or spell—the female officer running into the hallway toward the front door, and Brantson into the yard, searching for me.

Neither of them could possibly realize they've just witnessed a mystery that, despite their reams of case notes, photos, and surveillance footage, they'll never have the satisfaction of solving.

Behind me, the flesh-and-blood version of Landolin snaps his fingers. The blood-smeared kitchen and my parents' bodies are instantly swallowed by shadow magic, which coils across the surface of the mirror before dispersing, leaving me staring at my shaking reflection. The prince's arm is still banded around my waist.

With a strangled cry, I do the unthinkable... turn in Landolin's arms and blubber against the soft leather covering his chest. "I didn't fucking do it. I didn't kill them. All this time I've thought—"

"Yes, yes," he says, sweeping me off the floor and dumping me unceremoniously onto the sofa in the middle of the room. "Poor little human thought she'd gone insane and murdered her own dear parents. But, alas, you're not half as interesting as that. It was only the Wild Hunt collecting the dues of the Raven Realm."

My breath stutters. The room wavers. The world tilts, reality reshaped in a single breath. My parents—my cold-hearted, complicated parents—died at the hands of Landolin's monsters. It wasn't me. Not my madness. I've been torturing myself for years, hating myself... for nothing.

I wait for the relief to crash over me, but it creeps in slow, too tangled up in everything else. Pointless pity rises in my throat, burning like bile. They weren't good people. They didn't love me the way they should have, and yet they were all I had.

The Hunt killed them, and Landolin has known this all along.

My shame, my guilt—all of it, fed by his silence. He could've absolved me eight years ago, or like... wrote me a fucking letter or something.

I want to scream. I want to sob. I want to crawl out of my own skin. Instead, I sit there, shaking, rebuilding from the inside out.

I scrub a hand down my face, forcing a riot of emotions down deep. *Later*. I can fall apart later. Right now, I need answers.

"Tell me, what's the grand plan this time? Am I dancing like a mindless puppet again? By the way, my moves haven't improved much. Will I be thrown into your cells? Shoveling out the horse stalls? Something worse?"

"*Please*. Don't give me too many tempting ideas," he says. "Now that you've come of age, we can test you." He leans down and sniffs my hair. "Strange. You don't smell the same outside the human realm. At Gravenshade, your house was choked with the scent I expected."

"Expected? What does that mean? And while you're at it, tell me what sort of tests I'll have to take."

"Tests to confirm that you're who I believe you are."

"And if I am?"

"Then your fate is sealed—because you'll be of use to me.... and the Hunt."

"You knew where I lived. If I'm possibly so useful, why not retrieve me sooner?"

"The Merit Queen protected your whereabouts with a concealment spell. Old Druidic magic. Strong. We checked your home many times, but couldn't see, hear, or smell you. Merrin Fionbharr had forgotten about her brother's obsession with you. All I had to do was bide my time and wait for him to locate you in the Earth Realm. His presence near yours broke the spell."

Oh, *Wyn*. I hope Landolin never tells him that. Right now, he must be frantic with worry. Zylah, too. And what about Ollie and the other cats? How are they coping without me? Hopefully Zy's remembered to feed them—and open their favorite window—or I'll never hear the end of it when I get home.

If I'm lucky enough to ever return.

"And what happens if you've made a mistake and I'm not the person you need?"

White teeth flash in a nasty grin as shadows peel from the mirrors and twine around Landolin's boots like fawning cats.

"Don't forget to drink something," he instructs, ignoring my question as his dark head indicates a desk on one side of the window bearing a silver decanter and a goblet. "Food will be sent up shortly. Be sure to lick the plate clean. Your strength must be regained as soon as possible."

Yes, I'll be needing it to punch him square in the face and drop him to the ground in a puddle of leather-wrapped bullshit.

Landolin and his dark magic disappear behind the surface of the mirrored wall. Good riddance to the master of the Hunt. I hope he trips over his shadows and breaks his pompous, control-freak neck.

I check the door and find it locked. *Fuck.* What the hell am I meant to do with myself now?

Hurrying to the window, I peer through a veil of gray mist. There's nothing beyond it. No ground below, no distant mountains. Just black spires, slick with rain, jutting from dark brickwork turrets beside my room, grim and depressing.

What an ugly, miserable place.

I collapse in the desk chair, guzzle three glasses of water, and contemplate my options, of which there are few.

The mist outside is too thick to see through, the room's too high to jump from, and the castle's probably crawling with more guards than I've had intrusive thoughts today. And that's saying something.

So, *great.* I'm imprisoned in a gothic nightmare with not even a whisper of an escape plan. Love that for me.

I'm trying not to spiral, but to be honest, it's going poorly. My palms are clammy, my jaw aches from stress clenching, and my head feels like it might explode with worry.

Mostly about Wyn.

I don't know what to hope for. That he's safe at home with his perfect fae family? Or that he's on his way here, doing something reckless and heroic to get me out of this gloomy, grayscale prison?

But if my own parents could barely tolerate me, what are the odds a fae prince would risk everything to save me?

Slim to none.

So he's probably safe and cozy, wrapped up in bed—hopefully alone and not with a sexy fae beauty.

And there is one glaring bright side to this whole shitshow... apparently I'm not a murderer.

Yay!

Well, not yet, anyway.

CHAPTER 29

Summer

I t's day two at Landolin's court, and my mind is still a foggy mess of fear, anxiety, and exhaustion. I haven't slept properly or eaten much. It's hard to do either with a wall of mirrors opposite the bed that I'm pretty certain Landolin's watching me through, probably enjoying the show like it's some twisted version of reality TV—albeit a very boring one.

The Shade Prince still hasn't told me if I'm a prisoner or a guest. I've asked many times. Nicely. Then not-so-nicely. And his answer is always the same. Silence accompanied with a condescending smirk. Which, frankly, tells me everything I need to know about fae hospitality. Zero stars. Would not recommend. Might even set the place on fire.

Day and night, the city is shrouded in a murky dusk. I'm sure the sun must rise somewhere behind the purple and gray clouds that perpetually veil the sky, but I'm yet to see any evidence of its existence.

Outside my window, the castle's turrets twist up from the earth like blackened roots, as if the whole building was coaxed from the ground with magic rather than constructed with labor and tools.

It fits, I guess. Nothing feels right here. The walls, the shadows... they all seem like spies, taking notes on my every dull move. Probably reporting back to Landolin and his delightful father, who sounds like a beacon of warmth and goodwill. Said no one ever.

Even the air feels judgmental, like it disapproves of my very human existence.

I'm not cold or starving. Not shackled to a wall. Technically, I'm fine, but gods I miss Zylah's kooky snark and Wyn's... Wyn's *everything*.

Even his wolfy brooding. *Especially* the wolfy brooding.

And now that I've lost access to my anxiety meds, it's only a matter of time before the real fun begins. Brain zaps, emotional spirals, maybe a spontaneous sob-fest in front of Landolin's creepy mirror-surveillance system.

Can't wait.

But really, I should cheer up. So far, no one has hurt or even threatened me, and not only has Landolin delivered trays piled with food on a reliable schedule, he's also sent up books. Plenty of them.

Three yesterday afternoon, and I found five on my bedside table when I woke up this morning—unfortunately, all on the same gruesome subjects. Death and shadows. Burials and resurrections. Goddess-like females reanimating corpses. All illustrated in beautiful, but nauseating detail.

I've tried, but I can't concentrate on reading. I'm still reeling from the revelation of what happened to my parents.

I spent years punishing myself for something I didn't do, thinking that when my reckoning came, I would deserve worse than this. Starvation. Isolation. Maybe even death. But I was wrong about what I did. About who I am. Still, the guilt doesn't vanish just because the truth's out. It lingers. Probably always will.

When Landolin delivered this morning's breakfast, he asked what I thought of his gifts and whether I'd started reading them. I shrugged and begged again to know why I was here, when he planned to let me go, and if he knew where Wyn was.

"You'll find out soon enough," he said. "Wynter is surely on his way—to cause trouble and meet his death, of course, more fool him. But you'll be able to leave your room soon. Be patient."

Then he melted into the shadows of the mirrors. Rude, but also kind of impressive.

And now my stomach is growling with hunger, and I'm so bored I'd sell my soul for Wi-Fi and a bag of potato chips. Or at least a phone to pass the time mindlessly doomscrolling.

Maybe I wouldn't sell *my* soul. Landolin's would be better.

At lunchtime, just as I resolve to eat the entirety of whatever meal arrives, locks click, my door creaks open, and a servant enters my room carrying a tray balanced on thin arms. She's child-sized. Barefoot. Hair floating slightly as if caught in a gentle, persistent breeze. She looks like she belongs in a creepy, porcelain doll museum.

The creature hums—no words or obvious tune, just a soft, unsettling noise. She sets the tray down and produces a small, wilted silver flower, placing it neatly on the rim of the bowl of food, as if it's precious.

Then she turns to leave without so much as a glance.

"Wait," I call out. "What's your name?"

The girl stops, tilting her head so far sideways I worry it might snap off.

"Phaedra," she says, her voice a rough snarl.

"You're a servant here?" I ask.

"I'm a maid of the Hunt. One of their many pairs of eyes and ears that never miss a secret or a whisper. We don't make friends of human thralls."

"I'm not a thrall. Not anymore. I'm in my right mind."

At least I hope I am. How can I know for sure?

A thin grin stretches the fae's hollow-cheeked face. "Once a thrall, always a thrall, child."

Child? She's the one who has the face of a fourth grader and the general vibe of a Bond villain.

"Thanks for reminding me about my past trauma," I say. "Tell your master I insist on seeing something, *anything*, outside this room tomorrow."

"Who are you to make demands of the prince?"

"Someone who'll suffocate herself with a pillow if she doesn't get a change of scenery soon."

Phaedra chuckles, a low noise that grates down my spine.

As she shuffles toward the door, I address her stooped back, "Why do you call me a child when you look barely over the age of nine?"

Opaque eyes fix on me. "Nine hundred *years* would be closer to my age." She pauses and tilts her head again. "I was once a normal girl, like you," she says softly. "Before the Hunt. Before he made me into this."

"Landolin?" I ask, heartbeat skipping.

She shakes her head. "No, not him." And just like that, the soft note vanishes, and her expression shutters. "Eat your food. Try not to choke."

The snaggle-toothed grin reappears, then she exits through the door, leaving me staring at the silver flower on my plate as it crumbles to powder, sprinkling over half my stew like pretty, poisoned sugar.

The meal smells of mint and butter, so I guess it's technically food and, therefore, safe to eat. The side salad is glowing, the meat is oddly glossy, and the silver powder feels like a direct attempt on my life. Should I really be considering eating this?

My stomach groans.

Decision made.

Mouth watering, I scrape as much silver glitter off as I can and start eating. If I die in my sleep, at least I'll die slightly less hangry.

CHAPTER 30

Summer

The next morning when Landolin finally lets me out of my room, I get my first look at the City of Shades—Dorthadas, as he calls it. And it's nothing like the Emerald Court Wyn described while we hiked up Mount Cúig, with its glowing black-and-green stone and bursts of bright, playful magic.

This place is stripped bare. Grim, gray, and gloomy. Still beautiful, sure, but the kind of beauty you find in ruins or on dark, stormy days spent alone with a sad book in front of a roaring fire.

Honestly, I kind of like it, which isn't surprising for a girl who lives with ghosts and calls a haunted house her home.

Many of the castle's inner walls are made of trees grown so close together they've fused into dark, living barriers—surviving on magic instead of fresh air or light. My footsteps echo through the corridor as I trail my hand along one, and it shudders beneath my touch.

"*Whoa.*" I jerk back. "Do you always do that or am I just special?" I say to no one, because I'm lonely and bored and apparently talk to walls now.

"That depends," rumbles a voice near my ear.

I spin, and there he is, looming directly over my right shoulder. Landolin. Dressed in black velvet and leather, hands calmly clasped behind his back, eyes giving nothing away.

"I thought you were walking quite a distance behind me."

"I was, but I enjoy creeping up on humans," he says without a trace of a smile.

Makes sense. Leader of the Wild Hunt and all that.

"The castle walls are old," he continues. "And like most living entities, they enjoy being touched."

"Ew. I feel like I've been violated."

"Technically, you were violating *them.*"

A chill creeps down my neck. I hate it when the villain has a point.

I've never seen a tree, let alone a wall, react that way. Not even in Lake Grenlynn, and the Bywater's a notoriously spooky place. I still can't believe I'm in Faery, surrounded by myth and magic—and that's saying something, coming from a girl whose second-best friend is the sad ghost of a Victorian-era kitchen maid.

Which reminds me... I still haven't seen any ghosts in my room or the castle's corridors, and that seems off. The Shade castle must be thousands of years old. You'd think at least one tortured soul would be loitering around, howling pitifully. Maybe they're all on strike. Or maybe they took one look at me and bailed.

"Do you have ghosts here? Spirits of the dead?" I ask.

Landolin stops short, his black eyes locking on mine with unsettling focus. A flicker of something like interest crosses his expression, but he doesn't answer. Then without a word, he pivots and strides off down the hallway, coat tails flapping.

I hesitate, but my room is the last place I want to be right now, so I jog to fall in beside him. We climb a never-ending spiral staircase, passing servants with cold eyes and faces that almost look human, more so than Phaedra, at least.

Finally, we come to a landing, and the Shade Prince uses both hands to tug a pair of wall sconces—both flickering greenish-blue instead of warm gold. A wooden door shimmers into view, then slides open to reveal a broad terrace overlooking the town.

I step from the tower into the open air and march to the stone railing as the full impact of the view hits me. The city unfurls below, bathed in a grim daylight no brighter than a cloudy dawn.

Buildings carved from dark stone rise along winding streets that sprawl toward shadow-soaked hills and a forest so dense and still it looks painted onto the horizon. The light is weak, the air smoky, and the city extends so far I can't tell where the land ends and the dull sky begins. Much like the castle, it's lovely, if you like your beauty eerie and unsettling.

The city hums with activity. Not the familiar sound of cars and trains, but faint, hollow chimes and the rattle of cartwheels rumbling over hard stone. The occasional noise that could be an owl, or something more sinister, hoots in the distance.

From the direction of the woods, hoofbeats echo, slow and rhythmic, like multiple hearts beating together. It's not loud, exactly, but it's constant, a low background drone that makes my skin crawl and my brain whisper, *no thank you. Stay away.*

"By ghosts, I assume you mean wraiths. Lost spirits," Landolin says beside me, jolting me from my morbid thoughts.

Well that came out of nowhere. Did he really wait fifteen minutes to dignify my question with an answer?

"Yeah. Dead people's energy," I say. "What's left of souls too traumatized or stubborn to let go of their lives after death. Do you have them here?"

"A few. We'd like more. We're interested in... how shall I put it? Reanimation, if you like."

"Of the dead?"

Brushing a lock of hair from his eyes, he nods. "Have you dabbled?" He watches me closely and crosses his arms.

I think of Zylah and her menagerie of stuffed roadkill in our basement. My polite but persistent distaste for them. "In necromancy? No. Never."

Something like disappointment flashes over his features. "Shame," he says, his shadows curling around his wrist resting on the balustrade. His mouth hardens. "You may find you soon develop an interest."

Another shiver raises the hairs on the back of my neck, and a disturbingly low horn blows from across the valley.

"Is that the Wild Hunt out there?" I ask, pointing at the hills. "I thought they only rode at night."

"Essentially, it's always night here. And it will remain that way until..." He clamps his jaw and turns his face to the side, obviously kicking himself for nearly revealing some deep, dark Shade Court secret.

"I'd like to see more of the castle, if you'll allow it. I don't remember anything from my time here, but maybe if I wander around, something will click."

"A useless quarry. You won't remember it. The thrall spell was cast deep, but it would've waned a little during your time with the Merit's and then Wynter's court. You may have some memories of Talamh Cúig. Not that you'll have the opportunity to visit that dreary place again. It's beautiful, I suppose. All that glowing stone and clean air. No wonder Wyn's so soft." Then he winces, his hands tightening into fists.

I wonder what he was picturing to get that lie out? Wyn's lips? His earlobes? They're about the only squishy things on his body.

My stomach sinks. If that's not confirmation that Landolin's planning to keep me here forever, I don't know what is. In other words, I live here now. Lucky me.

"Landolin, why am I here? I'm just an average human. What's the point?"

"I told you—we need you. Didn't you ever read your mother's stories? For centuries, humans have played vital roles in the fae realms. My father never should have sold you to the Merits. I'll explain everything in time. But know this, for now, you're safe."

"Oh, great. That's comforting. Why did your father let me go if I'm so necessary?"

"You were on loan. Wynter's sister should never have interfered and returned you to the Earth Realm. But it doesn't matter now. Wherever you moved, the Hunt would've found you eventually once the Merit Queen's concealment spell was broken. This time, as a bonus, you've come of age."

"I'm twenty-five. You're a few years late."

He chuckles. "Better late than never. Come, I'll show you more of the castle."

Landolin leads me through a parade of unsettling wonders. A hall of statues that move their poses when I touch them, a courtyard of rambling black-petaled vines, glistening with a silver sheen under the sunless sky, a library where the books float about the room at random, whizzing past my face as if taunting me to pluck one from the air.

The halls are dim and close, lit by floating silver orbs that flicker as if they can barely be bothered and might sputter out at any moment. The polished stone floor slopes at odd angles and bone-white arches rise overhead like rows of glistening ribs, the air carrying smoke and the sweet tang of incense.

We pass rooms where rich drapes hang heavy over tall windows, and in one, hooded servants set a long dining table with polished black cutlery, moving with an eerie, deliberate grace. In another, a pair of wild-haired fae play a game with glowing pieces that hover slightly above the surface of the board.

When we reach a grand door decorated with bones and tiny skulls, Landolin won't let me peek behind it, muttering the words, "Shadow casters. Can't be disturbed."

The castle is grand in a dark, grotesque way. Many hallways seem to lead nowhere. Windows look out onto layers of fog, and flickering bursts of light reveal seven pale, pastel moons strung across the sky in a rainbow arc.

More than once I see movement behind half-closed doors, creatures that peer out before scurrying away, as if they're afraid their prince will scold them.

The courtiers we pass stare with hostile curiosity. Some smile aggressively. Some only scowl. One offers me a handful of glossy white berries, and Landolin shouts something in a guttural language, then squashes them under his boot. Poisonous, no doubt.

One woman has a face like cracked porcelain, her lips inked black and tiny sparks swirling in her eyes, like stars. A tall figure draped in a strange combination of layers of moss and fishing netting stands in a doorway, unmoving, antlers scraping against the arch above his head. I wonder if he's wearing a type of headdress or if the antlers are part of the faery's body.

Other fae vanish the moment I glance their way, slipping into shadows, seemingly dissolving between cracks in the floor like some of the unfriendly ghosts I see haunting Lake Grenlynn.

Landolin walks through the mayhem as if all of this is perfectly normal. I keep my chin up, counting silently in my head, and pretend I feel the same. The Shade Court fae would probably love it if I flinched or ran away. But I won't give them the satisfaction. Not now. Not ever.

We arrive in another courtyard, lower down in the castle, nestled between turrets and open to the sky. The space is empty, and our steps echo loudly in the rectangular space. The pool in the center reflects a sea of stars that can't possibly be real because it's still gloomy daytime and a layer of clouds covers the sky.

Landolin stops at the tiled edge, waiting for me to catch up.

That's when I notice it—just a flicker, like the glimpse of an afterimage, a shadow where it shouldn't be. Black tendrils of magic coil at the base of his neck, curling beneath the edge of his collar. And for a moment, it looks like they're burrowing into his skin, eating him alive.

"Do you ever raise the dead in your dreams?" he asks casually, as if picking up the thread of an earlier conversation. He directs me to sit beside the pool.

"What were those shadows doing?" I ask, nodding at his neck. "Looked like they were... eating into your skin."

He brushes his collar with the back of one hand, a flicker of fear flashing in his eyes before he shuts it down. "Just a trick of the light," he says.

"But—"

"Forget it. You were going to tell me about your dreams."

I tilt my head. "Dreams? I never remember them."

His lips twitch, almost forming a smile as he joins me on the ground, hugging his knees to his chest like a young boy. "Don't believe you."

I shrug. "Even if I did have such dreams, why would I tell the man who killed my mother and father about them?"

"I thought you didn't like your parents very much."

"That's beside the point. Why *did* you kill them?"

His shoulders drop as he releases a heavy sigh. "What happened that night wasn't my decision. I had no choice."

"We always have choices, Landolin. It comes down to bravery and what we're prepared to sacrifice to make the decisions that benefit others instead of ourselves."

His eyes track the ripples in the pool. "Put it this way... I wasn't about to choose a long and painful death just to save those two reigning champions of emotional neglect."

Begrudgingly, I have to agree with his reasoning. "*Who* made you kill them?" I ask.

"Best you don't know the details. Now be honest. You must recall *some* of your dreams."

"Sure, maybe the thrilling ones. Such as grocery shopping with no money in my bank. Group assignments for school. I study counseling, so one time I was even arguing with a couch about emotional boundaries. Wild, I know."

"School? Group assignments?" Landolin's eyes narrow, like he's picturing a circle of humans carving each other up with serrated blades.

"Relax," I add. "No weapons are involved. Just deadlines, blame, and mutual loathing."

Landolin doesn't crack a grin at my sarcasm. He stays still, like he's waiting for my words to make sense. Going by the look on his face, he'll be there quite a while.

Just when I think he might ask another question, a voice slices through the gloom behind him.

"We've got a problem."

Landolin looks over his shoulder, unfazed, as a figure steps from the shadows.

The stranger is lean, sharp-eyed, dressed in dark riding leathers still dusted with dirt and ash. His gaze skims over me, assessing, unimpressed.

"Irren," Landolin says. "What's happened?"

"There's news from the Carrion," Irren replies. "Two riders returned. One of them's flying a banner that doesn't belong to them."

"*Whose* banner?" the prince asks, getting to his feet.

"Yurendyl's."

Landolin's face doesn't change as he curses under his breath, but he lets a deep silence stretch for a few beats too long.

"Who else knows about this?"

"The riders. You. Me." Irren's tone is calm, but his eyes tell a different story as they shift my way. "And... her... the human."

"I know what she is, Irren. No need to point it out." Landolin gestures for me to stand. "You'll return to your room and stay there until I come for you."

Power radiates from him as he waves a palm in front of my face, shadows coiling up his arms before they wrap around me. My vision tunnels and everything goes black.

When I wake, I'm sprawled across the sofa in my room, feeling the oppressive presence of the wall of mirrors and a heavy cloak of loneliness settling over me.

At dinnertime, Phaedra delivers a fish-head stew without a word, and this time I don't bother asking any questions. I eat around the fishes' blank stares, my tears mixing with the rich, oily broth.

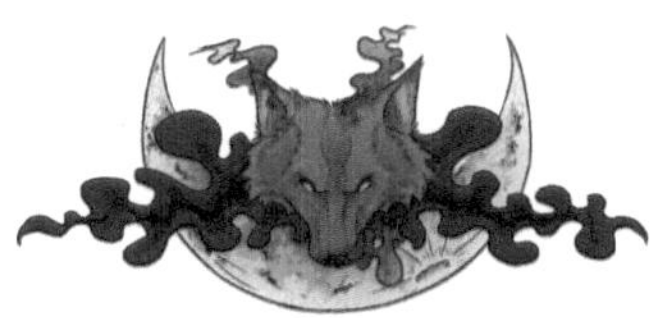

Later that night, I hear the Hunt galloping through the halls, the rhythmic echoes of their hoofbeats growing closer and closer. The clatter of bone against stone dragging me from a restless sleep and out of my bed.

As I press an ear to my chamber door, barely breathing as they approach, the hairs on my neck and arms stand on end. The smell of scorched earth and wet ash floods under the door, and my heart thunders against my ribcage.

By some miracle, the door's unlocked, and I carefully crack it open a sliver.

Twenty or more horses canter down the corridor, their ghost-white bones protruding from tattered hides. They look so different from when they appeared at Gravenshade with their black coats shining. Now, they seem like something straight out of a horror film, and their numbers have at least doubled.

Dressed in leather, some of the riders wear masks. Other's faces are painted with black and silver stripes. Not one of them speaks. The horses don't snort or even seem to breathe. They're ghostly, supernatural creatures.

Leading the charge is Landolin, a crown of moss-covered antlers on his head. He doesn't look at me. But somehow, I know he sees me—feels me watching as shadows rise around the Hunt and they ride straight through a solid wall at the end of the corridor, like phantoms torn from the worst kind of fairy tale.

I push the door shut and sink back against it, my heart hammering as hoofbeats echo into silence.

Okay.

New rule... don't open doors in the middle of the night.

Ever again.

CHAPTER 31

Wynter

The first thing I'm aware of is suffocating warmth. The second is the low hum of magic clinging to my skin, hot and itchy. I grunt and fling my arm out, hitting Ivor curled up beside me, snoring like a wild boar.

"Fuck, no." I sit bolt upright, holding my throbbing head. "*No.*"

The room is familiar. *Too* familiar. I'm surrounded by dark blue walls decorated with threads of shining copper that ray out from central discs, like beams in the Merit Sun Throne. Heavy velvet curtains are only part-drawn to let in a slice of bright morning light. This is the room I always sleep in when I visit Merri, which means...

I'm in the Merit Palace.

And I was supposed to be in the fucking Shade Court.

I throw off the covers and swing my legs over the side of the bed, reaching for the goblet on the nightstand.

The door opens.

Merri, my betrayer, enters.

Ivor jumps off the bed and trots toward her, hankering for pats—the traitorous lapdog.

"Don't start," she says, holding up a hand. The same hand that used to tug me out of trouble when we were young. "Please take a moment and listen before you bury me in the rubble of my own home."

Crossing my arms, I take a slow, deep breath through my nose. "What did you do?"

She has the decency to look vaguely guilty. This morning, her crown and finery are gone, and her red waves are half-fallen from their braids. She looks disheveled. Worried. Just as she fucking-well should.

"Wyn, you needed rest," she says calmly. "You looked like you hadn't slept in days, and I wasn't about to send you into the Shade Court like that. They'd eat you alive."

I return her fierce scowl. "How *long*?" I ask, raking my hands through my hair.

"Three nights."

I freeze, knuckle-deep in knots. "You put a sleep spell on me—your own brother—for three whole nights?"

She nods, silver eyes resting serenely on mine. "I couldn't wake you. The spell keeps you asleep for as long as necessary. You clearly needed the rest."

"Unbelievable."

"I'm your older sister. And you've long been impulsive and unpredictable. It's not in my job description to let my foolish brother fling himself into the Raven Realm without at least a decent nap and a change of proper clothes. You arrived wearing only a glamour after shifting, didn't you?"

"Who cares what I was wearing? Summer could be—"

"Alive. And waiting. If Landolin wanted her dead, he would have killed her eight years ago."

My jaw clenches so hard my teeth ache.

There's so much I want to say, all of it a tangled mess of guilt and fear. I'm so afraid I've already failed Summer and that she's dead. Or maybe worse... She might be being tortured as I sit here in comfort and luxury—suffering terribly. Or dancing like a puppet again until her feet bleed and she collapses on hard stone, breaking bones and spirit.

"How was she?" Merri asks, blinking back tears. "Before Landolin got to her."

"She's missing a year of memories. Thinks she killed her own parents. Take a wild fucking guess how she's doing."

"Likely traumatized."

"Yeah. She's a beautiful mess."

"The poor girl. When you see her, give her a hug from me."

"I will." I pause, then arch a brow. "Well then... do I have your permission to leave now, Your Majesty?" I ask.

Merri gestures to the side table. A fresh tunic, clean leathers, and a cloak folded neatly beside a satchel packed with supplies.

"If you've finished your tantrum, Wynter, get dressed. I'll take you to Chancellor Mareous who will help us open the portal."

Mareous—the sea witch whose wise counsel and formidable magic have been a pillar of Merit power for centuries—has always had it in for me.

"Must you?" I ask, ungratefully. "I don't think she likes me. Why isn't Riven helping us?"

"Meerade's hatchlings are learning to fly. He's supporting her. And Mareous has always liked you *too* much, if you know what I mean."

What? Does that explain her narrowed-eyed glares across the dining hall over the years? I thought she was picturing gutting me with her claws, not imagining her thighs wrapped around my waist.

After I've tugged on clothes, Merri enfolds me in a warm embrace. "Ready?"

Not really. Merit transfers hurt like seven hells, but I nod anyway and say, "Just promise you'll put me back together in the right order. You've only been doing this whole transmuting thing for seven years."

Merri's laugh tickles my neck. "I'll do my best. At least your wolf trusts me. Come on, Ivor, join us."

Ivor barks as he squeezes between us, then a wave of nausea hits me, violent and sudden, and my body dissolves in the magic.

We land on the beach, and the scent of an incoming storm wraps around me, fresh and briny, smelling a lot like Merri and her air magic. I take a moment to steady myself, let the nausea settle, then scan the rugged coastline.

Across the bay, black-and-white towers rise from the ocean, piercing the sky like twin spears. A single footbridge spans the water between them, narrow and impossibly long, connecting the sea to land with a ribbon of dark metal.

When Merri followed the Merit King to this city—after nursing him back to health when she found him wounded in our land—he wasn't exactly pleased to see her. Still, he settled her into the White Tower, the same place the old king (his asshole father) had bound Riven's mother's soul to the chambers. A test to see whether my sister would be approved by the queen who came before her. Of course, good-natured Merri passed with dignity and grace.

Rows of waves crash in slow arcs, rolling onto the black sand as they've been doing since time began. A circle of merfolk wait in the shallows, their wet hair glittering with tiny white shells, eyes opaque and distant.

Merri stands beside me, her face turned to the horizon as Ivor leans against my side. She takes my hand and squeezes hard. Then, the song begins.

It rises from the sea like the tide itself. Low and lilting, then sharp and sweet, notes coiling through the air like ribbons of magic.

Then Counselor Mareous glides in over the water. A fearsome goddess of the ocean. But not one I'd ever dare pray to.

Her hair is kelp green and silver, threaded with pearls that glow brightly in the sunlight. Long strands writhe around her as if her hair has a mind of its own, entwining like sea serpents down her back. Her skin is silvered, kissed with scales, and her eyes are the color of a stormy ocean.

She steps onto the shore barefoot, a train of water trailing behind her like a skein of translucent silk.

Merri moves forward, and I follow, my breath hitching hard in my throat. Mareous bows her head, and the merfolk do the same.

"Queen Merrin, everything has been arranged as requested," she says, her voice resonating with the rhythm of the sea. Steady, deep, and impossible to ignore. "The gate awaits."

Then her gaze settles on my face, trails to my boots, then back up again. "Prince Wynter, it has been too long."

"Several moon turns at least," I reply as I bow in greeting.

"You and Ivor do not drift this way often enough," she says with a slow smile. "Your presence always brings me great pleasure. If I could, I would see you more frequently, Prince of the Fertile Earth."

At least Mareous doesn't call me Prince of the Barren Earth, like the air mage who cursed me does. But judging by the way she's grinning at me now, I might feel more comfortable if she did.

The merfolk wade from the water and begin to chant, voices rising and falling like the swell of the ocean. Silver light winds around them, linking their arms, their hearts, their power as they form a large circle.

Mareous lifts her hands. "Merri, Wynter, Ivor, take your places in the center."

We do as she bids, and Mareous stands across from us, her fingers weaving invisible threads of magic through the air. Wild, ancient power builds in the boundary of the circle.

We join hands, Ivor standing between us, and my sister's air magic weaves around our bodies, bright and volatile, tugging at our cloaks and hair, eager to carry the spell forward. My earth magic has no place in this ritual, even so, the base of my spine thrums, pressure building like stone shifting beneath the ground, aching to burst free.

Mareous throws her head back, her jaw slack. Frothing water pours from her mouth and the outstretched cups of her hands, churning around our feet and rising to lap around our calves.

Silver light explodes in the sky above, wind and magic colliding in a deafening fury.

Merri whispers something, but I can't make out the words. She blows me a kiss, and then I'm thrown into the air. I must black out because it only seems like seconds pass before I land on hard ground, sand crunching beneath me.

Fuck, this feels wrong.

I look up. The sky is the color of brushed iron. The sun's nowhere to be seen. Just gray sand stretching in every direction, broken by jagged outcrops of stone and the twisted skeletons of fire-ravaged trees.

Not the Shade Court. Not one obsidian glass wall of the City of Dorthadas in sight.

"Of course," I mutter. "Of course we fucking missed the mark."

Ivor whines beside me, and I wrap my arms around his neck as he licks my face.

I pull myself up, brush sand off my tunic, and focus. The sand is dry and coarse, clinging to my fingers as I gather a handful, feeling for the pulse of the land in each grain. It's faint, buried deep, but the magic is definitely there. Northward, where a golden light shimmers. That's it—that's where Summer is.

With a long breath, I let go of my fae form.

The shift is quick. Skin to fur, thoughts to instinct. Pain, heat, then a full-bodied feeling of rightness.

I drop to all fours. Ivor pads up slow, chest heaving, eyes bright. We meet nose to nose as always. He huffs once, tail brushing mine as he moves beside me, then nudges behind my ear. Yeah. We should get moving.

I send him an image of the gate at the rear of Dorthadas—only used by traders and merchants—that I remember from visiting the city in my seventeenth year.

Then we run.

The gray-sand desert gives way to ghostly forests with pale trees twisted like stooped court elders, branches rattling in the warm wind. The ground is parched and cracked, scattered with bones and gnarled roots clawing through the dirt.

I wish I had thought to test the strength of my power in the Raven Realm before I shifted. While in wolf form, I can't summon so much as a single spray of dirt. But thank Dana, my senses are as sharp as ever, tuned to every shift in wind and approaching magic. It's not spell work, but it's enough to keep me alive out here and help me find Summer.

The air shifts.

Magic pulses ahead. Distant, but familiar. Shadow magic.

I nudge Ivor, and we run harder.

By my best estimate, we'll need to travel overnight to reach the Shade Court.

To get to Summer.

My mate is still alive. Thank fuck. I can feel her in my blood, in my bones, every strike of my paws upon the earth driving me closer. And this time, nothing and no one will stop me from keeping her safe.

Hold on, little sun.

I'm coming for you.

CHAPTER 32

Summer

On the morning of my fourth day in Dorthadas, I find my chamber door still unlocked, like it was last night. No explanation, no summons from Landolin. Just the absence of resistance—like the castle has finally decided to let me roam.

Which, of course, I plan to take full advantage of.

I wonder if I could escape. Run through the hallways, get down to ground level, find a door out of the castle. Out of the city.

And then what? Where would I go? I was unconscious when they brought me here. And I have absolutely no idea how to find my way back to Wyn's realm, or to Lake Grenlynn.

For now, I'm stuck here.

After dragging myself up and down a maze of staircases that practically hum with magical side-eye—as if they resent being walked on by a human—I finally retrace the path to the courtyard with the pool of stars.

I let out a slow breath as I step over the stone threshold, relieved to be in a space that might offer a sliver of peace... or a door to the outside—only to realize I'm not alone.

A female fae leans against a crooked pillar, casually tossing what looks like a small bone from hand to hand, reminding me of Zylah in her basement of creepy creatures... if Zylah had decided empathy was overrated and terror was more on brand for her.

The fae's eyes flick to mine, a sly smile on her pale-blue lips.

"Well, if it isn't our little human miracle," she purrs, unfolding her leathery black wings with slow, deliberate menace.

"Sorry, wrong room," I say, pivoting on my heel.

Best if I head back to my mirrored-surveillance suite. Sure, it's not private, but at least it's safe... *ish*. And the last thing I need—five days off my anxiety meds and one spiraling thought away from a full-blown panic attack—is a cryptic chat with a malevolent bat lady.

"Stay a while," she says. "We're all curious about you." She flicks the bone toward me. It arcs and lands at my feet with a soft clatter.

"Who's we? I don't see anyone else here."

"The Shadow Court, of course."

I squint at the bone. It looks like a bird's vertebra, I decide, stepping around it and keeping my tone flat. "I'm flattered to be thought of as *miraculous*. But I'm really not that interesting."

The bone vibrates, spinning on its own before flying through the air to rest on the fae's open palm. She tilts her head. "Landolin says you're the one. But I'm not so easily convinced."

My throat tightens, but I roll my eyes like I'm unbothered. "I'm not convinced either, so we have that in common."

"You've finally decided to stretch your legs," she says, her voice a dry rustle.

"Someone decided to leave my door unlocked."

"The castle doors unlock when you're ready to walk through them." She fishes another bone from her pocket and tosses it into the air. It flips once, twice, then lands neatly on her palm. "Speaking of walking, you move like someone unfamiliar with the shape of her own shadow."

"The shape of my shadow?" I say. "It changes depending on where the sun is. On the angles."

She smiles, all teeth and no warmth. "Strange. Landolin usually picks sharper assets for the Hunt."

"Assets?" I echo. "I wasn't aware I was a tool to be used by your prince and his merry little death cult on horseback."

Another lazy toss of the bone. "Oh, but that's exactly what you are. Although, not everyone agrees on how useful you'll turn out to be."

I fold my arms. "If you're trying to rattle me, you'll have to do better than talk in riddles."

The fae tilts her head. Hair as dark as oil and shimmering with a wet glitter slides over her shoulder. "You should ask Landolin what he gave up to bring you here. Or better... what he thinks you'll give him in return."

That lands like a stone in my gut. I try not to flinch, but I shift my stance slightly, and she catches it.

"You don't know what Landolin is, do you?" she murmurs, stepping away from the pillar. "That's delicious."

I lift my chin. "I don't really care. I just know I'm not the one he needs. I want to go home and let you fae get back to scheming and gossiping about someone else."

"Oh, sweet thing." Her eyes gleam with malice. "They're not done with you. Not even close. The Hunt doesn't ride for nothing, and it never makes mistakes."

I'm pretty sure she's wrong about that. Everyone makes mistakes, even the fae. Though I get the feeling they'd rather gnaw off their own tongues than admit it.

"What do they call you?" I ask, making a half-hearted attempt at diplomacy. Know thy enemy is my philosophy. Or at least know whose name to scream out when they stab you in the back.

She stops a few feet away, just outside striking distance, and I catch myself wishing for one of Wyn's swords. Not that I could do much more than swing it like a toddler with an overlarge glow stick.

"That's something I don't give out freely," says the fae. "What would you barter to know it?"

"Nothing. I'll make up my own name for you instead. Something dignified, like Crankthorn. Or Miss Grim and Vaguely Glowy."

She laughs, then her voice softens to an almost friendly tone. "I remember you from another lifetime ago. Always spinning like a fool. You were younger and in thrall to our Shade King, Moiron. They only let you out of your room for revels. Or to show you off to visitors from other courts. Such a sad, pitiful sight."

My mouth goes dry. The stone floor of the courtyard tilts just a little, her words digging into the aching hollow behind my ribs. Numbers whirl through my brain, but I can't seem to catch hold of one to start counting. My boots stay rooted, but my fingers twitch, desperate to reach for something solid.

"I don't remember any of that," I say flatly. "Just shadows and smoke. Constant noise. Screams that might have been mine."

She smirks. "Of course you don't. Memory is a privilege, not a right."

Whatever that means.

I take a step closer. "What happened to me back then? Tell me the worst of it. I need to know, or I'll never be at peace."

The smirk fades, replaced by something colder. She tosses the bone again and catches it, her eyes never leaving mine.

"You think you want the truth. But what you want is comfort. And they're rarely ever the same thing."

"Try me," I snap. "You seem the type to enjoy dragging pain out by the syllable."

Her smile returns, wider this time. "Very well. You danced when they told you to. Smiled when they made you. You were the court's little mirror—pretty, empty, and displaying only what the king wished to see. He kept you on a thread, you know, not a chain. A chain suggests resistance. You were more than happy to obey."

I swallow hard. "Why me?"

Black wings unfurl with a predatory grace. "They were waiting for you to grow up and become the one they needed. Maybe the king hoped you'd break into a million pieces in the meantime."

I suck in a slow breath, determined to ask the questions that have always plagued me. "Was I tortured? Raped?"

She leans in, her breath cool against my cheek. "No. You were to be Landolin's tool one day, remember? He did his best to keep you whole and hale. Protect you from his father. Ask the prince what he thinks you can give him."

Irren appears out of the shadows, his slate-colored eyes grim, chestnut hair tied back from his face with a string of leather. "Landolin needs to speak with you."

The female fae steps forward.

"Not you, Misery. The human."

I flash her a smug little smile. "Got your name for free, and to be honest, it couldn't possibly suit you better."

With a sigh, she pockets the bone and turns away, vanishing between two columns like Marie, Gravenshade's ghostly maid, used to do whenever I so much as glanced at the vacuum cleaner.

"Let's go," says Irren, his gravelly voice grating on my nerves.

He turns before I can ask where we're heading and strides off at a pace that demands I keep up or get left behind. His dark leathers creak with each step, the blade at his hip catching what little light filters through the stone latticework above us.

I fall in beside him, moving as fast as I can without breaking into a jog. After a few tense moments, I break the silence. "You always this friendly, or like most Shade Court fae, have you got a problem with humans, too?"

Other than the echo of our footsteps, no answer comes.

We pass under archways strung with creeping ivy, small white flowers dotting the black vines, and through narrow hallways where the walls absorb the light—matte black and textured like dried ash.

Today, the fae we pass barely glance at me, their eyes averted as they slip by without a sound. It seems someone's told them to steer clear. Fine by me. I have social anxiety anyway.

CHAPTER 33

Summer

"Are you going to tell me where we're headed?" I ask.

"Depends. Would you like to know?"

I sigh. "Of course I would."

"To the throne room," Irren replies, not slowing his pace. "Where Landolin is waiting."

"Wonderful," I mutter. "Maybe today he'll actually form a sentence that makes sense to me."

Still no reaction.

I glance at the curved blade hanging from his belt—nothing like any weapon I'd recognize from the human world. Its black edge is jagged, as if chipped from obsidian, and the hilt is wrapped in something that looks suspiciously like hair. Hopefully not human.

"That's a strange knife you're wearing," I say.

A muscle ticks in his jaw. "It's a hornblade."

"Nice. And does every member of the Hunt wear one, or just the charming ones?"

"Only the second in command."

"I see. What does it do best... call the riders forth or slice up your enemies?"

His mouth twitches, but it's more of a grimace than a smile. "Both equally," he says.

"How practical."

I swear I hear the mildest snort as he pats his weapon-slash-musical instrument with pride.

We climb a narrow set of stairs carved from stone that's so polished it looks wet. The air cools the higher we go, thickening with that smoky tang I'm learning to associate with the Shade Court's magic.

As we round a corner, I catch glimpses of rooms behind open archways. One is filled with books stacked in spirals, another with mirrors suspended in midair, all reflecting different scenes instead of the room itself—fields of bright flowers, ponds draped with willow branches, and bright-green, sunlit mountains that couldn't possibly exist in this gloomy realm.

Finally, we reach the entrance to the throne room.

Two monolithic slabs of obsidian doors rise before us, their shiny surfaces rippling with magic. Small, wraith-like faces shift across the stone—ghostly illusions trapped in mid-scream, mouths frozen wide as they drift in and out of view.

Guards stand motionless on either side of the doors, draped in hooded ash-gray cloaks that obscure their faces. They clutch long spears decorated with glossy, black feathers.

Irren doesn't slow, just nods at them once, and the doors open, not with a creak or a groan, but with the sound of hundreds of ghostly whispers pouring from the trapped faces billowing across the stone. And I thought Gravenshade Hall was creepy.

I steel myself and step inside.

The ceiling stretches so high it disappears into a gloomy mist above. Black stone columns rise like trees in a fire-scarred forest, marbled with veins of silver. The throne itself sits on a raised obsidian dais, flanked by wide, golden steps.

Behind it, a wall of glass reveals the realm's seven pastel moons, their light diffused through mist, painting the floor in strange, unnatural hues.

Irren stops just inside the massive open doors and jerks his chin toward the dais. "He's waiting."

I brush past him, heart hammering much harder than I'd like to admit. "Thanks for the warm escort. You really know how to set a girl at ease." *Not.*

Shaking his head, he grunts and stalks off—probably making haste to the castle's darkest corner, or wherever members of the Hunt go to brood about life.

Landolin sits on a throne carved from polished dark stone, its high, flaring sides rising around the base like jagged wings. The seat is wide but shallow, the back straight and unforgiving. No cushions. No ornamentation beyond the natural striations in the rock. It was made to be imposing, not comfortable.

The Shade Prince rises from the throne without a word and moves down the golden steps with unsettling grace.

He's dressed in black from shoulder to heel, but he wears no princely crown. His clothes are functional, layered leathers and dark cloth stitched with metallic thread that catches the light. A long coat drapes from his shoulders, the hem embroidered with silver patterns that look like shadows curling upward to embrace him.

Trying not to fidget, I stand in the middle of the hall and watch him approach. His dark hair is tied back today, loose and low. The closer he gets, I notice his ebony, gold-flecked eyes are calm and steady, not cruel and mocking like I thought they'd be.

He stops a few feet away from me, offering no smile. No greeting. Just waiting for me to speak first.

Fine. I'll take the bait.

"If this is the part where you kill me, Landolin, could we at least skip the smug monologue you're clearly rehearsing and get it over with?"

"I don't want to kill you, Summer."

That's a relief, especially since he can't lie. But I don't let myself relax too much. *Wanting* and *needing* to commit murder are two very different things.

"Then why did you have your henchman drag me here? For a chai latte and a chat?"

"Haven't you been begging to know why you're in my court?"

"You know I have."

"There'll be a midnight trial tonight," he says. "We need to ascertain if you can help the Hunt."

"Me? Partake in a trial? I thought you said it would be a test, like an exam or an interview. I can tell you right now you've got the wrong girl and save you the time and effort," I say. "I'm a big fan of girl power and battles in books and movies, but in person, I'm more into the curl-up-and-die strategy. So there's no point giving me a sword and throwing me in an arena."

"I disagree. The Hunt must know what power, if any, lies dormant inside you. It's time to call your gift to the surface."

"My gift?" I keep my voice low and flat. "Unless sarcasm counts, I'm tragically lacking in talent."

"That remains to be seen," Landolin says. "And it won't be a traditional battle with weapons and the like. You must know what gift I'm referring to."

Nope, I don't. Unless he's talking about my ability to see ghosts. But that's a curse, not a gift.

I think of Zylah, our inside jokes and late-night confessions, my cats, and of Wyn, promising to never let anyone come between us. Promising that we were forever.

I may never see any of them again.

Landolin stands still as stone, waiting for me to speak again—a classic cold-blooded manipulator move.

Once more, I play along.

"Is this trial something you personally need to happen?" I ask. "Or is it for the king?"

Wyn told me lots about Moiron Ravenseeker. Apparently, he's cruel and calculating. The type of fae who enjoys watching people break apart for kicks and giggles. In other words, a complete asshole.

I don't understand what the Shade Prince is up to yet. But I have a fair idea who's pulling his strings.

Landolin's gaze sharpens. "The trial's for both of us. I need the answer to be revealed as much as my father does. Probably more."

I shift my weight. "And if this supposed *gift* of mine doesn't show itself? What happens to me?"

He steps forward, slow and deliberate. "It will show itself, Summer. There's no other option."

His tone resonates with certainty, like he really believes I'm the one. That I'm somehow useful to the Hunt. But he's wrong.

When I eventually finish my counseling course, I'll have a purpose—helping others who've lived through trauma. Like I have. But for now, I'm just a girl whose own mother couldn't summon the energy to love her properly. Pathetic, really.

I tighten my arms around my ribs and bounce on my toes, teeth chattering. "What makes you so sure of that? I'm not being funny. I really want to understand."

Black eyes flick over me. "I know that you speak to the dead. Irren found your... What do humans call it? Profile? Post? Whatever it was, we watched you poke around crumbling houses, rambling on and on about the spirits you conversed with."

"I didn't think fae could use the Internet," I whisper, shocked he knows about my spectral entourage.

"We learned a lot about human technology from the Merits. Even Wi-Fi signals cannot defeat us." He tilts his head like an owl at midnight, locking on its prey. "Foolish of you to think they could."

He turns me by my shoulders and points at a small door tucked in a wall beside the dais steps. "Go outside and look around the city. Distract and calm yourself before tonight. I can *almost* promise you won't be hurt and that nothing bad will happen to you during the trial."

A defeated sigh slips through my lips. An almost promise from a fae is hardly very reassuring.

"Aren't you worried I'll escape?"

He laughs. "Not at all. Wards surround the city that activate when anyone tries to *leave* that the king would prefer stay. They sense betrayal, fear, and the intent to flee. The city walls are always watching and listening."

I blink. "The walls can sense what I'm thinking?"

"*And* feeling. It's old magic," he says. "Older than me. Maybe older than this court. It was built into the bones of the kingdom—a sentient energy focused on fear and guilt. If you try to leave with fear in your heart... it simply turns you around."

"So I'm stuck here forever," I say flatly.

"You're *contained* for the time being," he corrects. "There's a difference."

"Not sure I agree, Landolin."

He doesn't argue, just struts around me in a close circle, hands clasped behind his back, the click of his boots a measured rhythmic echo. "Someone will collect you from your room this evening, and you'll dine with the king before the trial."

Oh, goody. Lucky me. I hope they don't expect me to actually *speak* to anyone. Social engagements aren't my forte.

The narrow door creaks as he opens it, then thrusts me out into the chaos of the city.

"Have fun," he says with an arrogant wink. "Avoid anything with no eyes and too many teeth. They tend to love snacking on stray humans. Don't want you to miss tonight."

Maybe it'd be better if I *did* get eaten. At least then I wouldn't have to see Landolin's smug face again—or take part in his farce of a trial.

CHAPTER 34

Wynter

By the time we reach the outskirts of Dorthadas, my patience is one howl away from snapping. Rain and mud soak my fur, and my paws burn, caked with dried blood.

Beside me, Ivor huffs, his breath fogging in the chilly air. *Finally*, his sagging posture says. As if I'd dragged him all this way just to torture him.

The black walls of the City of Dorthadas rise ahead, a grim barricade brimming with dark energy. There's nothing soft or pretty about it. It's built to make you think twice about entering. Or turn back altogether.

Even if it's the last city I see, nothing will stop me from breaching the walls to find Summer.

The main gates are out of the question—too many guards, and even if we go through separately, two wolves entering the town in one day will definitely raise suspicions. So we skirt the curve of the wall instead, Ivor leading the way, recalling the route from our last time in Dorthadas.

We pass rooftops of city buildings draped in the realm's permanent gloomy dusk, fences made of bone and scrap metal, and a line of merchant carts loaded with goods waiting for inspection.

One cart in particular creaks forward, covered in canvas and smelling of root vegetables and damp cloth. I flick my ears toward it.

That one.

Ivor doesn't hesitate. We crawl deeper into the shadows of the wall, then leap.

Inside, it's cramped, the scent of overripe vegetables sharp enough to sting my eyes. I wedge myself between sacks, dig my claws into the wood, and brace for movement.

The cart jolts forward, and Ivor shudders beside me. I nip his ear, warning him to stay quiet and still.

The guards' inspection of the cart's contents is cursory, and we make it through the gate, lurching over cobblestones. The wheels slow, then stop. We wait three breaths, then crawl out the back, silently leaping to the ground.

I shift the moment we hit an alleyway.

Bones creak, skin shivers and stretches, pain shoots up my spine, and then I'm standing, naked, in a pile of rotting produce.

"Fuck. Typical Shade Court welcome." Scraping my feet clean on the ground, I summon the glamour of a local courtier—dark tunic, black cloak, sharper, meaner features, and blades tucked into every available sheathe and strap.

Next, I make Ivor look like a hunting hound with wiry gray fur, thin legs, and a long neck and snout.

He whines in protest.

"Don't worry," I say. "You look good. Almost pettable."

My wolf snorts and turns his back in disgust.

Dorthadas isn't a town for tourists. It's grim and unwelcoming.

Buildings crowd together, looming like they're conspiring against me. Crooked alleyways splinter off at odd angles, and most streets lead nowhere—or to claustrophobic dead ends where the air tastes like ash and blood, thick as a slaughterhouse floor.

Oppressive magic sticks to my skin, the weight of it amplified by the low light and the seven pastel moons arcing through the gloom above.

Not a place I want to linger.

We move fast, cutting through side streets, avoiding areas closer to the castle. I keep my hood up and my knives close. Ivor pads beside me, ears forward, tail low.

The fae don't look at us as we pass by store windows displaying typical Dorthadas wares—mirrors that show someone else's reflection, perfumes bottled in lacquered bone, with labels like *Crave* and *Wither*. So we must be doing something right.

The castle's shadow creeps over everything, all black stone and needlepoint towers, built to strike fear in newcomers' hearts, not invite fawning praise. Our heads down and ears pricked, we keep to the edges of the buildings and walls, listening to conversations, hoping to hear snippets about the court's new human acquisition.

And then I see her.

Summer—moving like the ground might give way beneath her. Which is fair, all things considered.

She walks fast, but her hands are clenched at her sides, jaw tight, and shoulders squared like she's daring someone to stop her. Her dark hair is pulled back off her face, and she's wearing a crimson dress over striped pants, a gold, filigree belt encircling her waist, and matching long earrings swaying from her ears. Shade Court trappings.

Nausea spins through me at the memory of the last time I saw her wearing such things—dancing while the Merit High Mage laughed and laughed.

Ivor tenses beside me, fur bristling down his spine.

"I know," I murmur. "There she is. Lucky for them, they haven't hurt her. She looks well."

Two guards follow at a casual distance. Not crowding her, but close enough to kill her if she does something Moiron wouldn't approve of.

A growl vibrates low in my chest as my hands curl into fists, nails biting into flesh. I don't shift, but the wolf within me lunges anyway, snarling into the space between us.

I see her, *my mate*, and every instinct inside me howls, clawing at the bars of my control. I want to rip through the guards, get to her. *Shield* her. *Protect* her. But I don't move. Can't move without getting her killed.

I reach for her thoughts but get nothing. Either I'm too far away, or my so-called skill has chosen the worst possible time to fail me. Damn this pathetic excuse for a gift.

We track them for several blocks until Summer stops at a market stall, inspecting an array of knives and daggers. The guards linger behind, one of them yawning like he's been on shift since the dawn of time. The other nudges him and mutters something low.

Summer seems blissfully unaware of their presence and strolls on.

Ivor moves closer to the guards, and I follow, pausing behind a cart loaded with carved obsidian, close enough to catch a few words.

"...immediately after the festivities in the Great Hall tonight. Out in the Hollow at midnight. Don't be late. You know what happened last time you displeased Moiron."

"Right," the other guard says, rolling his eyes. "I'm not the one who almost fell asleep during the last Marking of the Antlers ceremony."

The first one snorts. "The girl won't pass the trial anyway. Some say she's nothing but a low-born mortal. No gifts or talents that are of any use to us here."

The second leans in. "Landolin's invested in her. If she fails, he'll be the one to take the fall. Her too, of course."

One jerks his chin, and they fall in behind Summer. But I stand still, cold creeping up my back. Fury burning through my veins.

So, there'll be a trial of some sort in the Hollow tonight.

But what's the point of putting her through that? She's human. Can't fight. Has no magic. But for some reason, Moiron and his son believe otherwise.

The Merit High Mage—the one who brought Summer to Riven's court, where my sister met her—claimed Moiron believed she was important to Landolin's bond with the Hunt. That bond was long rumored to have been won from Yurendyl, its original custodians, by questionable means.

But they're wrong about her. And I intend to be there when they realize it.

Fortunately, I know the place the guards mentioned. The Hollow, a ceremonial pit carved into the hillside behind the castle. Ancient and steeped in enough blood and dark magic that it clings to the soil like rot, preventing anything beautiful from growing there.

Whatever it takes, I have to be there tonight. Failure isn't an option.

I could storm up to the castle door now and insist on an audience with Moiron, try to bargain Summer's way out of here. But given what I plan to offer him in exchange for her life, the presence of his entire court and the element of surprise will work best in my favor.

We peel off from the market crowd, Ivor and I vanishing into the gloom and cutting through the city toward the Hollow.

I know a path. It's old, uncomfortably narrow, and filled with the type of thorns that will tear out our fur and attempt to blind us. But it'll get us to the exact location where we need to hide until midnight, when the seven moons hang highest in the sky.

That's my plan.

And it better fucking work.

In wolf form, I take a back route through the eastern quarter of Dorthadas—a stretch of market halls and storage towers left to crumble when the court moved closer to the cliffs several hundred years ago.

It's quiet here, so different from the human realm. No cars, no sirens, none of the messy buzz of humanity. Just the wind rustling leaves and our paws crunching over debris as we head toward a tunnel beneath the hill that opens right behind the Hollow. I've used it before. A long time ago.

The tunnel entrance is still there. So are the vines... And the stones and collapsed ceiling I didn't account for. I stare at the heap of black rubble blocking the path.

Seven hells. Because nothing can ever go smoothly.

Ivor yelps, his body nudging mine like it's my fault.

The plan was simple. Find Summer, make sure she's safe, then make a grand entrance and crash Moiron's hoax of a trial. Ideally in that order. Turns out "swoop in and save the day" was more of a theory than an actual fool-proof strategy.

A soft whine sounds behind me.

I rumble a growl in reply. *Not helpful, Ivor.*

We backtrack, run up the slope, and take the longer route around because there's no other option, losing precious time. I move on instinct now, guided by scent—damp earth, trampled grass, the musk of prey drifting toward us on the wind.

The ruins east of the ridge look promising from a distance—low walls, open alleys, nothing that screams *immediate deathtrap*. But this is the Raven Realm. At this point, I wouldn't be surprised if a Cu Sith—a giant, green-furred hound—showed up to tear us to pieces. At least for me, it'd be over fast. It's Summer's fate that terrifies me in that scenario—the thought of no one left to fight for her.

Ivor sticks close to my side, ears flicked forward as he huffs short breaths. Like me, he hates the flavor of the air here. It tastes stale, like food left too long in the sun. Not that there's much sunlight in this gods-forsaken place.

We weave through the broken streets, vaulting piles of crumbled stone and thorny hedges. The Hollow can't be far now. I feel its malevolent energy tugging at my bones.

After a while, the sky above Dorthadas doesn't darken... it just deepens, turning the color of brushed metal, the moons beginning to flicker in and out behind the clouds.

The ground hums beneath my paws. Not the hum of natural energy flowing through the soil. Not the vibration of the Hollow. Old magic that feels like a trap.

Shit, I'd better...

I skid to a stop, but it's too late. A flare of sickly green light detonates across the stones—a spell set long ago, snapping into place.

I try to veer away, but dark energy slams into me, pain searing through every nerve. It feels like getting gut-punched by a mountain. And then I'm ripped out of my wolf skin like someone hooked me behind the ribs and yanked hard.

Flesh. Bone. Instincts shift back.

The last thing I feel before the world blackens is the cold bite of stone against bare skin. I don't even get a curse out before a dark cloud swallows me whole.

CHAPTER 35

Summer

I'm given no warning. Not even an official dinner invitation. A single fae guard with ash-rimmed eyes shows up at my door and shoves a dark purple outfit into my arms.

"Put this on," he says.

I inspect the mulberry-colored leather corset, laced to create a low-cut neckline. Embroidered vines curl over the long skirt that flows beneath it, the right side slashed with a deep split.

"Do you have anything in black?" I ask, aiming to annoy. "It's a little too festive for my liking."

His scowl tells me he has no patience for smartasses. "Hurry up. I'll wait outside the door."

After I wash my face, I change into the dress, leaving my hair loose and my anxiety running wild.

As promised, the guard is waiting beside my door. Without a word, he motions for me to follow.

"Any point in asking your name?" I say eventually, still pacing the endless hallways—two thousand and thirty-three steps so far.

"No."

"Right. Then at least tell me where we're going."

"Dinner in the hall," he croaks, his voice rough, like a crow choking on a fat worm.

"Sounds great," I lie, skipping to keep up with him. "As long as I'm not the main course."

The large black doors loom ahead. I hold my breath as they swing open, wink at one of the creepy, translucent faces drifting across the shiny obsidian surface, and step into the revel.

The hall feels different tonight—more claustrophobic, like the walls are inching inward. Cold radiates up through the stone, nipping at my ankles even through my boots. And the air carries a damp, metallic scent, like wet coins laced with smoke. Strangely familiar. Uncomfortably so.

A flicker of a memory strikes—my bare feet hitting this same stone floor, music that wouldn't stop, the pain of raw hunger twisting my gut as I spun and spun and spun.

I shove the memory down before it can finish unfolding. What the hell is going on? Landolin said I wouldn't remember my past at the Shade Court. Couldn't remember it. Is something changing?

The throne room is still vast and unsettling, but this time, more details leap out.

Twenty-six arched beams rise overhead like the ribs of a cage, while curtains of deep red amaranth flowers—love-lies-bleeding—drape from the rafters, swaying gently to the eerie music. Hundreds of floating orbs cast dim, shifting light over the courtiers, shadows crawling across their faces and robes.

The Shade fae wear masks, headdresses, and crowns, all crafted to resemble antlers, crow wings, snake heads, wolf snouts and other symbols of creatures from nightmares. They dance either out of time with the beat, too fast, or disturbingly slow, their movements erratic. Others watch from the edges of the dance floor, dark stone goblets cradled in their hands.

Landolin sits at the bottom of the golden steps that lead to the dais, as if he's been waiting for me. But when he catches my eye, he looks away without a greeting. Says nothing.

The king, Moiron Ravenseeker, perches on the throne, the seven glowing moons strung like party lights outside the window behind him. I could've sworn they were higher in the sky this afternoon, when I walked around the town, but I know better than to expect this place to abide by the rules of logic.

Antlers made of blackened metal crown Moiron's deep blue hair, his silver robes stitched with hundreds of tiny feathers. When he moves his hands, ash trails behind his fingers, and the red glow in his eyes sends a shiver creeping down my spine.

Flanked by guards, I take thirty-nine shaky steps to reach Landolin—who beckons me forward, wasting no time before leading me up the stairs to present me to his father.

Moiron sniffs, inspecting me like I'm a stain on his favorite cloak. "So," he says to his son, his red-hued eyes still trailing over me. "This is your thrall, fully grown."

I try to meet his gaze without flinching, but I find myself glancing away every few seconds. *Damn. Those ember-lit eyes freak me the fuck out.*

"The one and only," Landolin replies.

Moiron clicks his tongue. "Are you certain? She looks too soft."

I raise my chin. "Can you blame me? It's been a very long week."

Several fae nearby chuckle. Most just stare, probably hoping the Shade King's shadows will swallow me whole. Or worse, that he'll bludgeon me to death with one of his spiked arm bracers.

Moiron leans forward. "At midnight, you will stand trial, and we'll see what you're made of. Until then..." His fingers curl, and vines I hadn't even noticed shift beneath my feet, winding around my legs like ropes. "...Enjoy the revel."

"I'd probably enjoy the scenery more if I wasn't being gift-wrapped in vines like a sacrifice to the Shade Court's forest gods. Any chance you'll untie your decorative greenery?"

Embarrassment burns through me as the king lazily flicks a hand. I drop to the floor—flat on my ass—the vines still coiled tight around my legs. So that's a no, then.

Two fae close in, offering me a plate of cheese and sweet-smelling pastries. Even though I'm terrified of being put under a spell and becoming a thrall again, I'm so hungry that I gobble the food up and chase it down with a cup of wine, taking in the sights and sounds around me.

The hall hums with low music—plucked strings and something deeper, bone horns maybe, similar to the Wild Hunt's but quieter and slightly jollier. Laughter echoes off the stone walls. Should be a comforting sound, but to my ears it sounds malicious, even threatening.

Courtiers drift between dining tables in leather corsets, silk robes, and extravagant armor, showing enough skin to make a mirror in the mortal world blush. Their smiles are nasty, their pupils blown wide—like cats hunting in the dark.

Some look like monsters from childhood nightmares, rows of horns jutting from their brows. Their skin ripples as if something crawls beneath it—bodies scaled, bloodied, wrapped in smoky shadows. Many possess a wild, lethal beauty, their bodies poised to strike, like animals before they lunge for their prey.

I search for dancing humans in the crowd. Thralls, like I once was, relieved when I find none.

A small table rests between the king and Landolin's thrones, now cleared of food but still set with goblets and candles. I perch on the top step—just another curiosity in a grand museum of oddities.

The music winds up, growing louder and weirder. I spot a few familiar faces from the castle halls and my walk around the city, including Misery, the winged fae with the bone who tried to rattle me earlier today. She raises her cup in a mock salute.

Landolin watches me, somehow looking both bored and intense, and Moiron smiles like he's counting the ticket sales for my execution.

Hell, I wish Wyn were here, standing beside me, doing that growly, overprotective thing he does best. I wish I were back home at Gravenshade—Ollie head-butting my book in bed, while I read too late into the night, Mom's ghost muttering unsolicited life advice through the steam in the bathroom mirror. Anywhere but here.

My chest tightens like I've run a mile uphill. I clench my jaw, blink too fast, and try not to spiral and count my own heartbeat or the many doorways I could bolt through.

I don't have my meds. Don't have a plan. But I refuse to let the fear leak out. Not in tears. Not in twitches. Not even in the rate of my breathing.

No one here gets to see me freak out. I just have to stay calm, and if I can survive the trial, I can survive whatever comes after. I have to.

To stop the panic from snowballing, I shift my focus to earlier today, my thoughts a little muddled from the wine.

The city didn't offer any great secrets or unexpected comforts, but at least I was outside in the fresh air. Sort of. If you count alleys that reek of smoke, spoiled food, and the charming scent of frying offal.

The city butcher sold meat I couldn't identify—and didn't want to. A bookstore was stacked with volumes that whispered about me when I turned my back. I passed a musician playing a flute carved from something that looked disturbingly like a human spine, earning coins and applause from fae who danced around him five feet off the ground, wings flapping lazily as they spun.

I walked fast, told myself I was exploring. But really, I was mapping every exit and gate I could find. Every corner looked like it might open into freedom, but none of them did. And even if one had, the sentient wards would never have let me leave.

I'd never felt so caged under an open sky, grim and sunless as it had been this afternoon.

In the hall, the hum of conversation rises and falls around me. Goblets clink. Laughter creeps over my skin, making my flesh crawl. And eyes, too many to count, track my every breath, piercing through the space between us.

I stay where I am, having already shuffled myself and Moiron's vines halfway down the steps below the dais. It's the perfect spot—far enough away to be ignored, close enough to catch the voices drifting down from above.

Landolin and Moiron Ravenseeker speak in that careless, booming way that says they either don't care who hears them, or assume no one would dare to listen.

Well, I dare. And I *am* listening.

"What will you do if your trial reveals her to be useless?" Moiron says, his voice low but steady. "The court grows restless for an answer to your... predicament. Yurendyl have kept two of our Carrion for several days before sending them home carrying their banner. We need the right girl, and we need her *now*."

The Carrion. They were the riders Irren mentioned to Landolin yesterday in the courtyard. The secret he wanted kept. I wonder how the king came to learn of it, and what it all means for me.

"*This* girl is here now," Landolin replies. "And the trial *will* reveal her hidden talent. I wish it to be so, and there is no other option."

The trial. Fuck. I hope I won't be called upon to raise the city's dead warriors before vanquishing them all in a battle—because there's fat chance of that happening. If I had a secret magical gift, I'd know. I'm a ghost whisperer. That's about as impressive as it gets.

"And I ask again," snarls Moiron, "if she fails, will you sit quietly and watch me dispose of her, or make a fuss?"

"Let's worry about that when the time comes, Father." Landolin's laugh is quiet and humorless. "Besides, when have you ever cared about what I think?"

I risk a glance over my shoulder.

Moiron lounges with the lazy ease of absolute power, knowing no one would dare oppose him. Landolin stands beside his throne, arms crossed, eyes fixed on the floor as if willing the stone to swallow him, while shadows lick at his boots.

"I advise you not to take that tone with me," says Moiron. "Don't forget what happened last time you defied me. You lead the Hunt. And you will lead this girl to the truth of what she is or, alternatively, to her death."

Landolin doesn't argue. He simply nods. But when Moiron turns away, I swear the Shade Prince's jaw tightens hard enough to crack, and three of his shadows form the shapes of tiny spears.

The king rises, and the court falls silent, waiting for him to speak.

He barks out three sharp words, "To the Hollow," and the fae stream through the main exit like birds startled from trees, their piercing shrieks and laughter making me cover my ears.

CHAPTER 36

Summer

Having received no instructions, I stand frozen on the steps, watching the procession depart the Great Hall. No one tells me to move. No one tells me anything.

Then Landolin lifts his head and calls out in a clear, deep voice, "*Misery*."

At first, I think he's making some kind of dramatic statement—a commentary on the night. Or on me.

Then I see her. The bone-throwing fae from the courtyard.

She emerges from a shadowed alcove near the eastern wall—tall, skeletal-thin, and wrapped in strips of dull silk and leather, like someone stitched her clothes together in the dark and they somehow turned out pretty cool.

Long, midnight hair threaded with dried vines frames her narrow face. Her skin is the color of faded lavender, her eyes glassy and solid black. She walks barefoot, leathery wings raised, each step deliberate and at a pace so unnerving the fleeing crowd parts for her automatically. Chains between her ankles clink when she moves, and I can't help wondering if she's a slave from another court.

She stops in front of me, her unblinking gaze settling on my face, making my skin crawl under her scrutiny.

"Summer Brady," she says. "Come with me."

It's not even an order. Not really. More like she's giving a weather report. This is happening. Prepare accordingly.

I give a mock salute and rise. The vines restraining me have disappeared, but my legs have gone to sleep. I groan as I get up, glancing toward the dais. Landolin watches me with an unreadable expression.

Moiron doesn't look at me at all.

Misery turns and strides off, expecting me to follow without question. Every part of me says *stay put*. But I go anyway.

We exit through a side passage, not the main doors. The hallways narrow as we go, the air growing colder with every step. My heart thuds too fast, but I force myself to breathe through it. No panicking. Not yet. Counting to infinity? Totally reasonable under the circumstances.

I tell myself I'm fine. That Wyn would want me to be brave. So, I gulp in another breath and decide to do some delving, stealing a glance at her as we walk.

"Is that your real name? Misery?" I ask.

"Not even a fae parent would be so cruel as to gift their child such a fate," she replies.

"I don't know... have you noticed King Moiron's parenting style?"

No response. Not even a snort or a quirk of her lips.

"Are you a prisoner here, too?" I try again.

Silence.

"What's this test about? What will I have to do? You might as well tell me. Whatever it is, I can't escape it. Or *you*."

Not bothering to look at me, Misery speeds up. "You ask too many questions."

I could argue, but she's probably right. I might feel sorry for her if I knew what the Shade Court had done to her. And I probably don't *want* to know what they're about to do to me.

At last, the corridor opens onto a narrow outdoor path, lit by strings of floating lanterns that sway in the breeze. Up ahead, the courtiers come into view—hundreds, maybe thousands, forming a loose ring around a shallow basin carved into the ground.

The Hollow.

It's not a pit, like an old quarry. It's too clean, too deliberate. Almost as if something massive was pressed into the ground and then lifted away, leaving behind a smooth, circular scar, like a natural amphitheater.

I stop at the edge, where the air feels thicker, harder to breathe.

Misery speaks without turning. "Stand in the center and wait for the call. If you run, the Hunt will follow and strike you down without mercy."

I open my mouth to say something—maybe to beg for help—but she's already melted into the crowd.

And now I'm alone.

Well, not technically. Because the entire Shade Court is staring back at me.

I take one step down into the Hollow.

Then another.

And another.

The slope is shallow, but the intense silence humming in the night air makes it feel steeper, more dangerous. The crowd watches from the rim, their faces half-lit by hanging lanterns and the cold glow of the seven moons. I can't hear them talking, or even breathing. The fuckers. I suppose this is premium entertainment for them.

The ground under my boots is uneven and littered with old bones that gleam like sickening warnings in the moonlight. Sweat drips down my back, and the sound of my own rattled breaths is nightmarish, like I'm trapped in a dream I can't wake up from.

I make it to the middle of the pit without receiving any instructions. No one attacking me. Nothing. I'm filled with a sense that I've arrived in the part of my story, of my life, where I'll either perform a miracle or die trying. So, yeah, *go me*, I guess.

From the edge of the Hollow, Moiron Ravenseeker strides toward me.

His voice cuts clean across the space, echoing like a warning shot. "Summer Brady of Lake Grenlynn in the Mortal Realm. The Court calls upon you to serve."

I force myself to look up at him. He's standing tall in black-and-silver robes that shift with every movement, his shadows caressing his body. The fire in his red eyes is banked, now dark and cruel, and he stares at me like I'm nothing. Worthless.

I refuse to wither under such a gaze. I lift my chin and pretend he's my deceased but still opinionated mother. And no man, living or fae, has ever scared me half as much as she does.

Landolin stands beside the king, his hands clasped behind his back like he's afraid of what they'll do if he releases them.

Moiron speaks again. "There are claims your blood can call the dead from their graves and control them. That your breath whispers the language of the afterlife."

I blink. "That's not a class I remember signing up for."

A ripple of laughter from the crowd.

Moiron doesn't crack a smile. "This is not a trial of cruelty," he says. "It is merely a test of what sleeps inside you. A way to discern if you are the one the Hunt has waited for. And if the Hollow will stir at your command."

He gestures to a shape at the far end of the pit I hadn't noticed before, shrouded in shadow.

It looks like a body. Or what's left of one, wrapped in linen, resting on a slab of pale stone, like an offering that no one wants to accept.

"You will raise it," Moiron says. "If the power is yours, if you are indeed a dead waker, the corpses will answer."

Corpses? I take a breath, the taste of blood filling my mouth.

"How? How am I meant to do it? Do you have an instruction manual by any chance?"

The king scowls, and Landolin steps forward, passing me a hunting knife with a glossy, mother-of-pearl handle. "The same way you speak to your ghosts. Ask the dead to rise. And offer them blood, of course."

Blood? Oh, shit. Now I really want to go home.

"Them?" I ask, peering into the corner.

Near the slab is multi-layered pallet, each level holding maybe three bodies, so there are at least ten linen-wrapped corpses in the Hollow. Am I expected to raise them all, or will just one satisfy this ghoulish court's necromancy kink?

"And if I fail?" I ask.

"You won't," Landolin insists, which feels more like a demand than encouragement. "Do your best," he adds. "For you can do nothing more."

Well, that's certainly true.

I turn and face Moiron. "Your... Majesty... I'm absolutely sure you've kidnapped the wrong girl. Can't the Hunt just take me back home? Keep searching for the right one? I mean look at me... I'm nothing special. Why keep me?"

Moiron sighs. "The Prince of Earth's father, Everend Fionbharr, the wretched Prince of Air, once allowed his daughter, Merrin, to cheat our court at the Beltane ritual when she jumped the fires with Landolin, thus robbing us of our rightful, future queen."

The king's hair is the same deep blue shade as the streaks in his son's, but his eyes glow as red as a demon's. The resemblance is there, sure, but where Landolin carries his arrogance like armor, Moiron wields his like a weapon. I wonder, just for a moment, if—deep down—they're cut from the same cursed cloth.

Then I remember Landolin's vision of that night. The way he stood over my parents' bodies with blood on his hands and shadows crawling behind his back. And whatever doubt I had burns right out of me. I'm sure he's as rotten as his beady-eyed father.

"What does your court being cheated out of a queen have to do with me?" I ask.

"Everend's son, Wynter, believes you're his mate. That only you can free him from their mad mage's curse. Don't you see, you being the girl we need is the perfect alignment of both progress and revenge. Agreed?"

"No, not really," I mumble.

"Besides, you belonged to us first. Eight years ago, the Hunt sniffed you out at the place you call Gravenshade Hall and recognized the scent of fate. There is only one way out of the Hollow for you, girl. Best you get started."

Fantastic. I guess I should start composing my tragic last words, then.

The king and his son retreat, and with zero enthusiasm, I shuffle toward the pallet of the dead.

I study the corpse laid out separately on the block of stone. The linen is old and frayed, and the body is large. Probably male. Maybe a soldier. Or a laborer. Either way, he looks too far gone to be raised by *anyone*, least of all an anxiety-ridden mortal with self-esteem issues.

I don't know the first thing about raising the dead, and today's meds-withdrawal symptoms—nausea and brain fog—aren't exactly boosting my odds.

But apparently, I'm about to try anyway. Really hoping I don't vomit on a corpse.

Shit. There are definitely more bodies than I realized. Eleven, maybe twelve, laid out on tiered slabs of wood like a grotesque wedding cake. From a safe distance, I try to pick my lucky—or unlucky—test subject.

One corpse has a skewed jaw. Another is missing fingers. They smell of dry earth and rotting fabric, like they were recently unpacked from storage for the occasion.

I glance up at the crowd circling the Hollow, so many fae still watching. Waiting. Hoping I'll do something spectacular or fail horribly. Either would likely entertain them.

Taking a deep breath, I step forward.

The closest corpse is on the bottom tier—a small frame with its hands bound across its chest in a way that feels too deliberate. She... or he... could've been a prisoner. Empathy warming my heart, I crouch beside it and rest a hand lightly on what I think is a shoulder.

"Hey," I whisper, my voice raspy with nerves. "If you can hear me in there... now would be an excellent time to sit up and do something spooky. Like let out a shriek. Curse the king. Expel some gas. Anything you can manage would be great."

Nothing happens, which is fair enough. I can't believe I just asked a dead body to fart.

I shift to my knees and lean closer, rubbing the rough linen between my fingers. I speak again. This time a little louder. "Oh, Dead One, whoever you are, you're being summoned by Summer Brady, amateur ghost whisperer and very reluctant guest of the Shade Court. Your presence is... kind of required."

Still nothing. Not even a twitch. I try again, voice dropping to a reassuring murmur, the way I speak to ghosts back home when they're newly deceased and skittish.

"It's okay to come back now. You're safe. Just follow the sound of my voice..."

The corpse I'm touching doesn't stir, or breathe, or flinch. None of them do.

"This is ridiculous. Of course it won't work," I mutter. "Because I'm not the *actual* girl the Shade Court needs."

Wyn's dimpled grin flashes in my mind, and I suppress the urge to curl up in a ball and cry. I look up at the bodies on the higher tiers. More stillness. And no sign of any twitching limbs trying to rise.

Sitting back on my heels, I exhale a heavy sigh. Then, because this whole thing is already a nightmare and my head is about to explode with stress, I blurt out, "Is this like Sleeping Beauty for corpses? Do I have to kiss one of you poor suckers to wake you up?"

A couple of chuckles ripple through the court. I think someone even claps.

Hell. Could this day get any worse?

I lean in toward the dead guy with the lopsided jaw and mutter, "This isn't personal, okay? So don't get any bright ideas if you get resurrected." Then I gently tap my lips to its linen-covered forehead.

Still dead. Still stinky and unmoving.

"Right. Thought so."

I pull away, heart hammering. My hands are shaking. The kind of tremble that comes from feeling simultaneously ridiculous and absolutely terrified. This was never going to work. I talk to ghosts, not sacks of bones. I don't raise bodies. I don't resurrect spirits. I listen. That's what I'm good at, which is why I'm training to become a counselor.

But the fae are still watching. Every single one of them.

I glance toward the edge of the Hollow. Landolin stares back, his expression twisted with a mix of hope and guilt. Moiron stands beside him, stone-faced. The unfeeling bastard.

I look down at my hands. Then at the knife sticking out of my pocket, hesitating only a second before drawing it. It's not particularly beautiful or ceremonial—just practical, clean, dark steel. I press the edge of the blade to my palm. Just enough to bleed a little.

The pain flares sharp, and I hiss in a breath, then hold my hand over the corpse's face, letting my blood drip.

"Two drops in your eyes for sight," I whisper, my mind beginning to fracture. "One for your breath. And three for whatever's left in that skull that might bring you back to life."

My blood hits the linen drop by drop. Soaks in. And then... nothing.

Absolutely *nothing* happens.

I bleed into the silence as I stare at the crowd of fae who are vibrating with anticipation to call me a fraud and demand my death. My hand shakes harder. My mouth is dry. My heart pounds like a war drum.

Then something shifts in the air.

A gust of cold sweeps through the space, snuffing out three of the floating lanterns. The crowd stirs. Some murmur. A few draw blades just in case.

Then the body under my hands jerks. I jolt back, my pulse racing. It spasms once more... then goes still.

The crowd holds its breath. I hold my breath.

And then the corpse releases a hollow, gassy groan—a sick, bloated sound that makes my insides recoil.

Another lantern dies.

And just like that, the body stops moving. Whatever spark had flickered briefly inside it dies out.

The entire Hollow exhales.

Moiron steps forward. "That's enough. The human has failed."

Landolin's voice follows. "Summer... move back."

A shape flickers in the corner of my eye, faint and blurry. I glance toward the bodies, and that's when I see him. Not the corpse. The ghost.

He's hovering just above the pallet, a gray-skinned specter with a ravaged face, wearing the blood-slick tunic he died in. His mouth opens, and a terrible sound leaks out, a low, raspy whisper. It's barely audible, but somehow, the words are perfectly clear to me.

"King Moiron is a fraud."

My breath catches.

The ghost's head tilts, milky eyes boring into mine. "His Hunt was bought with blood. It feeds upon his son. But do not fear. The wolf is coming. Earth triumphs over shadow. It always does."

Then the ghost lets out a wail that curdles my stomach and vanishes, sucked backward into the corpse like smoke into a vent.

Well, I guess that settles it... this realm definitely has ghosts. Terrifying ones.

I sit in the dirt, blood dripping down my wrist, heart racing. Trying not to cry or throw up. Trying not to let them see my fear.

Above me, the court starts whispering.

At the edge of my vision, a dark cloud stirs—Moiron Ravenseeker's shadows—then something hits my cheek. *Hard.*

CHAPTER 37

Wynter

I come to with something slippery and wet dragging across my face. I blink, groan, and sputter. Ivor's on my chest, tail thudding like a mallet on packed earth. His tongue scrapes my cheek again, rough and urgent.

I squint blearily up at the sky. The moons look too high. I'd better be fucking hallucinating that.

So far, the plan's going *great*. Just brilliant. What an absolute shitshow.

"Off, Ivor," I rasp, pushing at him weakly. "Your tongue isn't helping."

I wipe a smear of blood from my chest, run my fingers over a gash on my thigh.

I'm cold, bleeding, and *of course* I'm fucking naked.

Flat on my back in the middle of a blasted ruin, dirt ground into my skin, blood dried at my temple. No clothes, no weapons—those two I can fix—and no idea how long I've been lying here while Summer's at the mercy of Moiron fucking Ravenseeker.

"Perfect. Couldn't be better," I croak, sitting up so fast the entire realm spins three times.

Scorched runes smolder in the dirt around me. Whatever spell I triggered burned itself out while I was drooling on my back. How long was I out? And how much time have we lost?

Seven hells. Stripped down to the skin, battered, and late. Thank fuck for glamours and the ability to shift.

Ivor scrapes his claws against the ground, then noses at my arm, anxious. I drag myself onto my feet, head pounding, the ground tilting.

Above us, those moons are definitely higher than they should be.

Way higher.

Panic fists my gut.

The trial. It's probably started already.

I snap into wolf form without thinking, barely managing to stay conscious through the nausea, and then sprint toward the Hollow with Ivor at my heels.

Trees and the dark shapes of ruined buildings blur at the sides of my vision as I pass. I don't stop to think what might be watching or following us. I don't stop for anything.

The longer I run, the worse the silence around me feels. I can't hear any sounds of the Shade Court up ahead. No crowd chanting. No Moiron booming out instructions. Nothing.

I push harder, paws bleeding over rough stone, lungs burning until I finally hear it—cheers and applause.

I glance up at the arc of moons again. I'm too fucking late, and Summer's alone down there with a court full of vultures.

By the time Ivor and I reach the upper ridge overlooking the Hollow, the crowd is hushed, the air strung tight with anticipation. My bones burn as I shift into my fae form and conjure a glamour of dark leather and a cloak that lashes the air like a weapon with every step. I shape it fast, brutally. I don't need to be pretty. I just need to be terrifying.

Pushing through the fae gathered on the Hollow's rim—judges, nobles, and observers—I move to the front with Ivor beside me. I scan the slope for a path down the hill, my eyes adjusting to the figures in the pit below.

"Where are you, Summer?" I whisper.

The Hollow glows dimly in shifting tones of green and silver—cast by torchlight burning at the edges and flames flickering from three braziers. Landolin stands near a ceremonial post at the center, arms crossed, dark hair whipping in the breeze.

Shadow magic vibrates against my skin, and I swallow hard, trying not to gag at the taste of it on my tongue. In the darkest corner, linen-wrapped bodies lie stacked on wooden pallets.

And then I see Summer.

Shoulders drawn back, her chin is set at a determined angle, but her posture is tense as if she's bracing against pain. There's blood seeping from her palm, a bruise blooming on her cheek.

Landolin presses a crystal vial against her lips, and Moiron's shadows swirl around her waist, chaotic like he's losing control. Or has already lost it.

Rage boils inside me, and I curl my fists, grinding my teeth. "Let's do this," I tell Ivor, conjuring a sword from the elements.

I descend the slope slow and steady, each step deliberate, shaking the earth. Let them see me approach. Let them wonder if they should stop me. Or run.

The court watches, murmurs dropping off one by one. No one tries to touch me.

Good.

Ivor keeps pace at my side as we move through the crowd and my glamour builds. It's fueled by anger, drawing energy from the Hollow itself—from the very ground I might be buried under before daybreak.

My skin darkens as I walk, veined through with gold and silver, resembling the ancient stone of the Dún Mountains near my home when the light hits them just right.

Thin layers of slate and gold dust cover my cloak. The edges appear worn and rough, trailing behind me as my feet strike the ground with deliberate thuds. Dust whirls up around me, the land rising to my earth magic, embracing me.

When I reach the center of the Hollow, I stop, feeling the ground pulse underfoot, the entire Shade Court's attention locked on me.

Let them see me stripped down—a cursed prince facing death. Whatever the price I pay tonight, it'll be worth it if they let Summer return home. If she's safe.

Dead silence falls over the Hollow. Even Moiron, perched on a broken column in his raven form, stops preening his gold-streaked feathers. His beady gaze drops to my bare, bloodstained feet.

As I step into the light, Landolin's jaw tightens, and his grip on Summer releases—an odd move considering the circumstances. She turns, seeing me for the first time since I entered the Hollow.

"Wyn," she breathes, stumbling forward—until Moiron shifts into his fae form and positions himself between us, silent and unyielding.

"Bit rude to start without me," I say, my voice echoing as wind drags my hair across my face and I step around the Shade King.

"Don't worry, Wynter Fionbharr, Prince of Dirt and Graves," says Landolin. "I'm happy to fill you in on what you missed."

"Not much by the looks of it," I say, loud enough for the courtiers to hear. "Testing the wrong mortal for zombie-raising magic is fucking embarrassing. Even for the Shade Court."

Wide-eyed, Summer rings her hands. It's the first time I've seen her clearly since Landolin stole her from our campsite.

Dark smudges line her eyes. Her dress is smeared with dirt, hair a tangled mess, and other than the bruise she looks well enough. And alive and beautiful.

"Who hurt her?" I snarl.

"Father's shadows got a little too close," says Landolin. "She's fine."

I'll be the judge of that. And I'll also make that fucker Moiron pay, no matter how long it takes.

"I failed their ridiculous test," she says, indicating the pile of bodies behind her.

"Not entirely," says Landolin. "One... burped. Perhaps that can be built upon."

She glares at him over her shoulder. "No, it can't. I promise you. If I tried for a thousand years, I couldn't resurrect a single fly, which *means* I can leave with Wyn now. Right?"

Her eyes cut to Landolin again, seeking the confirmation I know he won't give. As predicted, he stays silent.

Summer tries to move closer to me, but the Shade Prince tugs her back, and it takes everything I've got not to lop his head off with my blade and snatch her away. Trouble is, we wouldn't get far.

She attempts a smile. "I can't believe you're here. I'm so happy to see you, Wyn. You look... different. Incredible."

Summer's right. Of course I look amazing. I burned through most of my power crafting this damned glamour, gambling that I could bargain our way out of this mess. Every shift between forms takes more out of me in this realm, draining what little magic I have left.

Feigning indifference, I clasp my hands behind my back and circle Summer and Landolin. "At this point, I'm more relieved than happy. The other night, when I told you not to move, I didn't mean you should traipse around the campsite alone and get yourself carted off to the Shade Court."

"I know. I'm sorry. His shadows drew me out of bed. Believe me, I didn't want to go anywhere."

Gods, I've missed her. And she's going to kill me when she hears my plan to get her out of this miserable excuse for a royal court.

I flash her a grin. "Told you I'd always find you."

She doesn't smile again, but her shoulders drop half an inch. That's something, at least.

Landolin steps forward, his expression unreadable. "This is a closed space. Nothing that happens here concerns you. It's best if you leave."

"Looks open to me," I say, shrugging.

"The girl is under our protection. You have no right to interfere."

"I have every right," I snap. "She's not your toy or the Wild Hunt's sacrifice. She has given herself freely to me. Summer is mine."

Landolin tilts his head. "You're not a fae of this land, Wynter. What you say is of no consequence. The human was ours before you and your sister ever laid eyes upon her. Accept this and go in peace, maintaining the goodwill between our realms. Go!"

Shadows wind up his body, enveloping him in darkness. When he reappears, Summer is trapped against him, her back pressed to his chest, his arm banding her waist.

"That's my *mate*. Get your hands off my future wife."

"Wife?" says, Moiron, morphing into shadows then appearing in front of me. "Shouldn't you pretend she means little to you? Now that you've played your hand, we can ask anything of you in exchange for her safety and still maintain peace with your kingdom. You're as subtle as a landslide. Who taught you diplomacy? Your brainless, bonded wolf?"

The so-called brainless, bonded wolf bares his teeth beside me.

The Shade Court knows she's my mate. The entire seven realms probably does. Moiron's just playing games.

Summer's thoughts pierce my mind—sending me a message.

I'd rather you live than have to watch you die trying to save me. Please, Wyn. Be careful.

Ivor growls, ears back, hackles raised.

The Hollow hums around us, the court shifting and murmuring, eager to see spilled blood glistening in the pastel light of the moons. All hoping my next words will be foolish ones.

Landolin loosens his grip on Summer, his spine straight as a sword, and Moiron—dark-robed, red-eyed, black-hearted bastard—watches me with calculated calm.

"My diplomacy skills aside..." I raise my voice just enough to carry it to the edges of the crowd. "I have something you may be interested in bargaining for."

Moiron's head tilts the way a bird's does just before it pecks a creature's eyes out, his interest clearly piqued.

Pressing on before I lose my nerve, I say, "Summer Brady has no gift to give you. No grave-born power. Whatever you thought she was, she isn't it. Whatever the Hunt needs, it's not in her possession."

Gasps ripple through the crowd. Landolin's jaw tightens. Good. Let them squirm.

I keep my gaze locked on the Shade King's. "But you can still win a prize tonight. Something valuable. Something worthy... For a price."

He says nothing, only waits to see what I'm prepared to give up.

I exhale through my nose slowly, calming my racing thoughts.

Don't think about Summer behind you. Don't think about how fast her heart's beating. Don't let her fear stop you.

"I'm sure you know about my curse." I spit the words out like they burn. "So bury me in Dorthadas's soil. Curse lifted or not, if I remain buried for seven nights, the Elemental magic released when I rise—or die—will answer to your land."

A low hiss runs through the gathered fae. Not outrage. Excitement.

I push harder, my voice low and cold. "You're aware of the old law, Ravenseeker. *What the land buries, the land claims.* If I rise, I rise tied to your earth. You'll have more than walking sacks of reanimated bones to boast about—Elemental magic to nurture and remake."

Moiron's lips curve into something that might be a smile. Or a snarl. Hard to tell with a face like his.

Landolin folds his arms across his chest, suspicion in his gaze. "You offer yourself freely?"

"Yes," I say, my mouth dry as dust. "No bonds. No bargains owed. Simply let Summer leave this realm whenever she wishes. Give her safe passage home. I'll send a messenger through a portal to my sister and my parents, explaining what I've chosen and why. And if they come here and interfere, my life is forfeit. They'll have no claim to vengeance—no recourse, no retaliation."

A long, heavy silence, then Summer shifts her weight behind me. I don't dare turn. If I see her face, I'll break.

"*No, Wyn,*" she cries out.

A scuffle sounds, and I glance back in time to see Landolin's shadows crawl into her mouth, silencing her. Power moves through my gut, and the ground beneath the Hollow shakes.

"Settle down," says the prince. "This is only temporary. For her safety."

Moiron's eyes gleam like wet mulberries under the torchlight. His voice slides out smooth and certain. "Very well. I accept your terms, Prince of Earth."

He takes two steps closer, his shadows slithering ahead of him. "You will be buried by our hands. You will lie beneath our soil. If you rise, your magic strengthens our court. If you do not..." He spreads his arms wide in mock generosity. "We will mourn your failure with all appropriate dignity."

Laughter sparks from the crowd, loud and vicious.

"And the girl?" I say, forcing the words through my teeth. "Vow that Summer will be free."

"I vow that she will be given leave to sit at your grave," Moiron says, casually, as if discussing a disfavored pet. "She will be free to wait. Free to leave our realm should she wish it."

Free to rot inside if she chooses to stay. Which she definitely won't.

Landolin meets my gaze over the king's shoulder. There's no triumph there. No cruelty. Just... inevitability. He knows the cost I'm prepared to pay better than anyone—the leader of the Hunt with no mate. No key to solving his own curse.

Maybe he was never quite the monster I thought he was. Or maybe monsters just recognize their own.

To be respectful, I incline my head. Just enough to hide the surge of terror clawing at my ribs.

"So be it," I say, taking the king's outstretched hand. "Our bargain is struck."

Summer's thoughts slam into me. Pain, fury, heartbreak. I shut her out before the sound of her agony breaks me.

Beneath the Hollow, a tremor rolls through the earth—the old magic waking.

Let it tremble.

Let it remember me.

Because soon, we will be one.

CHAPTER 38

Summer

S unrise in the Shade Court is a joke. A sad one.

The light shifts from black to purple, then gray, never quite turning gold. A melancholy effect that suits the business of the day—burying the man I love alive.

This morning, all is quiet on the coastal cliffs, except for the wind roaring in off the sea, wild and wet, carrying the scent of brine and seaweed.

I stand near the edge, wrapped in a too-fancy dress Phaedra stuffed me into just after dawn. The bodice is tight, leather and bone laced over a neckline that dips too low. Embroidered vines twist up the full skirts, and the split on one side is scandalously high. I'm dressed for a revel or a wedding, not a funeral.

My hair hangs loose over my shoulders, and the bruise on my cheek has ripened overnight into the same deep purple shade as the dress.

After last night's ordeal in the Hollow, guards shoved us into separate chambers. I saw Wyn's as we passed. It had no windows. Just a cot, a pitcher of water, and several locks that clicked hard from the outside where an armed guard stood to attention.

I hadn't seen Wyn again until minutes ago, when two winged fae brought me out to the edge of the sea cliffs. The pre-dawn sky hung low and heavy, and the ground was damp beneath my boots.

And now, here he is—standing barefoot, cloak loose around his shoulders, watching Landolin dig his grave.

Yes. Wyn's *grave*.

What a terrible, foolish bargain he made with Moiron.

Seven days and seven nights beneath the earth, cursed to sleep until... what? Some magical deity decides to *maybe* give him a happy ending? Or will it just be a cold and lonely death?

I know the rules. Wyn told me. Cursed by a mad mage back in his own realm to be buried alive, and only true love can dig him out, help him rise. All very poetic. All very "Faery" and insane.

And yet, still, here we are.

I want to shake him. Ask him why now. Why not wait? Why not find a better plan, one that doesn't end with him lying in a hole, sacrificed to a court, to a land he despises.

Why jump headfirst into the ground before the curse demands it?

But I already know the answer. It's written all over him, plain as the bruise on my face. He said it out loud. Bargained for my release.

Because Moiron threatened me.

Because Landolin is still deluding himself I can be trained to raise the dead.

Wyn offered himself in exchange for my safety because he thinks it will save me. That he can cheat fate by rushing into its open jaws and hoping for the best. As if dying early somehow counts as a win.

Idiot. Brave, beautiful *idiot*.

The wind whips hair over my eyes, and I tug it away, my heart pumping erratically, pounding out my dread as I count up from the number seven. Why seven? I have no idea. But it often feels like a safer place to start than one.

Landolin is shirtless as he shovels, because of course he is. His hair is damp from sea mist, his muscles flexing with every clean, mechanical lift of the spade. He's halfway through digging a rectangular hole in the rocky ledge, and the thud of each shovelful landing beside it grates against my spine.

Wyn watches him for a long time before speaking. "Why don't you use magic?" he finally asks. "Save yourself some energy."

Landolin doesn't stop digging. He just smirks. "That would be cheating."

A laugh bubbles up my throat, followed by a scream. Somehow, I manage to suppress both. In the distance, a wolf howls. Poor Ivor. He's still out there, probably pacing madly, trying to get to us.

Instead of launching myself on Landolin's back and tearing his black eyes out, I just stand there, my almost-bare legs freezing in the icy wind, casually watching Wyn's grave get dug like it's compost being turned for a tomato plot.

Eventually, the hole is finished. It's not particularly deep, which gives me a small sense of relief.

Landolin wipes the back of his hand across his mouth and steps away, spade slung casually over one shoulder. "You bargain poorly for a prince of Faery," he says to Wyn. "My father said she would be free to leave. He did *not* say our city walls would *let* her."

I turn sharply toward him. "What the hell does that mean?"

Before Landolin answers, Wyn shifts. One second he's fae, the next he's a wolf mid-lunge, teeth bared and fur bristling. The raw growl that rips from his chest makes me want to run in the other direction.

Landolin doesn't flinch.

A shadow lifts from the ground and crashes into Wyn in the middle of the air, slamming him sideways onto a boulder near the edge of the cliff. He hits the stone hard and drops but doesn't stay down.

Wyn snarls, scrambles up, and leaps again. Another shadow whips around his hind leg, yanks him mid-jump, and hurls him across the rocks.

This time, he lands as a man, not a wolf—naked, bleeding, and wheezing through his teeth.

"Stop," I breathe. "Please... don't hurt him."

A dark aura of power haloing Landolin, he stalks toward Wyn, his face a mask of cool detachment. "If you do this, Wynter. Go gently into the earth, then I'll protect her, make sure she lives. Treat her well. I vow it."

Wyn spits blood. "And if I don't?"

"She's bought and paid for," Landolin says. "My tribute. And I can do whatever I like with her."

Wyn pushes himself upright, one arm wrapped around his ribs. "She's *mine*."

Landolin's voice doesn't change. "And what difference does that make? The Hunt has claimed her *twice*. If she isn't the one who can solve my little problem, then I'll find other uses for her. Things you wouldn't like to imagine."

He looks at me then, cold and calculated, and my stomach spasms with fear.

"So tell me, Wynter," he drawls, "is it to be *her* blood on my marriage bed... or another human's?"

Wyn lunges again, this time half-crawling before collapsing at my feet. He drags himself to his knees, shaking. "She's not your mate, therefore, you can't claim her," he snarls. "You need permission. A human parent. A bargain."

Landolin's mouth quirks. "I can take whomever I like, if they have no living parent."

The sea crashes below, and the ruthless wind tears at our clothing. The elements don't care what happens here. Who dies or who lives. And neither does Landolin.

Footsteps crunch behind us.

I turn and watch Phaedra, the servant who brought me breakfast and dresses I didn't ask for, coming toward us. She walks with small shaky steps, her gaze fixed on the ground in front of her feet.

"I brought water," she says, setting a silver goblet beside Wyn. "And bandages. You'll want them... before the burial."

Wyn doesn't speak or acknowledge her.

Phaedra glances once at Landolin. Her voice drops lower. "You think yourself clean in this, but you should know that carrying out your father's wishes leaves a stain upon your fate."

Landolin's eyes narrow. "Careful, Phaedra. I suggest you don't say another word."

"I'm only a servant," she replies, all innocence. "No one cares or remembers what I say." Then she turns and walks away, the soft rustle of her skirts swallowed by the wind.

I wonder how she knew to bring bandages, and that Wyn is injured. Unless...

I glance at Landolin. "You told her to bring that stuff, didn't you?"

He doesn't look at me. Just brushes dirt from his hands like the conversation bores him. "Have you forgotten you're in a magical realm? In this court, it's a simple thing for our shadows to speak to each other."

"Just when I think you couldn't get any creepier," I say.

"On your socials," he shoots back, "you call yourself a Paranormal Communications Director. So I predict with time, you'll fit in very well at the Shade Court."

"That was a joke, so don't hold your breath," I mutter, wondering if it's a fae thing—cleaning wounds before a burial—or just particular to Wyn's curse.

Wyn lifts the cup and drinks, the water running down his chin, mixing with blood. He stands tall, naked just like the first time I saw him, but bruised and unsteady.

With horror flickering in his eyes, he looks at me. "Don't wait for me, Summer. Promise you'll leave. Find a way out."

I step closer. "Wyn. I'm not leaving without you. Seven days the curse says."

"Don't wait. But if you do, and I don't rise, make them honor the exact wording of the bargain. Moiron promised to let you leave this realm. That means you must be allowed to pass through the city walls."

"You don't have the right to give up on us like that," I say, fists clenched at my sides. "Whether I stay or not, it's my choice."

He gives me a broken smile. "Too late. I gave up last night when I let them lock the door. The whole point of the curse is to surrender. And it's *your* best chance for survival. So do it, Summer, surrender."

"Well, that's your decision. Mine might be different."

Wyn leans in close. "I thought we'd have more time," he murmurs, his voice raw, exhaustion etched into the lines around his mouth.

"We do," I whisper. "We have forever. In seven days, I'll be here."

He swallows hard, eyes flicking up toward Landolin, then back to me. "Take care. Do anything but let them hurt you."

"I'm not the one being buried alive, Wyn."

"I'd be buried a thousand times over if it would keep you safe, little sun."

My throat tightens. I grip his hand hard. "Don't you dare stay down there forever. I'll be forced to work on my non-existent necromancy skills to get you back again."

"I won't," he says, flashing those killer dimples. "I promise."

I clutch his face between my hands and kiss him fast and hard. His lips are cool, mouth warm. Trembling, he kisses me back like a drowning man clawing for air. Behind us, Landolin lets out a pained sigh.

Ignoring the Shade Prince, Wyn presses his forehead to mine. "I love you," he breathes. "If this ends here, I'll wait for you in the afterlife. Forever if that's what it takes. I'll never stop hoping, Summer, believing that I'll see you again."

"Careful. That sounds like you might end up being the new ghost in my bathroom mirror, hanging out with my mom. Why wish *that* fate upon yourself?"

"Why? Because I never breathed properly until I saw you. Never lived until I touched your hand for the first time. Never—"

"Okay, I get it. You can haunt my lingerie drawer anytime you like," I say with a sad smile. "I love you so much, Wyn. I'll come find you. No matter where you are. I promise."

My hands drop as Landolin steps forward.

Wyn turns toward the grave. He squeezes my hand once before letting go.

Landolin snorts and gestures to the empty pit. "I've made something special for you. Close your eyes."

Wyn sighs and looks up at the sky, shaking his head.

"I mean it. Close them, or I'll close hers."

Wyn obeys. When he opens his eyes, a pale white headstone rests at the top of the grave. The inscription reads: *R.I.P. Wynter Fionbharr, Prince of Mud.*

"Very funny," Wyn says.

"You should hear my other options... Here Lies Wynter, Beloved By Dirt, Feared By No One. Gone to Ground, Finally Where He Belongs. May He Decompose In Peace. So many I liked, but in the end, I went for simplicity."

"Good choice," mutters Wyn.

In the distance, near a wind-swept blackthorn tree, I catch movement in the corner of my eye—a low, dark shape pacing. A glint of orange eyes in the gloom. Ivor.

He's pinned behind a shimmering ribbon of ward magic etched into the ground, dark shadows crackling at his paws like static.

Ivor's ears are flat, tail rigid, muscles tight with fury. He doesn't bark or howl. He just watches, silent and murderous, as Wyn steps down into the dirt, as if he's willing him not to do it. As if he's ready to tear the throat out of every Shade Court fae to stop this from happening—if only he could.

Wyn lays down. No theatrics. No grand speech. Just a barefoot prince climbing into the carved-out earth like he's settling in for a relaxing morning nap.

Terror claws at my insides. My body freezes, and bile rises with the panic.

Landolin takes a small stone amulet from his belt, murmurs something in the grating tongue of the court, and a violet shimmer passes over the pit.

"Wyn, is he allowed to do that? What's he—"

"It's fine," says Landolin. "I'm protecting the grave from harm. Would you prefer wild creatures dig him up before his time?"

"Why do you care if they do?" I ask.

Landolin leans on the shovel, looking at me like I'm a fool. "Because if he doesn't stay there for seven days and seven nights, our land won't receive the full quota of Elemental magic he promised us. It won't be as strong." With a shrug, he begins to bury Wyn alive.

After two shovelfuls, Landolin stops. "Shift into your wolf," he says.

Wyn's fists clench over his thighs. "Why?"

"For the usual reason. *Because I said so*, you Elemental mutt."

Landolin knows Wyn won't have access to magic in his wolf form. He wants him weak. Helpless. Less likely to rise. Dead or not, as long as he's still in the grave after seven days, the land will capture Wyn's residual magic. Landolin likely doesn't care if Wyn survives.

"Look, if you do this for me, Wynter, I'll show the human the real truth of what happened that night with her parents."

"The truth?" I yelp. "If the images you showed me in the mirrors were a lie, why would I trust anything you show me now, you evil prick?"

"I cannot lie, so ask if it's the whole truth, and I'll have no choice but to admit it."

Wyn gives me a quick nod. "He's right, Summer. And you deserve to know the full story."

"Good," says Landolin. "But let's get your wounds dressed first. I was so eager to begin, I nearly forgot."

CHAPTER 39

Summer

His wounds now clean and bandaged, Wyn sits up in the shallow grave and summons a glamour—just dark leather pants and nothing else. He's now officially in a Leather and Abs competition with the Shade Prince.

"So this is what passes for a grave in your court?" Wyn mutters. "Not even six feet deep. I'm quite offended."

Landolin frowns. "That's all you have to say? No crying or pathetic begging for your life?"

Wyn shrugs. "I'm saving the theatrics for my resurrection. Hurry up and tell her what happened. I won't shift until you do."

Shadows lick the edges of Landolin's boots. "I promised to show you the truth," he says to me. "Are you willing to see it?"

I nod, swallowing a snow-globe sized lump in my throat.

"Good," he says. "Then come here."

His hand brushes my forehead, and my breath ices over in my chest.

The vision starts differently this time.

No mirrors. No slow pan of the bloodied kitchen tiles. No sense of floating horror as though I'm a ghost watching it all unfold. This time, I'm right there. In the scene, just like I was eight years ago.

Feet on the stairs. One hand on the rail. My voice humming a nothing-song under my breath.

I remember parts of that night so clearly. And I also remember not remembering the rest. It's such a weird sensation.

I step down into the kitchen and stop.

Chopped cheese and tomatoes sit on a board on the counter near the stove.

That's right, I'd gone upstairs to grab my phone before I finished putting my pizza together.

My mother lies on the floor, her robe soaked red, legs twisted at a horrible angle. My father kneels beside her, a knife clenched in one trembling hand.

His shoulders heave. He mutters her name over and over, like a spell to undo whatever's happened.

Then he hears me. Sees my fingers pressed over my gaping mouth.

"Summer," he gasps. "No—no, baby, wait—"

I scream.

He jolts onto his feet, the knife still in his hand.

"Listen to me," he pleads, his voice cracking. "It was an accident. She slipped. I didn't mean..."

He steps toward me. I back up. Feet skidding on the wet tiles until my shoulder hits the door frame.

"Please," he shouts, reaching for me. "You weren't supposed to see. No one was. I had no choice. I need money. I..."

He grabs me, his hand clamping down on my arm. The knife comes up. My father's eyes are wild.

And then...

Darkness explodes through the kitchen, and shadows swirl in like a hurricane. Figures made of night and fury tear my dad away from me. He hits the wall with a wet crunch. Then the blade slashes across his throat before clattering to the floor.

Screaming, I fall. Screaming, I crawl on my knees. Screaming, I watch through eyes as wide as dinner plates.

Landolin stands near the stove, surrounded by smoke and shadow creatures that don't belong in a kitchen full of pizza mess and unpaid bills.

In the vision, he doesn't speak. Just watches me as the scene starts to melt.

Blood dissolves like ink in water. My father merges with the black fog. My mother's body fades away.

All of it... the horror, the wrongness. All sucked into the shadows, and then gone.

Then I'm back on the cliffs, my knees in the dirt, and the sunrise has barely shifted a shade.

Landolin watches me cautiously, his arms folded.

"You saved me?" I whisper.

"I did."

"Why?"

"I'd been watching the house for a while. Watching *you*, and hoping you were the girl I'd been searching for." His voice softens. "I couldn't let your father take you away from us. From the Hunt."

"But... Detective Perez said there were no traces of the murderer left behind. My dad's prints on the knife, or on the walls... there were none."

Landolin grins. "All wiped away with a quick pass of my shadows."

"When you showed me the fake version of events, you said the Hunt killed them. I thought full-blooded fae couldn't lie."

"I said it was the Wild Hunt collecting the *dues* of the Raven Realm—which was you. I never said a word about who killed your parents. Visions shaped by magic can show whatever their wielder wants. Even lies."

Damn reality-twisting fae. Can't trust a single one of them—except for Wyn. But he's a halfling, so technically he doesn't count.

My dad. My *dad* did it. Now that's a total mind fuck. He was an asshole, sure. Didn't even know how to hug me properly—too wrapped up in himself, his booze, his get-rich-quick-then-go-broke schemes. But I never thought he'd try to kill me.

Or Mom.

It wasn't some crazed stranger. Not the fae, Landolin's shadows, or any kind of magic. The monster was already in the house, and he was my own flesh and blood.

My skin crawls as the Hunt's horn blows in the distance, long and loud. My heart hammers in my chest. Nausea rises, and I bend and empty my stomach off to the side.

Fuck. I remember everything now.

The Shade Court. The spinning. The endless dancing. Twirling until my legs buckled and I collapsed because no one would help me stop. Then the laughter, like hyenas hovering over a fresh kill, all cruel stares and taunting grins.

I remember the sphere-lit halls of the Shade Court castle. The seven pastel moons. My skirts soaking in spilled wine. My wrists raw where the faeries' nails scraped my skin.

And then another Court. The bronze and metal hall. More endless dancing and a girl with red hair and silver eyes. Merri. Wyn's sister, who rescued me from the Merits, took me back to her birth home of green and gold—the beautiful Seelie palace.

And Wyn. I remember him from before, at his home in Talamh Cúig. Younger, less guarded, and always hovering in the background. Never teasing me, like the other fae, just... watching. Eyes fixed on me like he was reading his favorite book.

The whole time I was there, waiting for the thrall spell to weaken enough for their High Mage to finally remove it, never once did he touch me cruelly or laugh when I fell. And one time, I remember someone stepping between me and the guards and guiding me back to a comfortable, luxurious room, tucking me in safe.

It was him. My Wyn.

Flashing green eyes and a freckled scowl. A prince with dirt under his nails and fists clenched at his sides, always present, helping me rise.

"You were there," I whisper, staring down at him. "Talamh Cúig. The Elemental Kingdom. You were the Winter Prince. The one I knew I had to wait for."

The tortured expression on his face, the sweet silver patch of hair falling over his left eye—they break my heart. His throat bobs, but he says nothing.

"At the time, I thought I'd imagined you," I say. "Made you up to help me survive."

But I hadn't. He'd been real.

Finally, he gives me a dimpled smile. "Actually, my official title is Prince of Earth, not the Winter Prince."

Landolin looks down at Wyn. "You promised to shift."

Holding my gaze, Wyn whispers, "I love you. Never forget it."

Then, slowly, painfully, his limbs begin to contort. Fur ripples across his skin. Bones crack. I flinch as his body warps and twists, unable to look away. And then he's gone, and in his place stands a great dark-furred wolf, tail low, head bowed.

My beautiful Hank.

He leaps out, legs shaky, and limps into my lap.

I wrap my arms around his warm body, burying my face in his ruff, sobbing and breathing in the scent of earth, pine, home.

He licks my cheek once. That's all. Then he pulls away and pads back into the grave, curling up tight as if he's ready for a nap. Resigned to his fate.

Landolin picks up the shovel.

My breath saws in and out, short and ragged. "Landolin? There has to be another way."

"There isn't," he says, and begins burying my beloved wolf one shovelful at a time.

Wyn holds steady, doesn't grimace or blink, his eyes fixed on mine. In case he can hear me, I send him the same thought over and over.

I love you. I love you. I love you.

I bite my lip so hard I taste blood, but I don't cry. Not yet. Not while he's still watching me, which he does—right up until the dirt covers his eyes and swallows him whole.

The wind gusts over me, tearing my cloak from my shoulders, and Ivor lets out a long, mournful howl.

Landolin brushes his hands off and looks at me. "You should rest before you begin your vigil."

I don't answer.

He studies me a moment longer, then says, "You'll be at his side the whole seven days, I assume. Good. If he wakes early, know this, I'll be there. So don't run. Wait for me to arrive."

"Why the hell would I do that?" I snap, then turn on my heel before I say something I'll really regret.

Alone, I walk down the hill toward the castle, the wind dragging at my gown, the bruise on my cheek throbbing with every step.

I want to drop to the ground and bawl my eyes out, but I don't stumble. I don't fall.

I won't let myself. Not until the earth gives Wyn back to me.

CHAPTER 40

Summer

The wind is colder on the eighth night. Salt spray lingers in the air, stinging my chafed lips. It hasn't stopped howling since the pathetic excuse for a sun disappeared behind the jagged horizon hours ago, and neither have I.

I've barely slept. The stone bench the fae gave me to sleep on hasn't been used. If I lie down at all, I lie over Wyn, begging him to come back to me.

The grass around his grave has long since flattened beneath my pacing steps. I've worn the edges of my boots thin, but I'll never stop. Never leave. Not until he wakes.

Phaedra comes at dusk and dawn, always silent, leaving food I hardly touch—flatbread, goat cheese, figs soaked in red wine, and fresh water. Once, she left tea steeped in rosemary and another herb bitter enough to sting my nose. I didn't touch it. I was too afraid it might be poisoned.

Day and night, I talk to Wyn, pleading with him to wake, my voice low and cracked with exhaustion. Sometimes I sing songs or tell him silly stories, like the time I told a Gravenshade tour group the ghost in the drawing room hated loud voices. A total lie. But five minutes later, a guy sneezed, and the chandelier fell. No one's dared to speak above a whisper in there since.

I tell him every stupid ghost story I can think of. I bargain with gods I don't believe in. And sometimes I just sit here and count.

Wyn's been buried longer than the curse required. Almost eight nights. Does that mean he's already dead? Gone forever?

I've nearly given up hope of seeing him again, and the stress of not knowing if I ever will feels like having my heart carved out through my ribs with a blunt knife. It's agonizing.

Landolin came yesterday, on the seventh day. Didn't announce himself, of course. Just stepped out of the shadows like he'd opened a door in the air, then sighed like he was disappointed to find me still here.

"Come inside, Summer," he told me. "You've done enough grieving for several lifetimes."

I didn't respond. I just stared at him over Wyn's grave.

"You've made your point," he went on. "You're loyal, tragic, and stubborn as a rotted root. No comment? Fine, then. I'll make a blood vow for your safety, if that will help you walk away. Seven days have passed. He's gone. At least come inside and live in comfort. Unharmed. I promise the Hunt won't touch you."

"Why do you need a girl with necromancy skills?" I'd asked.

He smiled like he thought I was daft, then told me the less I knew, the safer I'd be.

I told him to go to hell. Told him I'd rather be buried alive with Wyn than be protected by someone who plans to collect human girls like trophies.

And then I turned my back on him and didn't say another word.

He stood there for a while, watching. Maybe expecting me to change my mind and follow him back to the castle.

But I didn't.

Tonight, the clouds hang heavier than usual, stretched low over the sea like a wad of wet cotton. The moons have vanished behind them, and I feel lonelier for it.

I'm so tired of waiting. Of hoping. Of not knowing if there's something I should be doing to bring Wyn back to me. Maybe there's a key to this, and I'm meant to chant something special. Or dance naked under the seven moons while pledging eternal devotion to the Shade Court gods.

For all I know, I was supposed to recite some ancient spell at midnight on the third day, and now I've missed the window and Wyn's just... stuck in there forever because no one gave me the curse's cheat sheet.

The wind picks up, and I shiver, wrapping my cloak around my stomach. Time to start pacing again. It's the only thing that keeps me warm. I brace my hand against the ground to stand, and something sharp bites into my palm. A broken root or a splintered stone.

But just before I push upright, a gray haze at the edge of my vision stops me. I close my eyes, then open them, relaxing my focus.

A translucent figure kneels beside the gravestone. Then another. And another. Three ghosts, half-formed and flickering like candlelight in the breeze. They say nothing, but I feel them, the weight of their stares and the hum of their presence heavy against my skin. One of them reaches toward my wrist, and the moment her finger grazes my wound, a shiver races through me.

The message is clear.

Give him your blood.

Of course. It's always tears or blood that does the trick in the old tales. Or your first born. Unfortunately, I don't have one of those to give away.

I nod my understanding, and the spirits vanish as my blood wells up fast. I let it drip into the soil, whispering a silent thank you.

One.

Two.

Three drops.

Nothing... Nothing... Nothing...

And then the earth stirs.

At first, it's barely a tremble, a slight undulation of the surface of the grave.

Then something breaks through the soil.

It isn't a wolf's leg or a paw. It's a man's. Or a fae's to be correct. Dirt-streaked, strong, perfectly formed. And Wyn's!

I scream. I laugh. I sob.

I'm on my knees before I know it, clawing at the grave with both hands, my nails breaking.

"Wyn? *Please.* Please be well. Don't be a zombie and eat me."

Fingers curl around mine, and I dig faster, frantic, until his face breaks through, filthy, gasping, and so, so beautiful. The most wonderful sight I've ever seen.

Something shifts beneath my hands—not just Wyn's body wriggling out of the dirt. The land is responding to his rising.

A deep, resonant pulse rolls through the soil like the heartbeat of a giant living underground. The beaten grass around the grave glows white, then shoots upright, thriving. Soil splits in jagged lines that shine a bright gold color, and stones and crystals burst through them, circling Wyn once before clattering down again.

Wyn moans, and a low hum builds in the air. The sound of roots twisting and rocks moving below the surface grates against my ears. The air is thick with magic, raising tiny hairs on my arms.

What the hell is happening?

And then like a dam wall finally cracking, the Elemental magic pours out of him, a flow of golden energy rippling from his mouth. It feels warm and nurturing, not destructive or frightening.

The land drinks it in.

The soil crackles where it touches Wyn's skin, absorbing power like it's starving. Vines twitch beneath the surface, then burst upward in quick spirals before crumbling into ash. The stone behind his back glows like molten silver, sputtering, before cooling again.

Wyn's breathing roughens, and his eyes flash open. They're too bright, too green, power lighting him up from within. "The land's taking some of my magic," he rasps. "It's also... binding part of me to it."

I touch his arm. His skin's hot, and his pulse is galloping.

"Can you stop it?"

He shakes his head. Dust rises in a wave from his shoulders, and the scent of petrichor and crushed rock fills the air.

"No. The curse is broken... but I'm still not entirely free." His breath stutters, and he grabs my wrist to steady himself, and then a narrow spiral of dirt coils up from the ground, wrapping around his forearm like a rope.

The magic flares gold, green, then an unusual earthy color—like moss painted yellow—as it sears into his skin. Wyn gasps and jerks once in shock.

When the glowing light fades, burned into the inside of his left forearm is a raised, branching scar that resembles the root system of a tree, deep and permanent.

"Shit," he mutters, his fingers tracing the pattern.

"What is it? Does it hurt?"

"No. It's a brand. The land took what it wanted, but it's marked me."

The wind cuts through the cliffside whipping waves of dark hair over his face.

"But what does that mean? Can they track you now?" I ask. "Will you be able to leave?"

He doesn't answer for a beat. Then, "I don't know. But I guess we'll soon find out."

"Have they taken all of your magic?" I ask. "Left you powerless?"

He frowns and conjures his usual glamour, the familiar black leathers forming over his skin. Smiling, he pulls me down onto his lap, and I breathe him in deep. Somehow, he still smells like clean earth and warm male.

Not that it matters. As long as he's alive, he could reek like mold and cow dung, and I wouldn't give a damn.

CHAPTER 41

Summer

"Wyn, you came back to me."

"Summer," he rasps. "You did it."

I throw my arms around his neck and try to crawl inside his skin. He's shaking, covered in dirt, but he's alive. He's alive.

"*We* did it. Together." I can't breathe, can barely speak. "I thought... I thought I'd lost you."

He holds me so tight it hurts. "You didn't. You won't. Not ever. I love you so much, Summer. I always have."

I pull back, blinking through tears. "Are you sure it's love? I'm a human who's been a thrall to two courts of Faery. How can you love someone so unworthy? My own mother didn't even like me, and my dad was possibly trying to kill me."

He flinches, pushing me back a little and scanning my face.

"Unworthy?" he says, wiping the tears from my cheeks. "Impossible. Nothing in life has meant as much to me as you do. From the moment I first saw you, I watched every twirl, every smile and frown, the slightest move you made. I was always there, Summer. All I wanted was to be by your side. If your mother can't see how perfect you are, that's her failure, not yours."

He takes a slow, steadying breath. His voice lowers. "You were placed under a spell, vile and temporary... but I was the one who was forever enchanted—by *you*."

"You didn't believe I could save you from the curse," I whisper. "If you had, you would've followed me straight to the Shade Court. What took you so long to get here?"

"I kind of told Merri I would never tie my fate to yours. That I'd keep you safe. Far away from Faery. Away from me. I needed her permission to come here so I could try to get you out. And let me tell you, it took some convincing."

I stiffen. "She thought she was doing us a favor by keeping us apart?"

"Precisely. Merri sometimes sees fragments of the future. Years ago, she saw me buried. Dying alone."

I swallow the lump forming in my throat. "She told you that, and you came here anyway."

"I would've crawled here if I had to. Anything for you, little sun. Simply name it."

We sit for a while, just breathing together. Then the questions rattling through my mind break free.

"How will we get out of here? The city walls are warded to prevent escape. We're probably stuck. I need to get back to Zylah. I can't bear to think of her wandering around Gravenshade alone, believing I'm dead."

Wyn hugs me tighter. "There'll be a portal in the city somewhere. We just have to find it." Then he says, "Summer... I heard things while I was down there in the dirt."

I brace my palms on his cheeks. "Were you conscious?"

"Sometimes. Not often. But when I was awake, the earth whispered secrets. It confirmed the Wild Hunt was stolen from its rightful court by a wager barbed with a trick. King Yurendyl lost the Hunt in a bet with King Moiron. Then Moiron bound Landolin to it with blood, and it's slowly killing him. Maybe that's why the Hunt needs a human necromancer. To break his curse. Or resurrect him when it does kill him."

I blink. "So the Hunt doesn't even belong to the Shade Court?"

"No. Once, it was bound by ancient, strict rules. And now it's corrupted, riding whenever its master sees fit. The Hunt is a weapon. But Landolin was never supposed to wield it. It also wasn't meant to be bound to a single soul. Not for this long. It's eating him alive."

Slow, deliberate claps break the stillness behind me. I twist at my waist to look around.

Landolin steps out of the mist, long sword dragging behind him, its tip rasping against the grass.

"Well, well. The Earth Prince returns. Did you give my regards to the worms?" he drawls. "Let me guess. The curse was broken by a single drop of true love's blood? Or was it seven thousand of her bitter tears?"

"Does it matter?" I ask, standing stiffly and climbing out of the shallow grave. My joints crack from kneeling too long. "Wyn has done what you asked and stuck to the bargain. The curse released him. He's free. So let us go."

"A demanding little creature, isn't she?" Landolin muses as Wyn lurches onto his feet, then toward the Shade Prince.

Landolin lunges forward, sword angled toward me. "Right now, you're extremely weak, Elemental," he says to Wyn. "I could kill her with a snap of my fingers. How would you stop me?"

"I likely couldn't," Wyn admits, standing tall, his face pale. "You have all the power here. As you said, I'm diminished. But If you hurt her, and I survived, I would track you. Hunt you. Torture you through every century of your miserable life. There would be no peace between our lands. My uncle, the king, would see to it. I would dedicate my life to your unhappiness. Don't think I won't."

Landolin laughs, the sound bitter and unpleasant as his shadows swirl around his scowl. "I believe you." He shrugs. "If you vow to never reveal what the grave told you, perhaps I will let you go."

Wyn bows and offers his hand to Landolin. "Of course, we both vow to never disclose to any other fae, person, or being what I learned while buried. Do you agree, Summer?"

I repeat the words of the promise Wyn made as he beckons me closer.

With no warning, he unsheathes a knife from his belt, slashes it lightly across his palm, Landolin's, and then mine. We press our hands together in turn, sealing our vow in blood.

"Good. I don't want a never-ending war with your court and your sister's court when I'm finally crowned king. Especially when Summer isn't the one I need after all... though she certainly smelled like it both times the Hunt took her. I am sorry for the pain I've caused. Perhaps one day you'll forgive my errors. My missteps."

Wyn's eyes narrow. "Explain something to me, Landolin. If you thought she was important all those years ago, why sell her to the mage from the Merit Court?"

Landolin's smirk fades. "My father sold her to torture me. It was a loan. She was always meant to return. But your sister interfered, and then we lost her."

I step forward, fury trembling through my limbs. Wyn doesn't stop me. He knows better.

"You call my kidnappings *missteps*?" I snap. "You treated me like your least favorite toy. You refused to let me go—out of jealousy, arrogance—and you were never even sure you'd stolen the right person. You let me believe I killed my own parents. You stole *everything* from me."

"Everything?" he says, his shadows winding up his limbs. "Now that's a lie. There was so much more we could have taken from you, Summer Brady. You were meant to be my bride. But your body was never assaulted. I made certain of that."

"Oh, wonderful. Should I thank you for your restraint? You destroyed my sanity. Robbed me of my self-worth. Made me believe I was capable of terrible, disgusting violence. You're a monster."

Landolin's expression hardens. "How soon you forget, human. I saved you from your father. My own father is a collector of your kind, and it is my duty to retrieve what he is owed. Promises were made prior to that night by your mother, but naive mortals never actually believe the Hunt will claim their dues. But we always do. King Moiron insists upon it, especially if the human might prove useful to his son and heir."

"And that's you," says Wyn, his voice low.

"Yes. This conversation has put me in a bad mood. Even so, I will give you leave to find your way back to Gravenshade and this Zylah person who waits for you."

Nausea rips through my gut at Landolin's revelation. My mother didn't just stop caring, she sold me to the fucking fae. How am I not a monster too, born of a murderer and a cold-hearted narcissist?

"Zylah?" I blurt, suddenly realizing that Landolin probably heard every word Wyn and I said while he was lurking around after Wyn clawed his way out of the earth.

"There was a reason I positioned your grave in this exact spot, Wynter," Landolin says. "I suggest you think upon it. Take your human and go before your sister and her husband come to retrieve you and turn my city to ash. Act swiftly if you wish to escape the shadows."

He gives us a mock salute, then vanishes in a coil of black smoke that folds in on itself, leaving a silver glowing outline in his place and an absence of smirking, arrogant fae.

I stare at the empty space. "Where the hell did he go?"

Wyn shakes his head, his freckles stark against his pale face. "He opened a portal. I don't know for sure, but I have an idea where he's gone. I really hope I'm wrong."

A howl sounds as Ivor breaks through the magical barrier, which dissolved along with the Shade Prince, and barrels toward us. He leaps up as Wyn crouches to greet him, licking his face.

Wyn strokes Ivor's fur, then straightens, eyes fixed on the horizon over the sea. "Are Zylah's parents dead?"

My heart stutters. "Yes. Car accident. She's practically lived at my house since grade school. I don't think my mom and dad ever noticed how often she stayed over. Her uncle lived a block away, and she hated him. Why do you ask?"

"Shit." Wyn rubs a hand over his mouth. "There's a rumor about how the Wild Hunt find their brides. By scent. Zylah's would be all over your home. To Landolin, you probably smell similar. It wasn't you he needed. It was her."

"But why couldn't Landolin and the Hunt see her? Why fix on me instead?"

His jaw tightens. "Yeah. That's what I can't figure out. Maybe something's shielding her—magically, I mean. We have to get back to Gravenshade Hall."

Wyn's eyes skim over me, then he summons a silver-hilted dagger and threads it through a black-studded belt. "You'll need this." He buckles it around my waist, then his mouth twitches like he's hiding a smirk. "Try not to stab me with it."

"Sorry. Can't promise I won't," I reply, my breath catching. "But I'll do my best not to fatally wound you. Where are we going?"

Wyn nods toward the cliff's edge. "Down there. It's the portal Landolin left open on purpose."

My stomach drops. "What?"

He grips my hand and calls Ivor over. "Do you trust me?"

I nod, and he tugs me forward. Then, together, we tumble off the cliff into the dark, churning sea below.

CHAPTER 42

Wynter

We crash through the surface of Lake Grenlynn, stumble onto the bank, and push up the hill, soaked to the bone and shivering. Ivor bursts out beside us, shaking water from his black coat, and immediately trots ahead, his ears pricked.

As we run, the woods claw at our clothes, branches snatching like the Hunt's own hands, trying to drag us back—back to the lake, where Summer nearly died when she was nine.

The hall rises through the trees, eerie and regal, its dark towers silhouetted in the dying light of the sun. Orange and gold bleed into purple as the day folds into itself. It's beautiful, the kind of twilight that makes predators bold and fools feel calm and safe.

"It's not even proper night here yet," says Summer.

"Nope. Realm jumping does a number on your body clock. You'll feel it later. Seven hells, I really hope we get to sleep in your comfortable bed tonight."

"How would you know what my bed's like? You haven't slept in it yet."

Shit. Guilt hits me hard. "I may have tried it one time when you were at work."

I stop just under the canopy of an old willow tree, dragging Summer against me. "Landolin's definitely here. Can you feel it? There's a smoky scent in the air from his magic, too."

"No," Summer says, tugging her impractical purple gown up her shoulders as she scans the decaying hall through the trees. "You're sure?"

"Yeah. Look." I nod toward the markings in the grass near the steps around an old fountain, half-melted into the soil. "His shadow magic leaves scorch marks. They're recent, too. That fucker set the portal to dump us in another city."

"Wait... he was trying to send us somewhere else?" She glances back at the shimmer hovering over the lake, already dissolving. "How do you know that? And how did you even change its course?"

I shrug. "I wasn't absolutely certain. But the portal felt wrong, not anchored by you and Gravenshade like it normally is. I was getting images of a vast red wilderness. Canyons."

Summer stares at me. "And you just... rerouted it?"

"I felt the shift, grabbed onto a thread from our last time inside it, and pulled us through Lake Grenlynn. It was easy. The lake wanted you back."

"Man, Landolin's diabolical." Her hand tightens in mine. "What's he planning?"

"My best guess? He's here to confirm what he suspects about Zylah. Probably can't take her without the Hunt, though."

"Shit." Silence stretches between us, then she asks, "So what do we do?"

I scan the Hall's upper windows. "We stay low and quiet. Don't draw attention until we know where he is and what we're walking into."

She gives a nervous laugh. "We're soaked and wearing formal wear. Not exactly blending in."

"Don't worry about blending in," I say, jaw clenched. I wave a hand, and the stones beneath us radiate heat, drying our clothes in seconds. "We just need to be fast."

Inside the manor, all is quiet. Our shadows stretch behind us like dark phantoms as we walk quickly but silently through the house.

The lamps flicker, highlighting the dust motes floating in the dimming dusk. Every creak underfoot threatens to give us away.

We pause outside the dining room. I motion for Summer to wait, listening. One beat. Two. Three.

Then we hear it. A low, familiar voice that makes my skin crawl. A second voice answers, light and breathy with fear. Boots hit hardboards, then there's the sound of scuffling movements.

Summer grips my arm. I nod once. It's definitely him. She stiffens beside me as we press ourselves further into the shadows, my muscles coiled, barely holding the wolf inside me at bay.

We slip into the room, Ivor padding at my heel with a low growl rumbling in his chest. I silence him with a single look.

The once luxurious space is in disarray, scrolled velvet chairs torn and set in a semi-circle around the hearth, a chandelier dangling askew.

We crouch behind an overturned sideboard near the entrance and watch the Shade Prince herd Summer's housemate into the bay-window alcove, the last of the sunset creating an orange halo around her hair.

Landolin stalks across the floor, circling Zylah. His expression is hungry, admiring, like he's just found the final piece of a puzzle he's spent centuries chasing. Perhaps he has.

Marie, the ghost maid, hovers above them wringing her spectral hands, her expression anguished. Landolin definitely sees her—his eyes keep flicking upward, scanning her—but he pretends otherwise. Zylah stands stiff and defiant, fists clenched at her sides. Her face is pale but furious, and when Landolin speaks, she pushes her glasses up her nose and bares her teeth in a silent snarl.

His voice is no louder than a whisper as he drives her out of the alcove and back toward the old fireplace, where soot blackens the brick and a shattered mirror reflects the room in broken pieces.

Summer leans in close, voice barely audible. "Why her?"

"Because he thinks she can bring dead things back to life," I murmur. "Like *he* might be soon."

Thanks to Landolin's father, the Hunt's blood bond is probably killing the prince slowly.

A sudden skittering sound breaks the tense moment, a clatter of claws on wood. From the dark hallway, Ollie, Summer's fierce, hairless cat, slinks into view, his tail held high like a banner of disdain.

He's followed by at least three more of Gravenshade's felines, their eyes shining black in the lamplight. Ollie pads straight up to Landolin and, with all the regal entitlement of a creature who's never feared a godsdamned thing in its life, rubs his flank against the prince's boot.

"Your name is like a blade slashed across my chest," Landolin says, ignoring the cat and drawing out each word like a lover's kiss. "*Zyyylahhh.* It's a quiet sigh, then the start of a song that continues for eternity." He smiles with pure glee. "Mistress of dead and broken things—owls, bats, foxes, and loons. All stitched together beneath your tender, trembling hands. *You're* the one I've been searching for. The one the Hunt couldn't see. *You.* Somehow hidden right under my nose for all these years."

Raising her palm, Zylah glares at him. "Sorry, speak to the hand. I've been warned not to talk to monsters."

His smile only deepens. "Oh, humans are fond of saying that, but you'll warm up to me eventually. And what makes you think I'm a monster? We've only just met."

"You have to be the reason Summer disappeared. *Both* times. What happened to her? I want her back. Now."

Landolin tilts his head, intrigued. "Why do you believe I had anything to do with that?"

Zylah's eyes narrow. "Because one of my birds started screaming your name the day Summer vanished and hasn't stopped the entire week she's been gone."

He blinks. "Excuse me?"

"Week?" Summer whispers. "I've been gone more like two weeks."

"Time works differently in Faery," I say. "Be quiet."

"My taxidermy," Zylah says, chin lifting. "Sometimes the animals I restore... I can hear them talk. That raven... he wouldn't shut up. Said the Hunter took the girl, wrapped her in shadows."

"What name did it speak exactly?" asks the prince.

"Ravenseeker. First, I thought it was just noise in my head. Thought I was losing my mind. But I knew Summer would never run away again. She'd never leave me here alone without telling me where she was going."

Landolin's expression sharpens, hungry eyes glittering. "Ah. So the bodies of the dead can speak to you. This makes so much sense. Confirms you're the one the Hunt *should* have taken in the first place."

Purring loudly, Ollie climbs Landolin's boot and sinks his teeth into his thigh. The Shade prick curses and jerks his leg as shadow tendrils burst from his body in all directions.

The cats scatter with yowls, darting behind the crumbling hearth and then into the dining bay. One of the shadows licks up the wall right in front of us, too close.

Landolin turns his head, eyes narrowing. Ollie darts forward and snarls, drawing the prince's attention away from us. A spear-shaped shadow shoots out from his extended palm, the impact sending the cat flying across the room.

My hand tightens on Summer's thigh, holding her in place. She flinches at the pressure. "Fuck," I whisper. "This is bad."

"We have to do something," she says, her voice shaky as her eyes flash toward me, wide and bright with panic.

Ollie races around the room's perimeter, behind the sideboard, then launches himself into Summer's arms. Landolin turns sharply and strides toward us, a bank of shadows tossing the furniture that shelters us aside with a single swipe of his hand.

"What the fuck are you two doing here?" he snarls.

"Heard you were having a party," I say. "Sounded a lot better than cliff diving in canyons."

Boom. Smug wolf-boy 1, angry Shade Prick 0.

"Well. Don't you two look wonderful in your court finery," he drawls, a chaos of gold swirling in his black irises. "Disheveled, yes, but far too polished for this crumbling old carcass of a house. Would you like to be sent back to the Raven Realm, where you'll fit in better?"

"Tempting, but no thanks," says Summer as Landolin draws his blade.

I shove onto my feet and drag Summer up with me. Zylah yelps as she lays eyes on us, storming over and grabbing hold of Landolin's arm. "Hey! Look at me. I'm the one you're here to hassle. Leave them alone."

He shrugs her off and stalks closer to us.

Magic pulses in my veins, tugging at the earth beneath us, and the floorboards tremble in response.

Landolin doesn't flinch as Zylah plants herself between him and Summer. The gleam in his eyes says he finds it amusing, enjoys it, which only makes her stand taller.

"I said back off, goth Thranduil," she snaps.

I shift forward, ready to attack, but then Zylah grabs Landolin's arm again, twisting it with startling precision before dropping her weight in a movement so fast and fluid it almost looks like magic. He actually stumbles. She follows with a sharp jab of her elbow to his throat and attempts to flip him over her hip like she's been battling fae princes her whole life.

Her moves are raw and messy. But they work.

Landolin hits the floor with a grunt, shocking the smugness off his face.

I stare, briefly stunned. Some elite fae warriors spend years perfecting moves like that, and Zylah does it wearing a strange hoodie with sequined bat wings.

"I've had just about *enough* of being manhandled by undead weirdos, thanks," she says, hands on her hips.

Landolin stays down longer than he needs to. Smiling. Studying her. "I'm not dead, love. I'm immortal. Which you must admit is a whole lot sexier."

Recovering from the shock of watching the deranged Landolin-and-Zylah show, I summon a ball of earth magic, but Landolin moves first, and the room erupts in chaos.

His blade swings toward me, a blur of shadow magic trailing behind it like smoke. I raise a wall of stone from the ground that crashes through floorboards with a thrust of my arm. His blade hits the wall, sparks flaring. I punch a spike of earth through from beneath his feet, but he leaps, cloak flaring like wings.

He lands hard, then sweeps his arms wide. The shadows rise with him, clawing and ferocious. One tendril lashes my shoulder, the pain burning like a firebrand. Another tangles around my ankle. I wrench free and slam both fists to the floor, calling to the magic down deep.

Instantly, it answers.

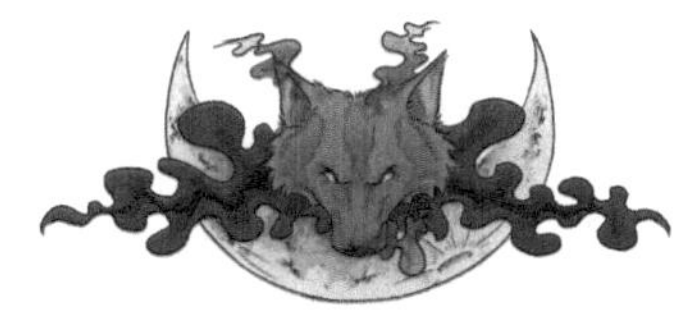

CHAPTER 43

Wynter

Stone beneath the house shatters, a fault line cracking the room, then a tree root thick as a man's torso rips through the floorboards, striking out like a whip.

Marie suddenly swoops low over the fray, screeching like a nightmare. Her form blurs as she hurtles through the largest shadow tendril wrapping around my leg, disrupting it with a burst of white light. The tendril recoils and dissipates. I flash her a grateful look, and she nods once and charges toward Zylah, attempting to use her translucent form to shield her.

Landolin dances back, but his shoulder clips the giant root, and he staggers, a snarl ripping from his throat. He condenses a bolt of shadows into a blade and hurls it. I dodge, but it skims across my ribs, scorching flesh. Pain flares, sharp and hot, but I stay on my feet. No time to flinch. No time to bleed.

As we circle each other, I wrench a thin wall of stone up between us. Landolin melts it with a ball of smoke so dark that it burns like pitch. Heat slams into me, blistering the air.

Fuck.

My whole body aches with exhaustion. Landolin's power isn't fading fast enough. It shouldn't even be holding this long, not without the Hunt to anchor it to the mortal realm. Whatever he's doing to keep it going, I hope it burns out soon.

"Wyn, be careful," Summer yells. I register her voice, but I can't look away from Landolin. Not now.

He surges forward, and we collide. "Try leading with your blade, not your ego," I grunt, shoving him back. "It's usually more effective."

Earth meets shadow as I drive jagged spikes up through the floor, and he counters with knives of black wind. The ceiling groans, then gives way. A chandelier crashes between us, spraying glass shards and dust.

He grins through bloodied teeth. "You're nothing but a self-righteous, prancing, Seelie bag of moss and mud, Wynter. And I'm bound to the most powerful force in the realms."

"Good for you," I say. "But I'm guessing you'll still bleed if I rip your throat out."

I drive my heel into the floor. Vines lash out, binding his arms. I tackle him onto the wall. We grapple, and he head butts me.

Landolin snarls something guttural, and I spit out blood and grin. "Sorry. I don't speak Old Dorthadian. Your tone reeks of desperation, though. That much is clear. How can I help send you back to that shithole you came from?"

"Fuck you, Wynter Fionbharr." He takes shadow form and slips through my grasp, every strike I make like hacking at fog.

But that doesn't stop me from chasing him, punching him. Over and over.

Finally, Landolin falters, flickering in and out of his material form as a root punches up through the floor and coils around his throat.

"You're losing, Huntless mutt," I growl.

Zylah ducks behind an overturned table, panting. Her eyes are wide, but her expression is furious. "Behind his right knee," she yells. "That's where the dead raven told me his curse was bound!"

So the grave whispers were true. And it's all tied to his father binding him to the Hunt—his greatest power and the very thing that's eating him alive.

Knife in hand, Summer doesn't hesitate. She sprints forward, ducking under a swipe of Landolin's blade that was meant for me, slashes and misses. Ivor lunges next, teeth bared, aiming for the prince's side, but he sails straight through him. Snarling, my wolf snaps at the shadowy haze, furious and confused.

While Landolin's focus is on Ivor, Summer drops low and crawls across the floor, her dagger glinting in what little light is left in the room. Then she surges up and drives the blade into the back of his leg.

The scream he lets out must erase any doubt Zylah ever had that he's human.

Dark blood gushes from Landolin's wound, a hiss sounding as it hits the air. He spins, wild with pain, and his shadows backhand Summer so hard she flies across the room.

Her cry rips through my gut, and everything inside me goes still... then shatters.

I roar her name and slam both hands to the ground. The floor splits open beneath Landolin, vines, roots, and jagged stone, surging up to seize him, dragging him down.

He thrashes, flickering between fae and shadow, screaming in a language older than time. Power shudders through the walls, brittle stone groaning beneath its weight.

"Enough," he bellows. "This solves nothing. *Ends* nothing. The Hunt is more powerful than the both of us. And it *will* be satisfied, Wyn. There's nothing either of us can do to stop it."

With a final, pulse of dark magic, he tears free from the vines, his body snapping back into its solid form again. His gaze lands on Zylah, and there's something reverent, almost worshipful, in his gaze.

"Soon," he says. "You'll come to me. You won't have a choice."

Then he dissolves into shadow, disappearing, and silence crashes down on our shoulders. A long moment passes before anyone dares to move.

Zylah draws in air like someone surfacing from deep water. Her shoulders tremble, but she's still on her feet. Her gaze darts to where Landolin disappeared, then to Summer, then to me. Voice thin but firm, she says, "He's not done. Whatever that was... it's not the end of it for me, is it?"

Marie hovers near the mantel, pale and shimmering. Ivor whines softly, then settles next to Summer, eyes fixed on the trail of ash on the floor as if he half-expects Landolin's shadows to rise again.

I kneel beside her, checking her pulse, her breathing, panic vibrating against my ribs. She's alive. Shaken. But alive.

The ghost girl drifts closer and bows her head, her mouth working silently as she wrings her hands.

"Thank you, Marie," Summer says with a soft smile. "For always being here when I need you. If not for your friendship, I wouldn't have survived this house, or my parents." She pauses, then adds, "Go on. Rest now. You must be tired from staying in the mortal realm so long and screaming like a howler monkey."

Marie nods, her glow dimming as she floats toward the shattered chandelier. She vanishes into the rafters, taking the last of the light with her. I don't say anything. None of us do.

The five cats trail after us as we make our way to the library. We light a fire in the hearth, and as shadows flicker across the walls, we watch them warily, Ivor's growls rumbling in his chest.

Zylah drops onto a threadbare armchair with Ollie in her lap and lets out a shaky breath. "Okay," she says. "So… just to recap, we were attacked by a shadow prince, one of my poorly stuffed birds might be psychic, and your cat is a tiny, hairless demon with excellent timing." She pauses. "Not saying I'm jealous, but my orange boy just screams at the ceiling and knocks over the bottles of embalming fluid on my workbench."

Summer lets out a breathy, half-crazed laugh. "Ollie's a menace. But he's my very own hairless menace."

Right on cue, the cat yowls and launches into her arms, and she buries her face in his wrinkled skin.

"He's a hero," Zylah says, cleaning her glasses. "Naked, rage-fueled, and deeply judgmental. Basically my kind of guy."

Even I crack a grin at that… before my brain catches up to reality. Zylah may not fully realize it yet, but there's a target on her back. A fucking big one.

"I wouldn't say that too loudly," Summer says, stroking Ollie's tufted head. "You might call Landolin back with that kind of talk, Zy."

Zylah's smile fades, her gaze fixing on Summer. "Seriously though, I'm so freaking happy you're not dead. I mean, other than the fancy gown, you look like a three-day-old shit in the sun, but you're breathing. That's a win, right?"

Summer leans her head back against the wall. "Pretty sure I bounced off a roof beam. Maybe I'm dead and this is just some weird afterlife."

"You think that I'd be here if this were the afterlife?" Zylah scoffs. "Please. I'm obsessed with dead things. I'll never get invited to a peaceful ghost party."

Summer huffs a quiet laugh, then sobers. "Landolin showed me the truth, Zy. I didn't kill my parents. Dad killed Mom, then Landolin's shadows killed *him* before he could hurt me."

Zylah's jaw drops. "I always hated your dad. Such an asshole. Must've been after her life insurance payout."

Summer wipes a tear from her face. "Definitely. Money was the only thing that mattered to him."

"Oh, honey," says Zylah. "You've always carried that guilt like a backpack full of bricks, and... I'm really sorry you had to do that for all those years. It must feel amazing to finally be free."

"Yeah," Summer says, her voice a broken whisper. "It's weird. I feel lighter, but not exactly better."

"Grief's a stubborn bastard," Zylah says. "But at least now you can tell it to get lost."

I clear my throat loudly. Ah, yes. All eyes back on me. "Given the circumstances, you both handled yourselves incredibly well. And, Zylah, your fighting skills were... surprising."

Zylah arches a brow. "Thanks. I've taken jujitsu classes since I was nine. But I definitely underperformed in there. I bit my tongue, screamed, and flung a very brave cat into a death zone."

"You also gave us the opening to weaken Landolin," I say. "And that raven of yours wasn't wrong."

Zylah exhales, then mutters, "I hate it when the spooky ones are right." Her gaze drifts to the fire. "What was that insane thing he said to me before he vanished?"

Summer sits forward, grimacing. "I think he's coming back for you. We have to figure out how to keep you safe."

Zylah nods slowly. "Great. Love that for me. Can we ask Detective Perez to arrest him?"

"Sure," I say. "Right after he arrests the ghost of the guy with the tooth collection in your attic. You know, the one with the big bag?"

Instead of laughing at my joke, Summer blinks. "I'm sorry. *What* ghost with *what* bag? And why didn't you mention him before?"

"Okay, but... is he like a dentist?" asks Zylah. "Or is it more of a teeth-trophy-collector, serial-killer situation?"

"I don't know," I reply. "Never asked. It's okay. I can banish him if he makes you uncomfortable. I thought you'd know about every ghost in this place."

"Not all of them. And we avoid the attic. The vibes are too creepy," says Summer. Then she holds her hand out, beckoning me closer. "Wyn, can your court do anything to help?"

I nod and sit beside her on the sofa, drawing her into my embrace. "Yeah. Don't worry. We'll find a way to keep Landolin at bay. Even if we have to hide Zylah at my home, the Elemental Court."

"So, exactly what kind of supernatural creatures are you and the shadow dude?" Zylah asks.

"Fae. The kind Summer's mom wrote about," I tell her.

"I can't run away to Faery and leave all my babies behind," Zylah protests, gesturing toward the basement where "*all the magic happens*" as she's fond of saying.

"Bring them with you," I suggest. "My family would be fascinated."

"I'll think about it," she concedes. "So Landolin's cursed? What does that mean exactly?"

Summer and I look at each other, the cut on my palm burning. "Can't talk about that now," I say. Or *ever*.

Zylah crosses her arms and frowns. "But he won't be coming back tonight, will he?"

I rake a hand through my hair. "Doubt it. He'll be licking his wounds and scheming with the Hunt. Working out the best time to strike again."

"Good." Zylah yawns. "After tonight's shit show, I really need to unwind. Feels like the perfect time to embalm an emotionally unstable chicken. The farmer said it died of anxiety. A cautionary tale for you, Summer."

She rises from the armchair, adjusts one of the buns in her hair, gives us clumsy hugs, and then heads down to the basement.

Summer's arms twine around my neck, and she drops a soft kiss on my cheek. "Speaking of my mother... we'd better go deal with the ghost of all my childhood trauma."

"Sure you don't want to get started on the dining room repairs first?" I tease.

"God, no. Banishings before decorating. That's always been my motto."

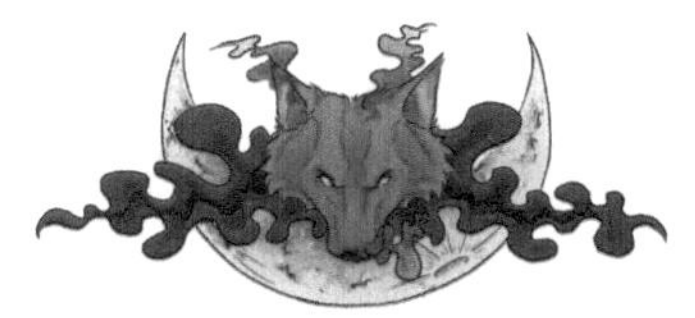

CHAPTER 44

Wynter

Summer sits cross-legged beside me in her bedroom, staring at an urn containing her mother's ashes. The cracked mirror leaning against the wall in front of us throws back our fractured, ragged reflections.

We're bruised, dirt-smudged, slumped shoulder-to-shoulder, but still breathing. Still together. And for once? Not running away from anything that's out to kidnap or kill us. And Ivor's asleep on the armchair in the bay window, snoring gently.

Summer's fingers release mine and tighten around the small bowl of salt. In her other hand, a stick of burning mugwort sends up a line of acrid smoke.

A shimmer distorts the air, and her mother appears in the mirror, slowly forming, her expression pinching into that of a woman who never learned how to be gentle or show love. She's still handsome, but it's a cold kind of beauty. Sharp-edged, like many fae from the crueler courts.

A soft whine sounds behind us, and I murmur for Ivor to go back to sleep. Everything's okay. He can rest now. We're safe.

Summer's mother flicks a silver wrap over a silky, dark blue top that looks suspiciously like human sleepwear. "Well, you appear to have been busy, daughter. And this is the wolf-boy, I presume? My name is Sorcha. Yours?"

"Wynter Fionbharr. Prince of the Elemental Court," I say, definitely not showing this woman the dimples Summer is so fond of.

"Mom," Summer says. "You sold me to the Shade Court. Why would you do that?"

Sorcha shrugs as if betraying her own child is no big deal. "Fame. Fortune. The usual. Not that it lasted long—your father saw to that, spending all of our money." She hesitates, then a flicker of something fragile crosses her face. "And they threatened me. Said if I didn't sign you over, they'd curse me with accelerated aging. Said I'd rot from the inside out, wrinkle by wrinkle, until I died a painful, early death."

I stay quiet. It sounds as if she's unaware her husband killed her. If she knew, maybe that smugness would vanish. Or maybe not. Either way, it's Summer's story to tell, not mine.

"They threatened you, then told you secrets," Summer says. "They made your stories better. And you gave the king your daughter in exchange for a wrinkle-free face and seeing your name on bestseller lists."

"No, not to the king," Sorcha replies coolly. "To his son—the one who leads the Hunt. He needed a human bride. Her blood on their wedding night. It's part of their rites, apparently. I wasn't given many details. They said you'd be fine—a princess, eventually a queen."

Summer flinches, her hand trembling around the bowl. "They'd have a hard time finding an unspoiled virgin of twenty-five years around Lake Grenlynn, Mother."

Sorcha's mouth tightens. "They didn't say it had to be first blood. Just fresh on the wedding night. Consent optional. The Unseelie don't care about something as trivial as a girl's purity. And why should they? We don't ask to see proof of a wiener's first sauce dipping, do we?"

Okay, that was kind of funny... but wait... *consent optional?* That burns like acid in my gut.

My magic flares at the edge of my control. The ground rumbles beneath the hall, and it takes every bit of willpower not to collapse the floor and watch the mirror tumble through it. Not that it would achieve much. Ghosts can't be buried a second time.

"They did tell me you might not survive," her mother adds, voice low and rasping. "They thought you might break, that you'd be too weak. Wondered if you were dark enough for their Court of Shadows. It seems they were right, since they spat you back out."

Summer's voice doesn't shake, in fact it sounds stronger. "You're the one who thinks I'm weak and strange. That's what you've always said. It was you who didn't think I was good enough for the dark fae."

"Because you weren't," her mother snaps. "Like an unwanted gift, you've been returned. You were a terrible daughter, and it seems an even worse tribute for the Shade Court, since they rejected you."

I squeeze Summer's hand as her whole body shakes.

"Rejected? We escaped. So fuck you, Mother dearest. I forgive you, but you can go lie in your grave for all eternity. Right now, please." Summer throws the salt, and it hits the mirror, bursting into sparks. Light explodes in the room as the glass cracks and splinters.

For one breathless moment, three ghostly women appear behind Summer—the gray ladies at last. Half-formed and dressed in tattered gowns from another age, their hands rest gently on her shoulders, backs straight, expressions solemn. They look like Summer's ancestors. Kin. They nod once, then vanish, sucked back into the veil that separates life from death.

Sorcha screams long and raw, the sound cutting off as her ghostly form shatters into tiny pieces. Gone forever.

Summer collapses into my arms, sobbing against my chest. "Did it work? I know I was meant to be all forgiving and loving, but I couldn't help telling her to get fucked. Did I completely ruin the banishing ritual?"

"No," I say, stifling a laugh. "You did just fine. When the spirit form shatters like glass, you know you've done the trick."

"Awesome. But listen, Wyn, if you say the word 'closure' right now, I might just punch you in the throat."

"Wouldn't dare."

Marie appears and drifts toward the mirror, hovering a moment like she's in mourning. Then she turns to Summer, reaches out as if to brush her cheek, then vanishes.

Summer watches the splintered glass for a long beat. Her breathing is uneven, her eyes distant. "Mom's really gone," she says quietly. "I always thought I'd feel something different when it happened. Relief, maybe. Or guilt. But I mostly feel kind of... empty."

I hold her tighter, vowing to dedicate my life to giving her the love she never got from her family.

"I hope Marie doesn't think I'll do that to *her*," says Summer, frowning.

"Don't worry. She looked pleased your mom's gone, too, if you ask me."

"Cool. Childhood trauma fixed, then." Arms wrapped around my neck, she grins up at me. "Shall we make pancakes?"

"How can you be hungry after everything that's happened tonight?"

"How can you *not* be after being buried in the ground for a week?"

"I've lost my appetite... for *food*. But maybe we can make pasta Alfredo for breakfast tomorrow. Right now, all I want is to crawl into bed with you and hold you too tight."

"That's all? Just hold me? If you could hear my thoughts right now..."

"Yeah," I say. "Shame that doesn't work in this realm."

I kiss her slowly, drowning in her comforting scent and warmth. Every part of me is aching from the fight, from my days buried in a grave. But it's nothing compared to the ache of nearly losing my mate.

"Give me time," I say. "I might be able to think of something else to do with you."

Summer laughs, her breath warm against the base of my throat.

"Tell me the truth, Wyn. Should we worry about Landolin coming back tonight? And Zylah? She seemed way too unbothered by what happened in the dining room."

I shake my head. "No, he won't return for at least a few weeks. He'll need to bring the Hunt with him if he wants to steal her. They can't leave Dorthadas until the next full moon, not if they want to run on maximum power. We've got time to plan."

She pulls back to study me. The skin under her eyes is smudged with weariness, but her green irises sparkle with mischief.

"Why do fae obsess over humans? We're powerless. Weak in comparison. Even in the old stories, it never made sense to me."

I smile, brushing a strand of dark hair from her cheek. "Guess we know what's good for us. And also, we have impeccable taste."

"Fair enough." Her hand drifts from my chest, trailing down my stomach. Then lower still. "Time for bed, then, I suppose."

"Stay there, Ivor," I command. "No matter what strange noises you hear. We're good. I promise."

He huffs out a long-suffering breath, wraps his tail over his eyes, and keeps snoring.

CHAPTER 45

Summer

We stumble toward the bathroom, grappling not with ghosts this time, but with each other and the thrill of being alive. Of being together.

I fumble with the faucets, then I'm in Wyn's arms, my back hitting the shower wall. He laughs, tripping over his feet and nearly tumbling us over the edge of the tub.

"Tell me again that nightmare is really over," I breathe, letting the warm water stream over my face, washing all the dirt away.

"It's over," Wyn says. "You're with me now. You're safe."

He presses closer and wraps my legs around his waist. A red mark is turning purple along his jaw, one of the many places where Landolin's shadows struck him. "Does that hurt?" I ask, brushing my fingertip over it.

He doesn't answer.

Instead, he cups my face with one hand, his thumb teasing the curve of my cheekbone, eyes greedily devouring me, like he's checking I'm real, not a dream.

Above the shower head, the floating, mangled body of a squirrel rotates lazily, like it's enjoying the mist and the show. I throw a washcloth at it. "I swear on my last clean towel, if you don't fade out in three seconds, buddy, your fuzzy little ass will be exorcised next."

It squeaks and disappears as Wyn laughs into my shoulder.

"When you dug me out of the grave, I didn't get to say it at the time, given Landolin's interruption," he mutters.

"Say what?" My voice comes out hoarse, sounding smoke damaged or maybe just turned on. Probably both.

His gaze is blistering. "That I would've stayed buried in Dorthadas's soil for you. Would've stayed there forever if it kept you safe."

I let out a breath that begins as a laugh and ends as a sob. "You almost did, idiot."

"Didn't." His forehead tips forward, resting against mine. "You called me back."

He closes his eyes for a moment, as if the trauma, the weight of it all, has finally caught up to him. "I didn't think I'd hear your voice again," he whispers. "Not in this world."

"I'll always be here for you," I murmur.

"I'm counting on it, Summer." His fingers glide down my neck, gently massaging in soap suds.

My knees shake at the longing and desire evident in his rough voice.

"Wyn." I release a trembling exhale, my fingers skating across the hard ridges of his stomach. "Are you hurt badly?"

"I'll tell you if you hit a tender spot. Keep checking."

I huff a breath. "That's not an answer."

He laughs into my mouth. "Okay, barely. Anyway, I don't feel pain when you're with me. Haven't I told you?"

His lips feather over the pulse on my neck, his teeth teasing, and then he bites down hard. Like a wolf claiming his mate.

"Mine," he growls. "Only mine. I'm going to fuck you so hard and make you forget every shitty thing about the last week. You'll remember only me. The feel of me inside you, making you slicker and slicker—losing yourself to everything except how I make you feel. Understand?"

"Yes," I moan. "Sounds perfect."

"*You're* perfect. And mine. Did I tell you that, too? Another man touches you, *ever*, and I'll rip his throat out. Eat his entrails for breakfast, lunch, and dinner."

"Way too much information," I say between ragged breaths as I fist his hard length, squeezing and sliding up and down, my thumb circling the tip.

Groaning, he watches me work him over, water and soap sluicing down our trembling bodies.

I tug his head up by a fistful of wet hair and kiss him, the sweet glide making my mind spin. His tongue slides into my mouth, and the kiss changes. No longer sweet or gentle. It's hungry and wild. A clash of lips and teeth and desperation that ends when he pulls away slightly, muttering breathless words.

"What?" I ask. "What did you say?"

"Nothing." His fingers tease along the seam of my entrance, then swirl over my clit, eliciting sighs and moans that I can't hold back. "Don't know what I'm saying," he rasps. "Can't think straight. All I want is to be inside you, little sun. Always. Can we do that?"

"Might be complicated," I tease.

"Fuck," he says, half-laughing, half-groaning. "Only you—you're the sunlight warming my grave. You're the roots that tether me to every realm, keeping me alive, feeding my soul. You're my *everything*. I would die for you. Kill for you. Do anything you asked of me. But right now, I need to feel you come on me while I howl your name out loud."

"God... what are you waiting for?"

Strong hands raise my hips, slowly impaling me on the glistening head bobbing against my stomach. We gasp, our eyes fixed on the sight of me stretched around his tip.

"Hold on tight," he says, then slams into me.

We moan between wet kisses as he sets a punishing pace, his body pressing mine against the tiled wall, one hand on my throat, the other on my breast. His head ducks low and he draws one nipple into his hot mouth, then the other, suckling and biting like a hungry wolf.

Every movement is frantic and greedy, peppered with laughter and low curses. He bangs his shin on the side of the bath. I hit my head on the wall. We don't stop or pause. Neither of us cares.

At one point he mutters something against my throat that sounds a lot like "seven hells I missed the taste of your skin," and I pretend not to hear it, so I don't fall apart then and there.

I slide my hands down his muscled back and dig my fingers into his ass, making him jerk. "Sweet Dana, I can't take much more of this."

"Dana?" I gasp as Wyn's pace becomes erratic and everything inside me tightens despite my best efforts to hold the intense orgasm at bay. "Who the hell is *she*?"

"A goddess. Nothing compared to you. We fae only speak her name to beg and complain. Right now, I need all the help I can get not to lose control... not to finish before you do."

He lifts my knee higher, spreading me wider, realigning his hips, and picking up speed. Water splashes off our bodies and all over the bathroom as the sound of slapping flesh fills the air, almost drowned out by our groans.

Wyn watches my breasts bounce with each pump, drives into the perfect spot that increases my cries and makes my nails dig deeper into his skin.

"Tell me there'll never be another. Only me," he demands.

"Only you, Wyn. Forever."

"Good. As it should be." His teeth clamp around the long muscle of my neck as he gives one last delicious thrust, grinding his hips into mine.

Crying out, I crash over the edge. He growls my name low in his chest and tumbles after me, wrapping me in an embrace so tight I nearly pass out.

"No knotting this time?" I tease when I finally catch my breath.

"Later. Too tired. But thank you," he says, dropping tender kisses along my jaw, my temple, my lips.

"What for?"

"For finally seeing me, loving me, remembering me, trusting me. If I had to wait a hundred more years, you'd be worth every torturous moment."

"Anytime. It's a pleasure, honestly," I joke.

Later, our limbs are tangled in my sheets as I lie on my side, tracing a scar on Wyn's hip with my finger. For a while, we don't speak. The rise and fall of his chest slows, and I press my foot against his toes under the covers.

"I should feel a lot better now that she's gone, right?" I say.

"Your mother? Do you?"

"No. I still feel... scarred from her selfish way of loving me... or not loving me. You know what's wild? I've spent years thinking there was a good chance I murdered my parents. Now it's hard to put that guilt back into its box."

"You're allowed to stop punishing yourself anytime now. You never did anything wrong. It's time to heal. Let it go," he says, hugging me tighter.

"You're right. And, hey, at least my mother's not floating above my bed critiquing my posture anymore."

"She had a point about the slouch."

I pinch the sharp blade of his ear playfully. "Get out."

Wyn smirks. "Make me."

"You couldn't be bothered doing the knotting thing before." I give an exhausted laugh. "I can't be bothered to kick you out. So just shut up and go to sleep, wolf-boy."

He squeezes my waist. "Anything you want, little sun. And you should sleep, too. We have a lot to talk about tomorrow."

The sheets are still damp from the shower, but I don't care. Wyn's scent is in them now—clean earth and pine—and I feel safe and warm.

Loved.

"You'll still be here when I wake up, won't you?" I ask, my eyelids already closing against my will.

He doesn't answer right away. Just wraps himself around me, tucking me against him. Then soft lips press against my forehead.

"I promise I'm not going anywhere without you, Summer. Never, *ever* again."

EPILOGUE

3 nights later Landolin

The vet clinic's flickering neon sign buzzes loudly, casting a sickly glow across the dark parking lot. Tonight, Zylah is the last to leave the building.

Yawning and stretching as she steps through the back door, she hefts her shiny, frog-shaped bag over one shoulder like it's full of rocks, waving to a human male pulling out in a low red car with no roof.

Gone are the scrubs she wore on her break, replaced by a black sweater that reads "Better Dead Than Alive" in peeling glitter across the front. Her strange, mortal-style skirt is short, fraying at the hem, paired with striped tights in garish, bright colors.

But it's her loose copper hair that makes my chest tighten around a sharply drawn breath. Long and wild, it tumbles down her back. No longer tied in twin coils that resemble horns. Instead, it flows, wild and untamed.

She seems tired and distracted, unconsciously humming a tune under her breath—one I'm positive she doesn't know the origin of.

But *I* do.

An Unseelie lullaby, crooned over bloodless babes in bark cribs, swaddled in nettles and ribboned lace. A song mothers sing to ease the dying of their ill children. Zylah hums it like it's of no consequence. But I'll teach her its truth.

When she's mine.

Orange hair. Amber eyes. Beautiful as a funeral rose.

Keys dangle from her hand—metal bones, a rubber bat with a missing eye, the name Zylah spelled out in cracked glitter, all jingling together as she strides through the near-empty parking lot.

She jabs the key into the door of her battered hatchback without looking around. Or checking to see who might be lurking in the shadows. Foolish girl. Another lesson she must learn.

My prize. My Mistress of dead things. Not the one I was promised, no. That offering was a trick. A bait-and-switch. Another prince's chosen, never destined to be mine.

But this sharp-voiced, tender-limbed mortal who stitches broken wings and collects the dead like heirlooms?

She's the one I choose.

This is the one I will take.

Keys half-turned in the lock, she hesitates. The air shifts, turns icy, her skin likely prickling. Something in her gut probably pangs, telling her to run. But she only shakes her head and mutters something about forgetting to eat dinner.

The car door creaks open... and she pauses again, frozen like a deer in the woods before the hunter's arrow lands. She glances over her shoulder, eyes unfocused. Unseeing.

I step from the shadows beneath the oak tree. No antlers. No clip-clop of hoofs. No jangle of the Hunt behind me. Only clear, silent intent.

"Hello, Zylah," I say, letting the shape of her name melt like butter on my tongue. "Remember me?"

The keys clatter to the ground. Her breath catches, eyes wide behind the glasses, lips parting before moving soundlessly.

She utters a single whispered word, hissed low and hostile: "*You.*"

Then she throws back her head and laughs.

**Thank you for reading Summer and Wynter's story!
I hope you check out Shadow's Fae, Zylah and Landolin's
tale.**

If you'd like to read more books set in this world, give the Black Blood Fae series a try.
Prince of Never, book 1, is about Wyn and Merri's parents and King of Merits is Merri and Riven's story, which both Wyn and Summer appear in as side characters. Note: the heat is lower.

**You can also try my dark, spicy enemies-to-lovers duet,
Courts of the Star Fae Realms.**

Gravenshade Vows:
Book 1, Summer's Fae
Book 2, Shadow's Fae

Courts of the Star Fae Realms:
Book 1, King of Storms and Feathers
Book 2, King of Fire and Flames

Black Blood Fae:
Book 1, Prince of Never
Book 2, King of Always
Book 3, King of Merits
Book 4, Prince of Then

And stay tuned for a book about King Ren from Courts of the Star Fae Realms and his stolen human bride.

Books are available in audiobook format and special print editions, including character art covers!

Thank you for reading Wyn and Summer's story! I hope you had as much fun hanging out with them as I did.
I love hearing from readers, and I'm so grateful for every lovely review I receive, no matter how brief.

Thank you so much for taking the time to recommend my books to other readers and for your wonderful support and enthusiasm.

Huge thanks to my amazing beta readers Amelie, Saskia, Ken, and Rosemary and to my wonderful ARC readers.

Until next time,

Juno
X

Juno Heart is obsessed with anti-heroes (and sometimes even growly cinnamon roll MMCs) who don't believe they deserve love.

When she's not writing, she's probably busy herding her cat and dog around the house, spilling coffee on her keyboard, or searching the local woods and alleyways for portals into another realm.

JOIN Juno's newsletter for new release and special deal alerts!

junoheartbooks.com
juno@junoheartbooks.com

tiktok.com/@junoheartauthor

amazon.com/stores/Juno-Heart/author/B07ZFZDV3X?

facebook.com/JunoHeartAuthor/

instagram.com/junoheart_author/

www.ingramcontent.com/pod-product-compliance
Lightning Source LLC
Chambersburg PA
CBHW030511120726

47904CB00005B/1417